ALFRED HITCHCOCK'S

TALES TO SCARE YOU STIFF

OTHER ANTHOLOGIES BY
ALFRED HITCHCOCK

Stories to be Read with the Door Locked
The Master's Choice
Tales to Send Chills Down Your Spine

FOR CHILDREN

Ghostly Gallery
Haunted Houseful
Monster Museum
Daring Detectives
Sinister Spies
Spellbinders in Suspense
Solve-Them-Yourself Mysteries
Supernatural Tales of Terror
and Suspense
Witch's Brew

ALFRED
HITCHCOCK'S

Tales to Scare You Stiff

Edited by Eleanor Sullivan

MAX REINHARDT
LONDON SYDNEY
TORONTO

British Library Cataloguing
in Publication Data
Alfred Hitchcock's tales to scare you stiff.
1. Horror tales, American
I. Sullivan, Eleanor
813'.01'0816[FS]   PS648.H6
ISBN 0-370-30298-2

© Davis Publications, Inc. 1978
Printed in Great Britain for
Max Reinhardt Ltd
9 Bow Street, London WC2E 7AL .
by Redwood Burn Ltd
Trowbridge, Wiltshire
First published in Great Britain 1981

Acknowledgements

Come Back, Come Back . . . by Donald E. Westlake; © 1960 by H. S. D. Publications, Inc.; reprinted by permission of the author.

Once Upon a Bank Floor by James Holding; © 1961 by H. S. D. Publications, Inc.; reprinted by permission of Scott Meredith Literary Agency, Inc.

Warrior's Farewell by Edward D. Hoch; copyright H. S. D. Publications, Inc., 1967; reprinted by permission of the author.

Adventures of the Sussex Archers by August Derleth; © 1962 by H. S. D. Publications, Inc.; reprinted by permission of Scott Meredith Literary Agency, Inc.

Don't Lose Your Cool by Dan J. Marlowe; © 1966 by H. S. D. Publications, Inc.; reprinted by permission of the author.

Bus to Chattanooga by Jonathan Craig; © 1964 by H. S. D. Publications, Inc.; reprinted by permission of Scott Meredith Literary Agency, Inc.

The Perfidy of Professor Blake by Libby MacCall; copyright H. S. D. Publications, Inc., 1970; reprinted by permission of Blanche C. Gregory, Inc.

I Don't Understand It by Bill Pronzini; copyright H. S. D. Publications, Inc., 1972; reprinted by permission of the author.

News from Nowhere by Ron Goulart; copyright H. S. D. Publications, Inc., 1971; reprinted by permission of the author.

A Case of Desperation by Kate Wilhelm; © 1964 by H. S. D. Publications, Inc.; reprinted by permission of the author.

The Books Always Balance by Lawrence Block; © 1963 by H. S. D. Publications, Inc.; reprinted by permission of the author.

The Second Debut by Arthur Porges; copyright H. S. D. Publications, Inc., 1968; reprinted by permission of Scott Meredith Literary Agency, Inc.

Sea Change by Henry Slesar; copyright H. S. D. Publications, Inc., 1969; reprinted by permission of the author.

The Green Heart by Jack Ritchie; © 1963 by H. S. D. Publications, Inc.; reprinted by permission of Larry Sternig Literary Agency.

Supply and Demand by James M. Ullman; © 1964 by H. S. D. Publications, Inc.; reprinted by permission of the author.

Contents

Come Back, Come Back . . .

by Donald E. Westlake

Detective Abraham Levine of Brooklyn's Forty-Third Precinct was a worried and a frightened man. He sat moodily at his desk in the small office he shared with his partner Jack Crawley, and pensively drew lopsided circles on the back of a blank accident report form. In the approximate center of each circle he placed a dot, drew two lines out from the dot to make a clock-face, reading three o'clock. An eight and a half by eleven sheet of white paper, covered with clock-faces, all reading three o'clock.

"That the time you see the doctor?"

Levine looked up, startled, called back from years away. Crawley was standing beside the desk, looking down at him, and Levine blinked, not having heard the question.

Crawley reached down and tapped the paper with a horny fingernail. "Three o'clock," he explained. "That the time you see the doctor?"

"Oh," said Levine. "Yes. Three o'clock."

Crawley said, "Take it easy, Abe."

"Sure," said Levine. He managed a weak smile. "No sense worrying beforehand, huh?"

"My brother," said Crawley, "he had one of those cardiograph things just a couple months ago. He's just around your age, and man, he was worried. And the doctor tells him, 'You'll live to be a hundred.' "

"And then you'll die," said Levine.

"What the hell, Abe, we all got to go *sometime*."

"Sure."

Abraham Levine was fifty-three years alive, twenty-four years a cop. A short and chunky man, he wore plain brown suits and dark solid-color ties, brown or black plain shoes. His hair was pepper-and-salt grey, trimmed all around in a stiff pseudo-military crewcut. The crewcut didn't go with the face, roundish, soft-eyed, sensitive-lipped, lined with fifty-three years' accumulation of small worries.

"Listen, Abe, you want to go on home? It's a dull day, nothing doing, I can—"

"Don't say that," Levine warned him. "The phone will ring." The phone rang as he was talking and he grinned, shrugging with palms up. "See?"

"Let me see what it is," said Crawley, reaching for the phone. "Probably nothing important. You can go on home and take it easy till three o'clock. It's only ten now and—Hello?" The last word spoken into the phone mouthpiece. "Yeah, this is Crawley."

Levine watched Crawley's face, trying to read in it the nature of the call. Crawley had been his partner for seven years, since old Jake Moshby had retired, and in that time they had become good friends, as close as two such different men could get to one another.

Crawley was a big man, somewhat overweight, somewhere in his middle forties. His clothes hung awkwardly on him, not as though they were too large or too small but as though they had been planned for a man of completely different proportions. His face was rugged, squarish, heavy-jowled. He looked like a tough cop, and he played the role very well.

Crawley had once described the quality of their partnership with reasonable accuracy. "With your brains and my beauty, Abe, we've got it made."

Now, Levine watched Crawley's face as the big man listened impassively to the phone, finally nodding and saying, "Okay, I'll go right on up there. Yeah, I know, that's what I figure, too." And he hung up.

"What is it, Jack?" Levine asked, getting up from the desk.

"A phony," said Crawley. "I can handle it, Abe. You go on home."

"I'd rather have some work to do. What is it?"

Crawley was striding for the door, Levine after him. "Man on a ledge," he said. "A phony. They're all phonies. The ones that really mean to jump do it right away, get it over with. Guys like this one, all they want is a little attention, somebody to tell them it's all okay, come on back in, everything's forgiven."

The two of them walked down the long green hall toward the front of the precinct. *Man on a ledge*, Levine thought. *Don't jump. Don't die. For God's sake, don't die.*

10

The address was an office building on Flatbush Avenue, a few blocks down from the bridge, near A&S and the major Brooklyn movie houses. A small crowd had gathered on the sidewalk across the street, looking up, but most of the pedestrians stopped only for a second or two, only long enough to see what the small crowd was gaping at, and then hurried on wherever they were going. They were still involved in life, they had things to do, they didn't have time to watch a man die.

Traffic on this side was being rerouted away from this block of Flatbush, around via Fulton or Willoughby or DeKalb. It was a little after ten o'clock on a sunny day in late June, warm without the humidity that would hit the city a week or two farther into the summer, but the uniformed cop who waved at them to make the turn was sweating, his blue shirt stained a darker blue, his forehead creased with strain above the sunglasses.

Crawley was driving their car, an unmarked black '56 Chevvy, no siren, and he braked to a stop in front of the patrolman. He stuck his head and arm out the window, dangling his wallet open so the badge showed. "Precinct," he called.

"Oh," said the cop. He stepped aside to let them pass. "You didn't have any siren or light or anything," he explained.

"We don't want to make our friend nervous," Crawley told him.

The cop glanced up, then looked back at Crawley. "He's making *me* nervous," he said.

Crawley laughed. "A phony," he told the cop. "Wait and see."

On his side of the car, Levine had leaned his head out the window, was looking up, studying the man on the ledge.

It was an office building, eight stories high. Not a very tall building, particularly for New York, but plenty tall enough for the purposes of the man standing on the ledge that girdled the building at the sixth floor level. The first floor of the building was mainly a bank and partially a luncheonette. The second floor, according to the lettering strung along the front windows, was entirely given over to a loan company, and Levine could understand the advantage of the location. A man had his loan request turned down by the bank, all he had to do was go up one flight of stairs—or one flight in the elevator, more likely—and there was the loan company.

And if the loan company failed him too, there was a nice ledge on the sixth floor.

Levine wondered if this particular case had anything to do with money. Almost everything had something to do with money. Things that he became aware of because he was a cop, almost all of them had something to do with money. The psychoanalysts are wrong, he thought. It isn't sex that's at the center of all the pain in the world, it's money. Even when a cop answers a call from neighbors complaining about a couple screaming and fighting and throwing things at one another, nine times out of ten it's the same old thing they're arguing about. Money.

Levine's eyes traveled up the facade of the building, beyond the loan company's windows. None of the windows higher up bore the lettering of firm names. On the sixth floor, most of the windows were open, heads were sticking out into the air. And in the middle of it all, just out of reach of the windows on either side of him, was the man on the ledge.

Levine squinted, trying to see the man better against the brightness of the day. He wore a suit—it looked grey, but might be black—and white shirt and a dark tie, and the open suit coat and the tie were both whipping in the breeze up there. The man was standing as though crucified, back flat against the wall of the building, legs spread maybe two feet apart, arms out straight to either side of him, hands pressed palm-in against the stone surface of the wall.

The man was terrified. Levine was much too far away to see his face or read the expression there, but he didn't need any more than the posture of the body on the ledge. Taut, pasted to the wall, wide-spread. The man was terrified.

Crawley was right, of course. Ninety-nine times out of a hundred, the man on the ledge *is* a phony. He doesn't really expect to have to kill himself, though he will do it if pressed too hard. But he's out there on the ledge for one purpose and one purpose only: to be seen. He wants to be seen, he wants to be noticed. Whatever his unfulfilled demands on life, whatever his frustrations or problems, he wants other people to be forced to be aware of them, and to agree to help him overcome them.

If he gets satisfaction he will allow himself, after a decent interval, to be brought back in. If he gets the raise, or the girl, or forgiveness from the boss for his embezzling, or forgiveness from his wife for his philandering, or whatever his one urgent demand is, once the demand

12

is met, he will come in from the ledge.

But there is one danger he doesn't stop to think about, not until it's too late and he's already out there on the ledge, and the drama has already begun. The police know of this danger, and they know it is by far the greatest danger of the man on the ledge, much greater than any danger of deliberate self-destruction.

He can fall.

This one had learned that danger by now, as every inch of his straining taut body testified. He had learned it, and he was frightened out of his wits.

Levine grimaced. The man on the ledge didn't know—or if he knew, the knowledge was useless to him—that a terrified man can have an accident much more readily and much more quickly than a calm man. And so the man on the ledge always compounded his danger.

Crawley braked the Chevvy to a stop at the curb, two doors beyond the address. The rest of the curb space was already used by official vehicles. An ambulance, white and gleaming. A smallish fire engine, red and full-packed with hose and ladders. A prowl car, most likely the one on this beat. The Crash & Rescue truck, dark blue, a first-aid station on wheels.

As he was getting out of the car, Levine noticed the firemen, standing around, leaning against the plate glass windows of the bank, an eight foot net lying closed on the sidewalk near them. Levine took the scene in, and knew what had happened. The firemen had started to open the net. The man on the ledge had threatened to jump at once if they didn't take the net away. He could always jump to one side, miss the net. A net was no good unless the person to be caught *wanted* to be caught. So the firemen had closed up their net again, and now they were waiting, leaning against the bank windows, far enough away to the right.

Other men stood here and there on the sidewalk, some uniformed and some in plainclothes, most of them looking up at the man on the ledge. None of them stood inside a large white circle drawn in chalk on the pavement. It was a wide sidewalk here, in front of the bank, and the circle was almost the full width of it.

No one stood inside that circle because it marked the probable area where the man would land, if and when he fell or jumped from the ledge. And no one wanted to be underneath.

Crawley came around the Chevvy, patting the fenders with a large calloused hand. He stopped next to Levine and looked up. "The phony," he growled, and Levine heard outrage in the tone. Crawley was an honest man, in simple terms of black and white. He hated dishonesty, in all its forms, from grand larceny to raucous television commercials. And a faked suicide attempt was dishonesty.

The two of them walked toward the building entrance. Crawley walked disdainfully through the precise center of the large chalked circle, not even bothering to look up. Levine walked around the outer edge.

Then the two of them went inside and took the elevator to the sixth floor.

The letters on the frosted-glass door read: "Anderson & Cartwright, Industrial Research Associates, Inc."

Crawley tapped on the glass. "Which one do you bet?" he asked. "Anderson or Cartwright?"

"It might be an employee."

Crawley shook his head. "Odds are against it. I take Anderson."

"Go in," said Levine gently. "Go on in."

Crawley pushed the door open and strode in, Levine behind him. It was the receptionist's office, cream-green walls and carpet, modernistic metal desk, modernistic metal and leather sofa and armchairs, modernistic saucer-shaped light fixtures hanging from bronzed chains attached to the ceiling.

Three women sat nervously, wide-eyed, off to the right, on the metal and leather armchairs. Above their heads were framed photographs of factory buildings, most of them in color, a few in black and white.

A uniformed patrolman was leaning against the receptionist's desk, arms folded across his chest, a relaxed expression on his face. He straightened up immediately when he saw Crawley and Levine. Levine recognized him as McCann, a patrolman working out of the same precinct.

"Am I glad to see you guys," said McCann. "Gundy's in talking to the guy now."

"Which one is it," Crawley asked, "Anderson or Cartwright?"

"Cartwright. Jason Cartwright. He's one of the bosses here."

14

Crawley turned a sour grin on Levine. "You win," he said, and led the way across the receptionist's office to the door marked: "Jason Cartwright PRIVATE."

There were two men in the room. One was sitting on the window ledge, looking out and to his left, talking in a soft voice. The other, standing a pace or two away from the window, was the patrolman, Gundy. He and McCann would be the two from the prowl car, the first ones on the scene.

At their entrance, Gundy looked around and then came over to talk with them. He and McCann were cut from the same mold. Both young, tall, slender, thin-cheeked, ready to grin at a second's notice. The older a man gets, Levine thought, the longer it takes him to get a grin organized.

Gundy wasn't grinning now. He looked very solemn, and a little scared. Levine realized with shock that this might be Gundy's first brush with death. He didn't look as though he could have been out of the Academy very long.

I have news for you, Gundy, he thought. *You don't get used to it.*

Crawley said, "What's the story?"

"I'm not sure," said Gundy. "He went out there about twenty minutes ago. That's his son talking to him. Son's a lawyer, got an office right in this building."

"What's the guy out there want?"

Gundy shook his head. "He won't say. He just stands out there. He won't say a word, except to shout that he's going to jump whenever anybody tries to get too close to him."

"A coy one," said Crawley, disgusted.

The phone shrilled, and Gundy stepped quickly over to the desk, picking up the receiver before the second ring. He spoke softly into the instrument, then looked over at the man by the window. "Your mother again," he said.

The man at the window spoke a few more words to the man on the ledge, then came over and took the phone from Gundy. Gundy immediately took his place at the window, and Levine could hear his first words plainly. "Just take it easy, now. Relax. But maybe you shouldn't close your eyes."

Levine looked at the son, now talking on the phone. A young man, not more than twenty-five or six. Blond crewcut, hornrim glasses, good

15

mouth, strong jawline. Dressed in Madison Avenue conservative. Just barely out of law school, from the look of him.

Levine studied the office. It was a large room, eighteen to twenty feet square, as traditional as the outer office was contemporary. The desk was a massive piece of furniture, a dark warm wood, the legs and drawer faces carefully and intricately carved. Glass-faced bookshelves lined one complete wall. The carpet was a neutral grey, wall-to-wall. There were two sofas, brown leather, long and deep and comfortable-looking. Bronze ashtray stands. More framed photographs of plant buildings.

The son was saying, "Yes, mother. I've been talking to him, mother. I don't know, mother."

Levine walked over, said to the son, "May I speak to her for a minute, please?"

"Of course. Mother, there's a policeman here who wants to talk to you."

Levine accepted the phone, said, "Mrs. Cartwright?"

The voice that answered was high-pitched, and Levine could readily imagine it becoming shrill. The voice said, "Why is he out there? Why is he doing that?"

"We don't know yet," Levine told her. "We were hoping you might be able to—"

"Me?" The voice was suddenly a bit closer to being shrill. "I still can't really believe this. I don't know why he'd—I have no idea. What does he say?"

"He hasn't told us why yet," said Levine. "Where are you now, Mrs. Cartwright?"

"At home, of course."

"That's where?"

"New Brunswick."

"Do you have a car there? Could you drive here now?"

"There? To New York?"

"It might help, Mrs. Cartwright, if he could see you, if you could talk to him."

"But—it would take *hours* to get there! Surely, it would be—that is, before I got there, you'd have him safe already, wouldn't you?"

She hopes he jumps, thought Levine, with sudden certainty. *By God, she hopes he jumps!*

16

"Well, wouldn't you?"

"Yes," he said wearily. "I suppose you're right. Here's your son again."

He extended the receiver to the son, who took it, cupped the mouthpiece with one hand, said worriedly, "Don't misunderstand her. Please, she isn't as cold as she might sound. She loves my father, she really does."

"All right," said Levine. He turned away from the pleading in the son's eyes, said to Crawley, "Let's talk with him a bit."

"Right," said Crawley.

There were two windows in the office, about ten feet apart, and Jason Cartwright was standing directly between them on the ledge. Crawley went to the left-hand window and Levine to the right-hand window, where the patrolman Gundy was still trying to chat with the man on the ledge, trying to keep him distracted from the height and his desire to jump. "We'll take over," Levine said softly, and Gundy nodded gratefully and backed away from the window.

Levine twisted around, sat on the windowsill, hooked one arm under the open window, leaned out slightly so that the breeze touched his face. He looked down.

Six stories. God, who would have thought six stories was so high from the ground? This is the height when you really get the feeling of height. On top of the Empire State building, or flying in a plane, it's just too damn high, it isn't real any more. But six stories—that's a fine height to be at, to really understand the terror of falling.

Place ten Levines, one standing on another's shoulders, forming a human tower or a totem pole, and the Levine in the window wouldn't be able to reach the cropped grey hair on the head of the top Levine in the totem pole.

Down there, he could make out faces, distinguish eyes and open mouths, see the blue jeans and high boots and black slickers of the firemen, the red domes atop the police cars. Across the street, he could see the red of a girl's sweater.

He looked down at the street, sixty-six feet below him. It was a funny thing about heights, a strange and funny and terrifying thing. Stand by the rail of a bridge, looking down at the water. Stand by a window on the sixth floor, looking down at the street. And from miles down inside the brain, a filthy little voice snickers and leers and croons, "Jump. Go on and jump. Wouldn't you like to know how it would feel, to fall free through space? Go on, go on, jump."

From his left, Crawley's voice suddenly boomed out. "Aren't you a little old, Cartwright, for this kind of nonsense?"

The reassuring well-known reality of Crawley's voice tore Levine away from the snickering little voice. He suddenly realized he'd been leaning too far out from the window, and pulled himself hastily back.

And he felt his heart pounding within his chest. Three o'clock, he had to go see that doctor. He had to be calm; his heart had to be calm for the doctor's inspection.

At night— He didn't get enough sleep at night any more, that was part of the problem. But it was impossible to sleep and listen to one's heart at the same time, and of the two it was more important to listen to the heart. Listen to it plodding along, laboring, like an old man climbing a hill with a heavy pack. And then, all at once, the silence. The skipped beat. And the sluggish heart gathering its forces, building its strength, plodding on again. It had never yet skipped two beats in a row.

It could only do that once.

"What is it you want, Cartwright?" called Crawley's voice.

Levine, for the first time, looked to the left and saw Jason Cartwright.

A big man, probably an athlete in his younger days, still muscular but now padded with the flesh of years. Black hair with a natural wave in it, now mussed by the breeze. A heavy face, the chin sagging a bit but the jawline still strong, the nose large and straight, the forehead wide, the brows outthrust, the eyes deep and now wide and wild. A good-looking man, probably in his late forties.

Levine knew a lot about him already. From the look of the son in there, this man had married young, probably while still in his teens. From the sound of the wife, the marriage had soured. From the look of the office and the apparent education of the son, his career had blossomed where his marriage hadn't. So this time, one of the exceptions, the trouble wouldn't be money. This time, it was connected most likely with his marriage.

Another woman?

It wouldn't be a good idea to ask him. Sooner or later, he would state his terms, he would tell them what had driven him out here.

18

Force the issue, and he might jump. A man on a ledge goes out there not wanting to jump, but accepting the fact that he may have to.

Cartwright had been looking at Crawley, and now he turned his head, stared at Levine. "Oh, no you don't!" he cried. His voice would normally be baritone, probably a pleasant speaking voice, but emotion had driven it up the scale, making it raucous, tinged with hysteria. "One distracts me while the other sneaks up on me, is that it?" the man cried. "You won't get away with it. Come near me and I'll jump, I swear I'll jump!"

"I'll stay right here," Levine promised. Leaning far out, he would be almost able to reach Cartwright's out-stretched hand. But if he were to touch it, Cartwright would surely jump. And if he were to grip it, Cartwright would most likely drag him along too, all the way down to the sidewalk sixty-six feet below.

"What is it, Cartwright?" demanded Crawley again. "What do you want?"

Way back at the beginning of their partnership, Levine and Crawley had discovered the arrangement that worked best for them. Crawley asked the questions, and Levine listened to the answers. While a man paid attention to Crawley, erected his facade between himself and Crawley, Levine, silent and unnoticed, could come in on the flank, peek behind the facade and see the man who was really there.

"I want you to leave me alone!" cried Cartwright. "Everybody, everybody! Just leave me alone!"

"Look up at the sky, Mister Cartwright," said Levine softly, just loud enough for the man on the ledge to hear him. "Look how blue it is. Look down across the street. Do you see the red of that girl's sweater? Breathe in, Mister Cartwright. Do you smell the city? Hark! Listen! Did you hear that car horn? That was over on Fulton Street, wasn't it?"

"Shut up!" screamed Cartwright, turning swiftly, precariously, to glare again at Levine. "Shut up, shut up, shut up! Leave me alone!"

Levine knew all he needed. "Do you want to talk to your son?" he asked.

"Allan?" The man's face softened all at once. "Allan?"

"He's right here," said Levine. He came back in from the window, signalled to the son, who was no longer talking on the phone. "He wants to talk to you."

The son rushed to the window. "Dad?"

Crawley came over, glowering. "Well?" he said.

Levine shook his head. "He doesn't want to die."

"I know that. What now?"

"I think it's the wife." Levine motioned to Gundy, who came over, and he said, "Is the partner here? Anderson?"

"Sure," said Gundy. "He's in his office. He tried to talk to Cartwright once, but Cartwright got too excited. We thought it would be a good idea if Anderson kept out of sight."

"Who thought? Anderson?"

"Well, yes. All of us. Anderson and McCann and me."

"Okay," said Levine. "You and the boy—what's his name, Allan?—stay here. Let me know what's happening, if anything at all does happen. We'll go talk with Mister Anderson now."

Anderson was short, slender, very brisk, very bald. His wire-framed spectacles reflected light, and his round little face was troubled. "No warning at all," he said. "Not a word. All of a sudden, Joan—she's our receptionist—got a call from someone across the street, saying there was a man on the ledge. And it was Jason. Just like that! No warning at all."

"The sign on your door," said Crawley, "says Industrial Research. What's that, efficiency expert stuff?"

Anderson smiled, a quick nervous flutter. "Not exactly," he said. He was devoting all his attention to Crawley, who was standing directly in front of him and who was asking the questions. Levine stood to one side, watching the movements of Anderson's lips and eyes and hands as he spoke.

"We are efficiency experts, in a way," Anderson was saying, "but not in the usual sense of the term. We don't work with time-charts, or how many people should work in the steno pool, things like that. Our major concern is the physical plant itself, the structure and design of the plant buildings and work areas."

Crawley nodded. "Architects," he said.

Anderson's brief smile fluttered on his face again, and he shook his head. "No, we work in conjunction with the architect, if it's a new building. But most of our work is concerned with the modernization of old facilities. In a way, we're a central clearing agency for new ideas in industrial plant procedures." It was, thought Levine, an explanation Anderson was used to making, so used to making that it sounded almost like a memorized patter.

"You and Cartwright equal partners?" asked Crawley. It was clear he hadn't understood a word of Anderson's explanation and was impatient to move on to other things.

Anderson nodded. "Yes, we are. We've been partners for twenty-one years."

"You know him well, then."

"I should think so, yes."

"Then maybe you know why he suddenly decided to go crawl out on the ledge."

Eyes widening, Anderson shook his head again. "Not a thing," he said. "I had no idea, nothing, I—There just wasn't any warning at all."

Levine stood off to one side, watching, his lips pursed in concentration. Was Anderson telling the truth? It seemed likely; it *felt* likely. The marriage again. It kept going back to the marriage.

"Has he acted at all funny lately?" Crawley was still pursuing the same thought, that there had to be some previous build-up, and that the build-up would show. "Has he been moody, anything like that?"

"Jason—" Anderson stopped, shook his head briefly, started again. "Jason is a quiet man, by nature. He—he rarely says much, rarely uh, *forces* his personality, if you know what I mean. If he's been thinking about this, whatever it is, it—it wouldn't show. I don't *think* it would show."

"Would he have any business worries at all?" Crawley undoubtedly realized by now this was a blind alley, but he would go through the normal questions anyway. You never could tell.

Anderson, as was to be expected, said, "No, none. We've—well, we've been doing very well. The last five years, we've been expanding steadily, we've even added to our staff, just six months ago."

Levine now spoke for the first time. "What about Mrs. Cartwright?" he asked.

Anderson looked blank, as he turned to face Levine. "Mrs. Cartwright? I—I don't understand what you mean."

Crawley immediately picked up the new ball, took over the questioning again. "Do you know her well, Mister Anderson? What kind of woman would you say she was?"

Anderson turned back to Crawley, once again opening his flank to Levine. "She's, well, actually I haven't seen very much of her the last few years. Jason moved out of Manhattan five or six years ago, over to Jersey, and I live out on the Island, so we don't, uh, we don t *socialize* very much, as much as we used to. As you get older—" he turned to face Levine, as though instinctively understanding that Levine would more readily know what he meant "—you don't go out so much any more, in the evening. You don't, uh, keep up friendships as much as you used to."

"You must know *something* about Mrs. Cartwright," said Crawley.

Anderson gave his attention to Crawley again. "She's, well, I suppose the best way to describe her is *determined*. I know for a fact she was the one who talked Jason into coming into partnership with me, twenty-one years ago. A forceful woman. Not a nag, mind you, I don't mean that at all. A very pleasant woman, really. A good hostess. A good mother, from the look of Allan. But forceful."

The wife, thought Levine. *She's the root of it. She knows, too, what drove him out there.*

And she wants him to jump.

Back in Cartwright's office, the son Allan was once again at the phone. The patrolman Gundy was at the left-hand window, and a new man, in clerical garb, at the right-hand window.

Gundy noticed Levine and Crawley come in, and immediately left the window. "A priest," he said softly. "Anderson said he was Catholic, so we got in touch with St. Mark's, over on Willoughby."

Levine nodded. He was listening to the son. "I don't know, mother. Of course, mother, we're doing everything we can. No, mother, no reporters up here, maybe it won't have to be in the papers at all."

Levine went over to the window Gundy had vacated, took up a position where he could see Cartwright, carefully refrained from looking down at the ground. The priest was saying, "God has his time for you, Mister Cartwright. This is God's prerogative, to choose the time and the means of your death."

Cartwright shook his head, not looking at the priest, glaring instead directly across Flatbush Avenue at the building across the way. "There is no God," he said.

"I don't believe you mean that, Mister Cartwright," said the priest.

22

"I believe you've lost faith in yourself, but I don't believe you've lost faith in God."

"Take that away!" screamed Cartwright all at once. "Take that away, or I jump right now!"

He was staring down toward the street, and Levine followed the direction of his gaze. Poles had been extended from windows on the floor below, and a safety net, similar to that used by circus performers, was being unrolled along them.

"Take that away!" screamed Cartwright again. He was leaning precariously forward, his face mottled red with fury and terror.

"Roll that back in!" shouted Levine. "Get it out of there, he can jump over it! Roll it back in!"

A face jutted out of one of the fifth-floor windows, turning inquiringly upward, saying, "Who are you?"

"Levine. Precinct. Get that thing away from there."

"Right you are," said the face, making it clear he accepted no responsibility either way. And the net and poles were withdrawn.

The priest, on the other side, was saying, "It's all right. Relax, Mr. Cartwright; it's all right. These people only want to help you; it's all right." The priest's voice was shaky. Like Gundy, he was a rookie at this. He'd never been asked to talk in a suicide before.

Levine twisted around, looking up. Two stories up, and the roof. More men were up there, with another safety net. If this were the top floor, they would probably take a chance with that net, try flipping it over him and pasting him like a butterfly to the wall. But not here, three stories down.

Cartwright had turned his face away from the still-talking priest, was studying Levine intently. Levine returned his gaze, and Cartwright said, "Where's Laura? She should be here by now, shouldn't she? Where is she?"

"Laura? You mean your wife?"

"Of course," he said. He stared at Levine, trying to read something in Levine's face. "Where is she?"

Tell him the truth? No. Tell him his wife wasn't coming, and he would jump right away. "She's on the way," he said. "She should be here pretty soon."

Cartwright turned his face forward again, stared off across the street. The priest was still talking, softly, insistently.

Levine came back into the office. To Crawley, he said, "It's the wife. He's waiting for her."

"They've always got a wife," said Crawley sourly. "And there's always just the one person they'll tell it to. Well, how long before she gets here?"

"She isn't coming."

"What?"

"She's at home, over in Jersey. She said she wouldn't come." Levine shrugged and added, "I'll try her again."

The son was still on the phone, but he handed it over as soon as Levine spoke to him. Levine said, "This is Detective Levine again, Mrs. Cartwright. We'd like you to come down here after all, please. Your husband asked to talk to you."

There was hesitation from the woman for a few seconds, and then she burst out, "Why can't you bring him in? Can't you even *stop* him?"

"He's out of reach, Mrs. Cartwright. If we tried to get him, I'm afraid he'd jump."

"This is ridiculous! No, no, definitely not, I'm not going to be a party to it. I'm not going to talk to him until he comes in from there. You tell him that."

"Mrs. Cartwright—"

"I'm not going to have any more to do with it!"

The click was loud in Levine's ear as she slammed the receiver onto the hook. Crawley was looking at him, and now said, "Well?"

"She hung up."

"She isn't coming?" It was plain that Crawley was having trouble believing it.

Levine glanced at the son, who could hear every word he was saying, and then shrugged. "She wants him to jump," he said.

The son's reaction was much smaller than Levine had expected. He simply shook his head definitely and said, "No."

Levine waited, looking at him.

The son shook his head again. "That isn't true," he said. "She just doesn't understand—she doesn't really think he means it."

"All right," said Levine. He turned away from the son, trying to think. The wife, the marriage—A man in his late forties, married young, son grown and set up in his own vocation. A quiet man, who doesn't force his personality on others, and a forceful wife. A practical

24

wife, who pushed him into a successful business.

Levine made his decision. He nodded, and went back through the receptionist's office, where the other patrolman, McCann, was chatting with the three women employees. Levine went into Anderson's office, said, "Excuse me. Could I have the use of your office for a little while?"

"Certainly." Anderson got up from his desk, came around, saying, "Anything at all, anything at all."

"Thank you."

Levine followed Anderson back to the receptionist's office, looked over the three women sitting against the left hand wall. Two were fortyish, plumpish, wearing wedding bands. The third looked to be in her early thirties, was tall and slender, good-looking in a solid level-eyed way, not glamorous. She wore no rings at all.

Levine went over to the third woman, said, "Could I speak to you for a minute, please?"

She looked up, startled, a bit frightened. "What? Oh. Oh, yes, of course."

She followed him back into Anderson's office. He motioned her to the chair facing Anderson's desk, himself sat behind the desk. "My name is Levine," he said. "Detective Abraham Levine. And you are—?"

"Janice Shapleigh," she said. Her voice was low, pleasantly melodious. She was wearing normal office clothing, a grey plain skirt and white plain blouse.

"You've worked here how long?"

"Three years." She was answering readily enough, with no hesitations, but deep in her eyes he could see she was frightened, and wary.

"Mister Cartwright won't tell us why he wants to kill himself," he began. "He's asked to speak to his wife, but she refuses to leave home—" He detected a tightening of her lips when he said that. Disapproval of Mrs. Cartwright? He went on. "—which we haven't told him yet. He doesn't really want to jump, Miss Shapleigh. He's a frustrated, thwarted man. There's something he wants or needs that he can't get, and he's chosen this way to try to force the issue." He paused, studying her face, said, "Would that something be you?"

Color started in her cheeks, and she opened her mouth for what he knew would be an immediate denial. But the denial didn't come. Instead, Janice Shapleigh sagged in the chair, defeated and miserable, not meeting Levine's eyes. In a small voice, barely audible, she said, "I didn't think he'd do anything like this. I never thought he'd do anything like this."

"He wants to marry you, is that it? And he can't get a divorce."

The girl nodded, and all at once she began to cry. She wept with one closed hand pressed to her mouth, muffling the sound, her head bowed as though she were ashamed of this weakness, ashamed to be seen crying.

Levine waited, watching her with the dulled helplessness of a man whose job by its very nature kept him exposed to the misery and frustrations of others. He would always want to help, and he would always be unable to help, to really help.

Janice Shapleigh controlled herself, slowly and painfully. When she looked up again, Levine knew she was finished weeping, no matter what happened. "What do you want me to do?" she said.

"Talk to him. His wife won't come—she knows what he wants to say to her, I suppose—so you're the only one."

"What can I say to him?"

Levine felt weary, heavy. Breathing, working the heart, pushing the sluggish blood through veins and arteries, was wearing, hopeless, exhausting labor. "I don't know," he said. "He wants to die because of you. Tell him why he should live."

Levine stood by the right-hand window, just out of sight of the man on the ledge. The son and the priest and Crawley and Gundy were all across the room, watching and waiting, the son looking bewildered, the priest relieved, Crawley sour, Gundy excited.

Janice Shapleigh was at the left-hand window, tense and frightened. She leaned out, looking down, and Levine saw her body go rigid, saw her hands tighten on the window-frame. She closed her eyes, swaying, inhaling, and Levine stood ready to move. If she were to faint from that position, she could fall out the window.

But she didn't faint. She raised her head and opened her eyes, and carefully avoided looking down at the street again. She looked, instead, to her right, toward the man on the ledge. "Jay," she said. "Jay, please."

"Jan!" Cartwright sounded surprised. "What are you doing? Jan, go back in there, stay away from this. Go back in there."

Levine stood by the window, listening. What would she say to him? What *could* she say to him?

"Jay," she said, slowly, hesitantly, "Jay, please. It isn't worth it. Nothing is worth—dying for."

"Where's Laura?"

Levine waited, unbreathing, and at last the girl spoke the lie he had placed in her mouth. "She's on the way. She'll be here soon. But what does it matter, Jay? She still won't agree, you know that. She won't believe you."

"I'll wait for Laura," he said.

The son was suddenly striding across the room, shouting, "What is this? What's going on here?"

Levine spun around, motioning angrily for the boy to be quiet.

"Who is that woman?" demanded the son. "What's she doing here?"

Levine intercepted him before he could get to Janice Shapleigh, pressed both palms flat against the boy's shirt-front. "Get back over there," he whispered fiercely. "Get back over there."

"Get away from me! Who is she? What's going on here?"

"Allan?" It was Cartwright's voice, shouting the question. "Allan?"

Crawley now had the boy's arms from behind, and he and Levine propelled him toward the door. "Let me *go!*" cried the boy. "I've got a right to—"

Crawley's large hand clamped across his mouth, and the three of them barreled through to the receptionist's office. As the door closed behind them, Levine heard Janice Shapleigh repeating, "Jay? Listen to me, Jay, please. Please, Jay."

The door safely shut behind them, the two detectives let the boy go. He turned immediately, trying to push past them and get back inside, crying, "You can't do this! Let me go! What do you think you are? Who is that woman?"

"Shut up," said Levine. He spoke softly, but the boy quieted at once. In his voice had been all his own miseries, all his own frustrations, and his utter weariness with the misery and frustration of others.

"I'll tell you who that woman is," Levine said. "She's the woman your father wants to marry. He wants to divorce your mother and marry her."

"No," said the boy, as sure and positive as he had been earlier in denying that his mother would want to see his father dead.

"Don't say no," said Levine coldly. "I'm telling you facts. That's what sent him out there on that ledge. Your mother won't agree to the divorce."

"My mother—"

"Your mother," Levine pushed coldly on, "planned your father's life. Now, all at once, he's reached the age where he should have accomplished whatever he set out to do. His son is grown, he's making good money, now's the time for him to look around and say, 'This is the world I made for myself, and it's a good one.' But he can't. Because he doesn't like his life, it isn't *his* life, it's the life your mother planned for him."

"You're wrong," said the boy. "You're wrong."

"So he went looking," said Levine, ignoring the boy's interruptions, "and he found Janice Shapleigh. She wouldn't push him, she wouldn't plan for him, she'd let *him* be the strong one."

The boy just stood there, shaking his head, repeating over and over, "You're wrong. You're wrong."

Levine grimaced, in irritation and defeat. *You never break through,* he thought. *You never break through.* Aloud he said, "In twenty years you'll believe me." He looked over at the patrolman, McCann. "Keep this young man out here with you," he said.

"Right," said McCann.

"Why?" cried the son. "He's my father! Why can't I go in there?"

"Shame," Levine told him. "If he saw his son and this woman at the same time, he'd jump."

The boy's eyes widened. He started to shake his head, then just stood there, staring.

Levine and Crawley went back into the other room.

Janice Shapleigh was coming away from the window, her face ashen. "Somebody down on the sidewalk started taking pictures," she said. "Jay shouted at them to stop. He told me to get in out of sight, or he'd jump right now."

"Respectability," said Levine, as though the word were obscene. "We're all fools."

Crawley said, "Think we ought to send someone for the wife?"

28

"No. She'd only make it worse. She'd say no, and he'd go over."

"Oh God!" Janice Shapleigh swayed suddenly and Crawley grabbed her arm, led her across to one of the leather sofas.

Levine went back to the right-hand window. He looked out. A block away, on the other side of the street, there was a large clock in front of a bank building. It was almost eleven-thirty. They'd been here almost an hour and a half.

Three o'clock, he thought suddenly. This thing had to be over before three o'clock, that was the time of his appointment with the doctor.

He looked out at Cartwright. The man was getting tired. His face was drawn with strain and emotion, and his fingertips were clutching tight to the rough face of the wall. Levine said, "Cartwright."

The man turned his head, slowly, afraid now of rapid movement. He looked at Levine without speaking.

"Cartwright," said Levine. "Have you thought about it now? Have you thought about death?"

"I want to talk to my wife."

"You could fall before she got here," Levine told him. "She has a long way to drive, and you're getting tired. Come in, come in here. You can talk to her in here when she arrives. You've proved your point, man, you can come in. Do you want to get too tired, do you want to lose your balance, lose your footing, slip and fall?"

"I want to talk to my wife," he said, doggedly.

"Cartwright, you're *alive*." Levine stared helplessly at the man, searching for the way to tell him how precious that was, the fact of being alive. "You're breathing," he said. "You can see and hear and smell and taste and touch. You can laugh at jokes, you can love a woman— For God's sake, man, you're *alive!*"

Cartwright's eyes didn't waver; his expression didn't change. "I want to talk to my wife," he repeated.

"Listen," said Levine. "You've been out here two hours now. You've had time to think about death, about non-being. Cartwright, listen. Look at me, Cartwright, I'm going to the doctor at three o'clock this afternoon. He's going to tell me about my heart, Cartwright. He's going to tell me if my heart is getting too tired. He's going to tell me if I'm going to stop being alive."

Levine strained with the need to tell this fool what he was throwing away, and knew it was hopeless.

The priest was back, all at once, at the other window. "Can we help you?" he asked. "Is there anything any of us can do to help you?"

Cartwright's head swiveled slowly. He studied the priest. "I want to talk to my wife," he said.

Levine gripped the windowsill. There had to be a way to bring him in, there had to be a way to trick him or force him or convince him to come in. He had to be brought in, he couldn't throw his life away, that's the only thing a man really has.

Levine wished desperately that *he* had the choice.

He leaned out again suddenly, glaring at the back of Cartwright's head. "Jump!" he shouted.

Cartwright's head swiveled around, the face open, the eyes shocked, staring at Levine in disbelief.

"Jump!" roared Levine. "Jump, you damn fool, end it, stop being alive, *die! Jump!* Throw yourself away, you imbecile, JUMP!"

Wide-eyed, Cartwright stared at Levine's flushed face, looked out and down at the crowd, the fire truck, the ambulance, the uniformed men, the chalked circle on the pavement.

And all at once he began to cry. His hands came up to his face, he swayed, and the crowd down below sighed, like a breeze rustling. "God help me!" Cartwright screamed.

Crawley came swarming out the other window, his legs held by Gundy. He grabbed for Cartwright's arm, growling, "All right, now, take it easy. Take it easy. This way, this way, just slide your feet along, don't try to bring the other foot around, just slide over, easy, easy—"

And the man came stumbling in from the ledge.

"You took a chance," said Crawley. "You took one hell of a chance." It was two-thirty, and Crawley was driving him to the doctor's office.

"I know," said Levine. His hands were still shaking; he could still feel the ragged pounding of his heart within his chest.

"But you called his bluff," said Crawley. "That kind, it's just a bluff. They don't really want to dive, they're bluffing."

"I know," said Levine.

"But you still took a hell of a chance."

"It—" Levine swallowed. It felt as though there were something hard caught in his throat. "It was the only way to get him in," he said. "The wife wasn't coming, and nothing else would bring him in. When the girlfriend failed—"

"It took guts, Abe. For a second there, I almost thought he was going to take you up on it."

"So did I."

Crawley pulled in at the curb in front of the doctor's office. "I'll pick you up around quarter to four," he said.

"I can take a cab," said Levine.

"Why? Why, for the love of Mike? The city's paying for the gas."

Levine smiled at his partner. "All right," he said. He got out of the car, went up the walk, up the stoop, onto the front porch. He looked back, watched the Chevvy turn the corner. He whispered, "I *wanted* him to jump." And he thought, "It's crazy. How would that have kept my number from being up?"

Then he went in to find out if he was going to stay alive.

Once Upon a Bank Floor

by James Holding

I usually buy a mystery story magazine to kill the tedium of a plane ride, but this time I didn't need it. The man who had the window seat beside me was better than any magazine.

He was middle-aged and dressed conservatively but rather carelessly. He had a double chin and bushy brows over gentle brown eyes. When I sat down in the aisle seat beside him before take-off, he glanced casually at me. I wanted to start a conversation but just couldn't do it. And he didn't say anything until we were airborne and had unsnapped our seat belts.

His opening remark was purely tentative, a friendly overture. He said, "I see you're a mystery story fan," his eyes going to the magazine in my hand.

"Not really a fan," I said, "but I find them a pleasant way to pass the time on a plane ride."

"I'm not really a fan, either," he said. "I read mystery stories as much to keep up-to-date on the new criminal techniques as anything else."

"That could mislead a lot of people," I said, making a pleasantry of it, "into thinking you were a crook reading your trade journals."

He grinned disarmingly. "It's not as bad as that," he said. "I work for a bank. Banks deal in money, and money draws criminals. I want to be ready for trouble if they try anything on the bank where I work, that's all." He added companionably, "My name's Colbaugh."

"Mine's Dickson," I said. "Glad to know you."

He said, "I was mixed up in a bank robbery once myself, at the Merchants National Bank in . . ." He named a small California town. "So I know how unexpectedly such things can happen."

"It sounds exciting," I remarked idly.

He shrugged. "You could call it exciting, all right." He leaned back in his seat and closed his eyes, evidently considering the amenities preserved.

But I wanted to get the story out of him, hear him tell it. "Tell me about it," I said.

"You'll be bored," he protested, opening his eyes again. "But all right. It's not a very long story. And it happened twenty years ago. I was a kind of assistant-assistant cashier at the bank—a clerk, really. We had a night depository at the bank where the town's merchants could deposit their cash for safekeeping after their stores closed up for the night. And as all the stores stayed open until nine o'clock on Thursday evenings in those days, there was always a good bit of cash to be found in our night depository on Friday mornings."

"I know how that goes," I said. "I own a sporting goods store in Fresno."

"Oh, really? That's a nice part of the country. Well, one of my jobs was to get down to the bank early in the mornings and clean out the deposits in the night depository so I could have them all tallied and on the assistant cashier's desk when he arrived for work at opening time. So I was always the first one there; other employees would begin to drift in about fifteen minutes before opening time, but I had the bank to myself for a good half hour each morning. And I kind of liked it, you know? It made me feel responsible to have the run of the place before anybody else got there."

I nodded comprehendingly.

"Well, one morning I left my house about eight o'clock as usual, and I was standing on my regular corner waiting for the bus that I rode to work, when a gray Ford sedan came along and stopped beside the bus stand and the driver leaned over and asked me if I wanted a lift downtown. I said sure and got in beside him when he pushed the car door open for me."

"In a mystery story," I said wisely, "you'd have been suspicious of the guy for offering you something for nothing. You'd have said no thanks and waited for your bus."

"Very probably. But it never entered my mind there was any hanky-panky afoot that morning. I got into the Ford and only then realized that there were two other men sitting in the back seat behind the driver and me. The thing that struck me most forcibly about them,

33

was that the one on the right held a long-barreled revolver of some sort in his hand, and it was pointed right at me. The gun didn't have any sights on the front. I remember noticing that in my shock and surprise."

"Sounds like a Woodsman with the sights filed off," I said. "Kind of a target pistol. I sell them in my store. That joker must have been a crack shot to work with a sporting gun like that."

"As far as I was concerned, he certainly was! I didn't say or do a single thing to attract attention to my plight, I can assure you, because the man with the gun told me not to. And that was a plenty good enough reason for me.

"We drove to the bank in dead silence, but at a very sedate speed. The driver stopped the Ford at the rear of the bank where I always went in, just as though he knew all about my daily routine. The bank backed on a narrow lane, or alley, and the rear door was used only by employees. At that early hour, the lane was deserted.

"The man with the gun said to me, 'Here we are, Buster. Out.' He motioned for me to get out of the car. He and the other man in the back seat got out, too. The gun-bearer was tall and blond and skinny, painfully thin. The other fellow was chunky and had fuzzy black hair growing down the back of his neck all the way to his collar, I remember that. The tall one said to the driver, 'Stay with the crate,' and then to me, 'Now, let's open up and go inside, if you don't mind.' His voice was cool and polite and unhurried, as though he did this sort of thing every day. Maybe he did.

"I couldn't see much point in arguing when that long gun barrel was poking into my back, so I got out my keys and opened the door. As I put the key in the lock, my sleeve pulled back, and I saw by my wrist watch it was only 8:15—still quite awhile before I could expect the bank guard or any of our other employees to show up. But I knew the time lock on the vault was set for just a few minutes before the bank opened, and I was pretty sure they couldn't do anything about *that*, unless they waited for opening time.

"We went inside. The tall man shattered any frail hopes I'd entertained with four words. He said to me, 'The night depository, Junior,' and I realized then that they *did* know what my routine was. They must have watched me for a few mornings to see what I did. I believe that's what they call 'casing the joint,' isn't it, Mr. Dickson?"

34

Colbaugh looked at me expectantly, as though wanting me to compliment him on his command of thieves' argot, derived, no doubt, from his reading of mystery stories. I said, "Yeah." It *was* strange to hear the expression come from the lips of this dignified middle-aged bank clerk.

"They forced me," he continued, "toward the night depository receptacle in the wall of the bank inside the front door. In those days, they didn't have solid ranks of all-glass, electric-eye doors for bank entrances the way we do now. Our bank just had a regular steel-frame front door with glass in it down to knee-height like any store door. And, there was a venetian blind on the inside of this door to keep the afternoon sun out of the eyes of Mr. Johnson, one of our vice presidents, whose desk was just to the right of the entrance. This blind was lowered after the sun moved around into Mr. Johnson's eyes every afternoon. And, it was left like that—lowered—until I came to work the next day, when I raised it as my first official act each morning on my way to clean out the night depository." Mr. Colbaugh turned his serene eyes on me and said deprecatingly, "You can see I had a lot of odd chores to do around the bank, Mr. Dickson. I was almost the janitor, really." He laughed before he went on.

"Even with the gun in my back, habit was strong in me that morning; I reached out automatically to raise Mr. Johnson's venetian blind on the front door as we went by. But the man behind me with the gun said, 'What do you think you're doing? Freeze!' I froze. I said, 'I raise this blind every morning. I was just going to draw it up . . .' 'Today,' he said, 'we won't raise it, Junior. If you don't mind. You think we want every jerk on the sidewalk to see what's going on in here?'

"I thought I ought to make some token effort, at least, to resist the robbers, so as we approached the night depository, I said, in what I fear was not a very convincing voice, 'I can't open this thing. It takes a special key. The assistant-cashier carries the only key, and he won't be here till the bank opens.'

"The short man didn't say anything, merely pulled a gun out of his pocket and went to stand beside the front door, looking out into the street through the slats of the lowered blind but hidden from the eyes of anybody outside. But the tall thin man jabbed his gun barrel harder than ever into my spine. 'Don't give me that, Buster,' he said. 'I know who opens this thing every morning. *You.* So fly at it. And don't make

35

me wait. My nerves are getting pretty jumpy.' He didn't sound a bit nervous to me."

"But *you* must have been," I put in.

Mr. Colbaugh nodded vigorously. "I was terrified. Almost stiff with fright. I got out my key to the depository box and opened it up as meek as Moses. What else could I do?"

"I would have done the same," I consoled him.

"This was Friday morning, and there was quite a large amount of cash and a lot of checks in the depository from the merchants' Thursday night receipts. The tall man grunted with satisfaction when he saw how much was there. 'Clean it out,' he ordered me, 'and put it in this.' He held out a black briefcase to me.

"I did as he said, but I moved as slowly as possible without it seeming too obvious. Maybe I could delay them a little, I thought. But, when the money and the checks were all in the briefcase, it was still only eight-thirty.

"I was beginning to wonder what they intended to do with me when they left. I didn't feel sanguine about that at all. I'd seen their faces. I could describe them to the police. I could identify them. And, I'd ridden in their Ford and could identify it, too, for I'd memorized the license number when I got out of the car at the rear of the bank.

"The tall man said, 'Lay down on the floor, buddy . . . on your back.' I did so. Right in the middle of the marble lobby. I felt very foolish, I can tell you. And very exposed, too. For the short man at the front door could keep me covered with his gun and watch out the door, too.

"The tall man took a look at his wrist watch. And just then the telephone rang. It was the telephone on Mr. Johnson's desk by the front door. It sounded like a fire alarm in that empty bank. I was so startled, I jumped, if you can really jump when you're lying flat on your back on the floor. The tall man stooped over me and prodded me in the stomach with his gun.

" 'Get that, you!' he barked at me. All his polite coolness was gone now. 'Answer that phone! And make it sound natural, Buster, or you'll never live to take another phone call! Move!'

"The phone was ringing for the third time. 'Hold the receiver away from your ear,' he warned me, 'so I can hear it, too.'

"I got up from the floor and went over and picked up the telephone, with the tall man right beside me. The short one hadn't said anything, but his gun was trained on me, now. I cleared my throat and said, 'Hello?' into the receiver, loud and clear. 'Is this the Farmers National?' came the tinny inquiry, as I held the receiver so the tall man could hear it.

"His gun was boring into my back. 'Yes, sir,' I said into the phone.

"'How late do you stay open this afternoon?' the voice asked. I looked at the bandit beside me and raised my eyebrows.

"'Tell him!' he whispered.

"I said into the phone, 'We close at three-thirty, sir.'

"'Thanks,' came the answer, and we could both hear the sharp click that sounded as the caller hung up.

"I put down the phone. There was sweat on my forehead and I felt sick. I looked at the short man's gun that was aimed at my mid-section from five feet away, and my knees shook. The tall man let out his breath in a 'whoosh' of relief.

"'Okay, Shiner,' he said to his pal, 'back to the door.' And to me, 'And you get back where you were, Buster.' He waved his gun at me. I lay down on the floor again.

"'Plenty of time, Shiner,' he called to his partner, then. 'Watch the kid, here. I'm going to take a look in the tellers' cages.'

"He went out of my sight, then, and I could hear him jerking open the cash drawers and swearing when he found them empty.

"I could see the minute hand on our big wall clock above the New Accounts desk moving with tiny jerks; one jerk for every thousand years, it seemed to me. It made four of these jerks by the time the tall man was satisfied that he wasn't overlooking anything in the tellers' cages. I could have told him we always locked up the cash in the vault.

"He came out into the lobby again where Shiner and I were, the briefcase in his left hand, his gun in his right. He motioned Shiner toward the rear door of the bank, the way we'd come in. So they weren't going to wait for the time lock on the vault. They were leaving. I could hear my heart thudding against the marble floor, as though the floor were a sounding board.

"Shiner left his post by the front door. 'What about him?' he asked the tall one, pointing his gun at me.

"'Put him out,' the other one said matter-of-factly, 'the way I told you.'"

Mr. Colbaugh turned and looked at me with a smile softening his mouth and crinkling up his eyes. "I can tell you, Mr. Dickson, I was awfully scared at that point. I didn't know whether they meant to kill me or just knock me out, or what. 'Put him out' could have meant anything. Then I saw Shiner reversing his gun in his hand and leaning over me and swinging the butt at my head, and that's all I saw for awhile."

I said, "The banking business has more hazards than I'd realized."

"It has indeed," he said. "I found out later that the bandits had another car waiting for them half a mile away, and that the Ford had been stolen. They were from out of state, it developed, and unknown in our town. So they didn't think it necessary to kill me. They just put me out of business while they made their getaway."

"So what happened?" I asked, the way a good listener should.

"The police took them easily as they emerged from the rear door of the bank," Colbaugh said. "The driver of the Ford was already in custody. The police had the bank surrounded."

We could hear the motors change pitch as our plane started to let down for a landing.

"The police!" I said, astounded. "Where'd *they* come from?"

"Johnny Sampson sent them."

I looked at him blankly. "Who was Johnny Sampson?"

"We went to high school together," Colbaugh said. "He was my best friend in the bank, a teller."

"What made him send for the police?"

"When he telephoned the bank and asked the closing time, I told him 3:30. But he knew it closed at 3:00. So that was his signal. To call the police."

I reached up for my hat and coat as I saw the airport runways coming up to meet us.

"You mean that telephone call was rigged?" I asked. "You had it all arranged with Sampson beforehand?"

"Sure." He smiled, pleased at my surprise. "That's what I meant when I said I liked to be ready for trouble at the bank. Johnny and I had it all worked out."

"Wait a minute," I protested. "Even so, how did Sampson know he should call you that particular morning? Did he do it every day?"

"Oh, no. Johnny was a bachelor," Colbaugh said, as though that explained everything. "He always ate his breakfast around the corner at Mother Hague's Coffee Shop before coming to work at the bank. He passed the bank entrance to get to the coffee shop at the same time every morning—8:20. And if he ever saw that the venetian blind on the bank's front door was still lowered when he went to breakfast, he was supposed to telephone the bank and ask what time it closed. If I answered and gave him the wrong closing time, call the police. If anybody but me answered, call the police. If nobody answered, call the police. You see how simple it was?"

"Very simple," I said, "if anything as complicated as that can be simple. What if you were sick and didn't come to work some morning and, therefore, failed to raise the venetian blind?"

"If I was sick, my wife phoned Sampson at his home before he went to breakfast and told him the venetian blind would be down when he passed it."

"How about Sampson, though? Suppose *he'd* been sick on the day of the hold-up?"

"An unlikely coincidence," Colbaugh said. "I guess that would have been just too bad for me and the night deposits."

I unfastened my seat belt as I felt the wheels touch down. "I'd say it was too bad for you anyway, wasn't it? You were the 'inside' man of your live burglar alarm system. You took the chances. You got knocked silly by the hold-up men, while your friend Sampson ate bacon and eggs in Mother Hague's Coffee Shop."

We stood up.

"Yes, that's true, I suppose," Colbaugh conceded. "But we were young. And, as you suggested earlier, it *was* exciting. You have no idea, Mr. Dickson, how exciting it is to see a gun butt being swung at your head and then not be sure until two hours later when you regain consciousness, that you haven't been murdered!"

I said, "Are you still with Merchants National?"

"Yes, still at the same old stand. So's Johnny Sampson. He's the president of the bank now."

"Good for him. Virtue's reward. And what's your job these days, Mr. Colbaugh?"

"I'm chairman of the board," he said, smiling. "Still taking the chances, you see."

"Now, I''ve got the whole story," I said ambiguously. "Right down to the present."

We walked down the ramp into the airport terminal together. I was slightly behind him. My topcoat was over my right arm. On impulse, when we got inside the terminal lobby, I pushed my forefinger into his back, under cover of my topcoat, and said, "Turn left, Mr. Colbaugh, and go into the men's room, will you?"

He reacted quite calmly. His eyes widened a little as they swiveled toward me. He stiffened slightly, and I could feel his back muscles come up under my finger for a second. Then he said, "The washroom? Why?" But he kept on walking.

"Now don't tell me that your assistant cashier has the only key to *this*," I said. "Here we are. Go on in."

We went in. It was a slack time; the washroom was empty, as I'd hoped.

When the door swished shut behind us, I took my forefinger out of Colbaugh's back and he turned toward me. He really looked at me this time, tilting his head back to gaze up into my face. And he got it right away.

He said, "You've taken on a good bit of weight since then, Dickson. And changed your name. Do you really own a sporting goods store in Fresno?"

"I was anticipating there a little," I said, smiling at him. "I *clerk* in a sporting goods store, and I have a wonderful opportunity to buy into it if I can raise two thousand dollars by the end of this week."

"Oh," Colbaugh said. "You're going straight, then?"

"I'm trying to, since I got out." I held up my finger. "I don't file the sights off my guns any more, you see?"

He said, "Why don't you swing a loan?"

"Did you ever know anybody who would lend money to an ex-con? I've tried."

"You didn't try our bank."

"I was going to. At least I went to your bank this morning to make an appeal to you personally, if you still worked there."

"Why didn't you?"

"I lost my nerve when I saw your line-up of loan officers and vice presidents. I knew they'd nix me for sure. It had to be you or nobody."

"So you followed me onto the plane, is that it?"

"Yes. I happened to see you walk through the bank with your hat and coat and overnight bag and get into the airport taxi. I recognized you right away. So, I followed you to the airport and bought a seat on the same flight."

He nodded, his face expressionless. "Two thousand dollars?"

"That's all. And I have no collateral, Mr. Colbaugh."

He allowed himself a tight smile. "You told Shiner to put me out that day, Dickson. He clubbed me with a gun. And remember I was just a kid."

"I know it. And I'm not proud of it. But think of it this way, Mr. Colbaugh. Wasn't your successful prevention of that bank robbery the first thing that made your bank management really *notice* you and Sampson? Isn't that what triggered the whole series of promotions that led you both to the top jobs you have today?"

I watched him narrowly, temporarily forgetting to breathe. For this was the only weapon I could use in my second hold-up of Colbaugh.

He didn't say anything for a minute, thinking it over. Then, his lips curled up a trifle, and I began to breathe again.

"You know," he said, "I think you're right, Dickson. It *was* through you that I first drew favorable notice at the bank. I never thought of it like that before, but in a sort of cock-eyed way, I suppose I owe you something for it. And so does Sampson."

"How about a thousand dollars apiece? You could call it a personal loan, Mr. Colbaugh. And I'll pay it back."

He made up his mind quickly. "I believe you will, at that," he said. He got out his checkbook and wrote out a check to cash for two thousand dollars. As he handed it to me, and we shook hands, he said curiously, "Why'd you bring me in here? Why not brace me in the plane or out in the lobby?"

I looked around at the bare white-tiled walls of the washroom and grinned at him. "No venetian blinds in here," I said.

Warrior's Farewell

by Edward D. Hoch

Some early morning fishermen had found the body, washed up on the sandy beach like a great dead whale cast aside by nature, and it was only a few hours until the authorities identified the man as Sam Zodiak, an unmarried used car dealer and petty gambler.

I read the item in the afternoon editions of the paper with great interest because at one time Sam Zodiak had probably been my best friend. He was a large man in every way, and when I first knew him he was an army sergeant, looking very much the part. That was something like fifteen years ago, in a place called Korea that most of the kids today don't even remember.

I was young and sort of frightened in those days—frightened of a place I didn't know and people I didn't understand. Prowling the streets of Seoul at night, lonely and far from home, I was thankful for the company of a man like Sergeant Zodiak. Unlike the others, he wasn't particularly interested in picking up any of the girls who cluttered the bars of the city, and he managed to stay reasonably sober during the hours we'd spend together.

"You know, Corporal," he'd say over a beer at a crowded back table in one of those smoky places, "I just look forward to doing my job every day. Sometimes I think the two most important words in the language are *war* and *justice*. And they're not a great deal different from each other, if you're fighting a just war like this one. They're invaders, and they got to be killed. It's as simple as that."

"You talk like a career soldier, Sarge." I liked to kid him about it.

"I'll stay in as long as they need me, that's for sure." He took the cigar out of his mouth. "Justice! That's what we got to deliver."

"What about when you get home?" I sipped my beer. "A lot of the fellows talk about going back to school."

"Hell, I'm too old for that. I'm over thirty already. No, I'm going to get me a little lot and sell used cars. That's where the money is. Then maybe I'll take off an afternoon a week and go out to the racetrack or something. I like to see them ponies run."

"They say it might be a long war here, Sarge."

He puffed on the cigar for a minute. "Well, then I'll stay a long time. First things first. We got to end this thing."

Two weeks later we went into battle together, one of the last big engagements before the truce was signed, and I saw for myself exactly what he meant. It was a bloody scrap, not far from the 38th Parallel, in an area of hilly farmland that had changed hands at least twice before. The planes had softened up the area, leaving only the old stone farmhouse standing roofless in the sun. We came over the hill with our rifles ready, backed up by a BAR and mortar team, and immediately exchanged fire with a retreating enemy squad. It was the better part of an hour before we'd taken the farmhouse and decided we could hold it till morning.

After an hour or so of scouting the area, we flushed out a Korean farmer who'd been hiding in a ditch. He didn't look quite right, but then none of them ever did to our eyes. He seemed friendly enough at first, and pretty soon the PFC who was guarding him put down his carbine to light a cigarette. It was his first and last mistake. The farmer made a dive for the rifle and got off two quick shots before I ran up and clubbed him to the ground with my own weapon. The PFC was dead.

"He's a North Korean officer," I said, ripping away the farm clothes to reveal the last vestiges of a uniform beneath. "I guess we came on too fast for him to get away."

"Damn spy!" Sergeant Zodiak muttered. He was the ranking non-com, and he had to decide what to do with the man. "Too bad you didn't kill him." The man was bleeding from the temple but otherwise seemed to be suffering no ill effects from my blows.

"It was faster to slug him, Sarge. I didn't want him spraying bullets around the place. Shall we send somebody back with him?"

"With the kid dead, we can't spare a man."

"We leave him tied up in the farmhouse, then. They'll find him to-morrow."

Sergeant Zodiak shook his head. "And let him kill somebody else, maybe? No, there's only one way to handle his kind." He reached out and took the carbine from me.

"He's a prisoner of war, Sarge!"

"Like hell he is! He's out of uniform. He's nothing but a spy and a murderer, and as such he can be executed."

"Without a trial?"

But Sergeant Zodiak half turned toward the prisoner and fired a quick burst from the carbine, ending the discussion. The man's head jerked back in the shock of death and he went down hard in the tall grass of the field.

We left him there with the other bodies, and nobody ever mentioned it again.

Sergeant Zodiak surprised me and everyone else when he didn't re-enlist for another tour of duty. He returned to the States with me, and we were discharged together in San Francisco. I moved east after that, spending a couple of years finishing my education at a little college in Ohio, but all the time I kept in touch with Zodiak, and an odd sort of friendship seemed to grow between us.

I saw him once after college on a trip out west, and we went on a two-day drunk that was unlike any of our subdued army outings. Sam had his used car lot and was making a pretty good living at it. Drinking together on that visit, I think we both realized for the first time the bond of friendship that existed between us. Six months later, when I married a girl I'd met in college, Sam Zodiak came east to be my best man.

After that, I didn't hear from him for something like a year, until he phoned me one evening and told me he was getting married. "That's great news, Sam," I told him, meaning it. "I was beginning to think you'd never do it."

"I want you out here for it," he said. "Best man, the whole deal."

"Just let me know the date and I'll be there."

Sam had left San Francisco and was living in a smaller ocean community in a neighboring state. I flew out there on my vacation, although the wedding was still a month away. I was anxious to meet the girl Sam Zodiak had finally chosen.

I never did meet Ann. On the very night I was flying out, an ex-mental patient who lived in the next block from her went wild and shot his wife. Then he went out on his front porch with the gun, saw Ann running across the street toward the house, and shot her dead. He wounded two others before the police managed to subdue him, and I arrived at the airport to find that tragedy had struck Sam Zodiak.

"I don't know what to do," he told me the next day. "I'm just lost and going around in circles. Ann was a nurse, always wanting to help people. We were just getting out of the car when she heard the shots and went running. Crazy! I should have grabbed her. I should have held her back. I should have done a hundred things."

"It wasn't your fault."

"The hell of it is, this fellow Gondon will get off free. There's not even a death penalty in this state any more."

"They'll put him away for a long time."

"A few years in a mental hospital and he'll be walking the streets a free man. I know."

I stayed for the week, trying to calm him, and I thought I'd succeeded pretty well. His prediction proved to be correct, though, and George Gondon was never brought to trial for killing Ann. The others recovered from their wounds, including his wife, and Gondon was sent to the state hospital for treatment.

I went back east to my own wife and, though the correspondence with Sam Zodiak continued, we saw no more of each other for three years. Then one day I received a brief letter from him, enclosing a newspaper clipping. It told how a man named George Gondon, recently released from a mental hospital, had been shot and killed during an apparent robbery. Sam's only comment on the clipping was a single sentence in his letter: *This is what I call justice, not revenge.*

Shortly after that, I changed jobs and became a purchasing expediter for a large chemical firm. One of my duties was a monthly trip to a supplier in Sam's city. Suddenly we were seeing each other again, on a regular basis.

One night, over beers, I asked him how he was doing.

"Darned good. The used car business is a little off, but I'm making it up at the track. Even own part interest in a racehorse now."

"That's great, Sam." I found myself trying to read the backward lettering on the neon sign in the bar's front window. "There's something I've been wanting to ask you," I said finally.

"Fire away, boy!"

"That clipping you sent me a few months back, about that fellow

45

who killed Ann."

"Yeah?" I could read nothing into his expression.

"Well, Sam . . . How should I say it?"

"I'll say it for you," he told me quietly. "It's no mystery, really. The thing's in the Bible. An eye for an eye, and all that stuff. There's not even a death penalty in this state anymore."

"I know." Suddenly my blood had turned cold.

"I know what you're thinking. You're remembering that time in Korea."

"No."

"I was right then, and I'm right now. He killed Ann, and nobody punished him for it. What was I supposed to do?"

I couldn't answer that. I didn't want to answer it. I just wanted to get away from there as quickly as I could.

After that, I started cutting down on my visits with Sam Zodiak. Sometimes I'd sneak into town for a day and not even tell him about it. I saw the signs for his used car place around town, and I knew he must be doing pretty well, but I didn't want to see him anymore.

About a year after George Gondon's death, the city where Sam lived was the scene of a particularly brutal sex murder involving a fourteen-year-old girl. She'd been found in the trunk of an abandoned car, and it took the police only an hour to trace the ownership of the vehicle and send out a ten-state alarm. The suspect was arrested in San Francisco a few days later and brought back to Sam's city under close police guard. The newspapers reported that the man had confessed to the killing.

There were maybe a hundred people outside police headquarters when the suspect, a young man named Asker, arrived. As he was led into the building between two detectives, a single shot from somewhere across the street hit him in the back of the head, killing him instantly. In the near panic that followed, the killer made a clean getaway.

I read the newspaper accounts of the killing with a gnawing sense of urgency. It couldn't be Sam Zodiak again, it just couldn't be, yet I had to know, to be certain. I arranged to fly out there the following weekend.

I wired Sam that I was coming, and he met me at the airport, smiling and friendly as ever, despite the fact that I'd seen little of him during the past year. "How you been, boy? How's the wife? Any kids yet?" He was the same old Sam, and I instantly regretted the suspicions which had been breeding in my mind; regretted them until I remembered Gondon and the Korean thing.

Later, over dinner, I ventured into the object of my trip. "I read about the killing of that fellow, Asker, at police headquarters. Awful thing."

"Awful? Asker's crime was awful, his killing wasn't."

"He hadn't even stood trial yet."

Sam Zodiak waved his hand. "What good would a trial have been? There's no death penalty in this state anymore."

"No." I lit a cigarette and tried to keep my hand from shaking. "Then you think his killing was justified?"

"Of course."

"Just like George Gondon's."

"Just like it. The people of this state never had a chance to vote on capital punishment. The legislature and the governor just got together and abolished it. You think that's right?"

"For some people it's hard to tell the difference between right and wrong. You killed Asker, didn't you?"

He eyed me slyly across the table. "Justice was done."

"Sam, Sam! What's happening to you?"

"It's not me—it's the modern morality—or lack of it." He focused on me with wide, intent eyes. "People look at me and what do they see? A used car dealer, a petty gambler. I suppose I'm the sort of guy who's supposed to have no morals at all. And yet, look at the rest of them! Condoning every sort of violence, every excess. The murderer today is to be pitied—because of his tragic childhood, or low IQ, or mental illness, or economic blight. They don't execute murderers any more, they send them to the hospital, or to prison for a few years. And then they turn them free to kill again."

I had to get out of there, into the fresh air where maybe it wouldn't seem so much of a bad dream. Sam paid the check and left with me, strolling at my side with one arm around my shoulders like the old army buddy he was. "I'm a warrior in the battle for justice," he said. "A warrior."

"I think you're mad," I told him. "How long are you going to keep this up?"

The sly look was back on his face, not entirely hidden by the night. "You're a buddy, so I'll tell you something. You'd never prove it to the police anyway, so I'm safe in telling you. There've been five of them now, five of them since last year. The others were downstate, and didn't make such splashy headlines."

"Five!"

"All criminals, all *murderers* who'd escaped the death penalty because of our laws."

We were strolling across the bay bridge, with the lights of the harbor obscured by the nightly mists. I turned to him, for a moment speechless from the horror of what he was telling me. Then I said, "You really think you have the right?"

Sam Zodiak stared straight ahead at the deserted bridge. "I have three others on my list already."

It was then that I pushed him with all my strength, saw him grasping frantically at the railing before he toppled over, with the beginnings of a scream cut short as he hit the murky waters below.

They found his body the following morning, while I was still in town, and though I read the account in the afternoon paper with a growing sense of relief, there was one thing that nagged at my mind—one tiny, troublesome thing.

When he'd realized what I was doing, in that last second before his face vanished from sight, Sam Zodiak hadn't looked really angry. Instead, there'd been a sort of challenge in his expression.

As if he were saying to me, *See what I mean!*

Adventures of the Sussex Archers

by August Derleth

One summer evening late in the 1920's I returned to our Praed Street quarters to find my friend Solar Pons slouched in his armchair contemplating an unfolded piece of ruled paper.

"Ah, Parker," he said, without looking up, "you're just in time for what promises to be an entertaining diversion."

So saying, he handed to me the paper he had just been studying.

It was cheap tablet paper, of a kind readily obtainable in any stationer's shop. On it had been pasted, in letters cut from a newspaper yellowed by weather:

PREPARE FOR YOUR
PUNISHMENT!

In addition, a printed drawing of an arrow had been pasted to the paper.

"It was directed to Joshua Colvin of Lurgashall, Sussex," said Pons, "and reached me by messenger from Claridge's late this afternoon. This letter came with it."

He fished the letter out of the pocket of his dressing-gown.

"Dear Mr. Pons:

"If it is convenient for you, I hope to call on you at eight this evening in regard to a problem about which my father will do nothing in spite of the fact that one such warning has already been followed by death. I enclose the warning he received. Since I believe you are fully aware of current crimes and mysteries in England, may I call your attention to the death of Andrew Jefferds of Petworth, ten days ago? Should it be inconvenient for me to call, a wire to me at Claridge's will put me off. I am, sir, respectfully yours.

Hewitt Colvin"

"I see by the newspapers beside your chair you've looked up Jefferds' death," I said.

"Indeed I have. Jefferds, a man with no known enemies—we read nothing of those unknown—was done to death at twilight ten days ago in his garden at the edge of the village by means of an arrow in his back."

"Surely that is an unusual weapon!" I cried.

"Is it not! But a profoundly significant one, for it also appears on the warning, and would then no doubt have some significance to Mr. Colvin." He raised his head and listened. "That is a motor slowing outside, and I suspect it is our client."

In a few moments Mrs. Johnson showed Hewitt Colvin into our quarters. He was a ruddy-faced man in his thirties, with keen grey eyes. He wore moustache and sideburns, and looked the picture of the country squire.

"Mr. Pons," he said without preamble, "I hope you'll forgive the abruptness of my letter. Six men have received a copy of the warning I dispatched to you—one is already dead."

"Ah," said Pons, "the significance of the arrow!" He waved our client to a seat, but Colvin was too agitated to take it, for he strode back and forth. "What have these six men in common?"

"All belonged to the Sussex Archers."

"Active?"

"No, sir. That is the background of my problem. They've been disbanded ever since Henry Pope's death twenty years ago. Pope was the seventh member of the Archers. He died like Mr. Jefferds—with an arrow in his back, an arrow belonging to the Sussex Archers. The inquest brought about a verdict of death by accident, and I've always understood that this was a true verdict."

"Let us begin at the beginning, Mr. Colvin," suggested Pons.

"It may be that is the beginning—back in 1907. As for now, well, sir, I suppose it begins with the return of Trevor Pope—brother of that Henry Pope who died two decades ago. He had been in Canada, came back to England, opened the old Pope house near Lurgashall, and went into a reclusive existence there.

"I'm not likely to forget my first sight of him! The country around Blackdown is great hiking country, as you may know. I was out one evening when I heard someone running toward me. I concealed myself in some undergrowth just in time to see burst out of the woods across a little opening from where I was hidden a short, dark, burly man surrounded by six great mastiffs, all running in absolute silence save for the sound of his footfalls. He looked inconceivably menacing!

"That was in May. Two weeks later I saw him again. This time I didn't hear him; he burst suddenly upon me, pedaling furiously on a bicycle, with his mastiffs running alongside—three on each side of him, and though he saw me, he said not a word—simply went past as fast as he could. Nor did the dogs bark. Mr. Pons, it was uncanny. In the interval I had learned his identity, but at the time it meant nothing to me—I was only twelve when Henry Pope died, and was off to school at the time.

"Then, late in June, the messages arrived."

"Sent to all surviving members of the Sussex Archers?" interrupted Pons.

"Yes, Mr. Pons."

"All six still live in the vicinity of Lurgashall? Petworth, I believe, is but three miles or so away."

"All but one. George Trewethen moved to Arundel ten years ago."

"What was your father's response to the warning?"

"He dismissed it as the work of a crank—until Jefferds' death. Then he wrote or telephoned to the other members and learned for the first time that all had received identical warnings. It put the wind up him for a bit, but not for long. He's very obstinate. When he goes out now he carries his gun—but a gun's poor defense against an arrow in the back; so my brother and I take turns following him and keeping him in sight whenever he goes out."

"You're here with his consent?"

"Yes, Mr. Pons. He isn't averse to a private inquiry, but seems determined to keep the police out of it."

"But are the police not already in it?" asked Pons.

"Yes, but they don't know about the warning Jefferds received. My father knew only because Jefferds had mentioned destroying it when he visited him a few days before his death—Mr. Pons, I'm driving back to Lurgashall tomorrow morning. Dare I hope you and Dr. Parker will accompany me?"

"What precisely do you expect of us, Mr. Colvin?"

"I hope you can devise some way in which to trap Trevor Pope before an attempt is made on father's life."

"That will surely not be readily accomplished. Six mastiffs, I think you said? And the man either runs or pedals as fast as possible. What do you say, Parker?"

"Let us go by all means. I am curious to see this man and his dogs."

"Thank heaven, Mr. Pons. It is little more than an hour from London. I will call for you tomorrow morning at seven."

After our client's departure, Pons sat for a few moments staring thoughtfully into the dark fireplace. Presently he turned in my direction and asked, "What do you make of it, Parker?"

"Well, it's plain as a pikestaff that Colvin senior doesn't want the police nosing about that twenty-year-old accident," I said. "And that suggests it may have been more than accident. From that conclusion it's but a step to the theory that Trevor Pope has returned from Canada to avenge his brother's murder."

"That is surely exemplary deduction," said Pons. "I am troubled by only one or two little aspects of the matter which no doubt you'll be able to clear up when the time comes. Thus far, we have no evidence to connect Trevor Pope with the warnings."

"It's surely not just coincidence that Pope's appearance in the neighborhood is followed by the warning letters. Their very wording points to him!"

"Does it not!" agreed Pons. "The intended victims are not told to prepare for death, but for 'punishment'. That is surely ambiguous! 'Punishment' for what?"

"Why, for the murder of Henry Pope, what else?"

"The coroner's inquest determined that Pope came to an accidental death."

"Inquests are not infallible, Pons; no one knows this better than you."

"True, but I incline a little to distrust of the obvious. Why warn these gentlemen at all if vengeance is the motive?"

"It is elementary psychology that avengers have a pathological wish to let their victims know *why* they are being punished. These warnings seem to have achieved their purpose, now that the first of the surviving Archers has been slain."

"But not yet to the extent of sending any one of them for the police. What coy reluctance to act!"

"If any proof were needed that Pope's death was not all it seems, that is certainly it."

"Is it? I wonder. These waters, I fear, are darker than we may at this moment believe. We shall see."

Thereafter Pons retreated for the evening behind a Guide to Sussex.

An hour after our client stopped for us next morning, we were driving through the quaint Wealden village which is Lurgashall, and then climbing the height of Blackdown, the highest hill in Sussex. Not far up the slope stood our client's home, a rambling stone house set behind stone gate piers and a yew hedge, with outbuildings down slope from it at one side.

Our client had wired his father of our impending arrival; as a result, Joshua Colvin awaited us in the breakfast room. He was a sturdy, middle-aged man wearing a fierce, straggly moustache, and a dogged look in his dark eyes.

He acknowledged his son's introductions in a gruff, self-confident manner. "You'll join me at breakfast?" he asked.

"A cup of tea, sir," said Pons. "I like to keep my mind clear for these little problems."

Colvin favored him with an even, measuring glance. "Sit down, gentlemen," he said. "You'll not mind my eating? I waited on your coming."

"By no means, Mr. Colvin."

We sat at the breakfast table, and would have been readily at ease had it not been for an almost immediate interruption. A young man, obviously just out of bed, burst into the room, his sensitive face flushed and upset.

"Father—I saw Pearson about again last night . . ." he said, and, catching sight of us, stopped. "I beg your pardon."

"Come in—you're late again," said Colvin. Turning to us, he added, "My son, Alasdair—Mr. Solar Pons, Dr. Parker. Now, then—Pearson. You're quite sure?"

"Certain, sir. Skulking outside the gate-posts. I got in at midnight."

"Pearson," put in our client, "is a beater my father discharged over two months ago. Been hanging around ever since."

"May I ask why he was discharged?" inquired Pons.

"He was party to a poaching ring," growled Colvin. "Sort of thing I

53

won't tolerate."

Alasdair Colvin, meanwhile, had swallowed only a cup of coffee. Then he got to his feet again, made his excuses, and left the room.

"Boy has an editorial position," said Colvin shortly. "Softening job. Lets him sleep late. Disgraceful, I call it."

Our host had now devoured a hearty breakfast. He pushed back from the table and sat, arms akimbo, hands gripping the arms of his chair.

"Well, sir," he said to Pons, "now you're here at my son's invitation, we may as well get on with it."

"Tell me something about the Sussex Archers, Mr. Colvin," said Pons.

"Little to tell, sir. Organized 1901, Disbanded 1907. Accidental killing of one of our members, Henry Pope. Never had more than seven members. Pope, Jefferds, myself. George Trewethen, Abel Howard, Will Ockley, and David Wise. That's the lot of us. All devoted to archery. We got together to practise it. That's the long and the short of it. All congenial chaps, very. Liked a nip or two, now and then. No harm in that. Had our own special arrows. That sort of thing. Competed now and then in contests with other clubs. Henry's death took the stuffing out of us and put an end to the Sussex Archers."

"The death of Mr. Pope would seem to warrant a few questions," said Pons.

"Twenty years ago, Mr. Pons," said Colvin with a mounting air of defense. "He's all dust and bone by this time. The coroner's inquest said accident."

"You insist on that, Mr. Colvin?" pressed Pons.

Beads of perspiration appeared suddenly on our host's temples. He gripped his chair arms harder. "Damn it, sir! That was the decision of the jury."

"Not yours, Mr. Colvin."

"Not mine!"

"I submit, sir, you accepted it with reservations."

"Since you're not the police, Mr. Pons, I may say that I did."

"Not an accident, then, Mr. Colvin."

"Murder!" Our host almost spat out the word. Once having said it, he relaxed; his hands slipped back along the arms of the chair. He took a deep breath; the words came out in a rush. "I don't see how he could

54

have been killed by accident, Mr. Pons. Nor do I know why he should have been murdered. We were all experienced archers, sir—*experienced!* We were not given to accidents. We were all close friends. There never was an uncongenial word among us. Besides, none of us had anything to gain by Henry's death. We had much to lose. We lost the one thing we prized among us—our archery. I've not touched my bow since the day."

"How was he killed, Mr. Colvin?"

"We were on the Weald, Mr. Pons. Woods all around us. We were separated, taking positions for distance in loosing our arrows. After we had discharged arrows we pushed forward to mark our distances and see who had shot his arrow farthest. We found Henry with an arrow in his back, dying. It was one of our special arrows—but unmarked."

"Unmarked?"

"Since we were trying for distance that day, we had marked our arrows individually. When we found our arrows later, we learned that Henry had discharged his." He paused, licked his lips, and went on. "All our arrows were marked that day, Mr. Pons—but the arrow that killed Henry wasn't marked. This wasn't brought out at the inquest, I need hardly say. Whoever killed Henry had brought along an unmarked arrow for that purpose."

"Was the Archers' schedule widely known?"

"Set up annually, sir," replied our host. "Anybody could have known it, if he were interested. Not many were."

"Is Mr. Pope's family still in the vicinity?"

"Henry was unmarried. A quiet man, retired early in life. Quite wealthy, too. His younger brother, Trevor, was his only heir. I remember what a time we had trying to reach Trevor—we didn't, in fact, get in touch with him until after Henry was buried. He was on a walking tour of the Scottish Highlands. He came back only long enough to take care of Henry's affairs, closed the Pope house on the far side of Lurgashall, and went to Canada. He returned only last May."

"And this, Mr. Colvin?"

Pons spread the warning our host had received on the table before him.

"Monstrous!" Colvin gave Pons a hard look. "I could be punished for many things, sir—but the death of Henry Pope isn't one of them."

"Was the arrow that killed Jefferds one belonging to the Sussex

Archers?"

"It was. No question about it. Fair put the wind up me."

"I should not be surprised," said Pons. "Now, then, about Pearson. How long had he been with you?"

"Ten years."

"You, too, have seen him skulking around?"

"Not I. Alasdair chiefly. Hewitt saw him on two occasions."

"Only recently, Mr. Pons," put in our client. "He seemed to be waiting for Father to come outside."

"Man knows my habits," growled Colvin senior. "He could find me outside any time he wanted to."

"I take it you've been married more than once, Mr. Colvin."

"Ah, you saw that Alasdair's no whit like him," our host said, jerking his head toward our client. "True. Married twice. Twice a widower. Alasdair was my second wife's son; I adopted him. A good, quiet boy, a little scatter-brained. Perhaps that goes with publishing."

"And Mr. Jefferds' murder," said Pons then—"does it occur to you that the same man who killed Henry Pope might have killed Jefferds? It's a possibility."

"Wouldn't it occur to you? But I tell you, sir, I'm at a complete loss as to who might have done it, and why."

"You've not been to the police," said Pons.

"Damn it, sir!—we've suppressed evidence. We don't want it to come out now. What good would it do? An arrow used by the Archers is the only thing that ties the two murders together. The *only* thing. Mr. Pons, I know! Henry Pope was an inoffensive man; so was Andy Jefferds. Who stood to gain by their deaths? Trevor Pope, who was miles away when his brother died! Ailing Mrs. Jefferds, who needed her husband alive far more than anything she might inherit! Such crimes are senseless, sir. But this is your game, not mine," finsihed our host, pushing back his chair and rising. "I leave you to my son."

So saying, he stalked out of the room.

Pons, too, rose. He turned to our client. "About Pearson, Mr. Colvin—when was the first time you saw him skulking around?"

"Why, I believe it was the night after Mr. Jefferds' death."

"But he *had* been about before?"

"Alasdair saw him before that—though he didn't mention it until I told Father I'd seen him. Then he came out with it—said he hadn't wanted to say it before and upset Father."

Pons stood for a moment deep in thought. Then a little smile touched his lips, and I knew he was off on a new line which pleased him. "Now, then," he said to our client. "We shall want to move about. Can you spare a pony cart?"

"Come with me, Mr. Pons."

Late that afternoon we drew up at a pub on the Lurgashall side of Petworth. We had spent the day calling on the other three resident members of the disbanded Sussex Archers—Will Ockley, a semi-invalid—David Wise, who was now a clergyman—and Abel Howard, a taciturn man of late middle age, who was still engaged in stock farming experiments—from all of whom I could not determine that Pons had elicited any more information than he already had.

In the pub we made our way to the bar and sat down. Pons ordered a gin and bitters, and I my customary ale. Since it was still early evening, there was little patronage in the pub, and the proprietor, a chubby fellow with sparkling eyes and a thatch of white hair, was not loath to talk.

"Strangers hereabout?" he asked.

"On our way to see Joshua Colvin on business," said Pons. "Know him?"

"Aye. Know him well."

"What sort is he?"

The proprietor shrugged. "There's some that likes him, some that don't. Has a gruff manner and a sharp way of telling the truth. Makes one uncomfortable."

"And his sons?"

The proprietor brightened. "Cut from different cloth altogether. Alasdair, now—he's a real sport. Comes in for the darts." He shook his head. "A bit of a loser, though—he's no hand for it. Still owes me five quid." He chuckled. "But Hewitt—well, sir, in business he's all business, and he don't come here much. But don't ye be fooled by that—he's an uncommon eye for the ladies. There's them could tell ye a tale or two about Hewitt and the ladies! But I ain't one to gossip, never was. Live and let live, I say."

"Does not a Mr. Pope live nearby?" asked Pons then.

The proprietor sobered at once. "The likes of him don't come here," he said darkly. "He don't talk to no one. There's them say they know why."

"And Mr. David Wise?"

"Aye—as close to a saint as ye can find these days." But abruptly he stopped talking; his eyes narrowed. He flattened his hand on the bar and leaned closer to Pons, staring searchingly at him. "Ye're asking about the Archers. Aye! I know ye, sir, damme if I don't. We've met."

"I don't recall it," said Pons.

"Ye're Solar Pons, the detective," he said, flinging himself away from us.

Thereafter he would say no more.

We took our leave soon thereafter, Pons not at all displeased by the proprietor's refusal to speak. "We have one more stop to make," he said. "Let us have a look at Trevor Pope."

Following the directions our client had given us, we drove down a lane into a Wealden hollow and came to a semi-Tudor house behind a low, vine-grown wall. It wore a deserted appearance.

Pons halted the trap at the gate, got out, and walked to the door, where he plied the knocker. There was a long wait before the door opened. An old servant stood there.

"Mr. Trevor Pope?" asked Pons.

"Mr. Pope doesn't wish to see anyone," said the servant. "He's going out."

Pons came back to the trap, got in, and drove up the lane to the road, where he turned off into a coppice, got out once more, beckoning me to follow, and tied our steed to a sapling. We circled toward the rear of the house, taking advantage of every tree, and had scarcely come into good view of it before there burst from the direction of the kennels half a dozen great mastiffs, and in their midst, running at dead heat, a short, dark man wearing a turtleneck sweater, tight-fitting trousers, and rubber-soled canvas shoes. They bore toward a woodland path which would take them around Lurgashall in the direction of Blackdown. The dogs made scarcely a sound; all that fell to ear was Pope's footfalls, and all that held to the mind's eye was the tense, strained expression on his dark face, and the clenched fists at his sides.

"What madness drives him to this?" I whispered, as they vanished.

"What, indeed! There must be an easier exercise. You cannot deny, however, that it is an impressive performance. Small wonder it startled

58

our client." Pons smiled. "It is now sundown. Surely he won't be gone long. Let us just go to meet him."

The course Trevor Pope had taken led in an arc away from the house; we were soon out of sight of it on a Wealden path that he and the dogs had followed. Pons paused suddenly at the edge of an open glade, where the path led down a slope toward Lurgashall. There he paused to look around.

"I fancy this will do as well as any place," he said. "Let us wait here."

The sun was gone, the afterglow began to fade, half an hour passed. Then came the sound of running footsteps.

"Ah, he is coming," said Pons.

Almost instantly the mastiffs and their master swept around a grove of young trees and bushes at the bottom of the slope within sight of Pons.

"Mr. Trevor Pope!" Pons called out in a loud voice and began to advance.

Pope came to a stop and heeled his dogs with a savage cry. He turned a furious face toward us, flung up his arm to point at Pons, and shouted, "Stand where you are! What in hell do you want?"

"To ask you some questions."

"I answer no questions."

"One, then, Mr. Pope!" Pons' voice echoed in the glade.

"Who are you?"

"Only a curious Londoner. You may have heard my name. It is Solar Pons."

There was an audible gasp from Pope. Then, "So they've sent for you!"

"One question, Mr. Pope!"

"Go to hell, sir!"

"Can you furnish me with an itinerary of your walking tour in the Scottish Highlands in 1907?"

There was a moment of pregnant silence. Then a fierce cry of rage, a curse, and Pope's furious words, "Get out—get out!—before I turn the dogs on you. You meddling nosy parker!"

"You may not have seen the last of me, Mr. Pope."

"You've seen the last of me, sir!"

Pons turned, and we went back the way we had come. There was no immediate movement behind us. When last I saw him, glancing over my shoulder as we were descending the slope toward the house and the cart beyond, Pope was standing motionless among his mastiffs, literally bursting with rage and hatred.

Once back in the trap, I could not help observing, "A violent man, Pons."

"Indeed," agreed Pons.

We rode in thoughtful silence until, just before reaching the stone gate piers of our client's home, Pons caught sight of someone slipping behind a cedar tree at the roadside.

He halted the trap at once, flung the reins to me, and leapt to the road. He darted around the cedar.

I heard his voice. "Mr. Pearson, I presume?"

"That's my name," answered a rough voice gruffly.

"What's your game, Pearson?"

"I got m' rights. I'm doin' no harm. This here's a public road."

"Quite right. Over two months ago you came to see Mr. Colvin."

"No, sir. Two weeks is more like it."

"You carry a gun, Mr. Pearson?"

"I ain't got a bow an' arrer!"

His inference was unmistakable. Pons abruptly bade him good-evening and came back to the cart. He said not a word as we drove on in the deepening dusk.

Our client waited for us in the hall. He was too correct to inquire how Pons had been engaged, though he must have drawn some conclusions.

"Can I get you anything to eat, gentlemen?" he asked.

"Perhaps a sandwich of cold beef and some dry wine," said Pons. "Just take it to our room, will you? I should like now to talk to your father once more."

"Very well, Mr. Pons. He's in his study. We just got back from his usual walk. It was my turn to guard him tonight." He sighed. "Father makes it very difficult; it angers him to catch sight of us behind him. Just in there, sir."

The senior Colvin sat before his stamp collection. His glance was more calculating than friendly.

"I'm sorry to trouble you, Mr. Colvin—but may I see your bow and arrow?"

Colvin leaned back, a baffled expression on his face. "Ha!" he exclaimed. "I wish I knew where they were. Put them away when Henry died, and then later put them somewhere else. Hanged if I know where they are now. That was twenty years ago, sir. Why d'you want to see 'em?"

"I have a fancy to see the kind of weapon that killed Mr. Pope and Mr. Jefferds—and may some day kill you unless I am able to prevent it."

"You speak bluntly, sir," said Colvin, flushing. "The bow I can't show you—but you'll find one of the arrows up there." He pointed to the wall above the fireplace and got up. "I'll get it down for you."

"No need, sir," said Pons. "I'll use this hassock to look at it."

He stood for a while before the arrow, which I thought an uncommonly long one, with a very sharp tip.

"I observe this arrow is sharp and lethal, Mr. Colvin. Is this usual?"

"Not at all, Mr. Pons. Average archery club wouldn't think of using tipped arrows. That was what made the Sussex Archers unique. Ours were all tipped. I told you, sir—we were experienced archers. Took pride in that. Took pride in the use of tipped arrows.—Until Henry died."

Pons retired from the hassock, restored it to its position, and bade our host good-night. Our client waited at the threshold to conduct us to our room, where our brief repast was ready for us.

"Is there anything more, Mr. Pons?" asked our client at our door.

"One thing. Does your father take his walk every evening?"

"At about sundown regularly, rain or shine. Only a severe storm keeps him in. He's rugged, Mr. Pons—very rugged."

"He usually follows the same route?"

"Roughly, yes."

"Is this route generally known in the neighborhood?"

"I should imagine so."

"Can you take time to show me tomorrow morning where he walked tonight?"

"Certainly. My office in Petworth can easily spare me."

"Thank you. Good night, sir."

Pons ate in contemplative silence, sat for a while cradling his Moselle, then got up and began to pace the floor in that attitude I knew so well—head clasped behind him. I knew better than to interrupt his train of thought.

After almost two hours of this, he paused before me. "Now, Parker, what have you to say of it all?"

"Little more than I said before. Trevor Pope flees through the dusk like a man trying to escape his guilt."

"Indeed he does!" said Pons agreeably. "I do not doubt but that Mr. Pope is the agent upon whose actions the entire puzzle turns."

"As I pointed out before we left Praed Street," I could not help saying.

"I recall it," continued Pons. "It does not seem to you significant that Pearson, who has been trying to see Joshua Colvin, has not yet been able to do so, though he knows Colvin's routine and could find him outside any time he wishes?"

"The fellow is clearly playing some game intended to put the wind up his former employer."

"That is surely one way of looking at it. Did it suggest nothing to you that each of the one-time Sussex Archers were questioned today held exactly the same views as our host? None would speak a word against each other, yet each was convinced that Henry Pope's death was not an accident."

"Theirs seems to be the only tenable view, the inquest notwithstanding."

"I submit it is an interesting coincidence, moreover, that Jefferds should be killed at twilight, the precise hour Trevor Pope is about with his pack of trained mastiffs."

"Would you have it otherwise?" I cried. "That was the hour for him to commit the crime! I suppose," I went on, "you've constructed a perfect case about Pearson."

"Pearson is certainly in the matter—up to his eyes, shall we say?—or I am dead wrong. Let me see," he went on, looking at his watch, "it is now after eleven. Inspector Jamison will certainly be at home by this time. Now if I can manage to reach the telephone without arousing the household, I will just have a little talk with him."

So saying, he slipped out of our room to place a trunk call.

When he came back, he vouchsafed no information.

Next morning Pons deliberately dawdled about the house until the trunk call he expected came at ten o'clock. He took it, listened, said less than ten words, thanked Inspector Jamison, and rang off. All this time our client had been standing by, waiting to be of service to us.

"Now I am ready, Mr. Colvin," said Pons, "to follow the course your father customarily takes on his evening walks."

"Come along, sir," said our client.

He led the way out of the house and struck off into the surrounding woods. Our course led down the slope of Blackdown toward the Weald, away from Lurgashall. Pons' eyes darted here and there. Occasionally he commented on the view to be had, and once he asked about the proximity of Trevor Pope's course.

"The two paths intersect at that copse just ahead, Mr. Pons," said Colvin. "That's where I saw Pope and his mastiffs."

We passed through the copse, which consisted of one very large old chestnut, surrounded by fifty or more younger trees. We had not gone far beyond it, when Pons excused himself and ran back into it, bidding us wait for him.

When he rejoined us, his eyes were dancing. "I believe we have seen enough, Mr. Colvin," he said. "I wanted especially to make sure that there *was* a point of intersection between your father's course and Trevor Pope's. It seems to serve the purpose for which it is intended."

"I am glad you think so, Mr. Pons."

Pons looked at his watch. "And now, if you will forgive me, we seem to have accomplished for the time being everything we can, and if you will drive us into Petworth, we can catch the 12:45 to London. Pray pay my respects to your father, and say to him I have every hope of laying hands upon the murderer of Mr. Jefferds within forty-eight hours."

"You've laid a trap for Pope then!" cried our client.

"We shall have to take the murderer in the act," answered Pons. "Pope is desperate. I rattled him severely last evening. Tell your brother to take exceptional care when he follows your father tonight."

We walked back to the house, and within a few minutes we were in our client's car on our way to Petworth, where we were deposited at the station.

No sooner had our client driven away, than Pons sprang into action. "Now, then," he said, "let us check our bags and spend a little time wandering about Petworth. We might take a bit of luncheon."

"We'll miss our train, Pons!"

Pons favored me with an amused smile. "We're not taking the train, Parker. We have an engagement this evening with a murderer. I expect to keep it."

Just before sundown we made our way into that copse of trees where Joshua Colvin's course crossed that of Trevor Pope. Pons had an objective in view—it was the old chestnut tree with a hollow at shoulder height and down one side of the tree—a low-branched tree dominating the copse.

"This is our rendezvous," said Pons. "If I am not in error, this is Joshua Colvin's night of peril. I hope to prevent his death and take his would-be murderer in the net. Now, then, up into the tree—well up."

Within a few moments we were out of sight up along the trunk of the old chestnut, Pons taking care to be along the far side, away from the direction from which Pope might come.

"But the dogs, Pons," I cried. "What of them? They're dangerous."

"We shall deal with them if the need arises," he answered. "Now, then, the sun is setting—we may expect Colvin to set out soon on his round. It will take him half an hour to reach here."

"And Pope as long," I mused. "How it all works out!"

"How indeed! Now let us be silent and wait upon events. Whatever you see, Parker—make no sound!"

The sun went down and the sky paled to the evensong of birds. Bats began to flitter noiselessly about. Then, promptly on schedule, Joshua Colvin entered the wood, his gun held carelessly in the crook of one arm, and passed within sight of the tree.

He had hardly gone before Alasdair Colvin sauntered into sight. The younger Colvin came straight to the chestnut tree and set his gun down against the old bole. He took from his pockets a pair of skin-tight gloves, into which he hastily slipped his hands. Then he reached into the opening in the chestnut tree and drew forth a bow and arrow!

At this moment Pons hurtled down upon him.

Startled at last from my almost paralyzed shock, I scrambled down the trunk and dropped after Pons.

Alasdair Colvin fought like a beast, with a burst of strength surprising in one so slight of body, but Pons and I managed to subdue him just as the elder Colvin came running back upon the scene, drawn by the sound of the struggle. Seeing the bow and arrow lying nearby,

Joshua Colvin understood the meaning of the scene at once. He raised his gun and fired twice to bring help.

"Serpent!" he grated. "Ungrateful serpent!" Then, spurning the prostrate young man, he turned to Pons. "But why? *Why?*"

"Alasdair was heavily in debt, Mr. Colvin. I suspect also that he was being blackmailed by Pearson. Your son killed Andrew Jefferds and planned your death in an attempt to recreate an old crime and pin it upon an old murderer."

"An old crime?"

"Henry Pope's murder. It was almost certainly his brother who slew him. Your paths crossed here, within minutes, though tonight, unaccountably, Pope is not coming—which would have served Alasdair grievously had he succeeded in his diabolical plan."

From the direction of the house came the sound of running footsteps.

On the train bound for London, Pons yielded to my inquiries.

"It seemed to me at the outset that, while not impossible, it was highly improbable that anyone would exact vengeance twenty years after the event to be avenged," he began. "And it would certainly have been the greatest folly to announce 'punishment' to those suspected of having committed the murder of Henry Pope, for this would surely focus attention upon Trevor Pope, the one man who might conceivably want to avenge his brother's death. It seemed therefore elementary that these messages were intended explicitly to do just that.

"Proceeding from this conclusion, I had only to look around for motive. Who would benefit at Joshua Colvin's death but his sons? Hewitt Colvin would hardly have enlisted my help had he been involved. That left only Alasdair. But what motive could he have? Curiously enough, it was the proprietor of the pub in Petworth who furnished a motive when he mentioned that Alasdair still owed him so trifling a sum as five quid—a motive strengthened when Jamison informed me this morning, in response to my request for an inquiry, that Alasdair was deeply in debt at the track and in various gaming houses—five thousand pounds.

"The plan was conceived with wonderful cleverness. A pity Jefferds had to die—a sacrifice to Alasdair's vanity. Everyone knew the elder Colvin's routine—and Alasdair knew that Trevor Pope would not be able to supply himself with an alibi at that hour. Moreover, the arrows and the bow Alasdair had taken from his father's storage and hidden in the tree could as readily have belonged to the late Henry Pope. Trevor alone knew there was no reason for vengeance against the Sussex Archers—for he unquestionably killed his brother; he alone had motive and opportunity—that vague walking tour of the Highlands enabled him to slip back, commit the crime—the Archers' schedule was set up annually, according to Colvin senior—and return to the Highlands to be 'located' after planned difficulties.

"Unhappily for Alasdair, two little events he had not counted upon took place. Pearson came upon him the night of Jefferds' murder—which also occurred at the hour Trevor Pope was out with his mastiffs—and very probably saw him with the bow in hand before he could conceal it. Though Pearson may have come originally to see the elder Colvin, he came thereafter to see Alasdair for the purpose of blackmailing him. You will recall the discrepancy between Alasdair's statement about seeing Pearson months ago, and Pearson's own claim, corroborated by Hewitt's failure to see him previously, that it was 'more like two weeks.' So Pearson suspected, and was thus in it up to his eyes!

"The other event, of course, was Hewitt's application at 7B. A neat little problem, Parker. Tomorrow, I fancy, I shall have a go at Trevor Pope's Highlands itinerary—difficult as that will be at this time."

But the solution of the secondary mystery was not to be Pons', for the morning papers announced the suicide by hanging of Trevor Pope, who, though he left no message behind, evidently saw in Pons' presence on the scene of his own dastardly crime the working of a belated nemesis.

Don't Lose Your Cool

by Dan J. Marlowe

Julio Martinez, the lean-bodied head gardener at Minnetonka Prison, sought out Piggy Larsen in a corner of the carpenter shop and handed him a folded-over square of paper. "I do not understand, Piggy," Martinez said earnestly. "Explain to me, please." His English was careful. He was a tall man with greying hair. The knees of his prison workclothes were dark with damp earth stains.

Larsen opened the note, read it, and laughed. He was a round little man with buck teeth. He sobered when he saw the tall man's expression. "It's a joke, Julio," he said hurriedly. "A gag, see?" He held out the note. " 'If you want to see your rabbit again, put two packs of cigarettes under the flat rock behind third base at the ball field before chow,' " he quoted. He turned the paper over. "That's all. Hand printed too. Who'd go to the trouble—" his voice died away. "It's a joke," he repeated.

Martinez flicked alight a large kitchen match with a heavy thumbnail, lit a cigarette, and flipped the still lighted match ten feet into a barrel of water in which two-by-fours were soaking. The match hissed out. "The rabbit is missing," he said gravely.

"Missing?" Piggy echoed blankly.

The tall man nodded. "From the flower bed. I have reported it to Murdoch."

"Oh," Piggy said in a changed tone. Murdoch was the chief guard. "Well, I mean, Julio, a wooden rabbit—'course I know how you sweat over the carvin' of 'em, an' the paintin' an repaintin' to get 'em just right. The duck, an' the goose here too. From across the yard they look real as real in front of your flower beds. But I mean, it's just a wooden—"

"It was bothering no one," Martinez said with a mildness of tone inconsistent with the smolder in his eyes. His glance went to the workbench where the carved figure of a goose awaited only paint to bring it to life. "As I was bothering no one."

"Well," Piggy said helplessly, waving the note, "what're you gonna do about it?"

"I hope that it is necessary for me to do nothing."

"Yeah," Piggy agreed uneasily. Martinez was serving a life term for the murders of his wife and her lover. The sentence had been life because he had been undeniably pleased with himself. In the inevitable test of strength two months after he arrived at Minnetonka, Martinez had inflicted fifty stitches worth of sharpened file upon the aggressor. When he came out of the prison hospital himself and served his ninety days in the hole, emerging as tranquilly as he'd entered, he was not tested again. "You got any idea who—?"

"I think the new one," Martinez said. "Spinnazola. He seems to feel the need to—push."

"Oh," Piggy said, and his voice changed again. "You don't want— listen, Julio, I mean, it's only a wooden—"

He stared after Julio Martinez' tall figure striding from the shop.

The next morning Piggy Larsen was bustling nervously about the carpenter shop when Martinez entered. Half a dozen prisoners were in the shop, including the burly Spinnazola. "Hey, Julio, you seen my seven-sixteenths—" Piggy began in a high-pitched voice, then fell silent as Martinez picked up a small, paper-wrapped parcel that had been placed on top of the carved goose.

The tall man opened the package and stared unbelievingly at the painted wooden head of a rabbit, its neck jaggedly snapped off. His dark features turned stark white, then dull red. His eyes barely focused on the note in the same rough printing as before: "The ante's gone up, Martinez. Four packs, or the duck is next."

"Don't lose your cool, baby," Piggy pleaded in an undertone. "It's a joke, see? Like practice." His pudgy hands danced frantically in the air. "Like finger exercises. It don't mean—"

Martinez didn't look at him. He didn't look at the men in the shop busily engaged in not looking at him. He addressed the wall in front of him in a carrying voice. "I ask that this foolishness stop," he said. "I ask it seriously."

68

When he turned, only Spinnazola met his eyes, grinning at him openly. Julio Martinez went outside to his beloved flowers.

In view of a dozen men that night, Martinez scaled the contents of a full pitcher of water fifteen feet. It splashed soggily the length of Spinnazola's cot, soaking it through. Martinez did it with the expertise of a man who has watered flowers from every conceivable type of container; not a drop spilled on the cellblock floor en route. Long after lights out Spinnazola could still be heard cursing. The rest of the cellblock was unusually quiet. Julio Martinez stretched out on his back on his cot with his hands folded behind his head, staring up at the ceiling.

In the morning he refused to talk to the dithering Piggy. Finished outside, he went into the carpenter shop and gathered up his carved goose and the bucket of turpentine with his paint brushes in it. He walked to the small room behind the laundry where he did his painting, alone. When he heard the squeak of the door and the hurried scrape of a shoe on cement, he turned his head to verify that it was Spinnazola charging him, knife in hand. "Wise man," the burly man growled. "This time it won't be no wooden—"

Julio Martinez flicked a large kitchen match alight with his thumbnail. With his left hand he picked up his bucket of turpentine and sloshed its contents at Spinnazola, striking him squarely in the chest.

The big man stopped, shocked, as the liquid splattered up and down his length. "Why, you—" he began furiously, and then his nostrils took in the odor of the turpentine. "No, no, no, no!" he screamed hoarsely.

Julio Martinez smiled, and flipped the lighted match.

Bus to Chattanooga

by Jonathan Craig

Janie June Hibbins was still sore from the strapping Uncle Elmore had given her yesterday afternoon, and every so often she would wince a little and shift her position in the rocker. It was hard to sew by the light of the coal-oil lamp, but she had had a lot of practice at it and she was within a few stitches of finishing the white cotton dress she was patterning on the one in the Sears, Roebuck catalogue.

It wasn't as if she'd done anything wrong, she reflected as she changed her position again. She hadn't. It was just that there weren't enough hours in the day to do all the work Uncle Elmore figured a healthy young girl ought to do. She didn't know how much longer she could stand it. Ever since Ma and Pa had died and Uncle Elmore had moved in, life had been just plain miserable. Uncle Elmore had always been one of the meanest men in the hills, and lately he had been getting even meaner. It had got so that all she had to do was look at him slantwise, and he'd go for the strap.

"Mind you keep your eye on that whiskey still, missy," Uncle Elmore had ordered her just before he climbed in his battered old car and started down the rutted road that wound through the Smoky Mountains for almost ten miles before it finally came out on the highway to Chattanooga. "I want that mash cooked right and proper. If it ain't, I'll be giving you a birthday present you won't like one little bit."

"Yes, sir, Uncle Elmore," Janie June had said.

"And don't be leaving the cabin after sundown. I don't want no female kin of mine spooning around in the dark with any of these young bucks around here. You hear me, girl?"

"Yes, sir."

"You better remember it, too. Unless you crave a whupping for a birthday present. How old will you be, anyhow?"

70

"Eighteen."

"Well, that ain't going to keep you from getting whupped. And being the prettiest girl on the mountain ain't going to keep you from it, neither. You just better learn to step a sight more lively, Janie June Hibbins."

"Oh, I will, Uncle Elmore."

"Fetch me a jar of 'shine. I plumb forgot."

Janie ran into the cabin, grabbed up one of the quart fruit jars she had just filled with corn whiskey, and rushed back to the car.

"Mind what I told you," Uncle Elmore called back as the car rattled off. "I don't keep that strap hanging on the wall just for show, you know."

Now, as Janie June took the last stitch in the hem of the dress and knotted the thread, she heard the banjo clock in the other room strike three. It was later than she'd thought, and she hurriedly hung up the dress and blew out the lamp and crossed to the window to watch for the bus to Chattanooga.

The bus came along up there on Piney Ridge at a few minutes after three, and on nights when Janie June was too troubled in her mind to sleep, she liked to watch for it and dream about how wonderful it would be if only she had enough money to run off to Chattanooga where there weren't any Uncle Elmores, or smelly whiskey stills, or hard work from sun to sun, or strappings that left a girl so sore she could hardly sit down. There was a full moon tonight, and Piney Ridge was so bright that Janie June could see almost as well as if it were daytime.

Just beneath the crest of the ridge, straight across from the cabin, Janie June saw something which made her forget about the bus completely. There, on the abandoned road that led down from the ridge through Nuzum's Notch, a car was moving very slowly with its lights out. As she watched, the car halted by the mouth of the China River Cave, where she had played so often as a child, and two men got out. She could tell they were men, but no more than that. They moved quickly, their shadowy forms merging briefly with the larger shadow of the car before they separated from it again and started toward the cave. But now they were carrying something between them, something that looked very much like another man. They were swallowed by the black shadow at the mouth of the cave for a few moments; then the

71

two of them came back alone, took what appeared to be a half-filled gunnysack from the car, and went back into the cave again. This time, they stayed inside much longer. When they came out, neither of them carried anything. They got into the car, still without having made a sound of any kind, and let the car coast down the road for a long way before they started the engine.

Janie June stared across the hollow at the black mouth of the cave, stark against the silver-gray of the moonwash on the surrounding rocks, for almost a full minute.

A person would be crazy to go up there, she told herself. A person would have to be touched, even to think about it.

She was still telling herself this as she went out to the other room, took down the lantern from the nail on the wall, picked up some matches from the box beside the cookstove, and set out for the cave.

She had been running up and down these hills all her life, and except for slowing down a little when she circled the grove where Uncle Elmore had his still, and which he had surrounded with trip-wires and deep, covered manpits as a protection against revenue agents and Sheriff Orv Loonsey, she ran all the way.

China River Cave—called that because, it was said, the small but rapid river inside it went all the way to China—wasn't much bigger than the cabin. Janie June lighted the lantern, set it on a rock, and looked about her.

There was nothing there. Janie June knew the cave as well as she knew her own room, and there was no place where even a half-filled gunnysack could have been hidden, much less a man's body. She picked up the lantern again and walked over to the edge of the underground river and stood looking down at the raging water. The river poured through the cave so fast that the water seemed to boil, and Janie June shuddered a little with the thought of what had happened to the man the other two had carried into the cave. The current would have sucked him out of sight in a second, and now the onrushing river would speed him through the bowels of the earth forever.

As Janie June turned away to leave, the lantern glinted on something in the dust just in front of her, and she picked it up. It was a narrow gold tie-clasp with the name *Duke* engraved on it in very small script. She studied it thoughtfully, and then threw it in the river. She wouldn't want anyone to know she'd seen *that*, because then they

72

might suspect she'd seen a whole lot more. She put out the lantern and left the cave.

As she started down the slope, Janie June saw headlights on the road that led to the cabin. They were still a long way off, but they were coming fast. That would be Uncle Elmore's car, she knew, and if she meant to reach the cabin before he did, she'd really have to hurry. What he'd do if he found her gone was just too awful to think about.

It was a good thing her skirt was so short, she reflected as she ran across Froggy Bottom and started up the opposite slope toward the cabin; this was no time to be hampered. She ran faster than she ever had before, even in the daytime, and every time she came to one of Uncle Elmore's trip-wires or covered man-pits, she leaped right over it, rather than lose the time it would take to run around it. But still, she had to circle around in back of the cabin, to keep herself out of the headlights of the approaching car, and she reached her bedroom window only half a minute before the car pulled into the yard. By the time she'd climbed inside, Uncle Elmore and some other man were already stomping across the creaking planks of the front porch.

Then Uncle Elmore was hammering on her door. "Wake up in there," he yelled. He was drunk, she could tell. Real drunk.

"That you, Uncle Elmore?" she called, trying to make her voice sound as if she'd only just awakened.

"You know durn good and well who it is," Uncle Elmore said. "Get yourself on out here, girl. We got company."

Janie June waited about as long as it would have taken her to put on her dress, and then she went out into the other room.

"Breakfast," Uncle Elmore said as soon as she appeared. "And don't let the grass grow, neither." He was bald and toothless, but his shoulders and chest were enormous, and when he moved his arms, the bulging muscles writhed beneath the freckled skin like so many snakes. He was sitting at the table with another, much younger man, and right now he had that mean grin on his face, the one he always got when he was mighty pleased with himself. "Eggs and ham and grits and taters and some of them damson preserves," he said. "Stir your stumps, Janie June."

"Yes, sir, Uncle Elmore," Janie June said as she hurried over to the cookstove.

The young man sitting at the table with Uncle Elmore had dark hair and eyes and a small, neat moustache, and he was every bit as good looking as Uncle Elmore was ugly. He smiled at Janie June and started to get to his feet.

Uncle Elmore laughed scornfully. "No need to get up for her," he said. "That's only Janie June. My niece."

"Good Lord," the man said softly.

"What in tarnation's wrong with you, Burt?" Uncle Elmore asked.

"You didn't tell me your niece was so pretty," Burt said.

"All it does is make her sassy," Uncle Elmore said.

"I never would have believed it," Burt said, staring at Janie June, occupied with her cooking.

"Hurry up with them victuals, girl," Uncle Elmore said as he turned on the old battery radio on the table. "I figure there just might be something interesting on the radio—eh, Burt?"

"Maybe so," Burt said. "My name's Burt Connor, Janie June."

"I'm right pleased to meet you," Janie June said.

Harsh and strident guitar music filled the room, and Uncle Elmore turned the radio down a little. "Fetch us a jar of 'shine, girl," he said.

Janie June took a jar of whiskey and two water glasses to the table and went back to the stove.

"You got a steady boy friend, Janie June?" Burt asked.

"No, sir," Janie June said.

Uncle Elmore laughed. "You're growing calf eyes, I swear, Burt," he said, filling his glass. "You must've seen a girl or two *some* time or other."

"I've seen a lot of them," Burt said. "But I never saw one as—"

"Hush!" Uncle Elmore said, the glass halfway to his mouth. "Listen."

". . . and the Chattanooga police still have no leads in the robbery and abduction of notorious gambler Duke Mahannah," the voice on the radio was saying. "Informed sources, however, have revealed that Mahannah's wall safe, which his kidnapers apparently forced him to open, contained almost thirty thousand dollars. . . . And now your Nightowl Newscaster would like just a moment of your time to tell you about—"

Uncle Elmore switched off the radio, downed the entire glass of moonshine in two long swallows, and winked at Burt.

"Well, now, what do you think of that?" he said. "Dang if it don't look like somebody's gone and stole that poor man's thirty thousand dollars." He shook his head and clucked his tongue. "'Course, you can't believe everything you hear on the radio, now can you?"

Burt smiled, his eyes still on Janie June. "No," he said. "You sure can't." He drank some of his whiskey, coughed, and drank some more. "You make good liquor, Elmore."

"Well, thanks," Uncle Elmore said. "I take my pains with it. Janie June, what's slowing up them victuals?"

"Don't rush her," Burt said.

"I'll rush her with a strap," Uncle Elmore said.

"Oh, you wouldn't do that," Burt said, laughing.

"I wouldn't eh?" Uncle Elmore said, reaching for the fruit jar. "How about some more 'shine in that glass, Burt?"

"Thanks," Burt said. "I don't mind if I do."

"Too bad we ain't got anything to celebrate, eh, Burt?" Uncle Elmore said, grinning broadly.

Burt grinned, too. "Yes, isn't it?" he said.

"Hurry up with that food, girl," Uncle Elmore said.

"Yes, Uncle Elmore," Janie June said. "It's all ready." She filled two plates at the stove and carried them to the table. "Can I go back to bed now, Uncle Elmore?" she asked.

"Why not stay up with us a while?" Burt said. "You like to dance, Janie June?"

"Go on to bed," Uncle Elmore said. "I want you pert and lively to-morrow. You hear?"

"Yes, sir," Janie June said as she opened the door of her room. "I was real glad to meet you, Mr. Connor."

"The same," Burt said, smiling. "I'll be seeing you again, Janie June. In fact, I just might be seeing you a lot."

Janie June bolted the door behind her and lay down on her bed with her clothes on and listened to the voices in the other room. An hour crawled by as the voices grew thicker and sleepier and the silences came oftener and lasted longer. Then there was a silence that stretched on for several minutes, and finally Uncle Elmore began to snore. When Janie June tiptoed to the door and put her eye to the crack be-tween it and the jamb, she saw that Uncle Elmore was asleep on his cot and Burt Connor was asleep at the table, his head resting on his forearm and his mouth slightly pursed, as if he were whistling.

Well, Janie June reflected as she crawled out the window, Uncle Elmore and Burt Connor wouldn't have thrown a bag of money in the river, the way they had poor Mr. Duke Mahannah's body, and that was for sure. She knew now what they'd done with the money—the only thing they *could* have done with it.

Twenty minutes later, the lantern beside her, Janie June was lying flat on her stomach beside the rushing water in the China River Cave, her arm in the water up to the elbow, feeling along the knobby surface of the undercut rock beneath her, probing for what she knew had to be there.

At last she found it—a taut wire tied to a fist-sized projection on the rock. The pull of the current on whatever was on the other end of the wire was so strong that the wire almost cut her fingers as she drew it up hand over hand, and if she hadn't been such a strong girl for her size she wouldn't have been able to pull it up at all.

It wasn't a gunnysack on the end of the wire, but a clear plastic bag as big as one, and it was more than half full of paper money.

Just as Janie June started to undo the wire from the gathered top of the bag, she thought she heard something. Her fingers seemed to freeze on the wire, and she crouched there, motionless, not even breathing. She heard it again—the sound of pebbles dislodged from the slope beneath the cave.

It had to be either Uncle Elmore or Burt Connor, she knew. Whoever it was, he'd kill her for sure. He'd know she knew what had happened to poor Mr. Duke Mahannah, and he'd kill her and throw her in the river.

She'd never thought so fast in her life. Whoever it was, he would already have seen the light of the lantern, so there was no use trying to do anything about that. But if he didn't already know who was in the cave, she still had a chance to keep from being caught.

That chance was to hide in the water. And since a wet dress would give her away later, she'd have to take it off. She dropped the bag of money back into the river, and then whipped the dress—which was all she had on—over her head and wedged it into the crevice between two rocks, where no one could see it. Then she slid into the water, and, making sure of each handhold before she trusted her life to it, worked herself back beneath the overhanging stone shelf of the river bank, just as she had done so many times in play when she was a little

76

girl. Only her head and shoulders were above the hissing surface of the water now, and she hooked her fingers over a small ridge in the rock and fought the savage tow of the current that threatened to tear her hands loose at any second and send her hurtling through the earth for all eternity.

She heard the hollow pound of heavy boots in the cave, and then Uncle Elmore's surprised curse when he found no one there. Swearing to himself steadily, Uncle Elmore began to pull up the wire attached to the money bag. The bag broke through the surface of the water, and a moment later Janie June heard the soft plop as Uncle Elmore dropped it on the cave floor.

Uncle Elmore's swearing broke off abruptly. "Burt!" he said. "I didn't hear you come in."

"I didn't mean for you to," Burt Connor's voice said. His voice was flat and cold, not at all the way it had been back at the cabin. "Caught you redhanded, didn't I?"

"What the Sam Hill are you talking about?" Uncle Elmore demanded.

Burt's laugh was ugly. "I kind of figured on you double-crossing me, but I didn't think it'd be so soon."

"Listen here—" Uncle Elmore began. "Hey, now! What're you doing with that knife?"

"You're a dead man, Elmore," Burt said. "Did you know that?"

"You got me wrong, Burt," Uncle Elmore said, his voice breaking. "I wasn't going to take the money. I seen a light up here and I—"

"Stop lying," Burt said.

"Get away from me with that knife, Burt!" Uncle Elmore yelled. "Don't do it, Burt! Burt, listen to me, I swear I never—"

"Good-bye, Elmore," Burt said, and then Uncle Elmore's body splashed into the water only a yard from Janie June's head, and in spite of herself, Janie June heard herself gasp.

The next instant, a big, hard hand had fastened on her wrist and was pulling her out of the water.

But when Burt had hauled her up beside him and saw that she was completely naked, he gaped at her in stunned disbelief and forgot for an instant to retain his viselike grip on her wrist. That instant was all Janie June needed to jerk away from him and dart for the mouth of the cave. Burt lunged after her, but his clutching hands slipped off her wet

77

body and he could not hold her.

Down the slope she raced, with Burt just behind her. His legs were longer than hers, but she knew every foot of the way and he did not. If only she could reach the cabin before he caught her, she could grab the rifle from over the fireplace and keep him from killing her.

And then, just as she was almost halfway across Froggy Bottom, she slipped on the dew-slicked grass and fell. She was up and running again almost at once, but now Burt was only a few steps behind her. As she started up the slope to the cabin, she cast a terrified glance over her shoulder and saw that he was even closer than she had thought, the knife in his hand flashing horribly in the moonlight. She'd never reach the cabin now, she knew; she was as good as dead this very second.

And then she remembered. The pits! The brush-covered man-pits around the grove where Uncle Elmore had his still!

The nearest pit was only a dozen yards away. She veered toward it, and at the last instant swerved to one side, hoping that Burt would crash through the thin layer of brush and fall into the deep pit below.

But it was not to be. Burt had changed his own course when he saw her change hers, and his pounding feet skirted the pit by inches.

He had her now for sure, Janie June knew. There wasn't any other pit she could lead him to without doubling back the way she had come. She could already imagine the knife sinking into her back, and she heard herself begin to whimper. She tried to run even faster.

Then she felt another sudden surge of hope, and she *did* run faster. She'd forgotten about the ankle-deep grass thirty yards ahead. It was the last one between here and the cabin, and it would be the last chance she'd have to save her life.

She reached the trip-wire a heartbeat before Burt did, leaped over it, and sprinted on. Burt's foot caught on the wire and he went sprawling headlong, his body skidding across the wet grass to come to a sudden stop against a stump.

Janie June ran into the cabin, jerked the rifle off the wall, and ran back out. She'd just have to shoot Mr. Connor, she guessed; there didn't seem to be any other way to keep him from killing her.

Burt Connor lay completely still, and as Janie June cautiously approached him, she saw that his neck was bent at an odd angle and that his eyes were wide open, staring at nothing. He was dead, she realized; the fall had broken his neck.

Janie June stood looking down at him for a long moment, and let it out very slowly. She would have to put Mr. Connor's body in the river, and that was going to be an awful chore. She wouldn't have any trouble getting it down the slope to Froggy Bottom, of course, and towing it across the slippery grass in the hollow wouldn't be too hard either. But pulling it up the far slope to the cave was going to be mighty tiring work.

Three hours later, when Janie June waved down the bus on top of Piney Ridge and climbed aboard, she was wearing her new white cotton dress and carrying Uncle Elmore's scuffed, twine-bound cardboard suitcase.

She found an empty seat, put the suitcase on her lap, and sat smiling out the window as the big bus roared back to life and started off down the mountain on its way to Chattanooga.

"Look how tight that girl's holding on to that old wreck of a suitcase," she heard a woman across the aisle whisper. "You'd think she had a fortune in there."

The Perfidy of Professor Blake

by Libby MacCall

To begin with, the whole thing was out of character, the Morrisons being the kind of people who always told the truth, no matter how unpalatable. They never cut corners on income tax returns—not even quite legitimate corners. Once, Mr. Morrison, who had forgotten to brake at a stop sign, had to appear in court and pay a ten-dollar fine. Once, Mrs. Morrison had an interview with a cop: her cleaning woman, arrested for shoplifting, had given Mrs. Morrison's name as a character reference. These incidents left them quite shaken.

Yes, the Morrisons were law-abiding people. Oh, they knew about the other kind. They'd had experience with dishonest persons. Plenty of it. When they first fell in love with archeology, they'd been incredibly gullible. In Mexico they'd bought a "guaranteed" pre-Columbian statuette. Back home in Riverview, New Jersey, their friend and new neighbor, Professor Blake, smiled tolerantly and pointed out the telltale marks of factory mass production. He hoped they hadn't been badly taken.

They had, by just how much they never told. Before their next trip—this time to Italy—they read and studied books he loaned them. They returned triumphant, proud owners of an Etruscan bowl. Professor Blake, again wearing that superior smile the initiate reserves for the tyro, showed them a photograph of the original (property of the archeological museum in Ravenna) and patiently pointed out the discrepancies between the real vase and their cleverly-crafted copy. At least, this fake was an expert one, handmade by a master of the counterfeiter's art.

The Morrisons' enthusiasm for archeology was entirely due to the influence of the neighbor. When Professor Blake moved into the house next door, he began, belatedly, to learn gardening. The Morrisons contributed cuttings and good advice. In return, they were invited to view some of the professor's color slides. Egyptian tombs and the temples of Southern India were a revelation to the Morrisons who, if they thought of them at all, thought of ancient civilizations as something kids studied in school. Their new friend brought the ruined buildings to life, peopling them with a colorful cast of characters: three-dimensional men and women who had servant problems and marital arguments. Mr. Morrison was fascinated by the Romans' advanced engineering techniques. Mrs. Morrison, easily able to contain her enthusiasm for drains, was enchanted by the jewelry and statuettes of semiprecious stone in the professor's collection.

That summer the Morrisons went to Mexico instead of making their usual visit to the Iowa relatives. Professor Blake helped them plan the trip, supplying introductions to friends and colleagues that enabled them to visit sites where actual digging was going on. That did it. They were hooked.

Their children, all grown, were doing well. There was no reason the Morrisons shouldn't spend their money on travel to distant places.

"Why," demanded their eldest, "are you suddenly ruin-happy? Go play shuffleboard in Florida. You might break a hip, wandering around those sites."

Mr. Morrison smiled the tolerant smile he reserved for generation-gap arguments and pressed the button on his new carousel slide projector. Onto the screen flashed a picture of a temple, precariously perched atop a steep flight of steps.

"That's why," he said. "That's a stiff climb. There are two hundred of those steps. But the view from the top—fantastic!"

"How do you get up there?"

"Walk, naturally," Mrs. Morrison said.

Her son stared at the screen, verified that each of the steps was a good two feet high, looked back at his mother's short legs and portly midsection. "That's a physical impossibility," he said.

"No, dear. It's easy. The guides get behind and boost." She giggled. "Try not to think about it, dear, since it seems to distress you."

That spring they stopped in Athens for a few relaxing days between excavations. Now that Mr. Morrison was retired, there was no longer any need to rush madly from site to site. They taxied up to the

Acropolis and settled down, hand in hand, on a huge block of stone in their favorite spot near the Temple of Athena.

"I never really believe this air," Mrs. Morrison said softly. "It makes me drunk, like champagne. We're so high, up here, I feel I could reach up and touch the sky."

Mr. Morrison squeezed her hand. "Don't do it," he said. "It might be dangerous."

"Dangerous?"

"Athena or Mercury might just reach down . . ."

"And I'd find myself jerked up to the ultimate heights?"

"Right. So don't do it. I'm not quite ready to let you join the gods on Mount Olympus."

"Mr. Mor-rees-sohn, is it not?" The fat gentleman confronting them was even shorter and more rotund than Mrs. Morrison. His smile glittered with gold. "You do not remember me!" His voice overflowed with sorrow. "I, who have sell you the most beautiful handwoven skirts in all of Greece without charge for the postage. All the way to Keokuk!"

"I'm afraid our minds were far away," Mrs. Morrison said. "Of course we remember you, Mr. Scopas."

"I have follow you." Mr. Scopas lowered his voice to a whisper, though no one was nearby. "I have close up my shop in order to do so. The matter is not one to be discuss within four walls." He turned to peer behind him, the back of his short neck bristling with suspicion. "These days, one is never safe."

"I told you this morning, we don't need a beautiful handmade carpet. You can skip the dramatics, man. A better offer won't change our minds," Mr. Morrison growled.

"Ah! It is no matter of a carpet. I speak now of a priceless object. Because you came to my shop from Professor Blake, I know you can appreciate it."

Mrs. Morrison shaded her eyes against the golden glitter of his teeth in the late-afternoon sunshine. "What sort of priceless object?"

"You know of the persecution of the royal family by the Junta? They have been force to hide. One—a second cousin of the King!—is an old customer. In order to eat, he must sell an item from his collection of antiquities. A tragedy!"

The little man was overacting. The Morrisons felt a strong inclination to laugh. "Lucky he's got things to sell," Mr. Morrison said.

The Greek sighed, a sigh so gusty it ruffled Mrs. Morrison's hair. "It is a tragedy that this magnificent Greek antiquity must leave Greece. But this man has children. So he parts from this precious ring. It is from Crete, where it was found in the Palace of Minos."

"And how can we be sure it's not a copy?"

"But no! This is real, made by a master craftsman, two thousands years before Christ! Think of it! You will present it to a museum, where your countrymen may look upon it and read, 'Generous gift from the collection of Mr. and Mrs. Mor-rees-sohn'! You will be a benefactor of the public."

"Okay. No charge for looking, is there?" Mr. Morrison was not ordinarily impolite, but he was anxious to terminate this idiotic conversation, though he feared it was already too late to recapture his shattered euphoria.

"Not here! You do not imagine I would carry it with me? We make an appointment. You come to my home and then I show, and you have opportunity to study it careful and verify the truth of my story. Here is my address. I am at home until nine in the morning. I do not suggest the nighttime. It is unsafe in the narrow streets of the Old City these days, with this vicious curdog of a Junta we have now. . ."

"What kind of guarantee do I get?" Mr. Morrison interrupted.

"Nothing in writing," the Greek said hastily. "It would not be safe, not for me nor for my client." He raised a pudgy hand. "I give my word of honor!"

"Not good enough. Sorry. I need a written guarantee from a recognized antique dealer."

"Impossible! Surely you know I would not cheat a friend of Professor Blake."

"Let's assume it's real. How do I get it through customs, with no bill of sale? Antiques come in duty-free only if you can prove they're real."

"A ring, it is so easy to slip through the customs."

"Smuggle it in? You must be crazy."

"You are making big mistake," Mr. Scopas said. "It is too bad. I had thought you more courageous."

"It's no use, Scopas. You can't needle me. Find yourself another customer."

With one last enormous sigh, the Greek gentleman turned his back

83

and departed, slipping and sliding over the rough stones in his shiny pointed shoes.

Mrs. Morrison laughed comfortably. "There was a time when we'd have fallen for a crazy story like that. We were inexperienced then."

"If," Mr. Morrison said, "he weren't such an obnoxious little creep, I'd have taken him up on it. I'd like to have a look. It is just barely possible he's telling the truth."

"We promised Professor Blake we'd never buy another artifact except through a reputable dealer," Mrs. Morrison said. "Besides, Scopas' apartment is sure to be full of fleas."

"Right! Just the thought of it makes me itch." Mr. Morrison pointed to a place between his shoulder blades which his wife obligingly scratched for him. "Whew! That's better. Let's try a few more shots in this light. Okay?"

"We must have a hundred slides of the Parthenon from here."

"Not one of them does it justice. Stay right where you are."

Unlike Mr. Scopas, his feet were sure on the uneven ground as he moved into position. Not for nothing had Mr. Morrison been a member of the mountain-climbing club in his undergraduate days. Mrs. Morrison, with a resigned shrug, arranged her red sweater over her shoulders. One of her wifely duties was to be equipped at all times with a touch of red, to serve as a spot of color against gray stone or green mountain. She owned, besides the sweater, a red pocketbook, a red raincoat, and a vast red straw shade hat. She looked terrible in red.

Next morning, following a restless night, Mr. Morrison woke early. In the other bed his wife slept on. He knew there'd be no going back to sleep for him. Might as well go and have a look at Scopas' ring—with no idea of buying, of course, but just for the fun of calling his bluff. He dressed quietly and slipped out.

He covered the distance rapidly, consulting his map of the city from time to time. Though a short man, only a couple of inches taller than his wife, he was thin and wiry. It wasn't fair, she had complained only last night. He ate far more than she did. He had no right to his slim figure while she suffered a steadily increasing girth. He had laughed and ordered more dessert for both of them. The layers of pastry were thin as tissue paper and oozed butter, honey, and other high-calorie, cholesterol-laden undesirables. "We'll walk it off tomorrow," he had said. It made no difference to him that his wife's figure did not show off a frock to good advantage. Besides, when hungry, she was cross, and that did matter. Nothing else upset her equanimity.

The home of Mr. Scopas was in a most unsavory neighborhood. The stench from the gutter was thoroughly uncivilized. Handkerchief to nose, Mr. Morrison sprinted up the four flights of stairs and knocked.

"Who is it?" came a whisper through the door.

"Morrison! Let me in!" he shouted, trying unsuccessfully to breathe in air without smelling it.

"Shhhhh!" The door opened, a pudgy, hairy hand reached out, clutched his sleeve, and drew him in. Scopas closed and locked the door. "So you come after all? Good! My wife sleeps. Come, we go in the kitchen."

They tiptoed down a narrow dark hall. In the kitchen, Scopas opened a battered tin box and took out several half-eaten loaves of bread. From behind them, he produced the end of a final loaf, green with mold. "Good hiding place, no?" His fat fingers fumbled in the moldy remnant. "Ah! I have it!" He wiped the ring on a grimy rag, no less unsavory than the moldy bread, then handed it to Mr. Morrison, who received it without enthusiasm and carried it to the narrow dirty window.

The ring consisted of a circular piece of some semiprecious stone— chalcedony, probably—set in silver and carved. It was hard to see clearly. Deciding to sacrifice his handkerchief to the cause of archeology, Mr. Morrison scrubbed a clean spot on the window pane. Now he could see the carving. It was a seated monkey, the figure distorted to fit the circular shape of the stone. Yes, both style and subject were quite typical of the Mid-Minoan period. An excited feeling began to grow in him. Surely nobody would go to this kind of trouble to create a fake. Would they? With an effort, he assumed an expression of doubt.

"Not bad," he said. "Not bad at all for a copy."

"You know it is no copy," Mr. Scopas replied with quiet assurance. "It is yours for fifty thousand drachmas."

Mr. Morrison did a rapid calculation. He had enough traveler's checks—he and Mrs. Morrison between them—so that he could pay Scopas and still finish the trip as planned. Just barely. If they were careful.

"It's worth much more than that," he said aloud. *"If* it's real . . ."

85

"But you will not pay more," Mr. Scopas replied with disarming candor. "The owner can live on the sum for a long time, perhaps until the Junta is overthrown and his family return to power."

Still uncertain—after all, he had been stung before—Mr. Morrison continued to hesitate.

"I hear my wife," Mr. Scopas hissed. "Better she not see you. Pay me and go."

Five minutes later, the signed traveler's checks were in the soiled fat hands of Mr. Scopas, and Mr. Morrison was hastening back to his hotel, the ring on the little finger of his left hand. He had put it on backward; all that showed was a narrow band of silver, the carved stone safely hidden in the palm of his hand. Now what? he thought. He couldn't wander around Greece with a clenched fist for the next two weeks. Nor did he care to admit his folly to his wife—not until Professor Blake had verified its authenticity. It must be hidden, not only from customs inspectors, but from Mrs. Morrison—an infinitely more difficult assignment. Where did people hide jewelry? Only diamonds were small enough to be pushed into a tube of toothpaste. There was no false bottom to the heel of his shoe. What did he own that was safe from Mrs. Morrison's tidying fingers? Ah, he had it! Shoe polish. By mutual consent, she was the laundress of drip-dries during their travels, while he attended to shoes. But what to do with the ring until he could arrange an unobserved session with his shoe-polishing kit? He was still seeking the answer to this problem when he reached his room to find that Mrs. Morrison had solved it for him. Her bed was empty and on the pillow reposed a note, stating that she had gone to the hairdresser. She hoped he had enjoyed his walk.

Using the handle of his toothbrush, he scooped polish from the kit, inserted the ring into the hole, replaced the paste, packed it down neatly, and washed the brown stains from his improvised tool. All that now remained was to present a cool and casual air to the customs and passport inspectors. Could he do it? He considered racing back to Scopas, shoe-kit in hand, to return the ring and retrieve his money and his integrity. But he rejected this thought even as it came to him. Too late for that. He shrugged, shoved the whole matter into the back of his mind, and went in search of a morning newspaper.

It was lunchtime when Mrs. Morrison returned, demanding to know how she liked the new hairdo the Greek operator had contrived. He did his best to be satisfactory. It looked just like the old one to him, but he had been a husband too long to say so. As soon as possible, he changed the subject.

"Let's go cash some of your traveler's checks," he said. "Mine are all gone."

Mrs. Morrison looked startled. "So are mine. I haven't one left."

"All of them? Impossible! You haven't paid for a thing since we left!"

"Not a thing . . . except the wonderful surprise I bought for your birthday, dear. Now don't ask questions. It was a lot of money, I know. But when you see it, you'll say it was worth it."

He tried vainly to remember what he'd admired during the last few weeks. That chess set in Ankara, maybe?

"It better be. Nothing for it, we'll have to cut the trip short." He laughed. "Never mind. It'll be nice to get home. Seems to me you've been talking about the grandchildren a lot lately."

"You're right. I start worrying that they'll forget me. Let's count up our cash and see how many days we've got left."

Mr. Morrison kept his bills in his wallet, his coins in his pants pocket. He counted it all carefully, while Mrs. Morrison was adding up the money in her pocketbook. The total was discouragingly small.

"That'll take care of the hotel bill and a taxi to the airport," he said. "Good thing we already have our return tickets. If all the flights are sold out, we may get pretty hungry."

Mrs. Morrison yanked open a dresser drawer. "Oh, I'm not finished counting, dear," she said. "There's some money in my brown antelope bag, the one you bought for me in Bologna. And there must be something in my little white evening bag—from that little shop next to the hump-backed bridge in Venice, remember?"

"Women!" But Mr. Morrison smiled as he said it, for the total when collected at last, was respectable. A call to Air Olympia brought good news: a cancellation had just come in. There would be no problem about changing the reservations to an early-morning flight. Since this was their last night, they decided to splurge by going out to dinner at the Grande Bretagne.

"Pack first, dinner afterwards," Mrs. Morrison said. "When we get back, we'll be full of good food and good wine and we won't want to be bothered."

They returned quite late after dinner. Mr. Morrison, having unlocked the door to their room, stepped aside to let his wife go first. She advanced into the room and then, with a small startled shriek, backed out again, treading rather heavily on Mr. Morrison's toe.

"Ouch! What the devil's the matter with you?" he shouted.

"There's a man . . . a man in there! Oh, dear, do be careful . . ."

Pushing her aside, Mr. Morrison catapulted himself into the room, just in time to see a foot disappear over the balcony railing. He ran out and looked over. A dim figure was running down the street. No use shouting; no one else in sight. He turned back into the room, which was a shambles.

"Oh, no!" Mrs. Morrison wailed. "All that packing to do over again!"

"Never mind the packing! What's he stolen?"

Mr. Morrison began rapidly to sort out their belongings. The shoe-polishing kit lay under a heap of tumbled sweaters. He contrived to drop it and in stooping to pick it up again, knocked it under the bed. He took his time about retrieving it and rose reassured. He'd managed a good look and ascertained that the smooth surface of the polish was undisturbed. If, as he was beginning to suspect, the thief had been after the ring, he'd been interrupted in time.

When at last all their belongings had been sorted out and repacked, they compared notes and decided that nothing was missing.

"He was probably looking for money," Mrs. Morrison said.

"Man, did he ever come to the wrong shop!" They laughed inordinately. Mr. Morrison felt his tension draining away. Again he wished he'd never got himself into this. He did not have the temperament for operations outside the law.

By the time they descended from the plane at Kennedy Airport, Mr. Morrison, though his heart was pounding, felt relatively calm—at least, calmer than he had expected to feel. He had lived through the coming hour so many times in imagination, nothing could be so bad as some of his fantasies.

The customs inspector was not one of the friendly sort. He poked and peered. "What's that?" he demanded, pouncing on a white powder in the bottom of Mrs. Morrison's carry-on.

She smiled disarmingly. "Soap flakes," she explained. "The box leaks. Isn't it a mess?"

The inspector glared. He wet his finger, dipped it in the powder, smelled it, tasted. Then he smiled too. "It *is* soap." He seemed surprised. "Okay. Close 'em up."

When they were safely out of hearing, Mrs. Morrison whispered, "Did he suspect me of smuggling in heroin? Surely no smuggler would be so careless as to spill it around loose!"

Her husband, who did not trust his voice, made no reply. Tomorrow, he was thinking, he would make some excuse to get out of the house alone and pay a call on Professor Blake.

As it turned out, no excuse was needed. Struggling to relaunch her household, Mrs. Morrison ignored him. He skulked next door with the ring.

"Scopas!" Professor Blake shouted subsequently. "That crook?" He covered his eyes with his hand. "Oh no! When I gave you the address, I warned you. His shop is okay for handwoven stuff, I said. But nothing valuable."

"Well, take a look and let me know the worst."

The professor took the ring and inspected it carefully. He whistled softly between his teeth. Mr. Morrison, annoyed to find that he was holding his breath, let it out with an explosive sound.

"Well?" he demanded.

"Can't be sure . . . yet." Professor Blake wrapped the ring carefully in his handkerchief before tucking it into his pocket. "Let you know in a few days."

Mr. Morrison went home to lunch.

"Where've you been?" Mrs. Morrison asked.

His weary mind went blank. He could think of no reasonable story. Fed up with the strain of keeping secrets from his wife, he blurted out the whole tale. At the end, Mrs. Morrison got up and ran out of the room. In a moment she was back, hand outstretched. In the palm lay a ring, chalcedony set in silver. What Mr. Morrison said then was not language a respectable middle-aged man customarily uses to address the wife of his bosom.

"I don't blame you," she said, when at last he ran down, having exhausted his limited stock of obscenities. "I deserve it. But you're just as bad."

"When did you go to see Scopas?" Mr. Morrison asked.

"It must have been just after you left. We probably missed each other by only a few minutes. When I woke up, you were gone, so I

89

rushed through my dressing and got to his place a few minutes before nine. I pretended I'd been to the hairdresser. I knew you wouldn't know the difference!"

"Where did you hide the ring, to get it past customs?"

"Here." She held out her left hand. "I told you I cut myself peeling an orange, but that wasn't true. This was just to hide the ring." She ripped off the strip bandage from the middle finger, revealing the undamaged skin beneath. "I can take it off now, you know. When I first brought the ring back to the hotel, I put it in my box of soap flakes. I thought of leaving it there, but at the last minute I changed my mind. Can you imagine how I'd have felt if I hadn't—when the customs officer got so nosy about the spilled soap in my carry-on?" She stood up. "Well, I might as well take this over to Professor Blake."

"Why bother? Just admit it: we got taken again, dear."

She set her jaw in an unaccustomed stubborn line. "I'm a pretty good judge of old jewelry by now. This looks real to me. The ring you bought is counterfeit. Mine's not."

"That's ridiculous! If Scopas is dealing in these fakes, he's got a dozen of 'em, all alike, one for every idiot that comes along."

"Maybe so. But I bet you he had a real one to begin with, to copy. Probably he ran out of fakes, so he sold me the original. Say! Maybe he did it by mistake! Oh, I hope so. Can you imagine his face when he realizes . . .?"

Her giggle and his booming laugh filled the room. Then, abruptly, he stopped. "You know, you might be right? I mean, about his having an authentic ring for copying. That's got to be it. And he sold it to me, because he knew darn well I'd be able to tell the difference." Suddenly he let out a shout. "Hey! How thick-headed can we be? That last night at the hotel . . . Scopas sent that guy to go through our baggage. He wasn't after money. He wanted that ring back!"

"Of course! It's a good thing we left in such a hurry. Heaven knows what he'd have tried next. Well, I'm taking this to Professor Blake, right this minute. We'll see who knows best."

It was several days before the professor summoned them.

"I have wonderful news." He beamed. "Scopas isn't quite as much of a crook as we thought. He actually sold you a fine specimen. Even taking into account the other ring—which is a fake, of course—you got a bargain. It's worth three times what you paid for the pair of them. I suggest you present this valuable antiquity to the museum." He placed one of the rings, which now rested on a bed of black velvet, on the coffee table. The other, he handed to Mrs. Morrison. "Wear it as a souvenir," he said.

Watching his wife slip the ring on her finger, Mr. Morrison grinned. "Wow! What a relief!" he said. "I don't like being made a fool of. Knew darn well that ring was the real thing."

His wife glared at him. "*This* is the ring you bought," she cried, holding out her hand. "It's easy to see the difference. This would never have fooled me!"

Together they turned on the professor. "Well?" Mr. Morrison added, "Mine was the real one, wasn't it?" as his wife shrilled, "Tell him he was the one who got cheated."

Professor Blake shook his head and smiled a benevolent smile. "Dear friends," he said, "during the tests, we put the two rings side by side. I haven't the slightest idea which is which. It doesn't matter. When you present the ring to the museum, a card will be printed to read, 'Gift of Mr. and Mrs. Morrison.' Congratulations to you both!"

For a moment the Morrisons sat in silence, glowering alternately at him and at each other.

"I don't believe you," Mrs. Morrison said at last. "You know which is which. You just don't want to tell us."

"You old devil! You did it on purpose!" Mr. Morrison cried.

The professor shook his head. "That would be most unethical. How can you suggest such a thing?" The lines of his face were stern. But Mr. Morrison could have sworn that he saw the suggestion of a twinkle in the professor's eyes.

I Don't Understand It

by Bill Pronzini

Well, I'd been on the road for two days, riding on the produce trucks from El Centro to Bakersfield, when a refrigerator van picked me up and took me straight through to the Salinas Valley. They let me out right where I was headed, too, in front of this dirt road about three miles the other side of San Sinandro.

I stood there on the side of the road, hanging onto the tan duffel with my stuff in it, and it was plenty hot all right, just past noon, and the sun all yellow and hazed over. I looked at the big wood sign that was stuck up there, and it said: JENSEN PRODUCE—PICKERS WANTED, and had a black arrow pointing off down the dirt road. That was the name of the place, sure enough.

I started up the dirt road, and it was pretty dry and dusty. Off on both sides you could see the rows and rows of lettuce shining nice and green in the sun, and the pickers hunched over in there. Most of them looked like Mex's, but here and there was some college boys that are always around to pick in the spring and summer months.

Pretty soon I come over a rise and I could see a wide clearing. There was a big white house set back a ways, and down in front an area that was all paved off. On one side was a big corrugated-iron warehouse, the sun coming off the top of that iron roof near to blinding you, it was so bright. About six flatbeds, a couple of Jimmy pickups and a big white Lincoln was sitting beside the warehouse. All of them had JENSEN PRODUCE done up in these big gold and blue letters on the door.

I come down there onto the asphalt part. Just to my right was four long, flat buildings made of wood, but with corrugated roofs. I knew that was where the pickers put down.

I walked across to the big warehouse. Both of the doors in front was shut, but there was a smaller one to the left and it was standing wide open.

Just as I come up to that door, this woman come out, facing inside, and sure enough she banged right into me before I could get out of the way. I stumbled back and dropped the duffel.

She come around and looked at me. She said, "Oh, I'm sorry. I didn't see you there."

Well, she was about the most beautiful woman I ever saw in my whole life. She had this long dark hair and green eyes with little gold flecks in them, and she was all brown and tan and her skin shined in the sun like she had oil rubbed on it. She had on a pair of white shorts and this white blouse with no sleeves. Her hands was in little fists on her hips, and she was smiling at me real nice and friendly. She said, "Well, I don't think I've seen you before."

I couldn't say nothing right then. I mean, I never been much good around the women anyway—I can't never think of nothing to talk to them about—and this one was so pretty she could've been in them Hollywood pictures.

My ears felt all funny and hot, with her looking right into my face like she was. But I couldn't just stand there, so I kind of coughed a little and bent down and picked up the duffel.

I said, "No, ma'am."

"I'm Mrs. Jensen. Is there something I can do for you?"

"Well, I heard you needed pickers."

"Yes, we do," she said. "The hot weather came on before we expected it. We have to harvest before the heat ruins the crop and we're awfully shorthanded."

I started to say something about being glad to help out, but just then this big good-looking fellow in a blue work shirt that had the sleeves rolled up and was unbuttoned down the front so you could see all the hair he had on his chest, he come out of the door. The woman turned and saw him and said, "Oh, this is Mr. Carbante. He's our foreman."

I said, "How are you, Mr. Carbante?"

"Okay," he said. "You looking for work?"

"Sure."

"Ever picked lettuce before?"

"No, sir. But I picked plenty of other things."

"Such as?"

"Well, citrus."

"Where?"

"Down in the Imperial Valley."

"What else?"

"Tomatoes. Grapes and apples and celery, too."

"All right," Mr. Carbante said. "You're on."

"I sure do thank you."

This Mrs. Jensen was still standing there with her hands on her hips. She looked at me. "I'm sorry again about that bump."

"Oh, it's nothing."

"Good luck."

"Thanks."

"I'll see you later, Gino," she said to Mr. Carbante.

"Okay, Mrs. Jensen."

When she was gone, around to the side, Mr. Carbante took me into the warehouse. They had a criss-cross of conveyer belts in there, and packing bins lining one wall, and there was a lot of Mex women that was sorting out the lettuce heads and putting the good ones off on one belt to where they were trimmed and graded and packed, and putting the ones that wasn't any good off on another belt.

We went into a little office they had there, and Mr. Carbante give me a little book to keep track of how many crates I was to pick, and told me what they paid for each crate. Then he said what bunkhouse I was to sleep in and the bunk number and what time they give you supper and what time you had to be up and ready for work in the morning.

He just finished telling me all that when this old bird come into the office. He had a nice head of white hair and pink cheeks, and he stopped where we was and give me a smile. He must've been close to seventy, sure enough, but his eyes was bright and he looked to get around pretty good.

Mr. Carbante said, "This is Mr. Jensen. He's the owner."

"How do you do, Mr. Jensen?"

"Glad to know you, son. You going to work for us?"

"Yes, sir."

"Well, that's fine."

"Yes, sir."

"Did you want to see me, Mr. Jensen?" Mr. Carbante asked.

94

"Have you seen Mrs. Jensen?"

"Not since breakfast."

"All right, Gino," Mr. Jensen said, and he went on out.

I said, "Mrs. Jensen was right here with you, Mr. Carbante."

"Never mind, boy."

"Yes, sir," I said. "Is that Mrs. Jensen's husband?"

Mr. Carbante's eyes got all narrow. "That's right. Why?"

"Well, nothing," I said, but I was wondering how come old Mr. Jensen had such a young wife. People sure do funny things sometimes, specially when they get old.

Mr. Carbante said, "You just mind your own business and pick your quota every day, and you'll get along fine here. You understand that, boy?"

"Sure, Mr. Carbante."

"Okay, then. You'll be down on the south side. There's a couple of Mex's out there who'll give you the hang of it."

Do you know how they pick lettuce?

The way you do it is, you have this long knife, real sharp, and you walk in along the rows, which are about two feet apart, and you clip off the heads in close to the ground and put them in these field crates you drag along with you. When you get a crate filled, you leave it in there between the rows and then a truck comes along and picks up the crates and takes them up to the warehouse.

Now, it don't sound like much, me telling it like that, but there's plenty of little tricks to it, all right.

These two men that Mr. Carbante had told me about give me some tips on how to tell which heads was to be cut, and how to tell which ones had been chewed up by the aphids, and which ones had got the mildew or been burnt by the sun. I took to watching this one big fellow, whose name was Haysoos. He was pretty near pure black from the sun, and had tiny little eyes and thick, bushy eyebrows. But he sure knew what he was doing in that lettuce, clipping away like nobody you ever saw.

After I watched him for a while, I got onto the knack of it and started right in myself. I had my shirt off out there, and it was plenty hot. I was burnt up pretty good from being down in the Imperial Valley, but down there you was working citrus and didn't have to pick right in under the sun like that.

Just as I got my first field crate filled up, who should come down the road but Mrs. Jensen and Mr. Carbante. They was just strolling along, side by side, her with this big floppy straw hat stuck up on her head. She was smiling, and every now and then she would wave to one of the pickers out in the lettuce. Every one of them was looking at her, sure enough.

She got up to where me and Haysoos was working and stopped and give me a nice smile. "Hello, there."

"Hello, Mrs. Jensen."

"How are you doing?"

"Just fine."

This Haysoos smiled at her with teeth that was all yellow and said something in Mex, but I guess she didn't hear him. She started off down the road again. Haysoos watched her. "*Muy bonita,* hey? Such a beautiful woman, a man's blood boils at the sight of such a beautiful woman."

"She sure is beautiful, all right," I said.

"She likes you, hey *amigo?*"

"She's real nice and friendly."

"Haysoos she does not like. Not big ugly Haysoos."

"Oh, sure she likes you, Haysoos."

"Carbante is who she likes, hey? Carbante and a thousand others."

He turned away and started in to pick again. I didn't know what he'd meant, but I didn't want to say nothing so I just turned away too and went to work in my own row.

The next day I was pretty sore from the stooping over, but I'd had a nice sleep the night before and it didn't bother me too much. I'd got the hang of picking the lettuce now, and I was clipping along at a nice pace.

One of the trucks come around with sandwiches and milk for us at noontime, and we sat there on the side of the road to eat. Well, while we was eating, here comes Mrs. Jensen down the road again.

She come right up there to where we was, smiling at everybody, and asked us if we all had enough to eat. Some of the college boys called out some things I didn't understand, and most everybody laughed, and Mrs. Jensen laughed right with them.

This Haysoos was sitting right near where I was. He kept watching

96

Mrs. Jensen. "Everyone but Haysoos, hey?" he said.

"How was that?"

"A man's blood boils."

He sure said a lot of funny things, that Haysoos.

Saturday come around before you knew it and that was when we was to get paid. After supper we all went to the office in the big warehouse with the little books we had and old Mr. Jensen and Mr. Carbante totaled up the number of crates we had picked and give us our pay, all in cash money.

When we was all paid, old Mr. Jensen stood up and said that he was going off to Salinas for the next few days on business, and that Mr. Carbante was to be in charge and if we wanted anything we should see him. After that he went out and got into his big Lincoln and drove off down the road.

I went back to the bunks then, but most of the other pickers, they was going off into San Sinandro to drink in the bars. A couple of them asked me if I wanted to come along, but I said I wasn't much for the drinking.

I lay down on my bunk and started to read this movie magazine one of the college boys had. I sure like to read them movie magazines, all about the Hollywood people and the houses they have and the fine clothes and everything. Someday I'm going to have me all them things, too.

Well, I lay there and pretty soon it got dark outside. But it was awful hot in there and I got up and went out to get some air. It sure hadn't cooled down much.

I walked down by the other bunks and come around the south end of the second one, and I heard all this commotion inside. There was a window right there and I stopped by that and looked inside to see what it was all about.

There was this bunch of pickers in there, about six of them, and they was all pretty well oiled up. They had a couple of empty wine jugs lying around on the floor, and they was passing this other one around from one to another.

And who should be right there in the middle of all of them but Haysoos. He was sitting on one of the bunks, his eyes all glassed over. He got the jug and took a long one out of there, and it passed on to

97

the next one. He wasn't whooping it up or nothing, like the rest of them was, but just sitting there on that bunk, kind of staring at the floor.

Well, while I watched, the rest of them started out the door and one had the wine jug. They called back to Haysoos, but he just sat there and didn't answer them at all. Then Haysoos was alone, and I heard the rest of them going off down the road singing some kind of Mex song.

Old Haysoos found another jug somewhere and had one you would hardly believe from it. He wiped off his mouth with the back of his hand and then stood up and wobbled around some. I could see his lips moving like he was talking to himself, but I couldn't hear none of it.

I got tired of watching him and went back to my bunk and lay down again, and it wasn't so hot anymore. Pretty soon I went to sleep.

I woke up right away when I heard the sirens. They was really loud.

I jumped off my bunk and ran outside, and there was a lot of the other pickers there, too, just come back from San Sinandro. They was all running up toward the big white house.

I commenced to running up there with them, and I thought how it must be that the big white house had caught fire somehow and what a terrible thing that would be. But when I got up there, I saw that it wasn't fire engines that had made the sirens, but police cars. There was three of them there, and a big ambulance, and they all had these red lights going round and round on their tops. There was a couple of policemen, too, holding the pickers back and telling them not to come any closer.

I wedged in there, and the pickers that had been there for a while was talking pretty fast.

". . . right there in the bedroom."

"She had it coming."

"They both did."

"Yeah, but not *that* way."

"Who found them?"

"Somebody heard the screams."

"But they didn't get him?"

"Not yet."

"He must have gone through the fields."

"They've got the roads blocked."

"We'll get up a posse . . ."

I said to one of the college boys who had been talking, "What is it? What happened?"

"You don't know?"

I said, "I was sleeping. What is it?"

Just then the front door of the big white house opened and two fellows dressed in white and two policemen come out and they was carrying two stretchers. They had to pass by where I was to get to the ambulance, and I looked at the two sheet-covered stretchers and what was on them.

I just couldn't believe it at first, but the college boys was talking again, telling about it, and I knew it had to be true. I turned away, sick as anybody ever was.

The one college boy put his hand on my shoulder. "Come on," he said, "we're going after him."

But I pulled away and run back to the bunks. I had to get away from there. I couldn't stay there no more.

You know what that crazy Haysoos had done?

He'd killed Mrs. Jensen and Mr. Carbante, that's what. He'd gone up to the big white house with that sharp, sharp lettuce knife of his and cut off both their heads.

I don't understand it, and I'm just so sick. A fine lady like Mrs. Jensen and a nice man like Mr. Carbante. Two of the swellest people you ever wanted to meet and know, and that crazy Haysoos had killed them both.

I just don't understand what could have made him do a terrible, terrible thing like that.

Do you?

News From Nowhere

by Ron Goulart

It was right there in the window, behind the dusty glass, next to scatters of tarnished metal jewelry, drooping peacock feathers, rusty faucets, collapsed hats and much-traveled suitcases: an enormous oil painting of Conway.

Conway, lean and smiling, wearing that broad-striped native poncho he'd always worn down there in Mexico, a small #1 brush cocked over his right ear and a wineskin clutched in his knobby right hand. Conway, smiling his gap-toothed smile, his big moustache bristling, and behind him the flat bright Mexican countryside; the view from the back room of the girl's house. Conway, a self-portrait he must have painted while they were down there all those months.

Right there in the front window of the News From Nowhere Junk Emporium, Conway smiled out on McAllister Street and all its run-down buildings and junk shops.

Andrew Paulin had forgotten to keep breathing. He coughed now and gasped in air through his open mouth. He was a tall blond man of thirty, about twenty pounds overweight and wearing a new gray suit. He'd been eating a chocolate almond bar and he threw it down toward the gutter. "Conway," he said aloud.

A heavy black woman in a green coat smiled at him as she passed.

Paulin licked his lips. He'd been in the News From Nowhere shop before. He liked to browse in the antique shops and junk stores that dotted San Francisco. Now that he only had to pretend to be working as a commercial artist he could take all the time he wanted to wander Union Street and Clement and McAllister. During the nine months he'd been back in San Francisco he'd been down here on McAllister as often as two or three times a week.

He went over to the door of the shop and grabbed the brass knob.

The knob spun around and around in his hand and nothing happened. Paulin pressed his shoulder against the grimy door and shoved. "Don't tell me he's closed?"

There were a dozen signs pasted on the inside of the glass door. *Hi Class Junque. Choice Items Come From Everywhere To Nowhere. In case of emergency contact owner at Oakleaf Hotel, Eddy Street.*

After trying the door once more, Paulin shaded his eyes and tried to see inside the long, narrow junk shop. He couldn't tell if there were any more of Conway's paintings inside or not. He turned away.

He went back around the corner and climbed into his sports car. "I should have gone back to that studio of his and gathered up all his stuff," he said to himself. He left the curb and headed for Eddy Street. "No, Conway had a couple of other places where he bummed studio space. There's really no way of telling where all he left his paintings. Now look, all that is back there is a picture of Conway in that fussy realistic style of his. New neorealism, didn't he call it? That's all it is. A self-portrait of Conway, so what. Nothing in it to link him with you. You might as well buy the thing and keep it out of sight, but you have to relax. Okay, it does show the girl's house, but nobody knows that besides you and Conway and the girl. And they're both dead."

The hotel clerk at the Oakleaf had grown fat since he'd been tattooed, and the snakes and flowers on his chubby bare arms were dim and distorted. "Who?" he asked Paulin.

"The old guy who runs the News From Nowhere."

"What's that?"

"A junk shop over on McAllister. You know the one."

"Oh, you mean Mac."

"Mac. Old guy who always wears a brown hat and rimless glasses."

"He's eighty-two, can hardly see anymore," said the fat sixty-year-old clerk. "Why you want him?"

"I want to buy something out of his shop."

"What?"

"A painting."

"Say, is this Tuesday?"

"Yes, it is."

"Tuesday Mac closes up shop and goes over across the Bay to visit his in-laws."

"You don't know where I might reach him?"

"Nope."

"What time do you expect him back?"

"Not till after ten tonight."

"Well, I'll call then."

"Switchboard closes sharp at ten. You'll have to wait until tomorrow," said the tattooed clerk. "That must be some terrific painting."

Paulin backed off from the brown wood counter in the Oakleaf's small lobby. "Nothing special, really."

Driving home toward his Russian Hill apartment, Paulin said to himself, "Don't go acting too anxious about the damn picture, now. I think you're right to want to buy it and get it out of the way. But don't make everybody wonder why. There's nothing to link you with Conway or the girl. Everyone—the papers, her family—accepted the crash. They believe she had an accident and was burned up in her car. Burned up along with the money she was carrying. You and Conway fixed that up. Just relax."

At the signal at the bottom of his street he glanced over and saw a Chinese man in a station wagon watching him. He must have been talking out loud, moving his lips. He had that habit and he'd have to watch it, control it. He made himself grin over at the Chinese and shrug. The light changed and he shot uphill toward home.

The shop door opened this time. Paulin stepped inside the News From Nowhere junk store, squinting. The long low room was dim, dusty. He stepped over a fallen tuba with a feather boa in its bell. "That's an interesting painting in the window," he said.

Behind a glass counter sat an old man in a brown coat-sweater. He had a soft brown hat pulled down low on his bald head. Sprawled on the streaked counter top were a dozen roller skates, a hacksaw, two cast-iron skillets, a Mason jar full of green marbles, three volumes of a 19th-century encyclopedia and two slices of whole wheat toast on a cracked china plate. "Far as I can tell," replied old Mac. He touched his glasses, leaving dusty prints on the thick lenses. "My sight is slowly diminishing."

"I think I might like to buy the painting. How much?"

"Far as I can see, it's the work of an authentic artist." Mac picked up the top slice of toast and broke it slowly in half. "Twenty dollars."

Pretending not to be that interested, Paulin said, "That's a little steep."

"Fellow yesterday offered me fifty."

"Why didn't he take it, then?"

"He might come back today and do just that. Twenty-five dollars. You want it?"

"I thought you said twenty."

"The more we have to argue the higher the price climbs."

"Well, okay. I'll buy it."

"No checks. Twenty-five in cash."

Paulin got out his wallet. "Have any more around by that particular artist?"

"Signed his name on it, didn't he? I forget what he calls himself."

"I didn't really notice," said Paulin, drawing out two tens and a five. "You wouldn't have anything else?"

The old man nodded. "One more. Out in back. Cost you thirty-five dollars, that one will. Want to take a look? Go on through the little door over there, push it hard."

"Guess I might as well," said Paulin. "He's an interesting artist, whoever he is."

"Likely he'll be famous someday and you'll make a fortune from your chicken-feed investment."

Paulin made his way around several small stuffed animals and to the door leading to the back room. He pushed and the door swung lop-sidedly open.

This room had a higher ceiling and was chill and damp. Great dark bureaus and chairs hulked around the room, piles of ancient magazines, clouded mirrors, more jars of marbles.

Here was another painting by Conway. Paulin inhaled, involuntarily bringing one hand up against his chest. This one showed the girl. "She was never very good-looking," Paulin said to himself. "The good-looking ones never seem to have money. Ugh, that awful peasant blouse she always wore, showing off all her blotchy skin."

He stepped closer to the big Conway painting, which was propped in a worn cane-bottom rocker. "When did he paint this thing? Maybe before I met him down there. He was trying to convince her she should be a patron of the arts even before I joined him. I suppose you should feel sorry for her, wanting everyone around her doing beautiful things." Finally he grabbed up the unframed painting. "But I don't really feel anything. I can live here in San Francisco for two or three years on that $50,000 we got out of her; longer if I take it easy. That's all I feel about her."

In the shop again, Paulin said, "A nice bit of work. I may as well take both of them. Thirty-five did you say?"

Mac rubbed at his glasses and leaned toward the painting. "I forgot it was a picture of a pretty girl. That should be worth fifty bucks at least."

"She's not all that pretty."

"Arguing merely ups the prices around here."

"Okay, all right. Here's the rest of the money."

After he took the cash, Mac bent and reached under the counter. A stuffed quail fell off a shelf and bounced on his stooped back. "Someplace I have some nice wrapping paper I can give you."

"I imagine you get items in from all over."

"From the four corners." Mac unfurled a spotted sheet of brown paper. "See if that'll fit around both of them while I dig you up a length of string."

"For instance, I wonder where these two paintings came from." Paulin watched the old man shuffling off into a corner.

"Mexico." Mac knocked a model train off a sprung sofa and clutched up a ball of twine.

"Really. Who brought them in?"

"Didn't get their names."

"Two people?"

"Man and wife, as I remember, brought them in over the weekend," said Mac, cutting off a piece of twine. "At least I presume they were man and wife. These days, and around Frisco, you never can tell. Couple in their early forties, did some touristing down in Mexico. Picked up these paintings, then decided they didn't want them after all. No accounting for taste. Here." He flung the string to Paulin.

Paulin had the two Conway paintings wrapped in the rough paper. He took the twine and tied up the package.

"You do that pretty well. Maybe you're an artist yourself."

"Yes, I am," replied Paulin. "You wouldn't know the name of the couple, would you? Where they might live?"

"This isn't a pawnshop," said Mac. "I have no need for biographical information."

It was a calm spring day, and Paulin had walked all the way from his apartment. Leaving the News From Nowhere shop, he put the wrapped Conway paintings under one arm and began walking back toward Russian Hill.

"That was just like Conway," he said to himself as he walked the bright mid-morning streets. "Painting her exactly as she looked, not flattering her at all. He had great confidence in himself, no need for flattery. Charming, smiling. Well, it didn't do him much good. He's been dead at the bottom of that canyon for almost a year now. Apparently he hasn't been found yet. I didn't figure he would be. With the girl it was different. We wanted them to find her and believe the $50,000 was with her; $50,000 she told her parents she was going to use for good works among the Mexican poor; $50,000 Conway and I convinced her would finance the three of us in a wonderful remote art colony for long happy years. What an unattractive girl."

High above, gulls circled in the clear blue sky.

"Smiling Conway," Paulin said to himself. "I still don't like the way he treated her at the end, teasing her. Not just knocking her out quickly and dumping her in the car. No, he wanted her to know he was going to kill her, that he'd betrayed her. A fine sense of humor, Conway's. Well, in a way that made it easier to do it to him. Using a variation on the original plan and dumping him unconscious in that wreck of a car of his and sending him to the bottom of the canyon way out there in nowhere. Yes, and I got rid of him in time to save nearly all the $50,000 for myself."

He was breathing in a more relaxed way and he stopped at a hot dog stand on Van Ness and bought a chili burger. He ate it as he walked, smiling now to himself.

He saw the third painting eight days later. This was the worst of all. "It's me," Paulin said, stopping on the rainy street in front of the News From Nowhere Junk Emporium. In this Conway painting, Paulin was sitting out in the red-tile patio behind the girl's house down there in Mexico. The girl was there, too, standing in an archway behind Paulin. Conway must have done that one from memory, because Paulin never posed for it. Conway was good at that. He could look at you once and remember everything about you. Paulin had seen Conway do a painting of his parents years after they'd died, and it was perfect.

Mac was taking some sort of oily gears out of a cardboard box, wheezing as he did. "You're in luck." He wiped his hands on his brown pants and touched his hat. "I got another of those pictures in, by the artist you like so much."

Paulin waited for the old man to mention it was a portrait of him, but Mac's eyesight must have prevented him from realizing it. "Yes, I noticed as I was passing."

"Sixty bucks for this one. I figure this particular artist is so much in demand, at least by you, I may as well cash in on it."

Paulin looked from the stooped old man to the painting in the shop window. It made him very uneasy having the picture there, showing him with the girl like that. "I'll take it. Did you happen to buy this from the same couple?"

Mac fished a wrinkled slip of yellow paper out of the sweatband of his brown hat and then clamped the hat back on his bald head. "Turns out these people got a dozen more by the same artist."

"A dozen?"

"Don't know if they want to sell them," said the old man. "See, when I showed interest they got the notion this particular artist was maybe hotter in the art world than they'd imagined. Many people suspect junk men are secret millionaires because of all the shrewd deals they pull. I'm going to have to go over there in my spare time and dicker. If it's worth it."

"I could go," offered Paulin.

"You'd cheat me out of my markup that way." Mac unfolded the scrap of paper. "Though maybe you could figure my commission in advance and then go and deal direct with these people."

"How much would you want?"

"I'd settle for one hundred."

Paulin sighed, got out his wallet. "Okay, all right. Who are they?"

"Name is Henderson and they just moved into a new place out near Stinson Beach. You know where that is, over in Marin County."

"Yes. Give me the address and phone number. I'll call them."

"Haven't got a phone as yet," said Mac as he handed over the slip on which he'd written Henderson and the Marin beach address. "Moving in, and you know how long it takes to get a phone installed. They tell me they're at home most every night."

Paulin took the address, crumpling it in his fist.

The fog kept coming in. The Henderson house sat alone, ringed by pine trees, at the end of a short road that climbed up from the beach. The low shingle house was dark, and Paulin parked his sports car away from it, off the road under some oaks.

The mist rolled in across the ocean and came swirling up over the cliffside behind the house, spinning through the trees.

"Now, if they aren't home," said Paulin to himself, "what difference does it make? If I can get the paintings without their seeing me, so much the better. It's likely all they have left will be here." He climbed quietly out of the car. "They must have bought this stuff from someone who cleaned out Conway's studio. Or maybe somebody who stored some of his paintings for him. When Conway didn't come back for a while, whoever had the stuff got tired of holding it and unloaded. Anyway, I'll have to see what these Hendersons have got."

The grass was high in the front lawn and, near a low rail fence, some sort of sign had fallen over. Paulin went directly to the front door and knocked. "Just in case someone is at home."

There was no response. After a moment Paulin slid a flashlight out of the pocket of his dark jacket and went quietly around the house. He found an unlocked window and raised it, then climbed in.

This was a bedroom. No paintings here.

He found them, seven pictures in all, lined up against one wall of the livingroom.

"Damn Conway," said Paulin. "I hadn't realized he'd documented our stay down there so well."

The three of them figured in most of the paintings: the girl, Conway and his smile, and Paulin. Even the girl's car, the one they'd put her in. There it was, sitting in the field near her house, with the three of them standing around, all looking happy. "Not expecting to die," he said.

Paulin checked out the other rooms in the Henderson house, but there were no more paintings.

He returned to the livingroom and studied the seven pictures again, swinging the beam of the flashlight from one to the other. "It's odd, in a way, so many of Conway's paintings should show up now," he said to himself. "You know, suppose this is some kind of setup? Oh, how

107

could it be? Conway's dead, at the bottom of that canyon, far away in Mexico." Paulin went closer to the paintings. "You don't know for sure, do you? All you did was knock him out and put him in his car and roll it over. You don't actually know he's dead. Of course he's dead. How could he have gotten out of there?"

Paulin picked up the painting of the three of them standing by the girl's car. "Conway's car never caught fire, you know. You should have climbed down there and made absolutely sure he was dead. But he was dead. If he wasn't, where has he been all these months? Suppose he did get out alive somehow. He'd know I was coming back here to San Francisco. You know how patient he was with the girl and how he loved to toy with her. Suppose the paintings are new? Maybe he's been watching me for months, figuring out how I live, the pattern of it. He could have made fresh paintings and bribed that nearly blind old man to put them on display. Now he's got you over here and he's going to torture you, like he did the girl, and find out where you've got the rest of the cash hidden."

Paulin put the painting back against the wall. "Stop scaring yourself. Conway's dead and it's only a coincidence these old paintings have turned up now. Gather them up and get out of here."

Something made a faint noise elsewhere in the house.

Paulin looked down at his free hand, shining the flashlight on it. He rubbed his forefinger slowly over his thumb, feeling what was there. Then he said, "Oh, God."

It was wet paint.

A Case of Desperation

by Kate Wilhelm

Marge was hungry. She had used her lunch hour to pick up some plastic dolls for the PTA Fall Festival, knowing she would have time to eat between two and three-thirty, before the small branch bank reopened for the Friday evening rush. Now it appeared she was going to have to wait for Mrs. Ashton to come and collect the dolls.

Ralph, the other teller, grinned commiseratingly at her and left. The manager, Mr. Redmon, stood by the door, waiting for the minute hand to click into place, but before he could set the lock, two people arrived. Mrs. Ashton pushed her way into the bank. A tall slender man in a windbreaker followed her closely. Marge sighed her relief.

"Marge, my dear," Mrs. Ashton began at the door, and continued with no change in volume as she crossed the floor. "You don't know how I rushed to get here in time. Did you get them? I've lined up six mothers to make dresses. Did you ask Warren?"

Marge pointed to the carton near the door. "Fifty of them," she said, "forty-five cents each," and realized that she had done it again. Warren had been half asleep when she returned from the PTA board meeting last night, and she had been too tired to start the annual argument about the parents' show.

"Fifty?" Mrs. Ashton was saying. "At two dollars, that will bring a hundred dollars. That's fine. I'll just give you a check for these now. Right place for it, isn't it?" She laughed, and began scrawling out the check.

The man in the windbreaker was still standing at the wall desk, thumbing through a small notebook. Marge wished he'd make out his deposit slip, or whatever he had to do, and get in behind Mrs. Ashton. She really was hungry.

Without looking up, Mrs. Ashton asked, "Will Warren play for us?"

"I didn't get a chance to ask him yet," Marge said; at the quick look of reproach, she added, "I'm sure he will." He'd swear and have her on the defensive for a day or two, but in the end he would play.

"That's fine. I'll put him down," Mrs. Ashton beamed.

The stranger at the desk was just standing there, probably listening to every word. Marge wished Mrs. Ashton would give her the check and leave. She'd call home and tell Annie to let the children eat early. Then she would broil a steak for Warren and herself later. He liked to have time for a leisurely martini. That would be the best way.

Mrs. Ashton waved the check back and forth, drying it. "Will you be home tomorrow? I have some extra tulip bulbs . . ."

It was ten past two when she finally left, with the dolls. Mr. Redmon locked the door behind her, and glanced impatiently toward the last customer.

The man looked up, and for the first time Marge saw his face. His features were clear and strong, almost boyishly sensitive, but he was unsmiling. He was taller than Mr. Redmon, probably six feet plus an inch or even two, but that might have been an illusion caused by his slenderness. He wore a grey hat and slacks, and a tan windbreaker over a white tieless shirt, and he carried a case that looked more like a tool box than a briefcase.

He was coming toward her. She started to smile, but didn't. Mr. Redmon looked frightened. She noticed for the first time that the man was keeping his right hand inside his jacket pocket. Her eyes widened as his deep blue eyes held hers.

"Don't get panicky, honey," he said softly, "but be careful, very, very careful." He pushed the black bag across the counter top.

It was as if she had been emptied of all thought, and there was only a hollow dread within her. It was happening here at her bank! Her fingers fumbled opening the drawer and then were pushing money into the case. Her eyes remained locked with his. It was forever—an instant—timeless, and he was reaching for it.

"That's fine, honey," he said. "Now just as carefully walk around the end of the counter and come out. Bring your purse."

She shook her head and took a step backward, away from him. For the first time she saw the gun pointed at the very still figure of Mr. Redmon. He nodded at her to obey. She walked around the counter and the three of them went back to the small office. The man taped

110

Mr. Redmon's mouth and tied his hands and feet, fastening him to his heavy mahogany desk. He lifted the receiver from the phone and set it on the desk.

"Listen, both of you," he said slowly. "I've been thinking of this for a long time, and I'm not going to be stopped. You tell them I have her with me." Mr. Redmon's eyes pleaded and he shook his head violently. The man ignored it. "I don't want to hurt her, but it will be up to them. And tell them," he said, clipping the words, "the only way they'll get me is dead. Just tell them I said that." He turned to Marge and motioned toward the door.

She didn't move, seemed unable to move. He took her arm. "Look at him, honey. He knows I mean every word I've said in here."

She looked from him to Mr. Redmon, and she found herself walking, the case dangling from her hand where he placed it. Using her keys, her car that was just outside the bank, he drove several blocks to an above-the-street parking lot with four decks. The car wound around the ramp to the top, along the narrow passageway to the rear.

"Come on, honey. We change here." He made her slide under the wheel to get out on his side. He unlocked the door of a blue car and she crawled in without being ordered. He reached behind the front seat and pulled out an overnight bag, putting it on the seat at her side before he got in. "You've been very sensible so far," he said, his eyes darting around at the other cars. "Just a little more now and you can go. Put this on." He handed her a pink blouse and, when she didn't move, he edged the gun out of his pocket. "Look, honey, you do exactly as I say or I'll knock you out and dress you myself." The chill of his voice was more frightening than the gun.

She had trouble with her trembling hands as s' ə unbuttoned her blouse, but finally handed it to him and put on the pink one. It was a little loose, not noticeably. At his command, she handed him her earrings and stared at the blonde wig he took from the suitcase. Impatiently he thrust it at her and she put it on. Then he put her things and his windbreaker in the case, pulled on a coat that matched his slacks, and added a tie. In all, it hadn't taken more than three or four minutes. "What are you going to do with me?" she asked.

He began backing out. "Just do exactly as I say and you'll have an adventure you can tell your grandchildren about."

"They'll catch you. They always do."

"No!" he said intensely. "For once I get to state the terms, and I'm not including being caught in them. Either I make it with the money, or they kill me. But they won't catch me!"

Marge shuddered and moved closer to the door.

"There's a sweater and a purse on the back seat. Get them." She was straightening up again when he stopped and tossed a half dollar to a white-coated attendant.

When they drove away she was shaking visibly, the first reaction of shocked, frightened obedience crumbling. Why hadn't she screamed in the lot? She felt as though she were coming out from a deep dream, only now being consciously in control of her actions. He couldn't act quickly enough to stop her if she could jump from the car at a stop sign or a red light. They were out of the downtown area, and she looked out trying to remember the next red light. About three blocks. If she could work the door handle . . . Cautiously she maneuvered one hand behind her back. She couldn't halt her gasp of dismay when he turned into a side street, and then into an alley. He stopped the car and pulled on the brake without turning off the ignition. Hope flooded her. Maybe he'd put her out there.

Casually he said, "I was in a prison camp in Korea and one of the guards taught me a kind of cute trick." His hand reached out and took her wrist as he spoke, and his fingers moved up and down as though feeling for a certain spot. Her eyes followed his fingers and then he was bringing her arm up behind her, her hand up to the shoulder blade, and higher. Pain exploded in her shoulder and she screamed. He released her, and massaged her back as she wept. "Every day he'd do that until I screamed. Sometimes he'd throw my arm out of joint, sometimes not. I never knew. Got so I screamed before he touched me. That seemed to please him." Marge sobbed into her hands. He waited until she stopped and then he said, "Sorry, honey. I didn't want to hurt you, but you might as well understand that this isn't a game. Your manager knew I meant it, and you might as well admit now that you do too. If I have to remind you again, you'll not use that arm for a long time. Keep off the door!" He flicked on the radio and drove out of the alley toward the turnpike.

They were on the toll road before the announcer cut into the music. "We interrupt this program . . ." He turned it louder and she listened to a recounting of the robbery, complete with their descriptions.

112

Marge stared dully ahead. They were looking for her car, for a man in a windbreaker, and a woman with dark brown hair. She was a blonde beside a man in a conservative suit traveling in a car filled with vacation luggage.

The music resumed and she said, "You thought of everything, didn't you? But they'll find my car and get your fingerprints from it. They'll call in the F.B.I."

He laughed. "They'll lift smudges from your car, just as they did in the bank. I was very careful." He glanced her way. "There will be road blocks and license checks; you remember to be just as careful, and there won't be any trouble."

"Where are you going to take me?"

"You stay until I think I can make it alone."

Her shoulder ached, and there was tightening in the back of her neck that she knew would bring on a violent headache within hours. The miles whizzed by at an alarming rate, and her expectations of an early pursuit faded as the monotony of the wind-filled ride wore her hopes to nothing. There had to be something he had overlooked. She leaned her head back against the seat and shut her eyes, trying to think.

At four-thirty he pulled off to the side of the road. "I have sandwiches," he said pleasantly, as if out for a Sunday picnic, "and a thermos of coffee. You did miss lunch, didn't you?" His voice was low-pitched, naturally soft, the sort of voice that was never heard in a group larger than three.

The headache had arrived by then. She nodded briefly. While they ate, he studied a road map. "There's a toll gate ahead about four or five miles," he said. "They'll probably be looking over all cars. Now listen. We are Mr. and Mrs. Robert Thorne, from Gary, on our way to Raleigh, North Carolina, to visit your parents on our vacation. They might search the car, but I don't think they'll go through the luggage unless they get suspicious. So," he looked at her levelly over the paper cup of coffee, "if you want to get back to your husband and those two children again, don't make them suspicious." He watched as she sipped the steaming coffee. "What's wrong? You sick?"

"Headache," she answered.

He reached across her to the glove compartment and found a bottle of aspirins. It was half empty. He shook out two and handed them to her, watching until she swallowed them.

When she finished her coffee, he put the thermos on the seat be-tween them. "Gives us a real homey touch, doesn't it?" He worked the car back into the traffic, heavier and slower now. "They're stopped up there, all right," he said, grimly satisfied.

Marge felt herself tensing and she worked her hands together, feel-ing the palms moist and clammy.

"What's your husband do?" he asked and she started at the sound of his voice. "Ease up, honey," he murmured. "Tell me about your hus-band."

"He's a classified salesman for the telephone company."

"Away a lot?"

"He travels in the state."

"Make good money?"

"Yes," she said sharply. "Why?"

"Just wondered. Announcer said you were the mother of two kids. If he's such a hot-shot, why are you working?"

"That's none of your business!"

"Granted. Own your home?"

"Please," she cried. "Leave me alone! I can't talk!"

"Oh, yes, you can," he snapped. "I asked if you own your home. You talk if it chokes you."

They were driving at twenty miles an hour in spurts, and on both sides drivers were honking their horns and hanging out the windows trying to see what was happening ahead. Marge's rigidity had de-creased at the persistent questioning, and she understood why he in-tended to keep it up.

"We have our own home," she said.

"Keep talking. Tell me all about it. When you got it, how much, what kind of furniture."

His hands gripping the wheel showed white at the knuckles, and a stab of fear went through her. What if he should panic? He might start shooting, or might try to break through the roadblock. She had seen it on television and in movies, and they always got killed. Almost hysteric-ally she chattered about the house. It was four years old, split level with hemlocks and junipers. The lower level was the workroom where Warren once made some lawn furniture that they didn't use. Joanne had a birthday party on the terrace last week. She was ten; Larry was eight and played Little League ball, first base unless Hank showed up, and then he played in the field.

The car in front of them was moving again, and he jerked their car as he followed. Marge's voice faltered. What had she been saying? They stopped in sight of the toll gate and she thought, *Now!* The police would recognize her. She had to be ready.

"Split level!" he snorted in disgust.

"What's wrong with split level?" she said staring at the car ahead and willing it to move on. The line moved like a measuring worm gathering itself in, inching forward, and stretching out again. A uniformed officer approached the car in front of them and spoke with the driver. On the other side another trooper glanced in the rear.

"I didn't say anything's wrong with split levels, if they are on hillsides." The robber yelled, and the officer at the rear of the other car turned to look.

Marge stared at him terrified. She started to speak, but her tongue was frozen and nothing came out. He said, still in a loud, rough tone, "If you have to have a split level, dammit, have it! But don't expect me to like it!" The policeman was within a few feet of them and she knew he could hear every word. "Now if you'll just shut up about split levels for the rest of this trip . . . Sorry, Officer."

"OK, Mac. License, please." He studied the license and compared the statistics with the man before he handed it back. Briefly he glanced at Marge, and she trembled with anticipation. He must see that something was wrong! She felt tears forming in her eyes, and inside she was screaming, *I'm Marge Elliot! Look at me! See the wig!* But he turned from them and flicked his eyes over the thermos and the luggage and fishing gear in the back, and waved them on. *She would scream! She'd make them notice!* She felt his hand tighten on her wrist and she went limp.

They picked up speed almost immediately. She felt weak from frustration. "You think you're so damned smart! I hope they catch you and let me testify. I hope you rot in jail for the rest of your life. You'll never get to spend a cent of the money."

"Wasn't planning to anyway," he said cheerfully and began to whistle. "Oh, we ain't got a barrel of money . . ."

"You've had good luck, but it won't last," she continued, oblivious of the song, knowing only her rage at the stupidity of the troopers, at the

115

clever way he manipulated her, making her play along with the grim farce, at her own cowardice.

"What's the name of your subdivision?" He was ignoring her outburst as if she were a petulant child.

"Pleasant View," she snapped.

"Oh, no! Pleasant View!" He grinned broadly at the flush that raced across her face.

It was the first time he had smiled, and it made him look incredibly young and vulnerable. Marge shivered at the thought. Him vulnerable! She thought of Warren, and irrationally she wondered if he would give Larry and Joanne their dinner on time. They liked to eat at five. What would he tell them? Mother is going for a ride with a bank robber; eat your pork chop. She shook off the thought. They were with Annie. He would be with the police somewhere, waiting to hear, smoking too much and swearing viciously, his face looking unshaved by now and dark with anger. Had he sworn so when she met him? She couldn't remember. Probably not, or she would have been shocked by it. *Yea, though I walk through the valley . . .* She pushed that aside also. That was her mother speaking through her mind, the conditioning of her childhood, behind her and meaningless now. It shouldn't be; she was very active in church work. She wished passionately she could return to the time when she knew someone would be there to take care of things when there was trouble. For so long she had been self-sufficient, needing no one; where was that strength now when she did need it?

She was roused from her thoughts by the slowing of the car, and reluctantly she opened her eyes. They were stopping at a filling station. She kept her eyes turned away from him so he couldn't see the sudden hope that bloomed in them.

"Forget it!" he said in a whisper. "You're not getting out, so relax." He told the attendant to fill it, and they sat side by side as the gauge clicked and the bell rang, as the spray covered the windshield and was wiped off, and they were again on the highway. The attendant had not looked at her once.

Marge felt that suddenly everything about her was too tight; her necklace was choking her and she pulled at it, finally taking it off and putting it on the seat between them. Her fingers twisted her rings around and around, and she became aware of the moistness of her

116

hands, and the heat of her girdle against her body. Her skirt was too tight, the band cutting into her waist, and her watch was uncomfortable on her wrist. She knew her feet were swelling; she felt herself swelling all over. The diamond on her finger caught the light and flashed as she turned it, and impatiently she pushed it around so only two narrow gold bands showed. There were red marks on the palms of her hands where she had gripped with her nails. She looked at the watch and compared it to the car clock, not believing it was running at all. It was Warren's Christmas gift from five years ago. "Go buy yourself a watch. Have it inscribed and everything. Pick out a nice one." In spite, she had picked out an exceptionally nice one and now she stared at it dully, and ran her finger under the band, relieving the pressure of it on her skin.

"Are you all right?" His voice startled her and she jerked reflexively. "There's a rest park ahead," he said. "We'll get out and walk up and down a few minutes. Don't faint on me now!"

Had she been near fainting? She thought probably she had. The tightness had gone into her chest, and breathing was a labored business. The car stopped and they were walking briskly, his hand firm on her arm, his steps setting a fast pace. Another car pulled into the small park, and he was stopping her before a rustic brown outhouse.

"I'm going to stand right here," he said curtly. "Don't get cute!"

There was nothing there. Nothing. Rough log walls, a smooth wooden seat with two covers, paper . . . Tears filled her eyes as she looked about wildly, and she felt defeat once more. She remembered her watch and yanked it off, leaving it on the seat. The newcomers were exercising a small dog, the man whistling cheerfully, his wife throwing sticks for the dog to retrieve. Marge walked back to the car, at his side, keeping her eyes on the ground. His grip was painful on her arm; the two other people ignored them, and they were driving away again.

"What did you do?" he demanded after they were again on the road. His fingers clamped on her wrist in a brutal grasp.

"Nothing."

"You're lying! I could see it on your face. You were scared and pleased with yourself. What did you do?" He was holding his anger under tight control, but it showed in the way he gripped the steering wheel, in the working of his jaw muscles, in the steely fingers that paralyzed her arm. He let go abruptly and flung it from him. He said no more until the park was out of sight and the emergency lane was clear of cars on both sides of the road. Then he pulled out of the driving lane and stopped the car. "Tell me!" His eyes burned into her, and she thought he was going to bring out the gun and shoot her.

"Nothing," she whispered. "There wasn't anything in there. I couldn't do anything!" She felt her heart beating as though it were going to stop completely after a last wild adagio of its own. Without reason or forethought, she twisted in the seat and began to fumble with the door. She had to get out! He pulled her back and slapped her, snapping her head back. She fell halfway across the seat, with her face pressed down against the plastic of the covering. "Please," she cried, "let me go! Please let me out. Tie me up, or knock me out, or anything. I have to get out! I can't stand any more!" She sobbed violently until there was nothing left in her. Wearily she pulled herself up and groped in the purse for a handkerchief.

"You've been saving that for a long time, haven't you?" She raised her eyes at the quiet of his tone. He sat smoking calmly, not touching her or even looking at her. His anger was gone, leaving his thin face thoughtful and withdrawn, almost resigned looking. "What's the matter, honey, can't a woman have a cry once in a while in a split level in Pleasant View?" It was as if he weren't talking to her, or even thinking of her, but of something far away. The car came alive and rolled back onto the highway.

"Leave me alone. Just leave me alone."

"Sure, honey. How old are you? Thirty-one, thirty-two? Doesn't matter. Your type I know," he said expressionlessly. "Out of school, into the marriage parlor, a few trips to the maternity hospital and presto, all through being a woman. Soon as the kids are old enough to start school you go to work, and for the rest of your lives, you're as independent as hell. What makes you so damned afraid of being a woman?"

She was too tired to protest. It was pointless to argue with a man who had a gun in his pocket.

He told her to fix her makeup. She obeyed silently. Then he said, "We're leaving the toll road at the next turnoff, and I want you to lie back with your eyes shut. You're a mess. I don't know how serious it was letting you out back there, and maybe I'll have to make you tell me about it. So be good to yourself and do it my way now."

The phrase, " . . . maybe I'll have to make you tell . . ." droned through her mind. She wouldn't tell him about the watch. He couldn't make her tell. She moved her shoulder imperceptibly, and the instant stab of pain made a mockery of her resolution. She couldn't ever remember being hurt deliberately before. To be hurt and made to cry out and cower, just because he was big and had a gun . . . She hoped she'd see him chained and helpless. She would sit in the witness chair and tell them how he hit her, and she'd be the calm one, and he'd know he was going to prison because of her. She wouldn't tell him! Not even if he did hit her or twist her arm . . . She cringed at the remembered pain, and at the thought of breaking again under his will. She couldn't humble herself again to him. She couldn't.

She was too afraid to lie outright. He'd know. He might even kill her if she lied now. At first, she had been terrified and it had worn off, and then he had hurt her and frightened her again, not the same way. She had become afraid of the pain and the humiliation of being hurt, not of being killed. Now she thought she might not live to see Larry and Joanne again. She felt her throat constrict, but she had no more tears, no more emotions to spend. She lay with her eyes shut, trying to plan.

"Why did you do it?" she asked after a long silence. "You said you weren't planning on using the money."

"That's right. But I needed it."

"Most people don't take up robbery. Most people are willing to work for the money they need."

"Work!" he said contemptuously. "You mean most people dream up ways to steal it without running the risk of arousing suspicions."

Marge swallowed her quick retort and said meekly, "I thought it might help if we talk. I won't try anything, I promise."

"I bet."

"About the rest room . . ."

"Later," he snapped. "There's the toll gate. Be asleep!"

She tried to look dead. The car stopped and change was jingled. He asked about a good restaurant. Inwardly, she could almost laugh. His asking about a restaurant like any innocent tourist! He was so clever, not overlooking a thing. And she had outsmarted him. When they caught him, she'd get the credit for keeping her head and giving them a lead.

He turned on the car lights and reduced speed as they approached the town. "About the rest room?"

"I left my watch in it," she said defiantly.

"I see. With your name on it, no doubt."

"My first name," she said. What if the woman merely kept it? Or if she handed it in and the police merely put it way down in a "lost and found" drawer? Just Marge and Warren on it; who would comment on that, or connect it to the robbery?

Music blared from the radio and he turned it down.

"Well?" Marge said. She looked away from the blazing eyes he turned on her.

"You want a medal? I don't believe you!"

"What do I care about whether or not you believe me! I've done nothing wrong!" She took a deep breath and said more calmly, "I will cooperate with you. Not because I want you to get away with it. I just don't want to be hurt again, and I don't want anyone killed. I hope they catch and execute you!"

"And you'd testify?"

"Gladly!"

He laughed, stopping it almost as quickly as it started. "Okay, that's fair enough. We know where we stand. I'll try not to hurt you so you can return home and send your kids to school so they can grow up to become substantial citizens like their parents. The boy can be like his father and the girl like you, making the same meaningless tracks on the same endless treadmill."

"That's insane!" Marge cried. "You make it sound shameful to be normal." She shook her head angrily. He had no right. He made her life sound hopeless and without purpose or meaning. Desperately she said, "You're sick. You said you were in a prison camp. They did something to you. They must have brainwashed you without you realizing it."

"Let's drop it," he cut in rudely. "The news is on."

They listened silently to a summation of the day's happenings, and a brief rehash of the robbery, with another description of both of them. Her car had been located and had given no clues that could be termed helpful.

They stopped at a drive-in and had hamburgers and coffee. Besides

120

the coffee they drank, he had the thermos filled for later use. Then they were speeding down the highway again, as before the stop.

Away from the turnpike she became aware of the mountainous nature of the countryside, and wondered vaguely where they were. It didn't seem very important. They had been driving over eight hours and she was too tired to care. Before the silence became too heavy to interrupt she asked, "Are you married?"

"Isn't everyone?" he said cynically.

Marge followed it up quickly. "Do you love her? Is the money for her?"

"A kid gets taken out of college and told to kill or be killed," he said instead of answering directly. "Finally, he comes home and there's a girl he kissed in another lifetime smiling at him, holding a ring in her hand. Bang, he's married and has a family! No time to think or wonder what it's all about. I don't know. Maybe I did love her, maybe I still do. I don't know. It doesn't matter. I had to get out of it. She'll use the money until she finds a new guy to conjure it up and hand it over, in exchange for the privilege of being told what to do. It's not her fault," he added, sounding sad. "She does what she has to. I guess we all do."

"If you didn't like it, you could have changed it without this. Others do."

"Do they? Or do they just change partners and go on dancing to the same tired music?"

"That's going to sound pretty stupid when they put you in prison."

"I'm not going to jail. Remember, honey?"

She felt a chill at the sureness of his voice. "I suppose," she said quickly, "you'll issue bulletins from time to time telling the rest of us about the better life, now that you've found it."

"People could use them, don't you think?"

"The first step, of course, is to rob a bank. A man can't just run off. He has to provide for his family."

"Honey," he said mockingly, "don't you realize that's all most men are doing now? Providing. How long since you thought of your husband as a man and wanted him?" His laugh was harsh when she sucked in an indignant breath. "Bulletins!" he said. "That's an idea. First, I'd kick out all that extra junk—PTA meetings every week, Ladies' Auxiliaries, socials, and I don't give a damn if they are for the church,

121

charity, or your old Aunt Suzy. A man gets tired of having his wife just coming in, or going out, or too busy on the telephone committee, or plain too tired. And every time a woman used sex as a club, she should become pregnant so she'd have nine months to meditate on its real meaning. There'd be damn few women able to hold jobs. Sex wasn't meant to be a club or a reward, and every time your men lose another round, you despise them a little bit more."

"Stop it!" she cried. She bit back her denial. She wouldn't give him the satisfaction of arguing with him. Why was she even listening to it? What did he know about her and Warren? After fourteen years no woman got excited . . . She clenched her fists and drew up the image of Larry and Joanne, but her own plan to broil steaks and have martinis kept intruding. She knew what would have happened afterwards, and then she would have told him about playing the piano for school. And the robber had heard back in the bank. He knew.

"I'm through. It's no good anyway," he said tiredly, the mockery and bite gone. "We're all on the same merry-go-round and it's going too fast to see beyond the next horse, too fast to realize that the same paths that lead to it, can take us away. Once you're on and the music starts, you don't get off again."

She glanced at his brooding silhouette. *You did*, she thought. They drove and she became numb with fatigue. She put on the sweater and tried to arrange her legs so she could be more comfortable. She must have dozed, for suddenly he was awakening her. She was dizzy with the motion of the car.

"Want some?" he asked, offering her coffee. She shook her head and huddled against the seat. "It will warm you," he insisted.

It wasn't worth quarreling over, and she drank it even though it was sweetened and bitter. "We'll stop in about an hour," he said. "There's a city about forty miles ahead and we'll find a motel." She stiffened and drew herself up and he laughed bitterly. "Don't be a fool. After I get some rest, you're out of it."

"What do you mean?"

"Just that. There were sleeping pills in the coffee. They won't take full effect for an hour or so, and you'll sleep about eight hours. By then, I'll be gone." He sounded very tired. "When we get to the motel I'll help you in. Don't start yelling if you wake up and find me helping you. If we have to pull out because of anything you do, I'll kill you."

122

His voice, desperate in his weariness, sounded of truth.

Sleeping pills, she thought. It would look perfect. A man and his wife not able to keep driving. He'd help her, and no one would notice anything. Occasionally she took sleeping pills and rolled about for hours before they had any effect on her. What if he overdosed her? If she could vomit . . .

"Relax, honey," he said, almost gently, and one of his hands covered hers in her lap. "Don't be scared now. You've been very brave, really. I couldn't tell from watching you a few times how you'd take it. I thought I might have to keep you out cold the whole trip, but you've been fine. You can be proud of yourself. Someday you'll look back on it and wonder if it really happened. You'll be a heroine on television, in the newspapers. Maybe a national magazine will buy your story. All the women in your subdivision will be jealous."

He continued to talk quietly, keeping her attention for a long time before her mind began to wander away.

"No one should have to take pills to sleep," she murmured when his words ceased.

"I know." His fingers pressed her hand.

She was drifting along a wooded path feeling alive with excitement at what awaited her at the end . . . It was so nice not worrying or planning, knowing someone was taking care of things. Her hand touched his, the warmth of it spreading through her body. She sighed and relaxed.

She felt his hands on her, and she was walking, haltingly. "Does this look all right for tonight, honey?"

She made the effort to mumble, "Fine."

"OK, just put the bag down there," he said to someone else, and she drooped on his arm. She was unutterably weary and her time sense was gone. He put her down on the bed and pulled a cover over her.

"I'm sorry," she started thickly, and subsided when his hand removed the wig. He was stroking her hair, pressing her head back down.

"It's all right," he whispered. "Sleep."

The dream returned. They were very far up the path and the merry-go-round was nothing, a blur in the distance. He was close to her and the excitement was a glow that enveloped them both, and she slept deeply.

"Marge! Marge! Are you all right?" Someone was shaking her and shouting. She was too heavy and tired to pull away.

Another voice, "Take it easy, sir. The doctor's coming."

She climbed up through layers of mist that held her back, and rough hands hauled at her and cold wetness shocked her face. "Darling! Wake up! What did he do to you?" She moaned softly and worked at opening her eyes. "It's all right, Marge," Warren said. "They got your watch; the men remembered the car. They're chasing him right now. He won't get away." He was sitting on the side of the double bed pulling at her.

She stared at him and shook her head. "They won't catch him."

"Snap out of it, Marge! You're safe now. Listen!" There was a distant, lost sound of a siren somewhere in the grey dawn. As Warren shook her, Marge heard the rapid, faint reports of guns firing. They sounded once more. The siren's wail stopped abruptly and the morning became silent again.

She slipped from Warren's hands and lay back on the bed. She was fully clothed, and very, very cold.

"Where is that doctor?"

Outside someone was shouting, ". . . over the cliff . . ."

Marge squeezed her eyelids together but couldn't contain the tears behind them.

"Don't cry, Marge. Please," Warren said helplessly. "It's over now. You heard. He's dead. You'll forget when we get back home, back to normal. Please, don't . . . . Did he . . . harm you . . . ?"

She shook her head blindly, unable to speak. When he leaned down and touched her, she jerked away from him and buried her face in the pillow, where her abductor's head had rested.

The Books Always Balance

by Lawrence Block

The first envelope arrived on a Tuesday. This marked it as slightly atypical from the start, as Myron Hettinger received very little mail at his office on Tuesdays. Letters mailed on Fridays arrived Monday morning, and letters mailed on Monday, unless dispatched rather early in the day, did not arrive until Wednesday, or at the earliest on Tuesday afternoon. This envelope, though, arrived Tuesday morning. John Palmer brought it into Myron Hettinger's office a few minutes past ten, along with the other mail. Like the other envelopes, it was unopened. Only Myron Hettinger opened Myron Hettinger's mail.

The rest of the mail, by and large, consisted of advertisements and solicitations of one sort or another. Myron Hettinger opened them in turn, studied them very briefly, tore them once in half and threw them into the wastebasket. When he came to this particular envelope, however, he paused momentarily.

He studied it. It bore his address. The address had been typed in a rather ordinary type-face. It bore, too, a Sunday evening postmark. It bore a four-cent stamp commemorating the one hundred fiftieth anniversary of the founding of a land grant college in the Midwest. It did not bear a return address or any other hint as to who had sent it or what might be contained therein.

Myron Hettinger opened the envelope. There was no letter inside. There was instead a photograph of two partially clad persons. One of them was a man who looked to be in his early fifties, balding, perhaps fifteen pounds overweight, with a narrow nose and rather thin lips. The man was with a woman who looked to be in her middle twenties, blonde, small-boned, smiling, and extraordinarily attractive. The man was Myron Hettinger, and the woman was Sheila Bix.

For somewhere between fifteen and thirty seconds, Myron Hettinger looked at the picture. Then he placed it upon the top of his desk and walked to the door of his office, which he locked. Then he returned to his desk, sat down in his straight-backed chair, and made sure that the envelope contained nothing but the photograph. After assuring himself of this, he tore the photograph twice in half, did as much with the envelope, placed the various scraps of paper and film in his ashtray, and set them aflame.

A less stable man might have ripped photo and envelope into an inestimable number of shreds, scattered the shreds to four or more winds, and crouched in mute terror behind his heavy desk. Myron Hettinger was stable. The photograph was not a threat but merely the promise of a threat, a portent of probable future menace. Fear could wait until the threat itself came to the fore.

A more whimsical man might have pasted the photograph in his scrapbook, or might have saved it as a memory piece. Myron Hettinger was not whimsical; he had no scrapbook and kept no memorabilia.

The fire in the ashtray had a foul odor. After it ceased to burn, Myron Hettinger turned on the air conditioner. The room was cleared of the odor in less than ten minutes.

The second envelope arrived two days later in Thursday morning's mail. Myron Hettinger had been expecting it, with neither bright anticipation nor with any real fear. He found it among a heavy stack of letters. The envelope was the same as the first. The address was the same, the type-face appeared to be the same, and the stamp, too, was identical with the stamp on the first envelope. The postmark was different, which was not surprising.

This envelope contained no photograph. Instead it contained an ordinary sheet of cheap stationery on which someone had typed the following message:

Get one thousand dollars in ten and twenty dollar bills. Put them in a package and put the package in a locker in the Times Square station of the IRT. Put the key in an envelope and leave it at the desk of the Slocum Hotel addressed to Mr. Jordan. Do all this today or a photo will be sent to your wife. Do not go to the police. Do not hire a detective. Do not do anything stupid.

The final three sentences of the unsigned letter were quite unnecessary. Myron Hettinger had no intention of going to the police, or of engaging the services of a detective. Nor did he intend to do anything stupid.

After letter and envelope had been burned, after the air conditioner had cleared the small room of its odor, Myron Hettinger stood at his window, looking out at East Forty-Third Street and thinking. The letter bothered him considerably more than the photograph had bothered him. It was a threat. It might conceivably intrude upon the balanced perfection of his life. This he couldn't tolerate.

Until the letter had arrived, Myron Hettinger's life had indeed been perfect. His work was perfect, to begin with. He was a certified public accountant, self-employed, and he earned a considerable amount of money every year by helping various persons and firms pay somewhat less in the way of taxes than they might have paid without his services. His marriage, too, was perfect. His wife, Eleanor, was two years his junior, kept his home as he wanted it kept, cooked perfect meals, kept him company when he wished her company, let him alone when he wished to be alone, kept her slightly prominent nose out of his private affairs, and was the beneficiary of a trust fund which paid her in the neighborhood of twenty-five thousand dollars per year.

Finally, to complete this picture of perfection, Myron Hettinger had a perfect mistress. This woman, of course, was the woman pictured in the unpleasant photograph. Her name was Sheila Bix. She provided comfort, both physical and emotional, she was the essence of discretion, and her demands were minimal—rent for her apartment, a small sum for incidentals, and an occasional bonus for clothing.

A perfect career, a perfect wife, a perfect mistress. This blackmailer, this *Mr. Jordan*, now threatened all three components of Myron Hettinger's perfect life. If the damnable photograph got into Mrs. Hettinger's hands, she would divorce him. He was very certain of this. If the divorce were scandalous, as it well might be, his business would suffer. And if all of this happened, it was quite likely that, for one reason or another, he would wind up losing Sheila Bix as well.

Myron Hettinger closed his eyes and drummed his fingers upon his desk top. He did not want to hurt his business, did not want to lose wife or mistress. His business satisfied him, as did Eleanor and Sheila. He did not *love* either Eleanor or Sheila, not any more than he *loved* his business. Love, after all, is an imperfect emotion. So is hate. Myron Hettinger did not hate this Mr. Jordan, much as he would have enjoyed seeing the man dead.

127

But what could he do?

There was, of course, one thing and only one thing that he could do. At noon he left his office, went to his bank, withdrew one thousand dollars in tens and twenties, packed them neatly in a cigar box, and deposited the box in a locker in the Times Square station of the IRT. He tucked the locker key into an envelope, addressed the envelope to the annoying Mr. Jordan, left the envelope at the desk of the Slocum Hotel, and returned to his office without eating lunch. Later in the day, perhaps because of Mr. Jordan or perhaps because of the missed meal, Myron Hettinger had a rather severe case of heartburn. He took bicarbonate of soda.

The third envelope arrived a week to the day after the second. Thereafter, for four weeks, Myron Hettinger received a similar envelope every Thursday morning. The letters within varied only slightly. Each letter asked for a thousand dollars. Each letter directed that he go through the rather complicated business of putting money in locker and leaving locker key at hotel desk. The letters differed each from the other only as to the designated hotel.

Three times Myron Hettinger followed the instructions to the letter. Three times he went to his bank, then to the subway station, then to the appointed hotel, and finally back to his office. Each time he missed lunch, and each time, probably as a direct result, he had heartburn. Each time he remedied it with bicarbonate of soda.

Things were becoming routine.

Routine in and of itself was not unpleasant. Myron Hettinger preferred order. He even devoted a specific page of his personal books to his account with the intrusive Mr. Jordan, listing each thousand-dollar payment the day it was paid. There were two reasons for this. First of all, Myron Hettinger never let an expenditure go unrecorded. His books were always in order and they always balanced. And secondly, there was somewhere in the back of his mind the faint hope that these payments to Mr. Jordan could at least be deducted from his income taxes.

Aside from his Thursday ventures, Myron Hettinger's life stayed pretty much as it had been. He did his work properly, spent two evenings a week with Sheila Bix, and spent five evenings a week with his wife.

128

He did not mention the blackmail to his wife, of course. Not even an idiot could have done this. Nor did he mention it to Sheila Bix. It was Myron Hettinger's firm conviction that personal matters were best discussed with no one. He knew, and Mr. Jordan knew, and that already was too much. He had no intention of enlarging this circle of knowledgeable persons if he could possibly avoid it.

When the sixth of these letters arrived—the seventh envelope in all from Mr. Jordan—Myron Hettinger locked his office door, burned the letter, and sat at his desk in deep thought. He did not move from his chair for almost a full hour. He did not fidget with desk-top gadgets. He did not doodle.

He thought.

This routine, he realized, could not possibly continue. While he might conceivably resign himself to suffering once a week from heartburn, he could not resign himself to the needless expenditure of one thousand dollars per week. One thousand dollars was not a tremendous amount of money to Myron Hettinger. Fifty-two thousand dollars was, and one did not need the mind of a certified public accountant to determine that weekly payments of one thousand dollars would run into precisely such a sum yearly. The payments, then, had to stop.

This could be accomplished in one of two ways. The blackmailer could be allowed to send his wretched photograph to Myron Hettinger's perfect wife, or he could be caused to stop his blackmailing. The first possibility seemed dreadful in its implications, as it had seemed before. The second seemed impossible.

He could, of course, appeal to his blackmailer's nobler instincts by including a plaintive letter with his payments. Yet this seemed potentially useless. Having no nobler instincts of his own, Myron Hettinger was understandably unwilling to attribute such instincts to the faceless Mr. Jordan.

What else?

Well, he could always kill Mr. Jordan.

This seemed to be the only solution, the only way to check this impossible outflow of cash. It also seemed rather difficult to bring off. It is hard to kill a man without knowing who he is, and Myron Hettinger had no way of finding out more about the impertinent Mr. Jordan. He could not lurk at the appointed hotel; Mr. Jordan, knowing him, could simply wait him out before putting in an appearance. Nor could he lurk near the subway locker, for the same reason.

And how on earth could you kill a man without either knowing him or meeting him?

Myron Hettinger's mind leaped back to an earlier thought, the thought of appealing to the man's nobler instincts through a letter. Then daylight dawned. He smiled the smile of a man who had solved a difficult problem through the application of sure and perfect reasoning.

That day, Myron Hettinger left his office at noon. He did not go to his bank, however. Instead he went to several places, among them a chemical supply house, a five-and-dime, and several drugstores. He was careful not to buy more than one item at any one place. We need not concern ourselves with the precise nature of his purchases. He was buying the ingredients for a bomb, and there is no point in telling the general public how to make bombs.

He made his bomb in the stall of a public lavatory, using as its container the same sort of cigar box in which he normally placed one thousand dollars in ten and twenty dollar bills. The principle of the bomb was simplicity itself. The working ingredient was nitroglycerine, a happily volatile substance which would explode upon the least provocation. A series of devices so arranged things that, were the cover of the cigar box to be lifted, enough hell would be raised to raise additional hell in the form of an explosion. If the box were not opened, but were dropped or banged, a similar explosion would occur. This last provision existed in the event that Mr. Jordan might suspect a bomb at the last moment and might drop the thing and run off. It also existed because Myron Hettinger could not avoid it. If you drop nitroglycerine, it explodes.

Once the bomb was made, Myron Hettinger did just what he always did. He went to the Times Square IRT station and deposited the bomb very gently in a locker. He took the key, inserted it in an envelope on which he had inscribed Mr. Jordan's name, and left the envelope at the desk of the Blackmore Hotel. Then he returned to his office. He was twenty minutes late this time.

He had difficulty keeping his mind on his work that afternoon. He managed to list the various expenses he had incurred in making the bomb on the sheet devoted to payments made to Mr. Jordan, and he smiled at the thought that he would be able to mark the account closed by morning. But he had trouble doing much else that day. Instead he sat and thought about the beauty of his solution.

The bomb would not fail. There was enough nitroglycerine in the cigar box to atomize not only Mr. Jordan but virtually anything within twenty yards of him, so the blackmailer could hardly hope to escape. There was the possibility—indeed, one might say the probability—that a great many persons other than Mr. Jordan might die. If the man was fool enough to open his parcel in the subway station, or if he was clumsy enough to drop it there, the carnage would be dreadful. If he took it home with him and opened it in the privacy of his own room or apartment, considerably less death and destruction seemed likely to occur.

But Myron Hettinger could not have cared less about how many persons Mr. Jordan carried with him to his grave. Men or women or children, he was sure he could remain totally unconcerned about their untimely deaths. If Mr. Jordan died, Myron Hettinger would survive. It was that simple.

At five o'clock, a great deal of work undone, Myron Hettinger got to his feet. He left his office and stood for a moment on the sidewalk, breathing stuffy air and considering his situation. He did not want to go home now, he decided. He had done something magnificent, he had solved an unsolvable problem, and he felt a need to celebrate.

An evening with Eleanor, while certainly comfortable, did not impress him as much of a celebration. An evening with Sheila Bix seemed far more along the lines of what he wanted. Yet he hated to break established routine. On Mondays and on Fridays he went to Sheila Bix's apartment. All other nights he went directly home.

Still, he had already broken one routine that day, the unhappy routine of payment. And why not do in another routine, if just for one night?

He called his wife from a pay phone. "I'll be staying in town for several hours," he said. "I didn't have a chance to call you earlier."

"You usually come home on Thursdays," she said.

"I know. Something's come up."

His wife did not question him, nor did she ask just what it was that had come up. She was the perfect wife. She told him that she loved him, which was quite probably true, and he told her that he loved her, which was most assuredly false. Then he replaced the receiver and stepped to the curb to hail a taxi. He told the driver to take him to an apartment building on West Seventy-Third Street just a few doors from Central Park.

The building was an unassuming one, a remodeled brownstone with four apartments to the floor. Sheila's apartment, on the third floor, rented for only one hundred twenty dollars per month, a very modest rental for what the tabloids persist in referring to as a love nest. This economy pleased him, but then it was what one would expect from the perfect mistress.

There was no elevator. Myron Hettinger climbed two flights of stairs and stood slightly but not terribly out of breath in front of Sheila Bix's door. He knocked on the door and waited. The door was not answered. He rang the bell, something he rarely did. The door was still not answered.

Had this happened on a Monday or on a Friday, Myron Hettinger might have been understandably piqued. It had never happened on a Monday or on a Friday. Now, though, he was not annoyed. Since Sheila Bix had no way of knowing that he was coming, he could hardly expect her to be present.

He had a key, of course. When a man has the perfect mistress, or even an imperfect one, he owns a key to the apartment for which he pays the rent. He used this key, opened the door and closed it behind him. He found a bottle of scotch and poured himself the drink which Sheila Bix poured for him every Monday and every Friday. He sat in a comfortable chair and sipped the drink, waiting for the arrival of Sheila Bix and dwelling both on the pleasant time he would have after she arrived and on the deep satisfaction to be derived from the death of the unfortunate Mr. Jordan.

It was twenty minutes to six when Myron Hettinger entered the comfortable, if inexpensive apartment, and poured himself a drink. It was twenty minutes after six when he heard footsteps on the stairs and then heard a key being fitted into a lock. He opened his mouth to let out a hello, then stopped. He would say nothing, he decided. And she would be surprised.

This happened.

The door opened. Sheila Bix, a blonde vision of loveliness, tripped merrily into the room with shining eyes and the lightest of feet. Her

132

arms were extended somewhat oddly. This was understandable, for she was balancing a parcel upon her pretty head much in the manner of an apprentice model balancing a book as part of a lesson in poise.

It took precisely as long for Myron Hettinger to recognize the box upon her head as it took for Sheila Bix to recognize Myron Hettinger. Both reacted nicely. Myron Hettinger put two and two together with the speed that made him a credit to his profession. Sheila Bix performed a similar feat, although she came up with a somewhat less perfect answer.

Myron Hettinger did several things. He tried to get out of the room. He tried to make the box stay where it was, poised precariously upon that pretty and treacherous head. And, finally, he made a desperate lunge to catch the box before it reached the floor, once Sheila Bix had done the inevitable recoiling in horror and spilling the box from head through air.

His lunge was a good one. He left his chair in a single motion. His hands reached out, groping for the falling cigar box.

There was a very loud noise, but Myron Hettinger only heard the beginnings of it.

The Second Debut

by Arthur Porges

The morning after was a rough day for the laboratory mice. Ordinarily Dr. Marek, like any good scientist, sacrificed them without either cruelty or compassion, but this time, even if his actions were not overtly sadistic, he took savage, irrational pleasure in each execution as if by robbing the little animals of their lives and complexes, he somehow mitigated last night's disappointment.

The biochemist had only two great loves—obsessions, actually—in life: his own specialty, and the piano. Finding himself without any ability at the keyboard, in spite of lessons from the best teachers, he had tried again, vicariously, on his younger brother Walter.

As the boy's guardian, their parents having been killed during the Hungarian rebellion, Dr. Marek had a free hand. So, from the age of six, Walter had been given the most rigorous and expensive musical education available. He had shown some talent as a pianist but no trace of real genius, even though there were many gifted Mareks among their ancestors. Unfortunately, the biochemist had succumbed to wishful thinking, and saw more in the boy than was there.

Walter's concert debut the night before had been a debacle. Technique, he had, but no insight; his Mozart was romanticized into bad Chopin; his Beethoven was thunderously empty; and he took all the storm and guts out of Bartok. The critics were merciless; how could anybody become so hopeless in a mere twenty years?

Heartbroken, Dr. Marek plunged more deeply into his work. He snubbed Walter, avoiding him like some unclean thing; and felt even worse on noting that the boy didn't realize what a flop he was. The idiot thought the critics were wrong!

Nor was it a matter of time and maturity; other pianists developed real musicianship early, or they never attained it. No, Walter simply lacked the prime requirement of his art. There was nothing to be done.

Then, not for the first time, Dr. Marek thought of Zygmunt Jankowski, the keyboard genius with the incredible fingers of a Horowitz, the musicianship of a Rubinstein, the personality of a Paderewski. Jankowski was great at eighteen, incomparable at forty—and finished at fifty-two, his prime, fingers smashed in a car accident. After that, he had disappeared. And to think that he, Dr. Marek, had dreamed of making Walter into another Jankowski!

But some dreams die hard, and Dr. Marek was only thirty. He turned his attention to the problem of mice and music, only half aware of what he sought.

He began by conditioning a group of mice to respond to a pure musical note. When they had learned this, after many trials, he killed one-third of the sample, extracted the RNA/DNA complexes from their brains, where they were concentrated, and injected them into untrained mice. These were then taught to recognize a simple sequence of notes, a primitive melody. Then their RNA/DNA extracts were given to a fresh group. In each case of a new collection, the conditioning required fewer trials. Finally, Dr. Marek had an elite group of mice that not only could recognize a theme, but respond to it when key and tempo were changed markedly; and with their extracts, previously untrained mice learned the same difficult chore with amazing celerity.

Now, mice are not men, and no scientist will extrapolate wildly from one species to the other but, since all life on earth is related, to bar inference completely would be just as unscientific as declaring unequivocally that mice equal men. So Dr. Marek did not stop with mice, but went on to cats, dogs, and even a few budget-straining chimps.

Two years later he sent for Walter, who had been scratching out a frustrated living by teaching music at a good but not highly-endowed college. The two brothers had seen little of each other since the concert, and Walter was understandably bitter. His own attempts to establish himself as a concert artist had failed; there were too many talented pianists with superior ability; and his technique, while adequate, could not compensate for his lack of understanding.

135

"You will live with me again," Dr. Marek told him crisply. He did not expect the order to be questioned, and it was not. When one has been dominated since the age of six by a strong-willed brother ten years older, revolt becomes impossible. Besides, was not Stefan a great scientist, well-paid and creative, a man too dedicated even to marry?

"Why do you want me?" the boy asked gloomily. "I have failed you as a pianist."

"That may be changed," was the cryptic reply. "Your trouble could have been due to a chemical imbalance. I mean to give you a course of injections. Then we shall see."

"What kind of injections?"

"You might think of them as a variety of vitamins; it doesn't matter. If they work, both your technique and insight will be much enhanced. But," he added sternly, "you must practice, eight hours a day. I've had the Bechstein tuned. Work, plus the injections, and who knows—by next year Walter Marek may surprise the critics."

The boy brightened. He knew little about biochemistry, but had unbounded faith in his brother.

"I shall work," he said eagerly. "It will be like old times again, Stefan."

"Except that I shall not be your judge," Dr. Marek said. "I was not objective. This time Madame Berrier shall listen to you."

She was a friend of Stefan's—a sometime mistress, in fact—and one of the greatest woman pianists of her generation. Walter knew she would set a high standard, and flinched a little. Those enormous, flaring dark eyes were hard to face when angry, brooked no mistakes.

The injections began at once, and were unpleasant. Dr. Marek was not a physician, and had no delicacy of touch with a hypodermic. He was used to laboratory animals, that squeaked or grunted, but couldn't berate him as ham-handed. Finally, however, after Walter's vehement objections, he acquired a finer needle, and improved his technique.

Both men were soon indifferent to such minor matters, because with startling speed Walter began to make progress. His fingers improved daily, so that the arpeggios rippled out in a smooth, dazzling stream, the ponderous chords sounded with precise synchronization and clangor, the trills vibrated like a snake's rattles. Bach was sounding as he should, and not like a composition by Tchaikovsky out of Chaminade.

Nor was there any self-deception involved. Those wonderful eyes of

Madame Berrier had first narrowed incredulously, and then shone opalescent as Walter played Schubert's "Wanderer Fantasy." Not since Edwin Fischer's performance had she heard anything to match it.

"Formidable!" she exclaimed, and kissed him.

A few weeks later, at the age of twenty-three, Walter Marek made his second debut as a concert pianist. The critics—the four who bothered—came to rend, since flaying a presumptuous incompetent is one of the major rewards of the profession; they stayed, after many encores thunderously applauded, as willing captives. Walter was a handsome boy, but now he glowed with fresh beauty, and his personality had acquired a flamboyant, careless charm that was irresistible. His performance was superb from the opening "Chromatic Fantasy and Fugue" to the last number, the difficult and exciting Chopin "Etude in A Minor," sometimes called "The Winter Wind."

From then on, his progress was phenomenal. He played with all the major orchestras, made innumerable brilliant recordings, and sold out at every concert.

One morning, his face troubled, Walter came to Stefan, and said, "I wonder if I'm going mad. Something very strange happened to me just now."

Dr. Marek gave him a sharp stare, his eyes narrowing. "What is it?" he demanded.

"You know I've never studied the Hammerklavier. Well, I was sight-reading the five movement today and, all at once, there I was, playing along without looking at the music." He laughed uneasily. "It wasn't much of a performance—after all, the Hammerklavier is a life work—but that I should know the notes . . . it disturbs and frightens me."

His brother became deathly white, looked years older, but his voice was steady as he said, "Come, Walter, it's not that unusual. You have heard others play it and you've listened to the old Schnabel records as a boy. You're a very talented fellow. Wasn't it Mendelssohn who came back from an oratorio that was kept secret, and transcribed it all from memory, just from hearing it? You are the same kind of genius."

"Thanks to your vitamins," Walter said in a low voice, giving Stefan a wondering stare.

"No," his brother said roughly. "You had the last of those six months ago. All they did was bring out the true Marek gift that is in your blood—and even mine, perhaps."

"I often wondered why you never took such injections," Walter said. "Your desire to play well was always greater than mine; we both know that."

"I didn't want them; I have my work," Stefan said quickly. "I developed them especially for you, but now their part is done. You are the finest pianist in the world; everybody admits that. Your prowess has earned unlimited acclaim."

During the years that followed, Walter consolidated his position as the best of the century. His specialty was Beethoven's "Hammerklavier" Sonata, a late and very difficult work of the composer. Walter played it much faster, and with more use of the pedal than other pianists, yet somehow kept the musical line under iron control so that the final impression was one of enormous excitement without the taint of eccentric phrasing.

Meanwhile Dr. Marek became more withdrawn and grim, spending long hours in the laboratory, and gradually giving up all teaching chores. Walter was too happy and creative now to fret about Stefan, but wondered occasionally, in a vague way, if his brother were ill. Certainly the man looked hag-ridden and tormented, aged beyond his years.

Still, after all these omens, Walter was shocked when Stefan died suddenly at forty-nine; and yet there was a guilty feeling of release, as if a shadow had moved away from him to reveal the sunlight in full strength.

Dr. Marek's colleagues, who honored the work, if not the man, wanted to publish his collected researches, and Walter, unwilling to have outsiders meddle with Stefan's papers, decided to do the basic screening himself. The notebooks were neatly shelved in chronological order, but two were oddly missing—the ones for the years of Walter's rebirth as a pianist. A careful search proved fruitless; either they were lost or had been destroyed.

There were, of course, some boxes of more personal papers, which cost Walter some pangs of memory: Stefan at eighteen, dark, handsome, self-reliant, and slightly grim, as circumstances in Hungary warranted; his parents, lost at six, he could not remember well, but his mother's face, full of vivacity and charm, made one old photo sparkle with life.

138

Then, in an envelope of clippings, Walter found some items that puzzled him greatly, since Stefan had no interest in crime. The one on top, dated sixteen years previously, was headed: "Gruesome Find on Skid Row." It came from the biggest town in the country, not far from their home. Walter scanned it wonderingly, then his attention sharpened. "The headless body of a derelict has turned out to be that of Zygmunt Jankowski, once called the greatest pianist in the world. After an accident in which his fingers were hopelessly mangled, he vanished, and was lost until now. Whether he was killed for a few coins, or was the victim of thrill-seeking perverts who have preyed on skid row bums for some years now, is not known."

Walter read on. This was no ordinary man, but Jankowski, so tragically dead. " . . . married the beautiful French singer, Claudine Michaud, who committed suicide when he disappeared." Suddenly Walter felt a terrible pang at his heart. He saw a woman's face, hauntingly beautiful in its modeling, planes, and color; and a low, sweet voice, full of love and anguish called his name . . . *his* name? No; she sang, "Zygmunt, Zygmunt . . ." and the harsh Polish syllables were pure melody in his ears. He shook his head as if to clear it; this was surely a mental aberration.

Unwilling to probe further, Walter skimmed the other clippings. The murder was not solved; there was more biographical material on Jankowski, though. One sentence caught his eye. It read: "Jankowski was celebrated for his dazzling, unorthodox interpretation of the massive 'Hammerklavier' Sonata of Beethoven. He played it extremely fast, sure of his flawless technique, but always with perfect control, so that there was no suggestion of mere caprice . . ." *How very odd,* Walter thought; *it might be a description of my own approach . . .*

Sea Change

by Henry Slesar

From the day Jane Brissom gave her the invitation, from the moment the travel folders were in her hand, Margo Wheeler underwent a pronounced transformation. Her students, the indifferent, mopheaded teen-agers who yawned their way through her lectures on English Grammar, noticed it first. They smiled more. They kidded with her after class. They seemed to recognize that she was almost as young as they were, and just as interested in getting some kicks out of life. When she was tired, wearied by teachers' conferences, bored with grading papers and untying the snarled word-knots of her students' compositions, she would lean back, say the magic words, and feel herself restored. A month in Europe! Two weeks on a transatlantic liner, and a month abroad! Was there anyone else so happy?

Maybe Jane Brissom, Margo thought, but she doubted it. At forty-five, a matchstick of a woman with watery eyes, random features, and a pitted complexion, Jane Brissom needed more than a vacation to make her happy. Margo couldn't resist the small, secret smile when she thought of Jane, although it was cruel, and rank ingratitude on her part.

Two nights before the sailing, she went to Jane's apartment and found her in the helpless confusion of packing.

"Look at this mess. Just look at it!" Jane said in anguish. "It's like an old clothes sale. I just don't see *what* I'm going to wear."

"Why, you have some very nice things," Margo said. "I always thought your clothes had such . . . taste." She wrinkled her small, pretty face. "Of course, if you hadn't loaned me that money, you could have gone out and bought a whole new wardrobe. I feel like such a *stinker*, Janey."

"Please, Margo, I *want* you to come along. It wouldn't be any fun all by myself. You're doing me a favor, really."

"Some favor," Margo laughed. Then she whistled as Jane picked up a glittering, bib-style necklace from the bureau and placed it forlornly against the flat, protruding bones of her chest. The necklace, with strings of multi-faceted stones, was a fire in the dim room. "Oh, Janey," Margo breathed, "what a hunk of jewelry!"

"Yes," Jane said sadly. "It was the only thing of Mother's I didn't sell after she died."

"Is it real? Are those real diamonds?"

"Oh, they're real, all right. The last time it was appraised I was told it would cost eleven or twelve thousand to replace. It might be worth even more now." She lowered the necklace, and with its borrowed light gone from her face, she seemed older and more haggard than ever.

"Could I try it, Janey? Just for a minute?" She took it in her hands.

In the mirror, the flashing fire around her throat, Margo looked at herself with exultation.

"Oh, it's beautiful! You've just *got* to take it with you, Janey. I mean, if you think it'll be safe . . ."

Janey smiled. "I've never had any occasion to wear the darned thing, so safe or not, I'm taking it. Besides, I've got my protection." She reached into a suitcase and produced a clumsy, black-handled revolver, holding it as casually as a shoe.

"Janey! You mean you're taking a gun along?"

"Don't make a fuss about it. We've had this old gun in the house ever since I was a little girl. It's just another part of the inheritance, that's all."

"Is it loaded?"

"Of course it's loaded. And don't think I won't use it if some *man*—" She flushed, and put the gun back into the suitcase. "Never mind about the gun, it's only sensible for two women traveling alone to have protection. And from what I've heard about Paris—" She snapped the suitcase shut. "Well, I'm ready for them."

Margo smothered a giggle.

The idea didn't come to Margo until morning. She thought she had dreamed it at first, but it was a waking, fully-conscious dream. She was so excited that she telephoned Jane at eight-thirty, and extracted a sleepy invitation to come over.

The older woman was still in her nightdress, a cotton bag that encased her thin body from neck to ankle.

"It's an inspiration!" Margo said. "That's what it is!"

"What is?"

Margo sat on the bed and curled her shapely legs beneath her. "Look, let's face it, Janey. We just won't have any fun at *all* on this trip if we don't—well, you know—meet people. *Men.* And you know as well as I do that there's nothing deadlier than two schoolteachers on a cruise—"

"I don't know anything of the kind," Jane said stiffly.

"But everybody *laughs* at that sort of thing, it's an old joke. The mousy schoolmarms on their sabbatical—"

"Well, I suppose there's something to that."

"But that's what I mean, Janey. Why do we *have* to be what we are? Why do we have to be schoolteachers? Why couldn't we pretend we're the kind of people who *belong* on a luxury liner, first-class passengers and everything? Why, the necklace alone—"

"Don't forget, it's only *one* necklace. We couldn't very well take turns, could we?"

Margo lowered her voice.

"Janey what if *one* of us pretended to be rich? I mean *really* rich. With that necklace, who would doubt it?"

"One of us?"

"It has to be only *one*, don't you see? As you said, there's only one necklace. But more important, the *other* one could be sort of a—servant. A maid, you know. Then there wouldn't be any *doubt* about how rich we were. One of us, anyway."

Jane walked over to her.

"Are you really serious? You mean we should pretend to be some kind of heiress and servant? For the whole trip?"

"Wouldn't it be *marvelous*? Can't you see the *impression* we'd make? We'd have every man on board in the palm of our hands! Who knows?" she tittered. "We might even meet a *real* millionaire!"

Jane folded her arms. "And who gets to play Cinderella? No, never mind, let me guess."

"Why, *you* do, of course, silly. You didn't think I was suggesting that *I* be the one? It'll be fun, really. I'll be your lady-in-waiting, and you

142

can be very, very *grand* in your umpty-thousand dollar necklace—"

The older woman smiled. "You know, I really think you mean it, Margo."

"Of course I do!"

"Well, I wouldn't think of it. It just wouldn't be fair."

Margo chewed her polished thumbnail.

"All right, then!" she said brightly. "We can do it another way. We can take turns!"

"Turns?"

"Of course! We're going *both* ways by ship. We have *two* cruises, don't we? You can be the millionairess one way, and I can be her the other!" She hugged herself joyfully. "Oh, Janey, wouldn't that be fantastic? You're just *bound* to meet some fine, wonderful *man*."

The word was like a bullet. It made Jane Brissom spin about, but she wasn't injured; she was suddenly radiant with a hope that had been suppressed for a lifetime.

Ten minutes later, they tossed a coin and Margo Wheeler won the Europe-bound trip.

They called the ship a Queen, and when Margo first saw its imperious bow and regal funnels, she felt as if in the presence of majesty. Jane was more practical; she took charge of luggage, tickets, and tips, and even before they boarded, they were playing their parts: Margo, the spoiled rich girl, accustomed to red carpets; Jane, the servant, rolling it before her.

In the stateroom, Margo produced a surprise, a bottle of champagne, and Jane rang the steward's button to ask for glasses. The steward was a wiry cockney with a wise, handsome face and bright, merry eyes, and he guessed their relationship at once. He poured Margo's drink for her gallantly, and gave Jane a companionable servant-to-servant wink on his way out.

"To Europe!" Margo said, lifting her glass.

"To you, madam," Jane said respectfully. Then they giggled like the schoolgirls they taught.

There was a "welcome aboard" party the first night out. Margo wore a powder-blue gown with a low neckline, ideal for the real glory of her attire. Jane put it around her neck herself, touching the diamond-encrusted strands lovingly.

"How does it look?" Margo asked, twirling before the mirror. "Does

143

it look as good as I think it does?"

"It's lovely," Jane said flatly.

"But I feel so *awful*. I mean, wearing *your* necklace—"

"A bargain's a bargain," Jane said. Then she put on a severe black dress with cuffs and collar. The mirror image was depressing, but she smiled gamely. "I *look* like a servant, don't I?"

"You look *fine*, Janey."

"Yes," the older woman said.

The party was slow in starting, the passengers diffident with each other. Then the band played with determination, and the drinks began to flow, and the dancing started, and with the suddenness of a popping cork, the festivities were under way. At their center, glittering, gleaming, dazzling with inner and outer radiance, was Margo Wheeler. From the sidelines, Jane watched her necklace sparkle in and out among the dancing couples, watched Margo tango with one man and meringue with another, saw her laughing with a gold-braided officer and sharing a drink with a bold-eyed man in evening dress.

At eleven-thirty she danced by Jane's table and waved. "Hi, Jane," she said gaily. "Listen, would you be a dear and get my stole?"

"Your stole?"

"You know, the one with the sequins. I'm going for a walk on deck."

"Oh," Jane said. "Yes, of course, miss," she added.

Jane left the party at twelve; Margo didn't return to the stateroom until two. She made just enough noise to wake Jane, then she apologized.

"It's all right," Jane said. "Did you have fun?"

"Did you see *him*?" Margo said. "Oh, Janey, he's a dream. His name is Gordon Baylor, and he's in investments or something. Listen, would you mind very much if I changed dining room tables? He's asked me to. You wouldn't mind, would you?"

"Why should I?" Jane said dryly. "I'm only your servant."

"Oh, I wish *you* could meet someone, Janey. That would make everything perfect." She sighed happily, and started to get ready for bed. Just before she turned off the light, she said, "Oh, would you mind doing me a favor, Janey? That blue knit suit of mine got awful rumpled in packing. Would you iron it for me?"

"All right," Jane Brissom said.

Margo didn't see Jane until late the next morning; she had risen early and gone out on deck. Margo was strolling with Gordon Baylor when she spotted Jane in conversation with the room steward. The little cockney bowed and moved off as they neared.

"Good morning, Jane," Margo said coolly. "Gordon, this is my maid, Jane."

The man with the bold eyes nodded indifferently and looked away. "Let's go on forward," he told Margo. "The captain's an old friend of mine; I'll introduce you."

"That would be lovely. Oh, Jane," Margo said casually, "you won't forget about ironing that suit? And be sure that my black formal is ready for tonight, won't you?"

"Yes, miss," Jane said, in a choked voice.

They moved off together, but their voices carried in the ocean breeze. "She's a gem," Margo was saying. "She's been with me for years."

In the deck chair, Jane sipped her bouillon and grimaced.

That afternoon, Margo returned to the cabin for a change of clothes, and found Jane writing a letter. She told her the exciting news: the captain was having a small party in his quarters that night. Jane became flustered, and worried over her clothes, until Margo said, "Oh, but you're not invited, Jane. I mean, I'm awfully sorry, but you *couldn't* be, really."

"Not invited?"

"Well, it's only a small party, and I couldn't very well ask my—well, my maid, could I?"

"No," Jane said bitterly. "I guess you couldn't."

There was no doubt that Margo Wheeler was having the time of her life. She found a wellspring of small talk and coquetry that she never knew she possessed; she seemed to catch fire each night from the glittering necklace that never left her throat. Gordon Baylor was getting interested; she knew he was intrigued, awed by her obvious wealth, impressed by the maid who jumped at her every command. And Margo made her jump; she didn't miss an opportunity. When Jane began to mutter and complain, she'd remind her that her turn would come on the return trip; but Jane, whose conquests amounted to nothing more than servant-to-servant conversations with the cockney steward, grew lonelier, more bitter, and more miserable with every hour of the voyage.

On the fourth night, when Margo staggered into the stateroom at one-thirty, intoxicated by champagne and her own success, Jane was waiting up with folded arms.

"All right," she said coldly. "I've had enough."

"What's that?"

"I'm sick and tired of playing servant, Margo."

The younger woman blinked, and touched the diamond strands. "But it's just two more days. Two more days and we'll be in Le Havre—"

"I don't care! I'm not having any *fun*. I'm not meeting anyone—"

"But the return trip—"

"I don't *care* about the return trip. I want this farce over now. There are half a dozen nice men I could have met if they didn't think I was your housemaid."

Margo only half-stifled a tipsy giggle. "Really, Janey? You really think that's true?"

"What do you mean by that?"

"Oh, for heaven's sake!" Margo said, flinging her stole to the bed. "You think it would make that much difference? Honestly, Janey, sometimes I think you have no sense at all! You wouldn't have a *chance* with a decent man, servant or not. So you might as well face the truth."

Jane gasped. "How can you talk to me like that?"

"It's true, isn't it? You've got as much chance to get a man interested in you as—as—" She floundered for a simile, and then dropped onto the bed. "I'm tired," she sighed. "Let's talk about it tomorrow."

She was asleep almost at once, fully clothed, the diamond necklace still coruscating around her neck. Even the hateful glare of her roommate's eyes didn't disturb her peaceful slumber.

"I'll show you," Jane Brissom whispered. "I'll show you, damn you!"

In the morning, Margo apologized. "Gosh, Janey, I don't know what came over me. I guess I was drunk; that's all there is to it. Let's not let it spoil things, huh? It's only two more days—"

"Very well, Margo, we'll forget it."

"You're sure you're not angry?"

"No, of course not," Jane said.

"There's a party in the main ballroom tonight. For everyone. You'll be there, won't you?"

146

"I'll see," Jane said, not looking at her.

Jane didn't attend the party. She sat up in the stateroom until it was over. When Margo waltzed in at three, still giggling over the evening's hilarity, her lipstick smudged and her gown rumpled, Jane was sitting quietly in the armchair near the porthole, looking out at the turgid sea with a strange air of tranquility.

"You should have been there!" Margo said breathlessly. "Jane, it was absolute heaven. We danced under the stars . . ."

"I'm glad you enjoyed it."

"Gordon wants me to meet him in Paris. He knows all about it; he's been there umpteen times—"

"Am I to be your servant in Paris, too?"

"Of course not!" Margo tittered. Then she set her face in a pout. "You're not still angry with me, are you? About those silly things I said last night?"

"They weren't silly," Jane said coldly. "They were true."

"Oh, no, Janey—"

"They were true, Margo. I can't get a man. I never could. Not the way you can, with lipstick, and a permanent, and some pretty jewelry. It's harder for me." She stood up, and held out her hand. "I'll take the necklace now, Margo."

"Take it?" Margo looked bewildered, and touched the diamond strands protectively. "But we still have another day to go, Janey. There's the big farewell party tomorrow night—"

"You can do without it. I need it now."

"But what for? Janey, you're not going to tell anyone about—well, about our arrangement?"

"I don't intend to spoil your fun. I simply want the necklace. There's something I want to do with it."

Margo stared at her, and then laughed brassily.

"You *are* going to wear it! You think you can *still* get some man interested, don't you?"

"Give me the necklace, Margo."

"I won't!" Margo shouted, stepping backwards and stamping her foot. "What good can it do you now?"

"That's not your affair. It's my necklace and I want it back."

"I won't give it back!" Margo's voice rose toward hysteria. "It's mine until we reach Le Havre. That was the agreement. It's mine! It's mine!"

Jane's unlovely hands became fists. She shivered, as if cold. Then she turned to her bunk, and lifted the pillow. She brought out the awkward, black-handled revolver; her grip on the butt was insecure, but the wavering muzzle was trained in Margo's direction.

Margo didn't believe it for a moment. She sat down limply on her bunk, and stared incredulously at the dark, menacing hole of the weapon.

"For heaven's sake, Janey," she whispered, "put that awful thing down."

"I want my necklace, Margo."

"You're crazy! You're absolutely crazy, Janey! You could—kill me by accident—"

"It wouldn't have to be an accident," Jane said with loathing. "I could kill you gladly, Margo, believe me!" Her anger made her hand shake, and Margo cowered against the wall.

"Please, Janey, you don't know what you're doing—"

The older woman took a step forward; Margo shrieked and leaped from the bunk toward the wall. Her hand slapped at the steward's call button, and she punched it vigorously, over and over. Then she whirled to face her roommate, and there was more fury than fear in her eyes.

"I'll have you locked up!" she screamed. "I'll have them put you away!"

Jane hesitated, turning uncertainly toward the door. In another moment they heard footsteps and a genteel knock.

"Steward, ladies!" said the cheery voice.

Margo smiled triumphantly, called, "Come in!"

The door opened, and the wiry cockney steward entered. Jane lowered the revolver sadly, and stared blankly at the porthole. Outside, the sea rolled by silently.

The steward glanced between them, and the merriment went out of his face.

"What is this? What's going on?"

He went to Janey and took the gun from her limp hand.

"You fool," he said hoarsely. "You want to wake the whole ship?"

"She wouldn't give it to me," Jane said weakly. "I tried to make her give it to me—"

The steward smiled thinly. "I'm sure the lady will be reasonable." He turned to Margo. "Won't you, lady? You won't make trouble for us, will you?"

"Trouble?" Margo said. "What are you talking about?"

The steward came closer, his manner more obsequious than ever. His arms shot out, and his large hands locked on Margo Wheeler's throat. She made no sound, and hardly struggled. She looked toward Jane with round, terrified eyes, but Jane only watched with quiet interest. Margo made one last rally for freedom from the ever-tightening grasp, but it was too late. Without air, there was no strength. Then, without air, there was no life. She closed her eyes and died.

The steward lowered her lifeless body slowly to the cabin bunk. When he straightened up, he looked at Jane and clucked.

"Would have been better my way," he said. "If you'd just swiped that bloody thing." He shrugged his neat shoulders. "Well, this way there won't be any complaints. I'll get a trunk or a laundry bag, and over the side . . ."

"The necklace," Jane said dreamily.

"Ah, yes, the necklace. Your mistress' pretty necklace." He bent down and unhooked it, held it up to the light. "We'll have a good time in Paris on this, ducks, see if we don't." He put it in his pocket, and went to the door. "I'll be back in five minutes. Good job, old girl. We working people got to stick together."

He pinched her cheek before going out.

The Green Heart

by Jack Ritchie

We had been married three months and I rather thought it was time to get rid of my wife.

I searched the greenhouse and its shed, but they contained only such non-toxic items as grafting wax, powdered limestone, Sphagnum moss, and the like.

I returned to the house. "Henrietta, where do you keep the poisons? I mean the sprays and things like that for the garden?"

"But, dear," my wife said. "We use the organic method. No sprays or chemicals of any kind. We enrich the soil nature's way with organic materials—leaves, grass clippings, and especially spoiled hay. A healthy soil produces healthy plants and insects simply do not destroy healthy plants. What did you want the poison for, dear?"

"I saw a beetle on one of the shrubs."

She smiled mildly. "One mustn't kill beetles indiscriminately, William. So many of them are beneficial."

I studied her. "Henrietta, I've been meaning to ask you, just where do you buy those dresses you wear?" I had also meant to ask, "And why?" but I did not.

She glanced briefly at a mirror. "Every month or so I just phone Elaine's shop and have her send over three or four dresses."

"Don't you ever try them on before you buy them?"

"There's no need to, dear, Elaine knows my size." She looked down at her dress. "Do you like it, William?"

"It fits perfectly. However, the next time you feel the inclination to buy another dress, I think that we'd both better go to Elaine's and look over her stock first."

When my father departed this world, he left me an inheritance which was just short of adequate. By that I mean that it was necessary for me to dip into my capital in order to exist in a civilized manner. During the course of fifteen years that capital, of course, diminished to non-existence. In short, at the time I met Henrietta, I lived on credit.

I have never felt that work is a duty, a pleasure, or a challenge, and I have always suspected that those who enjoy it are basically masochistic.

I had existed forty-five years without the necessity of stooping to labor, and I felt that it was manifestly unfair to expect me to do so now.

There remained one last recourse. Marriage.

I have never been against that institution for others. I realize that the average mind must occupy itself with something, whether it be labor, comic books, or marriage. However, I have always cherished my position of independence and the prospect of becoming a member of a "team"—even if that team consisted of only two people—was acutely depressing.

Yet I was penniless, and it was necessary for me to dip into marriage.

Once having arrived at that decision, I now attended the functions of my set with an appraising eye. Desperate though I was, I found myself rejecting one prospect after another. Eventually I extended my search to afternoon teas—and at one of them I first glimpsed Henrietta.

I was not impressed. Her clothes were not exactly out of fashion, but one had the impression that she had purchased them blindfolded. She was a small, fragile-appearing woman who sat alone in a corner, smiling faintly to herself, and one had the feeling that she had wandered in accidentally and now was not quite certain of how to get out.

I had been stifling a yawn, when Henrietta spilled her cup of tea.

The hostess' eyes darted like arrows. "Really, Henrietta!"

She blushed scarlet. "I'm sorry, Clara. I was thinking of something else."

Clara's shoulders twitched. "Why can't you be more careful? I've just had the rug cleaned."

It occurred to me that a woman who dressed as Henrietta did, did so because she was either poor, or too rich to care. When the chattering resumed, I turned to Hawley Purvis who was sitting at my right. "Henrietta? Would she be one of the Bartons? The ones who lost practically all their money last year?"

151

"Good heavens, no!" Purvis said. "She's a Lowell. Has that fabulous place on the Lakeview Road. Fifty acres or something like that and scores of servants."

"Married?"

"No. Never has been."

I stared across the room at Henrietta. A maid approached her with the teapot. Henrietta seemed alarmed at the prospect of again holding a full cup of tea. She was about to refuse, but she was too late. The maid poured.

Henrietta held the cup gingerly between the fingers of both hands.

I rubbed my jaw speculatively. Fifty acres? Scores of servants? I watched Henrietta covertly. She consumed half the cup of tea, and after five minutes her mind evidently wandered again. The cup slipped from her fingers and the contents spilled over the rug.

Clara's face turned livid and she shrieked. "Henrietta!"

This time Henrietta paled. If she could have fainted, I am positive she would have.

I rose and elaborately poured the contents of my own cup onto Clara's rug. "Madam," I said stiffly. "Take your damn rug to the cleaners and charge the bill to me." It was the moment for action.

I offered my arm to Henrietta and we left.

The greatest obstacle to my marriage plans did not come from Henrietta, but from her attorney, Adam McPherson.

I made his acquaintance one week after Henrietta and I announced our engagement. He came to my apartment, introduced himself, and then stared at me stonily. "How much do you want?"

"For what?"

"How much do you want to call off your marriage to Henrietta?"

I frowned. "Did she send you?"

"No. This is my own idea. I'm offering you ten thousand."

"If you will turn, you will find a door behind you. It is the way out."

He was not intimidated. "When I heard about you, I had you investigated. You are penniless and in debt to any number of establishments, including Curley's Rug Cleaning Service." His lips tightened. "You are marrying Henrietta for her money."

"Really? And what, besides the state of my finances, makes you so positive about that?"

"I have had your acquaintances polled. They unanimously agree that

152

you are as capable of a tender emotion as a fish. A cold fish, they all specified." He reiterated his offer. "Ten thousand dollars."

What was a paltry ten thousand compared to Henrietta's millions? "Henrietta and I are deeply in love," I said firmly. "I would not part with her for less than . . . for *all* the money in the world."

"Twenty thousand."

"Never."

"Thirty. And that's absolutely final."

"So is my 'No'. Is this *your* money you are offering?"

"Yes."

"And what is your motive?"

"I do not want Henrietta to make a mistake she will regret all her life."

I ventured a guess. "Have you ever asked her to marry you?"

He nodded glumly. "About four times a year for the last twelve years."

"And her sentiments?"

"She regards me as a dear trustworthy friend. Very depressing." A thought suddenly brightened his face. "Do you *really* love Henrietta?"

I used a word strange to me. "Passionately."

He rubbed his hands. "Then of course you would have no objection to signing a document disclaiming all rights to Henrietta's money?"

"Henrietta would never consent to anything like that."

"I'll ask her."

"I'll wring your neck." I regained control of myself. "If it is your interest to see that Henrietta is happy, undoubtedly you have noticed that she has achieved a certain euphoria since I met her."

He admitted it reluctantly. Then he sighed. "All right. I will not oppose the marriage further."

"How good of you."

He studied me a moment. "Henrietta needs to be protected."

I agreed. "She is rather simple."

He corrected me. "Ingenuous." He went to the door and then turned. "I suppose you know that she teaches at the university?"

I blinked. "Henrietta?"

"Yes. Associate Professor. Botany. Donates her entire salary to charity."

So that was why she had never been home on weekdays, except for

153

the evenings. "She never told me."

"Probably forgot," McPherson said. "She's absentminded about some things."

Henrietta and I were married three weeks later. It was a small private ceremony marred only by the fact that McPherson arrived drunk and burst into tears as I slipped the ring on Henrietta's finger. She was excited and cried.

We spent our honeymoon in the Bahamas, where Henrietta collected an incredible number of ferns and various tropical vegetations for further study at home.

When we returned to her estate, I endured a week of bad service and poor food while I occupied my time by checking the household accounts.

The day Henrietta returned to teaching at the university, I called the servants together. They regarded me with uniformly narrow eyes and a collective insolence.

I attacked the keystone first—the housekeeper. "Mrs. Tragger. Front and center."

She folded her arms. "What is it?"

I smiled with infinite sweetness. "There is something about you which puzzles me. Why do you go about with that perpetual frown upon your face?"

She frowned.

I spoke gently. "I should think that you would be bubblingly happy. Gay. Absolutely hilarious. Whistling day and night. After all you have successfully managed to pad the household accounts to the sum of eighteen thousand dollars in the last six years."

Her face darkened. "Are you accusing me of . . ."

"Yes."

She glared. "I'll sue immediately."

"Please do. As soon as you are released from prison."

Uncertainty flickered in her eyes, but she said, "You can't prove a thing."

It would have been difficult. However I showed my teeth. "Madam, I *can* prove it for the satisfaction of any judge or jury. Yet I am inclined to be generous. Do you have a suitcase?"

She blinked. "Yes."

"Splendid. Then pack it at once and leave. You are fired."

154

She seemed about to utter something profane and devastating, but perhaps the nature of my smile changed her mind. She licked her lips and glanced at her audience. Finally she harumphed and stalked out of the room.

I turned next to the chauffeur, an unshaven creature who evidently slept in his uniform. "Simpson."

"Yeah?"

"Do you think that we ought to junk our cars?"

"Huh?"

"I really believe that in the interests of economy we ought to get rid of them—one and all. According to our records of gas consumption and mileage, I find that not one of them gives us more than one mile per gallon."

He shifted his feet. "Them figures are probably wrong somewhere."

"Possibly. But you need worry about them no longer. I presume that you too have a suitcase?"

He glowered. "Only Miss Lowell can fire me."

I smiled. "Miss Lowell is now Mrs. Graham, and if I find you on the grounds one hour from now, I shall regard you as a trespasser. I will not shoot you in the head. That is impenetrable. However, enough of you remains so that I cannot possibly miss."

I did not dismiss all of the servants—only seventy percent of them—and I had half of those replaced immediately by a reputable employment agency.

That evening dinner was on time, served flawlessly, and satisfying to the palate.

Henrietta did not notice the food—she seldom does—but toward the end of the meal she happened to glance at the serving maid and frowned thoughtfully. "Are you new here? I haven't seen you before."

"Yes, madam."

Henrietta turned to me. "What happened to Tessie?"

"I dismissed her. Also quite a few of the others. I replaced some, but only those necessary to the proper functioning of this house. Was it essential for you to have *three* personal inadequate maids?"

"Three? I'm sorry, William. I didn't know I had *any*. Mrs. Tragger does all the hiring. And besides I've never seen any of them. I dress myself." She looked at me hopefully. "Did you fire Mrs. Tragger?"

"Yes."

"And the chauffeur?"

"Yes."

Her gaze was one of profound admiration. "I was always a little . . . *afraid* . . . of them. Especially the chauffeur. He always seemed so put out when I asked him to drive me anywhere. So I always took a bus."

After a month I had the immediate estate functioning with reasonable efficiency and honesty on the part of the servants.

And now, at breakfast, I pondered my next step—independence, with wealth. And that called for the quite permanent disposal of my wife.

Poison? Yes, an agreeable method, but could I purchase any without having to sign some sort of a register?

I had never killed anyone, yet I had the feeling that I could murder with a certain equanimity. Not that I would linger for the death agonies, of course. I would tactfully leave the room.

"Dear," Henrietta said. "Have you ever thought of teaching?"

"Teaching?"

"Yes, dear. There's an instructorship in history going to be open this fall and there seems to be no prospect of filling it. So many teachers have majored in the sciences lately. They consider it more patriotic, I suppose."

Rat poison? Somehow the idea seemed too plebeian.

"All you would need is a B.A.," Henrietta said. "And you have that. And I think it would be so nice if you and I left together for the university each morning."

"I haven't the slightest inclination to teach. I much prefer to spend my time learning."

"But just learning is selfish."

"Me? *Selfish?*"

"I don't mean you specifically, dear," she said hastily. "I just meant that learning is *taking* and teaching is *giving*. And if you taught, you would feel useful."

"I dislike feeling useful. It is much too common." I suddenly remembered Ralph Winkler. Possibly he would have poison lying about his premises. He and I had been roommates in college and he had majored in chemistry, or some such trade.

After breakfast I looked up Ralph's address in the phone book and arrived there forty-five minutes later. It was a painfully neat house set behind twenty-five feet of precise lawn.

Ralph poured coffee and settled back in his chair. "I haven't seen you at any of the alumni meetings."

"Ralph," I said. "I wonder if you might be able to lend me a little—"

His eyes clouded reminiscently. "Remember good old Gillie Stearns?"

"No. It doesn't necessarily have to be arsen—"

"He could wiggle his ears," Ralph said. "Became an anthropologist."

I glanced out of the window at what appeared to be apple trees.

"He's the one who wrote that term paper on the appendix," Ralph said.

"Who did?"

"Stearns. Nobody knows what the function of the appendix really is, but it was Stearns' theory that the way to have a healthy appendix was to wiggle—"

"I see you're quite a gardener," I said.

"Orchardist. I have five apple trees, two peach, and one pecan." He frowned slightly. "The pecan doesn't seem to produce."

"Aren't you supposed to have *two* pecan trees?"

"I never thought of that."

"Ralph," I said. "Do you spray? I mean your fruit trees? Often?"

I had touched his subject. He rose enthusiastically. "William, follow me."

I took my cup along.

He led me through the house, into the back yard, and to the garage. He selected a key from an impressive ring and unlocked the door. "I keep the car parked on the street. Not enough room in here." He opened the door and stepped aside. "See for yourself, William."

I received the immediate impression that I had entered a combination garden shop and pharmacy. A riding mower, a tractor, and various accessory attachments occupied the floor space. The shelves lining one entire side were filled with bottles, jars, cans, and cartons. An assortment of manual spray guns hung on the walls. "How big is your place, Ralph?"

"A full quarter of an acre."

My eyes ran over the shelves and I made a random choice. "What's in that little red can in the corner?"

"Just about the strongest stuff I have," he said proudly. "It'll kill anything." He pointed to a gas mask and a rubber suit hanging on a peg. "I have to wear that when I spray. Can't leave an inch of skin exposed."

I stared at the can. "And you spray this poison on your apples?"

"You've never seen better ones in your life, William. Not a sign of sooty blotch, calyx end rot, or Brooks fruit spot."

"And you eat these apples?"

"Perfectly safe. The spray eventually washes off through wind and weather. Besides, I always peel the ones I eat."

I finished my coffee and handed him the cup. "Would I be imposing if I asked for a re-fill? I'll wait here and browse."

While he was gone, I pried open the red can with a screwdriver. The contents were a sickly yellow dust. I filled an envelope, gingerly licked the flap to seal it, and put it back into my pocket.

Ralph returned with my cup. "Remember good old Jimmy Haskins?"

"No." I took the cup. "What do you think about the organic method of raising apples?"

A chill descended. "Most unscientific."

"We have about forty apple trees on our place," I said. "We never spray."

His lips tightened. "There are all kinds of people in this world."

I had the impression that he regretted bringing me the coffee. There was no point in departing on such a frigid note. I searched my memory and then chuckled. "Remember good old Clarence? The one we all said could get his haircut in a pencil sharpener?"

"Yes," Ralph said coldly. "He's my brother."

I did not, of course, intend to poison Henrietta in our own home. That would lead to the inevitable autopsy and the equally inevitable electric chair.

But an earlier conversation with Henrietta had given me a splendid idea.

"Dear," she had said. "Every summer I go on a field trip for a week or two. Would it be all right if I went this year?"

I had been about to tell her that I had no objections—providing that she did not expect me to go with her—but then a thought had occurred to me. "Where will you be going?"

"It would be a canoe trip, William," she had said. "The Minnesota woods."

"You've been taking trips like this alone?"

"Oh, no. I usually go with some of my students. But this year I was hoping that . . . that just you and I could go. We could hire a guide if you think we'd need one, but actually I don't think that would be necessary if we didn't wander from our camp."

The idea of battling mosquitoes was not inviting, but I smiled. "Of course I will go with you. And we will not require a guide."

My problem had been solved. We would be alone in the middle of nowhere. I would simply kill her and bury her.

Then I would inform the authorities that my wife had wandered away from our camp and been lost. There would be a search, of course, but Henrietta would not be found.

And the actual method of the murder itself? I had dallied with shooting, stabbing, strangling, and bludgeoning. I eventually rejected them all. They required a primitive violence which is foreign to my nature. This morning I finally decided that poisoning was the civilized procedure.

When I returned from Ralph Winkler's home, I put the poison under lock and key.

In the evening, as usual, Henrietta brought her notes and reference books into the livingroom and worked on her latest paper for the Botany Journal. I put a stack of records into the phonograph and settled under a lamp for another review of Henrietta's accounts.

After a while I turned in my chair. "Henrietta, there's one item which keeps recurring. Every month you withdraw two thousand dollars from one of your bank accounts. The money seems to disappear. At least I can't find any accounting for it."

Henrietta hesitated. "I'm afraid it's blackmail, dear."

"Blackmail?" Perhaps I had underestimated her. "What in the world have you done to be blackmailed for?"

"Nothing, dear. It's because of Professor Henrich. You see, he and his wife adopted a child. Only it wasn't through a regular agency. Black market, they call it. And they thought that everything was fine. But a year later a man came to them and claimed that he was the child's father. He seemed to have evidence to prove it and he wanted the baby back unless. . . ."

159

It was obvious. "Unless Professor Henrich paid?"

"Yes. First it was one hundred dollars a month and then gradually he was paying five hundred. But the professor and his wife simply couldn't afford that for long. They had to dip into their savings and when those were gone Professor Henrich came to me to borrow money. He more or less broke down and told me the entire story. And so I took over the payments."

"*You* took over the payments? How could Henrich possibly *allow* you to do something like that?"

"But he doesn't really know what I'm doing, dear. I just told him that I'd talk to Smith—that's the name of the blackmailer. And later I told the professor that I'd managed to frighten Smith away by threatening to go to the police."

"But obviously you didn't."

"No. I thought it over and realized that there wasn't any actual *proof* that Smith was a blackmailer. He always insisted on cash from the professor. And so if I failed to *prove* to the police that Smith was a blackmailer, he might become very angry with my interference and actually take the child back. I was in a dilemma and money seemed to be the only way out."

"Five hundred dollars at first? And then more and more? Until today it is two thousand dollars a month?"

"Yes, dear."

I rubbed my forehead and eyes. "Don't you realize that eventually it will be three thousand? Four?"

She shook her head. "No. Two thousand is my absolute limit. I told him so when he asked for two thousand five hundred. He seemed disappointed, but he accepted the situation." She smiled. "I can be very firm when I want to."

I had difficulty speaking. "Just how much have you given this contemptible wretch?"

"I'm not positive. About fifty thousand dollars by now, I imagine."

"*Fifty thousand dollars* of my . . . of *our* money? To a man who neither sows nor reaps?"

She nodded. "That reminds me, William. You'd have only three classes a day. That's because instructorships are usually given to students who are also working for advanced degrees and the university doesn't want to overload them. Would you like to work for your M.A.

too?"

"When are you going to see Smith again?"

"He comes here the first Monday of each month. He's very prompt and he always phones me on the Sunday before to remind me to get to the bank for the cash Monday morning."

I went to the liquor cabinet and made myself a stiff drink. "When he phones next, let me talk to him."

The call came Sunday afternoon and Henrietta handed the phone to me.

"Would you please leave the room, Henrietta," I said. "I am always a bit embarrassed when I reason with people."

When she was gone I spoke into the mouthpiece. "You've received your last cent, you miserable parasite."

"Who the hell are you?"

I explained precisely and then added, "I control every penny which leaves this house and you are no longer included in our charities."

"In that case I'll take the kid away from the professor."

"I doubt very much if you can. Your references aren't exactly the best—as Professor Henrich and his wife, and I and mine will gladly testify in any court."

"Look, mister, I can still make a lot of trouble. A lot of trouble."

"You are welcome to try." But then something occurred to me. A man deprived of a two thousand dollar a month income has a tendency to turn ugly. Undoubtedly he would keep an eye on us. And when Henrietta disappeared would he put two and two together? Blackmailers are notoriously suspicious. Would he approach me and demand money for silence? And if I did not pay, would he see to it that I was caused considerable embarrassment with the police? Would he cause the authorities to resume the search for Henrietta a bit more diligently—with an eye directed toward the sub-surface of our last encampment?

There is only one way to deal with a blackmailer—be he real or potential.

"Just one moment," I said. "Do you have proof that you are the father of the child? Real proof?"

"The professor saw the papers."

"But I haven't. I doubt if you have any proof at all. But if you do, bring it here Monday evening. No proof, no money." I hung up.

I explained to Henrietta that I wanted to see Smith alone when he came—to further reason with him—and on Monday evening she returned happily to the university to attend a lecture on the shallow root systems of the Sequoias.

When she was gone, I saw to it that the servants retired to their quarters and then went to the liquor cabinet in the study.

I opened the envelope containing Winkler's yellow powder. How much of this stuff was sufficient to kill a human being? I didn't know. I solved the problem by pouring the entire contents into a bottle of Scotch.

Smith arrived at eight-thirty. He was a somewhat bulky man with long arms and his hairline initiated approximately one inch from his eyebrows. He was expensively, if not tastefully, dressed.

I closed the door of the study behind us. "The proof, please."

He revealed marigold yellow teeth and removed a revolver from his pocket. "This is just so that you don't get any funny ideas." Then he put the gun back into his pocket and handed me an envelope.

I examined the contents. The papers were originals, not photostats, and apparently authentic. I wandered over to the liquor cabinet as I studied a hospital birth record. I made myself a bourbon and soda and then looked up as though I'd suddenly remembered he was still there. "A drink?"

"What you got?"

"Scotch?"

"That's it."

I poured a generous glass and handed it to him. He drained the entire contents and smacked his lips. "Good stuff."

That confirmed a suspicion of mine. People who drink Scotch have no sense of taste.

He extended the glass. "How about making that wet again?"

"Gladly." His simian aspect reminded me of good old Gillie Stearns and I asked a question. "Can you wiggle your ears?"

He seemed a bit saddened. "Used to be able to. But ever since my appendix got took out I lost the touch."

When I noticed that his coloring seemed to verge toward purple, I hastily put the papers back into the envelope and returned them. "These seem to be in order. And now if you'll excuse me, I'll get you the cash. I have it in the library safe." His color grew worse.

162

I went to the library and sat down. I finished a pipe and then returned to the study.

Smith lay on the floor, quite dead, and it appeared that his departure had not been a pleasant one.

I withdrew the envelope from his pocket and then slung him over my shoulder. I carried him through the French doors to the automobile he'd parked in the circular driveway.

I drove towards the outskirts of the city, following a bus line. When the area seemed relatively unpopulated, I turned off and parked the car.

I walked back half a dozen blocks before I boarded a bus.

Perhaps Smith's picture would appear in the newspapers when his body was found. If it did, and Henrietta noticed it, I would explain that a man like Smith undoubtedly had many enemies and that one of them had killed him. I felt confident that she would accept that explanation.

At Fremont Street, I left the bus and walked the two blocks to Ralph Winkler's home.

He opened the door and regarded me with distinct inhospitality. "Yes?"

"Ralph," I said. "We've been having a little trouble with field mice in our apple orchard."

His economic smile indicated vindication. "So organic gardeners have field mice problems?"

"I'm afraid so. I wonder whether you might have something potent—some chemical—which might enable us to get rid of them?"

I was welcome instantly. He stepped aside and we journeyed through the house and to his garage.

He surveyed his pharmacy. "What'll you have? I've got compounds here that will throw mice into convulsions."

I recalled the messy decline of Smith. "Basically I'm a humanitarian. Do you have something gentle, yet still lethal?"

He was disappointed in me. "Very well. I suppose I have something like that here . . . somewhere. But you really should try Cyclolodidan. I use it all the time."

"Do you have field mice?"

He nodded glumly. "Can't seem to get rid of them."

When Henrietta returned at eleven that night, I told her that Smith would never bother her or Professor Henrich again. "Threatened him with the police and twenty years in prison. He left here shaken, trembling, and penitent."

Henrietta gazed at me admiringly. "You seem to be able to get things done, William. I feel so safe with you."

During the week, Henrietta usually lunches at the university, but at twelve-thirty the next day she came home breathless and smiling like a child. She waved an envelope. "It's been accepted."

"What has?"

"*Alsophilia grahamicus.*"

"*Alsophilia grahamicus?*"

"A tropical tree fern, William. I discovered it during our honeymoon and when I couldn't classify it, I realized that it might be a true species. So I named it after you—that's the grahamicus part—and sent it to the Society for verification."

I rolled the words on my tongue. "*Alsophilia grahamicus.*" Rather pleasing. Perhaps I might yet become a footnote in some textbook—my bid toward immortality.

"Are you pleased, William?"

"That was very thoughtful of you."

"I'm having the tip of one frond put into a plastic token so that you can wear it always."

That evening Adam McPherson appeared for dinner. It had been his habit to do so the first Tuesday of every month for the past ten years and after our marriage Henrietta had still chosen to honor the standing invitation.

I met him at the door. "McPherson, I want a word with you."

He regarded me for a moment. "Really? What a coincidence. It was my intention to speak to you too." He glanced about. "Where is Henrietta?"

"Upstairs grading some term papers."

I led him into the study and came directly to the point. "McPherson, you are Henrietta's lawyer and comptroller. Surely you must have been aware that prior to my appearance this household was run in a most strange manner—padded payrolls, superfluous servants, astronomical household expenses."

He nodded. "Of course."

My eyes narrowed. "And yet you did nothing about it?"

"Why should I? After all, I am the one who was responsible for the entire glorious arrangement."

"You baldly *admit* that?"

"Certainly." McPherson went to the liquor cabinet and surveyed the contents. "It was quite a profitable arrangement for me. Kickbacks, you know." He looked back at me. "Henrietta is an excellent botanist, but she has no accounting ability whatsoever. And she trusted me."

I felt the impulse to strangle. "I do not care how messy this is going to be, I intend to prosecute."

He was not perturbed. "If you do, I shall see that you join me in prison—or possibly worse. For murder."

I was, of course, temporarily quieted.

He brought forth a bottle and a glass. "Several years ago I noticed that Henrietta regularly withdrew five hundred dollars from one of her bank accounts. It was a relatively insignificant sum, but she seldom uses cash, and I became curious. I asked her about it and when she proved uncharacteristically evasive, I questioned the servants—who were under my command, so to speak—and eventually ascertained the existence of Mr. Smith. Further investigation on my part—if one may use that term for eavesdropping—established the reason for his monthly visits."

McPherson poured liquor into his glass. "Smith had a limited imagination. He was apparently satisfied with five hundred dollars. But I was not." He smiled. "Therefore I approached him with the proposal of prison or cooperation. Naturally he chose cooperation. Of the two thousand he eventually received monthly from Henrietta, one went to me."

I stared at the bottle he still held in his hand. It was the Scotch which had eliminated Smith. I had forgotten to dispose of it.

McPherson put the bottle back on the shelf. "When Smith informed me that *you* wanted to see him personally, I wondered what you were up to now—after all you had already ruined one of my sources of income. And so I drove here last night, parked on the street, and waited for him to come out of your house. It was my intention to question him immediately about his meeting with you." He smiled. "His car came out of the driveway, but *you* were driving." He looked at his glass and then at me. "Can I make you a drink?"

"No, thank you," I said. "But by all means, please help yourself."

165

He savored and then finished the contents of his glass. He coughed appreciatively and reached for the bottle again. "I followed you. And when you walked away from Smith's car, I looked inside. Smith lay on the floor, obviously dead. I did not pry into the manner of his death and left immediately. How did you kill him?"

"I stabbed him in the back," I said.

He smiled. "Please do not attempt the same with me. I am wary and will remain at arm's length." He tried to stay alert.

And now *I* smiled. "I cannot expose you without being exposed myself? And so it is your intention to resume bilking Henrietta's estate? With my passive cooperation?"

He nodded. "Exactly."

I noticed that his complexion was changing to a more colorful hue. "We will discuss this further after dinner," I said pleasantly. "And now I shall see if Henrietta is ready."

I retired to the library, smoked a pipe, and returned to the study.

McPherson was dead.

I removed his car keys from his pocket and carried his body to his car outside. I deposited him in the trunk compartment and parked the car on the street.

I returned to the house just as Henrietta came down the stairs. "Is Adam here yet?"

"No, my dear."

She smiled. "He's rather fond of me. It was very thoughtful of him to cry at our wedding."

We delayed dinner half an hour and then sat down without him.

At ten that evening when I went out for a walk, I disposed of McPherson's car in the same manner I had used for Smith and returned by bus.

Henrietta was considerably shocked when she read of McPherson's death and the police were puzzled. Henrietta recovered, but the police remained puzzled and the days passed.

At the end of the semester, Henrietta and I packed and drove north to the Minnesota lake country. We rented a canoe, purchased supplies, and bravely proceeded into the wilderness on a warm Saturday afternoon.

Since we proceeded downstream, the paddling was not particularly tedious and the first hour passed pleasantly.

166

However as we approached the first white water, I realized, a bit too late, that the occupation of running rapids is a bit specialized.

I would gladly have paddled to shore and portaged, but I found that we were in the grip of the current. We had no choice but to hold on and attempt to steer.

We safely rode two-thirds of the rapids and I had reached a faint optimism, when suddenly a jagged rock appeared directly ahead. I endeavored frantically to avoid it. However, the after end of the canoe smashed into the obstruction and we turned over.

I found myself tumbling in the rushing water, grasping wildly for some handhold, but my fingers merely slipped off the wet rocks. Suddenly I found myself falling. I plunged deep into the water. When I fought my way to the surface, I discovered that I had successfully passed all obstacles and now floated in a relatively quiet pool at their base. Then I relaxed.

I swam to shore, climbed the bank, and looked back upstream.

Henrietta clung to an outcropping of rock just before the drop into the pool. She was pale and her eyes looked toward me for help.

I shouted, "Henrietta, let go of that rock. You'll be carried into the pool below. It's perfectly safe."

She looked down and then at me. "But I can't swim."

I blinked. *She couldn't swim?*

I felt my heart beating. This was the opportunity! There would be no need for poison. There had been a canoe accident and she had drowned. It was as simple as that. And I would walk back to the nearest habitation and tell the story.

I raised my voice again. "Hold your breath and let go of that rock. I'll be waiting down below and I'll bring you to shore."

I took off my soaking shoes, my trousers, and my shirt. Then I smiled at her and waved my hand. "All right. Let go."

She did not hesitate.

The current caught her and she plunged over and down into the pool.

I turned my back toward the water. All I would have to do now was wait. How long? Five minutes? Ten?

I looked down at my clothes. The round plastic token containing the tip of frond had fallen out of my pocket and lay on the grass. *Alsophilia grahamicus.*

167

I found myself trembling.

I had killed Smith and McPherson and they had deserved to die. But does one kill a child?

A child? Yes, a child-woman and she loved me. And in my own way I had grown rather . . .

I cursed savagely and plunged into the water.

I found Henrietta immediately and brought her to the surface. She was still obeying my injunction to hold her breath, though rather desperately.

I grasped her and began backstroking towards the shore. "You may breathe now, Henrietta. But only through your mouth. Not your nose. Taste the air and if it has water in it, spit it out and try again."

When we reached shore we sat in the sun. But it was still a bit cool and so I held her.

She looked up at me. "I'll always be able to depend on you, won't I, William? All the rest of my life?"

I almost sighed. "I'm afraid so."

And in September I would probably be teaching at the university.

Suddenly I looked forward to it.

Supply and Demand

by James M. Ullman

Gus climbed from the car and strolled up the walk. He was heavy set and fairly tall, his square face frozen in a permanent sneer. He rang the bell. A young woman gazed through the screen door. Gus said, "I wanna see Stan. I'm an old friend. A *real* old friend."

Hesitantly, the woman held the door open. Gus stepped into a living room where two small boys wrestled before a blaring television set. Elsewhere in the house, an infant squalled. The woman hurried to the kitchen and Stan came out. Slight, lean, and in his mid-thirties, Stan wore old clothes stained with black dirt; a garden tool jutted from a hip pocket.

Gus lit a cigar. "Hi, kid. Remember me?"

"Gus? I'll be darned, it's good to see you," Stan said, not meaning it at all. Nervously he glanced at the kitchen, where his wife soothed the infant. "Things are a mess here. Let's talk in the rec room." They went downstairs and Stan added, "How are you? I've been out of touch."

"I know." Gus eased into a wicker chair. "The other guys forgot you. If they saw you today, they wouldn't recognize you. But I kept track." Gus flicked ashes to the floor. "After Korea, you made college with the GI Bill. Then you married a nice girl and moved to the suburbs, strictly legit. You always was smart, Stan. Smart enough not to be arrested, even though you brainstormed all them two-bit burglaries the guys on our block used to pull."

"That was a long time ago. With me, things are different now."

"I'll bet. And I think it's swell, how you work for J. Newton Laverage, the biggest stockbroker in town. That's why I'm here. I got a financial problem, and I remembered my old buddy Stan, hobnobbing with the big shots, sitting there with all the inside dope. Maybe Stan can help."

Stan smiled. "I'll try. But you have an inflated idea of my importance. I'm just one of several dozen registered representatives in the firm. J. Newton Laverage hardly knows I exist. As for inside information, all I know is what I read in the *Wall Street Journal*."

"Sure. Not that I believe you. But anyhow, you remember Nick?"

"Of course." Uncomfortable, Stan licked his lips, which had gone very dry. "In the old days, he fenced the stuff we stole, and now he's a very big man. He gets a cut from every racket in the city."

"That's Nick. Well, I'm into him for a lotta dough. A deal went sour, and you know Nick. If you can't pay, he gets rough. At the moment, I can't pay."

"Gus, if you want to borrow money, I'm afraid . . ."

"Naw, I wouldn't ask for that much. But the last few years, Nick and some of the other big boys have been plungers in the stock market. Nick especially. He has a lot of cash, and he likes to invest it."

"I see. But how does that concern me?"

"It's simple. I figure if I give Nick a tip on a stock that's sure to go up, he'll cancel the debt I owe him. He could lay so much money on that stock that his profit would be four or five times my debt. And he'd be real grateful, because he's always complainin' how whenever he buys a stock, it goes down. It's hurtin' his pride."

Stan lit a cigarette and tried to keep his voice calm. "Gus, I hate to discourage you, but it can't be done. I could give you the names of thirty or forty stocks likely to go up, but I couldn't guarantee any of them would. Not even J. Newton Laverage could do that. The price of a stock is determined by a complex set of factors . . ."

"Stan, boy." Gus leaned forward, smugly sure of his logic. It had taken Gus a long time to reach this conclusion, but once formed in Gus's mind, any conclusion was irrevocable. "Let's level. You're a born schemer. Every kid on the block knew that. And a schemer like you wouldn't waste time in Laverage's office unless you got a sure thing in the market now and then. All you brokers hear about sure things, it's common knowledge. But don't worry, I won't tell Nick who gave me the tip. You're my secret. Just tell me why the stock will go up. Nick don't buy no stock without some reason, even if they all do go down."

"You're asking the impossible."

"It better not be impossible." Gus's pig-like eyes glittered. "You never did go for rough stuff, did you? But for me, this is serious. So if

170

you don't gimme the name of a sure thing in two weeks, there'll be plenty of rough stuff." Gus arched his brows toward the ceiling. "You got a nice wife up there. Cute kids, a cozy home. All sorts of things could happen, y'know? The cops could never pin it on me. And if you went to the cops, you'd have to tell 'em about the old gang, and when J. Newton Laverage heard about it you'd lose your job. So think it over."

Gus still lived in the old neighborhood. Based on the first floor of an ancient apartment building, he collected tribute from every petty racket flourishing on eight slum blocks.

One September morning Gus wandered to a window, a beer in one hairy hand and a cigar in the other. Something about a slim figure hurrying down the narrow street caught his eye. Sure enough, it was Stan, dressed now in grey flannel suit, his sandy hair covered by a high-crowned, short-brimmed hat. Under his arm, Stan carried a large carton.

Gus was waiting at the door when Stan climbed the stairs. "You're three days early," Gus observed. He studied Stan and was pleased at what he saw. Stan had been pale and distraught when Gus left the house in the suburb. Now he appeared serene and confident, much like the Stan of old. "It didn't take long to get the name of that stock after all, did it?"

Gus waved Stan to a dining room table. They took chairs and Stan said, "That part hasn't changed. Neither I nor anyone else can just give you the name of a stock and guarantee its price will rise."

"I warned you . . ."

"Hold on." Stan began unwrapping the carton. "I'm going to give you something much better than a tip. Gus, I'm going to show you how to *make* the price of a stock go up."

"Quit kidding."

"It's no joke. I won't pretend the idea came to me out of the blue. Confidentially, I've been toying with a scheme like this for years. And I can't claim I enjoyed your visit the other day. But I'll admit, it took you to inspire me to work out the details. If I do say so, it's a beautiful plan. I'm going to borrow to the hilt and cash in on this myself."

"I didn't think going legit would stop you from schemin' completely. What's in the box?"

"A tape recorder."

"Hey . . ."

Stan set the recorder on the table. "Relax. I'm not going to make tapes. I'm going to play some, and then leave the machine here after I go. But first, let me explain something. Most people buy and sell stocks merely by calling their broker on the telephone and placing the order."

"I know. Nick does that all the time. He picks up the phone and says, 'This is Nick. Get me a hundred so-and-so,' or 'I want youse to dump my oil stock.'"

"Exactly. The broker recognizes a good customer's voice and executes the order without question. And J. Newton Laverage's customers include some very wealthy men. They don't bother with small fry like me; they talk to Laverage personally. Some of them are so rich that just by buying enough of a stock, they can make the price rise instantly."

"If that's true, why don't they do it every day?"

"The law of supply and demand. If there's only one big buyer kicking the price up, the price will fall right back down as soon as he stops buying, and he'll be stuck with the shares he bought at a higher price. I'll explain it another way. A stock rises whenever more people want to buy it than want to sell it; it falls when more people want to sell than want to buy. For instance, suppose a customer calls J. Newton Laverage and asks him to buy a huge block of stock in a company where ordinarily, there's very little trade; meaning ordinarily, there are only a few buyers *or* sellers. When Laverage places the order, the price will start up almost immediately. If the price was a dollar, there soon won't be any sellers left willing to part with the stock for a dollar, and Laverage will have to bid more. When he runs out of sellers at two dollars, he'll have to buy from people unprepared to sell until the price reaches three, and so on. Of course as the price keeps going higher, more and more sellers are attracted to the market, until ultimately more stock is offered for sale than Laverage wants to buy. When that happens, the price will start back down."

"Okay. But what's our angle?"

"Just this. The customer who calls Laverage with a big order is going to be you."

Gus frowned. "Look, kid. I ain't no actor. How can I fool Laverage

172

into thinkin' I'm a business tycoon?"

"You'll understand after I play this tape. I've had a recorder hooked into Laverage's private line all week. Listen."

Stan shoved the recorder's PLAY button. The plastic reels began to turn.

On the recorder, a cultured male voice drawled: "This is Laverage."

"Newt?" The question was phrased in a hoarse, barking, almost unintelligible croak.

"Yes, Hank. Good to hear from you."

"How's da market?"

"Quiet. Some interest in the rails, that's all."

"Swell. I want ya to pick up a thousand Pennsy and a thousand Com Ed."

"Pennsy's already jumped to 45. Why don't I place the order at 44½, in case the price dips later?"

"Naw, don't fool around tryin' to save nickles and dimes. Buy at da goin' price, whatever it is. And buzz me at the hotel soon as ya know wot we got it for."

Someone hung up. Stan pushed the STOP button and leaned back, smiling.

"Who," Gus asked, "was Laverage talking to?"

"Henry W. Braun, the scrap king. He cleaned up in metals during World War II and has pyramided his profits a hundredfold since. He's a financial genius, but his formal education stopped at the second grade. You'll have no trouble imitating his speech mannerisms."

"I heard of Braun. But his voice, that weird squawk, what's wrong with it?"

"He had a throat operation last year and it didn't turn out right. With practice, Gus, I'm sure you can croak well enough to convince Laverage that you're Hank Braun. I'll drill you thoroughly on what to say. I've even picked out the stock we'll move—Fireball, Inc. They make washing machines, but that doesn't matter. What does matter is, ordinarily only a couple hundred shares of Fireball change hands daily, and for months the price has hung steady at about six dollars a share. When the supposed Hank Braun tells Laverage to buy a huge block of Fireball, the price will skyrocket."

"Won't Laverage get suspicious? I mean, if Braun is such a genius, why would he wanna knock the price to the moon? Like you explained, the price will drop like lead when he stops buyin', on account nobody else was willin' to pay more than six bucks a share before, and probably still ain't."

"A good question. And most rich men spread a big purchase over weeks and months, instead of buying all at once, so they don't disturb the price too much. But Hank Braun is impetuous and eccentric. He's done this sort of thing before, but he always comes out ahead because he's deduced the price will ultimately go higher than what he paid for it anyway. When Braun wants a stock, he wants it today, no matter what it costs."

"Uh-huh. But suppose the real Braun calls Laverage the same day I do?"

"Gus, Braun has no real home. He hops all over the country, checking his business interests. Laverage is Braun's broker here, but Braun also has brokers in every other big city he visits regularly. He only calls Laverage when he's in town, usually from a hotel suite kept ready for him, whether he's in the city or not. Laverage never knows if Braun is here until he gets a call. For a small bribe, I can get a key to Braun's suite and a guarantee you won't be disturbed while you're in there. After you give Laverage the buy order, you'll have to remain in the suite to receive calls Laverage will make to you, reporting on the progress of the purchase. Tentatively, I've decided you'll stage your act on October 25th, between 2 and 3:30 p.m."

"Why then?"

"For two reasons. First, Braun's private pilot has an account with us, and he mentioned casually the other day that during the last week of October Braun is scheduled to visit a throat specialist in Canada. By October 25th, everyone will have forgotten that remark, and it's not the sort of thing Braun would tell Laverage, since he's very sensitive about his voice. And second, October 25th is the date of Fireball's annual meeting. It begins at 2 p.m., the very minute Laverage will start buying the stock heavily. Nothing important will happen at the meeting, but investors all over the country will note the coincidence and *think* something happened. Some of them will jump in to buy Fireball too, in hopes of a quick profit, and they'll kick the price up even further. Meanwhile, as the price goes higher and higher, you, I, and Nick will be the sellers. We'll unload all our Fireball before the market closes at 3:30 p.m. When the bubble bursts the next day, we'll all be collecting fat checks from our brokerage houses."

Gus sat deep in contemplation. "It's crazy, but I like it, Stan, I'm beginnin' to like it a lot."

"It's a cinch." Stan rose. "If Braun returns unexpectedly, or if I learn Laverage knows Braun is in Canada, I'll tip you off and we'll postpone it. But you can tell Nick to start buying Fireball now. Warn him to buy just a little at a time, at the lowest price he can get it for. It's nearly two months until October 25th, and Nick should be able to acquire a sizeable block of Fireball at reasonable prices by then. I'd advise you to borrow more money and do the same. And play the tapes on this recorder so often you can imitate Braun's voice in your sleep." Stan smiled. "As for J. Newton Laverage—he and Braun will have one wonderful long-distance brawl on October 26th. No doubt their dispute will wind up in the lap of the Securities and Exchange Commission. But by that time, you'll be free of your debt and Nick will be rolling in dough."

The car pulled to the curb on a quiet side street around the corner from Braun's hotel. Gus started out of the back seat. One of the two men in front turned and said, "Remember, Gus. If this don't work—"

"Stop worryin'. If anythin's wrong, we postpone it to next week. But if I'm still in the hotel at 2 o'clock, the price of Fireball will start up at two minutes after two."

"It better. I'll be in a booth in a cigar store, talkin' to Nick, who'll be talkin' to his broker on another line. And if Fireball don't go up far enough by 3:30, you might as well ride to the roof of that hotel and jump off."

"Thanks for the encouragement."

Scowling, Gus walked from the car. He rounded the corner, strolled into the crowded hotel lobby, and headed for the elevator bank. He rode up to 18 and then walked down to 16, Henry W. Braun's floor. A key provided by Stan opened the door to the suite. One room had been furnished as an office, and Gus pulled up a chair and sat behind the desk. Everything had gone well so far. He picked up the phone, dialed the Laverage company, and in his normal voice asked for Stan.

"Gus? It's all set. Braun is still up in Canada. Anyone see you go in there?"

"Naw. But what's with Fireball? Nick had to pay nine bucks a share for the block he bought yesterday. It's already up three points since September."

"I know. There's been a lot of buying interest in the last few weeks. Nick must have invested a fantastic sum."

"It ain't just Nick. I didn't mention no names to him, but I gave him a rough idea how I'd rig the price, so Nick told all his friends. All the big boys are in on it—the Chicago mob, the New York crowd, the guys in Buffalo, Miami Beach, Las Vegas . . ."

"No wonder the price has been rising. I should have guessed. A chronic market player like Nick always shares a hot tip with his friends. But that's just a sample of what'll happen when Laverage executes the mammoth buy order *you're* going to place. Did you tell Nick to instruct his broker to sell Fireball when it reaches 13?"

"Yeah. You sure it'll go that high before starting to go down?"

"It'll go higher. But it wouldn't pay to be too greedy. If Nick ordered the stock sold at 15 and it only went to 14, he'd be stuck with it when the price tumbles tomorrow. But if he sells at 13, he'll make a nice profit, since he only paid from six to nine dollars for his shares."

"Nick understands that. All the boys got sell orders in around 13. But Stan, I'm worried. Nick went overboard, tellin' all his pals and investin' a huge chunk of his own dough. If Fireball don't reach 13 . . ."

"It will. Gus, you've got Braun's voice down pat. And we've drilled a dozen times on what Laverage might say to you, and what you should say to him. It's nearly two. Laverage just returned from lunch. So good luck."

Gus depressed the hook. He closed his eyes and took a deep breath. He cleared his throat, raised the hook, and dialed the Laverage company again.

A girl said: "J. Newton Laverage. May I . . ."

"Lemme talk," Gus croaked, "to Newt."

"Of course, Mr. Braun."

The girl made the connection. Gus began to perspire. At least, he had fooled the girl. . . .

"This is Laverage."

"Newt? Hank Braun. How's da market?"

"Good volume, Hank. The average is up about three dollars, with the aerospace issues leading the advance. About that General Dynamics you bought last month . . ."

"Never mind Dynamics. I wanna buy into Fireball. Two hundred thousand shares."

There was a pause. Then Laverage said: "That's a big order. Fireball has already climbed recently. If you're willing to take your time, I think I can pick it up in small blocks for less than it's selling for now. The last quote was 9¼. You know what'll happen if I buy two hundred thousand shares all at once."

"I know. But buy at da market price anyhow, I got my reasons. And buzz me at da hotel soon as you hear anythin'."

Gus hung up. He sank back in the chair and lit a cigar. Nervously he puffed, his eyes on the clock. Fifteen minutes later, the phone rang.

"Hank?"

"Yah," Gus squawked.

"We bought twenty thousand shares of Fireball so far, but the price is already at 10½. Are you sure . . ."

"I'm sure. Keep buyin'. You're doin' fine."

Gus lit another cigar. Laverage called again at 2:35 to admonish.

"I don't like it, Hank. We have forty thousand shares now, and the last sale was at 12¼. Fireball's annual meeting is today . . ."

"You think I don't know dat?"

"Well, then you know nothing will happen at the meeting. But all sorts of wild rumors are flying around. Speculators all over the country are starting to buy Fireball, hoping to sell it a few minutes later at a higher price. They're bidding against you, and if this keeps up . . ."

"Just buy more stock. I want them two hundred thousand shares before the market closes. Or do you want I should get another broker?"

"Of course not, Hank. Whatever you say."

Laverage's third call came at 3:14 p.m.

"We have a hundred and eighty thousand shares now. The price held at 13 for a while—an awful lot of sellers came into the market at 13—but the last quote was 13⅜."

"Swell."

The phone rang for the last time at 3:35. Laverage sounded weary.

"Hank? We got it all. We picked up the final block one minute before the bell. But you had to pay dear. The closing price was 14⅛."

"Dat's okay. You couldna done better. I sure appreciate it."

"I've run a quick tabulation. Your average price for the 200,000 shares was a little under thirteen dollars." Laverage hesitated. "Hank,

I don't want to presume on our friendship. But I just can't help wondering why . . ."

"I can't tell ya now, Newt. But you'll learn soon. Real soon."

Gus hung up. He mopped his brow. That was that, and as Stan had emphasized so often, the next step was to get out of the hotel—fast.

Gus rose. He wiped the telephone with a handkerchief to eradicate fingerprints. He opened a window and emptied the cigar butts from the ash tray. He washed the ash tray and set the chair back against the desk, leaving the room exactly as he had found it.

Quickly, Gus walked out of the suite. His exit was unobserved. He took the stairs to the 14th floor and rode an elevator to the lobby, which was happily packed with conventioneers.

Gus edged through the mob and into the revolving doors. On the street, for the first time in weeks, he began to relax. His stride became jauntier; his face contorted in an unaccustomed smile. He lit another cigar, turned the corner, and approached the car where Nick's trusted lieutenants waited.

"Hi, boys. You talk to Nick?"

The driver said: "Yeah, just now."

"What did he say?"

"He said to do this."

The barrel of an automatic pistol snaked from the car window. The gun barked four times and Gus tumbled backward. He sprawled dead on the pavement.

With a squeal of tires, the car roared away.

J. Newton Laverage put his signature on a check. "There you are, Stan. A little bonus. And forget those youthful indiscretions you mentioned. I'm not going to allow a man of your business acumen to leave our firm. Beginning tomorrow, you're a junior partner."

Stan mumbled his thanks, picked up the check and fingered it.

"Poor old Gus," Laverage went on. "Sitting there in the suite you rented down the hall from Braun's, thinking I was actually buying all that Fireball, taking my word for it when I told him the price was rising to 10, 11, 12, 13! Well, I suppose we had to go through with that charade, but it does seem hard on Gus . . ."

"If you knew him as I did," Stan replied, "you'd conclude nobody deserved it more."

Bird Island

by Ross Brown

I recall the birds swooping as the launch nosed beside the jetty and, as we stepped onto the island, a small girl curtseying, presenting us with flowers. Hardfaced fishermen in cloth caps stood staring at this, the return of the local girl with her foreign husband. They turned aside when I waved to them.

"Shy," Kirsti whispered to me. "They must become used to you." She squeezed my arm and tried to smile, but a solemnity clouded her features as she glanced around the small gathering. "Ragnvar is not here," she said.

I didn't answer. Instead I was thinking, so this is Steinsvik, capital of Bird Island, with its sturdy wooden houses bunched around a bay, a tangle of masts and rigging—and birds; Steinsvik, our future home, where I would become a village grocer. Yes, after years of watching roads and sea lanes slip past, I was to domesticate myself by good-naturedly ladling out sugar and slicing bacon.

A man sacrifices a lot for a woman, I considered; not only his privileged indifference toward time and money, but his starting to shave every day, polishing shoes, wearing a tie. It's hard. Yet the effort is tolerable when the woman's like Kirsti.

When we had met, I'd just signed off a Norskie freighter and sat in a seaman's mission, opposite a girl who drank black coffee with a nervous desperation. She told me she had answered an advertisement for a maid's position, and soon despaired of scrubbing pots in a sleazy hotel. She headed for the mission and Norwegian accents, during her few free hours.

After that we met frequently . . . Well, we began to share a flat and eventually got married. Physically, we suited each other. I wanted to take Kirsti to central Australia, for she had the same yearning as myself

179

for freedom and space; but I delayed, doubting whether she could withstand the summers, especially when her natural environment was the Arctic, a region she spoke of with compelling zest. Somehow, in this vacuum between our two worlds, we spread my wages as bartender and made our mediocre existence contented.

Then her father died. Letter after letter arrived from her surviving kin, brother Ragnvar, asking her to return and manage affairs in the grocery store. She studied the letters and sat by the window for hours, staring through the TV aerials and chimney pots. She was obsessed with a melancholic silence I could not break. I had no choice.

When I saw the wind seeping through her raven hair, her eyes reflecting the strange beauty of chilled waters, I was happy to have brought her home.

Bird Island—you'll find several places with this appropriate name on a map of Norway, but not this one. Inside the polar circle, it is a remnant of land dumped unlovingly by the ice-sheets that once ground over the north. Its vegetation extends to moss and flowers, its trees are straggly specimens. At first, I concluded that its 150 inhabitants were masochists, subjecting themselves to uncivilized effects and lack of conveniences from the mainland. I had varying impressions, some right, many wrong.

For instance, Ragnvar: we met friends and relations during that first week of settling-in, yet Kirsti's brother made no appearance before a week. In looks, as well as manner, he was odd. He had the same sleek hair as his sister, yet a livid scar flashed from beneath his right eye to his jaw. He kept his head averted, and always seemed to be in profile. I had no doubts about his tenacity. They said he received his stigma as a youth, an accident in the store, and he sat—with his cheek flapped open and blood streaming—in a boat for three hours while it was rowed to the mainland. Now, he lived away from the premises and just hovered around the village.

He was polite without being friendly toward me. Other villagers soon became attuned to my presence, and my gropings with their dialect. True, the children often followed me in the streets and curtains quivered as I passed houses, yet when people saw me standing behind the counter of the store, and day by day fulfilling their orders, translated by Kirsti, I earned smiles and mundane comments about the weather.

180

"Have patience with Ragnvar," pleaded my wife. "He is narrow-minded. He has never been away from the island. But he can be warm and lighthearted. Try to understand him."

"Kirsti, I promise."

I always promised. I wanted to please her, but it was often difficult because my northern woman had bewildering periods of despondency that defied any placatory attempts of mine. She could be expressive, buoyant, and then there were whole days without her conversing with me.

However, I was not irretrievably entangled with problems of human relationship, not when there were the seasons and aspects of Bird Island with which to contend. Summer thrust itself upon us—nightless days, and still more birds. In the thousands they circled around the trawlers, clustered around men gutting fish, stole morsels and ran insolently along the waterfront. Constantly, with the rush of the ocean, came their piercing shrieks, combining in an impelling, stimulating rhythm.

Autumn came and the birds headed south, searching for daylight and warmth. Kirsti and I watched them winging overhead, and I mentioned casually, "Heading for the sun, like normal people should do." Kirsti appraised me severely and I had to convince her I was joking. The grass shriveled with the cold of the approaching winter and perpetual darkness.

Winter, with the weather reports and their monotonous pronouncements of snow, or ice, or gales, was combated by the villagers. This was an indoor time of fraternization, of card playing, singing to an accordion, swigging homemade brews, but never with Ragnvar present. His aloofness aggravated me. When I spoke, he mumbled an unintelligible reply. Yet I wasn't averse to enforced obstinacy. I'd met harder characters than Ragnvar. To hell with him, I decided.

However, Kirsti said, "I think about him a good deal. He should leave here, go to the mainland and mix with other people, go where there are girls to meet. Here, he is introverted and lonely."

I nodded, containing my opinions about his personality.

"He needs help," she went on, and then was reticent for a moment, holding something back. She looked away from me. "We must help. I think we should invite him to live here. After all, this is partly his home, where we grew up together."

It was a month before I agreed to this. Then I did so, believing he could help with certain jobs.

He came, dour and estranged, avoiding all work. Each day he brooded around the waterfront of Steinsvik. At home we treated each other with unflinching reserve and, diplomatically, never clashed to use the bathroom, or even to eat our meals together.

"I'm fed up with this," I told Kirsti. "It's gone on much too long."

"Yes," she acknowledged. "But I have discussed this with him. I think he's embarrassed, and perhaps you must share the blame. He cannot really understand everything you say in Norwegian. Your accent is not always good."

I was annoyed. "Embarrassed! Then don't accuse my imperfect speech. It's probably his pretty face. Tell him I'm not interested in looking at it!"

I had to duck my head. Kirsti had been holding a cup, and now it screamed past my ear. Her dialect rolled out, her eyes narrowed, her cheeks flushed. I had to grab her by the shoulders and shake her. "Take it easy!" I demanded. I pushed her down into a chair and held her tight until she calmed down.

"What is it, Kirsti?"

She shook her head, admonishing herself. "Don't speak like that again," she sobbed.

"I didn't expect it would affect you like this."

"But you don't understand," she said, covering her face with her hands.

I attempted to pacify her once more, but was pushed aside. Rebuffed, I grabbed my jacket from behind the door and went out.

Well, there were limited means of releasing emotions in this confined place, and for the moment my wife had spurned me. I didn't seek encouragement from a bottle, had no children, had no intriguing work or artistic interest to fling myself into. Instead, I walked. I wandered over the island, the wind pulling at my clothes, trying to get this situation into perspective. Okay. What was a worshipper of sun and sand doing in this unblessed mite of a land? Just there for the sake of his wife, existing from day to day? No, not at all. I knew the island's compensations: no traffic lights, no factory sirens, no rat-race. Sure, I liked it here. A sort of magnetic, northern romanticism clutched at my inner fantasy; it spilled out when I watched the great ocean sucking at the shore, tumbling over rocks, the birds eternally circling and screeching their dirge.

I had an affinity with Bird Island, even if it wasn't my dream of home, but a paradise with a balanced climate that also stabilized a person's mental attitude.

No children, though; last winter one of the fishermen, with eight children, had dug me in the ribs and laughingly emphasized that the long, dark nights had the benefit of increasing the population. Still, while knocking around the world, I had often sensed that someone, giving birth somewhere, was trying to recall my face—only that someone wasn't my beautiful Kirsti.

Returning to the house, I was determined to adapt myself to these circumstances, to befriend Ragnvar and, simultaneously, to right any psychological obstacle that was probably stopping my wife and myself from producing a child.

But excuses come easily. The house remained a tomb. Ragnvar moped about, conversing in monosyllables. Kirsti hindered my intentions; she even suggested we sleep in separate beds, making the trite excuse that it would enable her to stretch out and sleep properly. Conceding to her wish also dampened my own feelings.

That winter came early. Dark, cheerless, it lasted interminably. Like a sulky child, I watched the skies and felt a sudden gratification when they were blanketed by the myriads of birds that brought spring. I awaited them with a camera, sent across from the mainland. I had become an amateur bird watcher, and roved around the island with birds ducking and squawking around my head, begging for the pieces of bread I carried.

"Where are you going today?" Kirsti would ask as I packed my haversack with camera, films, and food.

"There's some skuas diving for fish in the eastern bays," I would say.

"Perhaps . . . perhaps Ragnvar could go with you?"

"Perhaps he could," I would reply, for the hundredth time. "Kirsti, he's welcome with me any time, but I would like him to show a little human exuberance and not hide when I approach. He's hardly out of the room now. It's a waste of time even offering to help him."

As usual, she would move to the window and gaze at the sea, locking in her thoughts.

That was the situation. My wife developed the grocery business, I snapped pictures of birds, and Ragnvar vegetated. Absurd! I decided the three of us would face each other and talk, sit down and communicate for the first time, thrash this frustrating affair into a state of common sense.

Moods, however, like the weather, changed swiftly on the island. I was astounded when, through the medium of Kirsti, Ragnvar offered to guide me to a nesting-place of terns. On the west coast of the island, facing the brunt of the ocean, jutted some foreboding pinnacles of rock. Ragnvar had once guided some British ornithologists there and he knew the area well.

"Go with him," Kirsti implored. "It is best for all of us. It is a chance to come close to him."

When a week of continual rain and mist cleared, we set out. Instead of clambering overland and wasting energy, we would circle the island by boat. "See you in a couple of days," I told Kirsti, by the jetty. She kissed me passionately. I stepped into the boat, started the outboard motor, turned to wave, but Kirsti had gone.

Ragnvar didn't speak as we slipped over the calm waters. He hunched in the stern, keeping his fishing line clear of the propeller. I ate sandwiches and scanned the island.

The boat glided into a natural haven. Ragnvar cut the motor and made a line fast to a rock. He pointed up a hill and, noncommittally, we began the ascent: two men clad in woolen caps, windbreakers and high leather boots. The sea swelled, the birds cried. I felt that this morbid scene needed human intervention and tried to speak to my companion, but he just grunted and kept his head angled toward the ground. Okay, I would reserve my breath for the climb.

We stood at the base of the lime-streaked rocks. They could be climbed without ropes or pitons, but we had to be careful. Ragnvar led the way, the bulky pack making his slight body top-heavy. He never looked back. I sweated and panted, but kept close to him. When he reached a platform facing a cave, I was immediately behind him.

"Here," he said.

Inside the cave I pumped the stove and made coffee. Ragnvar was fiddling around with his gear, searching deep in his haversack. His face was thoughtful. Then he held up a bottle of brandy, somewhat self-consciously, mentioning that it had been smuggled in from the mainland. My smile mirrored his; it was the first time we'd had any link of pleasantry together. We poured the alcohol into our coffee, warming our bodies.

"We have not had this opportunity before," he said. "There is no interference. We can talk," and he did talk, at first haltingly, then with ease. He said that, even though he had brought me to this place, he considered the birds a mere addition to our environment, and saw nothing novel in studying them. "Birds are a nuisance," he said. "I don't want to insult you, but I think your hobby is slightly comic."

"A year ago I would have thought like that, too," I admitted. "I suppose it's all part of getting to know one's surroundings."

"Yes," he said quietly. "You must do that."

I rose to my feet. "I'll get some photos while the light's still bright."

He said that he would just rest for a while, and leaving the cave, I reasoned that we'd have deeper subjects to discuss later.

I heard the cries of countless birds concentrated in one spot and edged forward on my stomach, holding the camera ready. Overhead sentries shrieked wildly, threatening to dive. With caution, I distributed food, then lay still for an hour, allowing the terns to condition themselves to this friendly invasion of their territory. I finished off a roll of film commenced earlier that day, and retreated to the cave.

Ragnvar wasn't in his sleeping bag, as I had believed, but was seated cross-legged, his back against a wall. In his cupped hands he held a tin mug, and before him lay the brandy flask.

"You asleep?" I asked.

He stirred, his head wobbled. "You talk about sleep!" he cried. He threw his head back and high-pitched laughter echoed in the cave. His face was hideous in the half-light.

I moved closer to him.

"You have been asleep since you came here," he said seriously.

"I'll excuse you for getting drunk and acting like a fool. But first I want an explanation," I demanded angrily.

His tone was scornful. "Haven't you noticed the relationship between Kirsti and me? Do you think it is just a feeling of kinship? I'm only her half brother—or hasn't she told you that? She came back here for me, and won't be satisfied until you are out of the way."

In this remote cave, with the sea crashing and the wind muttering outside, I was prepared for a settlement. Now! "Get up!" I demanded.

He stood shakily, asked, "Have you heard of the people of the mountains who tested their manhood in a way we can test ours now? They faced each other and were tied by the left hand. In their right they held a knife, and they slashed at each other until one man was left."

I backed away from his wide-eyed stare. "You're insane!"

He withdrew his knife. "We won't bother about tying ourselves together. Just take out your knife. The victor may not be in one complete piece, but he can return to Kirsti."

I had seen knife fights before, and I knew the best method of protection—run! But here, this was difficult. Crazed Ragnvar stood between me and the cave's entrance. Instinctively, I clasped the bone handle of my knife, flipped it from its pouch and flung it at Ragnvar. It clouted him on the head and sent him reeling against the wall. I raced into the open, momentarily safe—but weaponless.

He came after me, cursing. I ducked behind some rock outcrops and hid behind boulders, trying to avoid him. I picked up large stones, ready to crash one on his head, and tossed them in different directions, but he was not misled. Despite his frenzy, his feet were nimble. Watched by birds, we conducted this desperate stalking.

"Foreigner!" I heard him call. "Have no fear. You won't have to live with your scars. You won't have to sit by a mirror half the day and contemplate your defilement. Yours won't be a love-mark, a brand of joy and mental suffering, a stigma . . ."

I heard the voice, and I wanted to force elaboration from it, but there was no time. Glancing up, I saw that Ragnvar confronted me. He grinned, holding the knife in his outstretched hand, then switching it from one palm to the other. He knew how to handle it.

I tried to watch the knife, his eyes, his feet, and at the same time reach for a stone to hurl at him. Neither of us spoke. He came closer, making me back-pedal slowly, toward the screaming birds. Everything confused me—the grey skies, the cliffs, this man who was a potential murderer, the vision of Kirsti smiling wistfully, the sea, the birds.

The birds, the birds, beating, flapping, screeching, the sky black; a moving wall of red beaks, wings, claws, whirling close, pressing in— terrifying! Ragnvar glanced up as the terns skimmed his head, slashing with his knife and ripping a couple from the air. I flattened myself against the cliff face, somewhat safe from the convulsed motions, fearful of this inexplicable animal power. Protecting my face with my hands, I

186

peeked through, saw Ragnvar, hands high, being knocked off his feet. He yelled, a horrible, agonized plea for mercy, for understanding, then was on his hands and knees, attempting to crawl away. Covered in birds, pecking, scratching, fighting, he was a bird, a bleeding mat of feathers. He raked the ground with his knife, then lay flat as a huge black-crowned tern dug at the back of his head. He whimpered, rolled. The birds sang exultantly. Stones gave way under his body. He slithered, uttering a final sob—then vanished.

I faced the cliff, pawed it, belted it with my fists, demanding that reality return to this unbelievable scene. I turned. The air was cleared. Futilely I called, "Ragnvar! Ragnvar!" but could see only a litter of feathers, a few dead birds, shreds of clothing and blood. Approaching the edge of the precipice, I looked below, hundreds of feet below, at swirling, innocent sea.

In the cave, I lit the stove and made coffee and drank to quell my shivering. I stared at the empty bottle, Ragnvar's haversack. I talked to myself, repeating everything I could remember that he said in those last moments, analyzing his statements, accusations, his motivations, the outcome of these events. Outside, the sea's hiss had been replaced by an insistent thrumming. Heavy rain flooded down the rocks, removing traces of the slaughter.

I drank myself alert with coffee as that dreadful night passed, and I knew what I must do.

Before daylight broke, I moved down to the boat and slid away from Bird Island. I did not look back. Two hours later, landing on the mainland, I jammed Ragnvar's haversack under a thwart, loosened the bung, and pointed the boat seawards again.

Later that day, muffled in a woolen cap and scarf, I boarded the southbound coastal ferry and mingled with tourists, but the sea and the birds made me a recluse in my cabin. In Bergen, three days later, an old acquaintance of mine sold my camera, loaned me money, and procured a passport. I bought an airline ticket.

Each day I slave with a gang that repairs railroad tracks. At night, alone, I use the bottle to oppose the birds, yet the cry of a man tumbling over a cliff persists. Piteously he shrieks, "Kirsti!" and as the ocean eddies around me, I know that a woman stands by a window and waits for a boat—and one man—to return.

Daisies Deceive

by Nedra Tyre

The door to the library opened gently.

She looked up from the desk at which she was sitting. She had been turning through a portfolio of flower prints as if she were waiting for something. Now she realized what it was she had been waiting for.

It was death.

She watched her grandnephew cross the vast uncarpeted parquet floor.

"Aunt Amanda," he said, "I didn't know you were still here. I came down to get something to read in bed. I'm too tired to drop off to sleep."

He was lying. He had waited to come back down until his brothers had gone to bed and had fallen asleep. He had planned this very carefully.

"It's awfully stuffy in here, Aunt Amanda. Do you mind if I open a window?"

She didn't answer and he didn't wait for an answer. He opened one of the casement windows. Though the air wasn't cold, she shuddered; that wind was coming from her grave.

In all her long life she'd never before known fear. But she knew it now.

He was going to murder her and there was nothing she could do to stop him. If she called out no one would hear her; the servants had gone home hours ago. Lou Barnes, her half deaf companion, was asleep on the third floor. Her other grandnephews were in the guest wing. They were all asleep or he wouldn't have ventured back downstairs.

She kept leafing through the portfolio. Her alert old brain tried to latch onto hope. She was done for. But perhaps he might not get away

188

with her murder. She had a good friend in the Homicide Squad of the Police Department. She could trust his competence. She remembered having made a joke not many months ago by promising him she would leave a clue if she were ever murdered.

"Do you have anything good to suggest for me to read, Aunt Amanda?"

He went to the shelves. His strong hands played across a row of books. They reached for one. There was no pretense at making a real selection. He was the greedy one among her four grandnephews; she had always known that.

Hope flickered once more—not for her life, but for pointing toward her killer. She took one of the flower prints from the portfolio and set it on the desk. She placed a heavy paperweight on top of it. Then she closed the portfolio and put it on the edge of the desk. That was the last lucid action of her life before fear and terror overwhelmed her. Panic made her dart toward the door, but there was no escape from the reach of his arms or from the heavy poker he had grabbed up from the fireplace. Only a little way from the desk her life was struck from her.

The murderer wiped the poker and set it back in its place. There was nothing else to tidy up; the palatial house was quiet; he eased out of the library and mounted the imposing stairway. When he reached the second floor he made the various turnings to the guest wing in which his three brothers and he had their rooms. He wanted a bath, but it might wake someone and he must not call attention to being up and about. He undressed and put on his pajamas and got into bed. He wondered how long it would be before the estate could be settled. But he wasn't too concerned. Money would be welcome any time. He fell asleep at once.

Downstairs the wind from the open window grew strong, it swept across the frail dead woman on the floor and it fluttered the edges of the print of a daisy anchored down with a paperweight on the desk.

Lt. Williams of Homicide had never before worked on a case in which the victim was an intimate friend. He was heartsick over Amanda Hollace's murder. He had been very fond of her; she had been a cultivated woman and a charming one; and very generous. Of course with a fortune that size she could afford to be generous. Her wisdom showed in the manner in which she had provided for her grandnephews who were her only living relatives; she had made them liberal allowances, but she hadn't settled any money on them while they were young. She believed that a man must learn to make his own way; and she had been proud of her nephews' accomplishments. One was an account executive in an advertising agency; one was in law; the other two were investment bankers.

Williams had first met Amanda Hollace at the women's club when he had talked there on juvenile delinquency. She had liked his talk and had asked him to her house to continue the discussion. Ever since he'd been a frequent dinner guest. From the beginning they had liked each other very much and his affection for her had increased. He admired her quick wit and intelligence. She had a lively interest in crime. Murder especially piqued her. One night she'd said: "If I'm ever murdered, John, I'll leave a clue for you. I simply couldn't embarrass a dear friend in Homicide by being the victim of an insoluble crime." How her eyes had sparkled when she'd said that. What a joke it was. They had both laughed.

The trouble was that few victims ever had the time or the opportunity to leave a clue.

It was usually the murderer who betrayed himself through carelessness or haste. But Miss Hollace's murderer had been neither careless nor in a hurry. He had left no hints as to his identity. It had to be one of the grandnephews, Williams was positive of that. It couldn't be anyone else. The servants had long since gone home, clear across the city, when the murder had been committed. Miss Barnes, the companion, couldn't have killed Miss Hollace. She couldn't have. She felt too affectionately toward the elderly woman. So it had to be one of the nephews.

But they all acted grief-stricken. Each one as Williams talked with him recounted his love for his great-aunt, his gratitude for her unfailing generosity and understanding; their father's suicide had left them destitute; prep school and college and travel would have been beyond them if it hadn't been for their Aunt Amanda; she'd seen them through their efforts to get jobs, had written proper letters to proper persons; they were all doing very well indeed.

"I can't believe it," Stewart Allen said. "It's impossible to think that anyone could have hated Aunt Amanda enough to kill her. Her death must have been an accident. A thief must have been surprised by Aunt Amanda in the library."

"But nothing was taken, Mr. Allen."

"Good lord, after a man has committed murder he wouldn't have enough composure to rob a house."

"Some murderers have great composure. Now, then, tell me exactly what you did last night."

Afterward, Luther Allen's account didn't vary from Stewart's. They had said good night to their aunt about ten-thirty and had gone upstairs to bed. They were exhausted from their long trips for their annual visit to their aunt.

The other two brothers, Gowan Allen and Laurence Allen, might have been actors reading for the same part; their stories were identical to Stewart's and Luther's. They, too, had been very tired after their long journeys and had said good night early to their aunt and had gone to their rooms to bed.

One of the brothers had to be lying. But Williams could detect no lie. One of them had needed money and had decided it was time for Miss Hollace's riches to be divided in four equal parts, and he had murdered her, and this morning they had all waked up very wealthy men.

The Medical Examiner and the photographers and most of the Homicide Squad had been busy in Miss Hollace's library, so Williams had talked with the Allen brothers in an upstairs sitting room. Just as Williams' last interview had ended Sergeant Moore called up that they'd finished in the library, and Williams stood at the head of the broad stairway to watch Miss Hollace make her final exit from her mansion. Then he went down the stairs and entered the library.

He sauntered around the room and stopped at the desk. Miss Hollace must have been sitting there when her murderer had come in. At least she had been sitting there, according to her nephews, when they had left her to go to bed. The desk was bare except for a portfolio of some kind and a flower print weighed down. He moved the paperweight and picked up the print. It was a daisy; its botanical name was in italics—*chrysanthemum leucanthemum*. There was no reason for the print to have been removed from the portfolio. No reason at all. And it had been anchored down in the way a person would leave a note for someone to read.

191

This must be the clue that Miss Hollace had promised to leave for him. Somehow she had found a way to tell him who her murderer was.

He took the print over to an armchair and sat down. For a long time he looked at the daisy, wondering what it meant.

All he could think of was that a daisy would never tell.

What possible significance could the daisy have? Miss Hollace must have been looking at the portfolio when the murderer had entered.

The print had to have reference to someone who had been in the house the previous evening and was still there. Well, there were two bankers, a lawyer, and an advertising executive—no daisy among them. Then the daisy must refer to a family joke. Or perhaps one of the nephews was married to a woman named Daisy. Come to think of it, marguerite was also a name for a daisy. Maybe one of them was married to a woman named Marguerite. Or Margaret. And in that split second left to Miss Hollace the only clue she could point to was the murderer's wife instead of the murderer himself.

Once more Williams summoned the brothers. He felt he must be careful. He mustn't give away the fact of the print. He mustn't reveal too much.

He tried to be cagey as he talked again with the Allen men. As before, they were pleasant and cooperative, but nothing they said helped. None of them was a gardener. None of them cared for flowers. None of them knew a woman named Daisy, let alone was married to one, or to a Marguerite or Margaret.

Luther said: "Our mother was fond of flowers. But I remember she liked only flowers with fragrance. So she wouldn't have cared for daisies. I'm damned sorry, but that's all I know about flowers in relation to our family."

Stewart and Gowan and Laurence were equally damned sorry and equally uninformative.

Williams accepted all their answers. He had to. But he knew one of them was a murderer.

A clue had to be in the print. Miss Hollace had left a clue for him, he was positive. And he must be methodical in finding out what the print of the daisy meant. He needed help. Flowers had meanings and he intended to find out what they were—red roses for true love, and all that. There would be books at the Public Library with such information.

When he asked for help at the Reference Desk in the Public Library a young woman handed him a small book entitled *The Language of Flowers*. He thumbed through its pages eagerly. But the meanings assigned to daisies gave him no clue; they were innocuous, relating to innocence and farewell, with no hint at murder or death by violence.

He returned the book to the Reference Desk. "Young lady," he pleaded, "can you help me? Can you think of any reference—perhaps in poetry—to a daisy that might describe an evil person or an evil action?"

She thought for a moment, then shook her head. "Offhand I'm afraid I can't think of anything. Poets loved lilacs and violets, myrtle and daffodils and primroses, roses and columbine and hyacinths and tulips and lilies. I can't think of a single reference to a daisy. Can you give me a little time to work on it? I can look through some books and ask other members of the staff, and if there's no help here we can telephone the English Department at the University."

While she searched he sat and waited. He doodled. He filled scratch paper with sketches of daisies. He eavesdropped on her telephone calls. He was tempted to peer over her shoulder while she riffled through reference books.

After a while she came back with some poems that mentioned daisies. But none of them was of any use to him. None pointed in any way to Miss Hollace's murderer.

Someone came just then to the Reference Desk to take over from the librarian who had been trying to help him. As the young woman picked up her pocketbook to leave she told him how sorry she was not to have given him the information he needed.

He thanked her and sat back down at the table. He couldn't accept failure. But it seemed that he would have to.

He got up and left the Library. As he went through its revolving door he suddenly realized that he'd had no lunch. He wasn't hungry but he felt weak. He was disgruntled and disappointed and frustrated. Next door to the library he saw a small cafe; he entered it. It was just past the regular lunch hour and the place was empty; he could have his pick of tables or booths. He went toward the back and a young woman smiled up at him.

"I'm so sorry about the daisy," she said. It was the young librarian. "I feel like a doctor who hasn't been able to relieve a patient's pain when I can't help a patron. But please don't give up hope. Sometimes it takes us weeks—even months—to get the right information."

Weeks. Months. A murderer couldn't be allowed to run loose that long.

He asked if he might sit with her.

"If you like," she said. "Is it too nosey of me to ask what you wanted with the information about a daisy? If it's personal I'll keep it confidential, I promise."

"I suppose you know Miss Amanda Hollace was murdered last night."

"Yes, I know. It's awful. She was such a generous person. She donated the children's wing of the library and the gallery."

"I'm working on her murder."

"You mean you're a policeman? You don't look like one."

"I don't know whether to take that as a compliment or not. Anyhow, I don't feel like a policeman at the moment."

He told her then about finding the print of the daisy.

"And you think the print points to a particular person? Who could it be?"

"A policeman can't discuss suspects."

"But you're looking for help. After all, there must be certain persons you're suspicious of?"

"I'll tell you in the strictest confidence I think it must be one of the four heirs—the Allen brothers—Stewart, Luther, Gowan, or Laurence."

The librarian had raised her coffee cup to her lips; she set it down without taking a sip. "Then the answer's simple. But, after all, you'll have a case to prove, won't you, and I'm sure that's never simple. But gowan's what a daisy's called in Scotland and northern England, so Gowan Allen must be—"

Lt. Williams didn't let her finish. He smiled at her. He leaped up from the booth and thanked her. He liked intelligent women and he liked them pretty. He would pay proper homage to this girl's intelligence and prettiness as soon as he had time. Right now, though, he was on his way to pluck a daisy, a daisy of a grandnephew, otherwise known as Gowan.

Dead Duck

by Lawrence Treat

The squad car stopped in front of the Brooklyn precinct-house and Perinsky, the big, reckless-looking detective, got out first, then Burson, the man he was bringing in. They went up the steps together.

Burson felt his stomach muscles twitch, contract. He sniffed at the air. He was a dark, slender young man, high-nosed, with serious, grey-green eyes. His mouth quivered slightly, and he compressed his lips. You weren't there, he told himself. Remember that, and stick to it. They can't prove otherwise. Even if the pair on the stoop speak up, they only saw you briefly; they can't be sure.

Burson was aware that the next half hour would be crucial. Convince them he hadn't seen Karen in almost a year, and he was safe. But one misstep, and he was a dead duck.

It had been only twenty minutes since Perinsky walked into Burson's commercial-art studio and identified himself.

"Mr. Clyde Burson?" he had said. He kept slapping his teeth down on a wad of gum, as if he had to use up some of his surplus energy. "We'd like to talk to you, over in Brooklyn."

"What about?"

"You know your wife's dead, don't you?"

Burson's head lifted with a jerk. "Karen—dead? What happened to her?"

"You tell us."

But Burson had read enough books to be familiar with the way the police worked. They took the offensive; they acted as if they knew everything; they tried to throw you off balance and make you slip up. So Perinsky's approach and his refusal to give out information during the ride to Brooklyn was orthodox procedure. No worry on that account. In fact, Burson derived a kind of strength from the detective's ample self-confidence and felt, illogically, that Perinsky was on his side.

Perinsky's hand touched Burson's arm now, protectively, and steered him towards a door. "This way, Buster," Perinsky said amiably. He knocked and entered a cheerless room of cracked walls, hardwood chairs and metal filing cabinets. "Lieutenant," he said. "Here's Clyde Burson."

Burson stiffened at the sight of the stocky, sandy-haired man seated at the desk. To Burson, the blue eyes looked cold and mean, the mouth a thin, ominous slash.

"Sit down, Mr. Burson," the police officer said. To Burson's astonishment, the voice was pleasant, soothing, almost gentle. "I'm Lieutenant Malliner. You know why you're here, don't you?"

Burson sat down uneasily. "Not exactly," he said, picking his words carefully. "Mr. Perinsky said Karen, my wife—she's dead."

"When was the last time you saw her?" Malliner asked.

"Close to a year ago, I guess."

"What did you bust up about?"

"We didn't get along, and so we parted by mutual agreement. Perfectly friendly."

"Expecting to get a divorce?"

Burson nodded. "We were negotiating."

That much was true. And on record, although it didn't hint at Karen's vindictiveness and her obstinate, spiteful refusal. He thought of the hysteria with which she'd screamed out, "Never, never, never! You'll have to kill me first!"

Malliner said bitingly, "You forgot to ask how she died."

"I didn't get the chance. Tell me, please."

Malliner handed Burson a sheet of blank paper. "Would you write your name on this?"

Burson took it, frowned. "Oh. I guess you want my fingerprints."

"That's right," Malliner said crisply. "And we got them." He snatched the paper and gave it to Perinsky. "Okay, Lou."

Burson cleared his throat. He shouldn't have said that. It marked him as a wise guy, prepared to withhold, deny, evade. Regretfully, he watched Perinsky walk past him. The door closed with an echoless bang, and Malliner rubbed his hands together.

"Where were you yesterday afternoon?" he asked.

"I went to a movie at Radio City. I had to wait on line quite awhile."

"What time were you there?"

"Well, from three to six, at least."

"Then how come two people saw you go into Mrs. Burson's house in Brooklyn at five o'clock, and come out at five-thirty?"

Burson betrayed no emotion. "They were mistaken," he said flatly.

"When you came out, you were upset. You stumbled on the steps and almost fell. They thought you were drunk."

The red-headed guy, Burson told himself, and the woman who looked like a janitress. She'd probably discovered the body and notified the police, but in any case she must have been on the premises this morning and have been questioned immediately. As for the identification of Burson, it could have been made from the dozens of pictures of him in Karen's album.

"Well?" said Malliner. "Did you expect to get away with your movie story? We run into that one every day in the week. No trouble cracking it."

Burson's hands balled up into fists. He lowered them and dug the knuckles against his thighs. "Lieutenant," he said. "What happened to Karen?"

"Homicide," Malliner said, staring intently. "She was stabbed, with a kitchen knife."

"Oh." Burson licked his lips. A green-handled kitchen knife, imbedded deep in her chest. She'd fallen near the window, and her eyes had been wide and staring. Her dress had been rumpled and he'd smoothed it down and tucked it under her legs.

"Got a girl friend?" Malliner asked.

Elise, small and soft and dreamy, and willing to go to the ends of the earth with him. "Clyde," she'd whispered, "if only we were free to be together, for always. We could be so happy."

Burson wiped the sweat from his forehead. "I don't want to bring anyone else into this."

"Who is she?" Malliner demanded. "Do you think we're so dumb we can't locate her?"

Burson shook his head. They wouldn't have to look for her. She'd come running to him as soon as she found out where he was.

"Elise Vandyke," he said in a low voice. "295 East 73rd."

Malliner jotted down the address, pressed a button, handed the paper to a uniformed cop who had come in, and whispered something. The cop went out. Perinsky strode in and gave Malliner a note. The lieutenant read it, crumpled it up.

"Still claim you weren't there?" he asked Burson. "And that you hadn't seen her in a year?"

Burson nodded. "Of course."

"Then how did your fingerprints get on her bureau?"

"Her bureau?" said Burson. He'd wiped his prints; he'd been careful about that. Had he missed up on the bureau, or was Malliner trying to put something over on him?

"You think I'm bluffing, don't you?" Malliner said. "Well, I'm going to give you a little advice. You sit down with yourself and come out of your dream world. Would I risk bluffing about fingerprints and get a confession based on fraud, so I can get blasted in court and maybe lose my job? You're an intelligent man, and you got sense enough to see I'm laying it on the line."

"But I didn't kill Karen. I couldn't kill anybody."

Malliner shot forward and hammered out his words like the thuds of a battering ram. "You don't have a chance," he roared. "I'll find out everything you did. I'll know every damn thought you had in your head. I'll lay you wide open, Burson. Because I hate killers."

Then he eased up. And after a moment or two, he forced a grin, baring his strong, even teeth.

"She told everybody," he said, "that she'd never give you a divorce. So there's your motive. I wish every case was as easy as this one. That's all for now."

Perinsky tapped Burson on the shoulder and led him out of the room.

"Look, Buster," the big detective said, as they went down the corridor, "get wise to yourself. Your best bet is to admit it, because you can't buck the Lieutenant. Not you."

Burson shook his head. "Find out who really killed her," he said in a tight voice. "You have the wrong man."

Perinsky shrugged and led him to a side room. There, under the jaundiced eye of a bored-looking cop, Burson sat down dejectedly.

Was he being smart? It had taken Malliner just about ten minutes to accuse him of murder. And while he waited here, twenty cops, or maybe fifty or a hundred of them, were piling up the evidence. Detectives knocking on doors and showing his picture and saying, "Know him? Then tell us—"

Tell us about the scraps he used to have with his wife, before he left her. Tell us how she created scenes, stirring him up to an anger he could hardly control. Tell us how she used to shriek at him, "You hate me! You want to get rid of me! You want to kill me!" Until finally, in rage and exasperation, he'd almost agree.

Tell us how he and Elise yearned for each other and could do nothing about it, and how he'd made the appointment with Karen for yesterday afternoon. "Don't worry, darling," he'd said to Elise. "I won't be soft this time. By Sunday night, we can plan on getting married. I promise it."

Would they get that statement out of Elise? Would they?

He thought of lab men with cameras and microscopes, analyzing the evidence in Karen's apartment and tracing his actions step by step. They'd recreate his frantic search of her desk. He'd pulled out every paper and ransacked every drawer. How could he explain that?

He held his face in his hands and groaned. Knowing Karen, he was certain she'd had a lover, and must have whipped him into a frenzy and screamed at him the same way she used to scream at her husband. "Kill me—that's what you want—go ahead and do it!"

Sure. Tell that to Malliner, and the lieutenant would have one more link in his chain of evidence. Admit she'd answered her bell when he had rung it, and it would prove she'd been alive when he got there. Every word of truth that he could utter would merely bolster the case against him. Malliner had his fall guy; he had Clyde Burson.

At three P.M., Perinsky brought Burson back to the lieutenant's office. A couple of other men sat at the far side of the room, but they didn't count. This was between Malliner and Burson, and it was personal.

"Well?" Malliner began. "Ready to talk?"

"If you'd investigate," Burson said shakily, "instead of trying to railroad me, you'd find out who did it."

"I've investigated," Malliner said drily. "You had an appointment with your wife yesterday afternoon. You'd decided to get tough with her, and so you stopped at the corner bar for a couple of quick ones. You were drunk, Burson. Even the bartender noticed."

A double scotch, Burson told himself. But he hadn't been drunk.

Merely upset, trying to steel himself for the ordeal.

"At five P.M., you went up the steps to her house. The janitress, Mrs. Kurtz, and a tenant named Rayburn saw you go into the vestibule and lean down to ring her bell."

That was right. Still blinking from the sunlight, he had bent down to examine the name-plates. You had to ring the apartment you wanted, so that they could press the buzzer that released the lock of the downstairs door.

"She answered your ring," Malliner said, "and you went up and stayed for a half hour. You had a violent argument, and you stabbed her with a kitchen knife. Then you went through her desk. You grabbed every paper and every letter. What were you looking for?"

"Nothing," Burson said. "I wasn't there."

"You came out at five-thirty, looking sick. Green in the face, is the way Rayburn described you."

And why not? Burson thought. When you find the body of your estranged wife—she's just been killed and you realize the jam you're in —who wouldn't look green?

"At quarter of six," Malliner said evenly, "you called Miss Vandyke and canceled your evening date. You told her you hadn't seen your wife, that you just couldn't face her. But you lied, Burson."

Sure I lied, Burson thought. I wasn't going to drag Elise into it; I didn't want to make her part of the horror. But I failed there, too.

"Why don't you try to find out who saw Karen yesterday?" Burson demanded jerkily. "Why pick on me? There were other people in the building. What about them?"

"Ten apartments," Malliner said. Five of them empty, tenants were in the country for the weekend and can prove it. Then there's a little old lady about eighty-five years old, who hardly has the strength to lift a knife. Two couples were home, with company, and we checked them out. Then there's the girl on the second floor, her boy friend was with her and they were looking at television, and finally there's this guy Rayburn, who saw you."

"Rayburn," Burson exclaimed. "What about him? What's *he* like? How do you know *he* didn't kill her?"

"Because he was on the stoop talking to the janitress, and the pair of them saw you go in. Look, Burson, we know our business, we been at it a long time. We looked at every possibility and there's only one answer. You."

"But I wasn't there."

"Your fingerprints were."

It went on like that for hours, while Malliner demolished him piece by piece. Fingerprints, with blown-up photographs that he couldn't argue himself out of. Traces of blood on the shoes he'd worn yesterday. Threads from his jacket caught on the splintered edge of Karen's desk. Proof, crushing and overwhelming.

Malliner hammered at him; Perinsky pleaded with him; the others took turns sniping at him. But it always came back to Malliner, who went at Burson with the single-minded malice of a deep grudge. No reason for it. Just two men who'd disliked each other on first sight.

Burson fought them off and shook his head haggardly, but gradually the hope and the will drained out of him. His mind would go blank, and he'd glance at Perinsky, who'd nod encouragement.

"Go ahead, Buster. We know you were there, so why not admit it?"

Why not? What difference could it make? Then they'd let up; they'd stop badgering him; he could rest. And he was tired, tired. He couldn't hold out against the weight of facts. Why kid himself? He wasn't even a good liar; he believed in truth and justice and the good will of men. And where was he getting, this way?

He rubbed his forehead and leaned back. He tried to speak, but his voice choked up and his words stuck. His hands trembled and his stomach rumbled and he had trouble breathing.

"I was there," he sobbed out. Strangely, he felt relief, almost a sense of peace. The problem was out of his hands now. He'd done his best, and he'd lost.

"I did go there," he said, "to her apartment. And I found her lying on the floor. Dead. It must have happened just a little while before I got there. I picked up the phone and I was going to call the police and then I was afraid you'd accuse me. It looked bad, and so I put the phone down and I began looking around. I lost my head. I can hardly remember what I did. After awhile I realized I was acting like a fool, so I wiped off some prints and then I went downstairs and took the subway home."

"Who let you into her apartment?" Malliner asked crisply.

"Nobody. The door was unlocked. She was always careless that way; she'd unlatch the door and then forget about it."

201

"Did you lock it when you left?"

"No. I just went out."

"It was locked in the morning, when Mrs. Kurtz found her."

"Then somebody locked it," Burson said.

"How did you get into the building?"

"I rang her bell."

"If she was dead," said Malliner, "how could she let you in?"

"That's just it," Burson said excitedly. "That's what I've been racking my brains about. The killer must have been there when I rang. Somebody who knew I was coming and counted on it."

"Meet anybody on the stairs?"

"No. He must have escaped. Through the skylight to the roof, or else down the fire escape."

"The fire escape had wet paint, and nobody went down it. And the ladder to the skylight was jammed. It had dust on it that hadn't been touched in weeks."

"Then where did he go?"

"Yeah," Malliner said. "Where did he?"

"There was somebody," Burson said slowly. "There had to be."

Malliner leaned forward and said slyly, as if he hoped Burson would fall into some kind of a trap, "Maybe you rang the wrong bell, huh?"

Burson lifted his head. "Lieutenant, I'm telling you the truth, every word of it. I could say sure, I rang the wrong bell, but I didn't. I examined the name plates and I rang hers, and I remember it because she was still using one of my visiting cards and she'd written *Mrs.* in front of my name, in red ink."

"That's right," Malliner said. He smiled broadly, and Burson sucked in his lips. He'd been tricked. He'd had his chance and flubbed it.

Malliner stood up. "Lou," he said to Perinsky, "let's take a trip over to Mrs. Burson's place and he can show us exactly what he did. Including where he got the knife from, and how he killed her." Malliner grinned. "This is going to look good, Lou. We'll have it all wrapped up before Homicide or the big brass know what we're doing."

They went out a side entrance. Burson sat in back between Perinsky and the lieutenant. A pair of detectives got in the front, and the car rolled out to the street, turned, and sped west.

"I know what must have happened," Burson said. "The killer knew I was coming, so he waited for me to ring and then he pushed the buzzer and hid while I came upstairs."

"You show me where he hid," the lieutenant said. "No closets, no bathrooms, no nothing."

"Then he went into another apartment," Burson said hoarsely. "Rayburn lives there, he must have killed her."

"He was out on the street when you rang, and he's got *you* to prove it."

Burson sank back. He had the growing conviction that Rayburn had killed her, that Karen had driven him to it in one of her hysterical outbursts. But how show it? There was no breaking through the circle of evidence. Either Burson's mind was too weary, or else there were no weak spots. He wondered for a moment whether he really could have killed her.

"No," he said in a loud, stubborn voice.

Perinsky's big, warm hand patted Burson's knee. "Take it easy," the big detective said. "You got a long ways to go."

Only a few people noticed them as they stepped out of the car. Burson and Perinsky led the procession, with Malliner a step behind and then the pair of detectives. Perinsky loomed over Burson as he opened the glass door of the vestibule and Burson stepped inside. He continued to hold the door open for the others.

"The sun was shining," Burson said, "and I waited here a few seconds. I had trouble adjusting my eyes. Then I recognized my visiting card and I pressed the button. Like this." He bent down and pushed the second bell from the end.

Malliner said, "What are you trying to pull? That's not her bell. That's Mrs. Henshaw's, the old lady's."

"It's the one I rang," Burson said.

"You told us you recognized your own visiting card, with *Mrs.* written in red. Remember?"

"Yes, but—"

"Well, look at it."

Burson glanced down and saw his mistake. Then a buzzer sounded, and he turned and pushed the door. An idea began to form hazily, but he couldn't think straight.

"Show us where a guy could have hid," Malliner said.

Burson scanned the corridor. No closets on this floor. And undoubtedly none anywhere, else Malliner wouldn't have been so sure. And yet—

Burson's legs were weak; he felt out of breath before he was halfway up the first flight. The staircase was narrow and he seemed to be dragging Perinsky, who held Burson's arm and was squeezed between him and the wall.

Burson said, frowning, "You want me to do exactly what I did on Sunday, don't you?"

"Yes."

He mounted uncertainly. No closets on the second floor, no possible hiding place here. Merely two doors to two apartments, and a brass knocker on each. He turned, started up the next flight. The detectives, alert, ready to jump him if he tried to break free, hemmed him in. He could hear voices talking from somewhere above.

"Somebody's up there," he said.

Malliner answered. "Sounds like Inspector O'Shea's voice," he said. "He's going to see us wrap it up, huh, Lou?"

Perinsky grunted, and Burson began the ascent of the next flight. At the third floor landing, he stopped.

"I misread her apartment number," he said. "I thought it was 3A instead of 5A." With Perinsky watching him alertly, Burson marched to the rear door. He rapped sharply with the knocker. "I went in here, and she told me where I could find Karen's apartment."

Malliner started to object, and then the door opened and a small, white-haired old lady smiled up at him.

"I rang your bell," Burson said, hoping she'd recognize him.

"Oh, did you? What do you want?"

"Remember last Sunday?"

"Of course I do." Her eyes beamed happily. "It was such a beautiful day."

"Remember me? I was looking for Mrs. Burson."

She frowned. "Mrs. Burson? Why, she's the one that—" The little old lady's lips quivered, and she backed away in fright.

Malliner said to her, "Ever see this man before?"

She shook her head. "No. Should I know you, young man?" She hovered expectantly. When nobody answered her, she withdrew shyly and closed her door.

Malliner swung Burson around. "Come on," he said. "Whatever you were trying to pull, it didn't work."

204

"She's mixed up," Burson said. "Don't you see that she's half senile and can't remember anything?"

"She said she'd never seen you before, didn't she? And that means she didn't see you Sunday."

Burson felt himself droop. He'd almost broken through the circle, but it was closed again, tighter than ever. And his idea was still vague, amorphous. Suppose the old lady had recognized him, then what? Then—nothing.

When Burson reached the fourth floor, he had to slow up and lean against the bannister. He was all in; he didn't want to go any further. He listened to the voices upstairs. They were louder now, and yet blurred, as if they came from Karen's apartment.

"Did you wait here?" Malliner said. And when Burson made no reply, Malliner added gruffly, "Come on, get going. The sooner you show us, the sooner you'll get this over with."

Burson didn't move. Malliner seized Burson's arm and gave it a sharp wrench. The pain, like a sharp slap, cleared Burson's mind. Almost immediately, it went blank again. He trudged forward on heavy, dragging feet. On the fourth floor, he saw a name on the front apartment. Richard Rayburn.

Burson glanced up at Perinsky. The big detective eyed him queerly, as if sensing Burson's inner excitement, and then dropped an admonishing hand on Burson's shoulder. Burson felt a solid, healthy strength flow through him. Something in his mind seemed to bump down, then lift and leave a strange, lucid clarity. He said in a loud voice, "I know—I know—I have it!"

Perinsky muttered under his breath and Malliner began swearing, and Burson yelled out in a high, piercing voice that drowned out both of them.

"Rayburn!" he shouted. "It had to be somebody in the building. Rayburn—he switched the name plates downstairs, Karen's and the little old lady's. I rang the old lady's bell on Sunday, 3A, the second from the end, and *she* answered. But I didn't make a mistake, because yesterday, Sunday, Karen's name was second from the end."

Burson heard someone coming down the stairs and he saw the shape of the inspector who was listening intently. Burson went on in the same shrill, excited voice. "Don't you see? Rayburn killed her before I came, and later on that night he put the name-plates back the way

205

they belonged, and so the proof is right there, waiting. Rayburn's fingerprints are on the back of the two name cards. On the backs—"

Rayburn's door shot open and a burly, red-headed man charged out and made a wild dash for the staircase leading down. The two detectives grabbed him and held him fast. He yelled, "Let me go, let me go!" But his eyes, lost and scared, betrayed him.

The inspector snapped out, "Malliner, what the hell were you trying to pull?"

Burson let out a loud guffaw, then he relaxed and sighed deeply. "Thanks for your help," he said. "Buster." And he smiled.

He'd see Elise this evening. Their troubles were over.

Vengeance on the Subway

by Patrick O'Keeffe

Whenever I read that someone was killed by an oncoming train in a New York subway station and the death is reported as either accident or suicide, I always wonder whether it wasn't something else.

My mind will invariably go back to the *Orinoco,* on which I was the young bosun on her last and fatal voyage. She sailed from Philadelphia, with general cargo for Caribbean ports, under Costa Rican registry, but was American owned and operated and paying close to the American scale. I was not long out of the Marine Hospital after two months with an ulcerated leg, caused when I got foul of a wire hawser, and I was broke, so I took the first job to come up, regardless of flag.

The first assistant engineer, Polanski, was a sadistic brute from the Pittsburgh steel area. The only good thing said about him was that he knew marine engines from cylinder tops to tail-end shaft, perhaps the only reason the chief engineer carried him. There was no taking it easy below for the gang on that ship. During his watch, and sometimes when off watch, Polanski prowled in and out of the engine room and fire room and along the shaft alley, just to be mean. He worked the day men like coolies. He made life miserable for his little Greek wiper, keeping him busy every minute of the watch and giving him the slushiest bilge-cleaning jobs. Everyone expected that some day the little wiper would drop a heavy wrench from a grating onto Polanski's head.

One or two of the gang muttered about getting even with Polanski ashore up some dark alley, but they didn't get a chance. He never stepped off the ship. He was too tight-fisted. He'd brought a bundle of true-crime magazines to sea with him, bought in some secondhand store, you can guess, and all he did in his time off was lie in his bunk, reading them. Anything he ran out of, like razor blades and shaving

207

soap, he'd get someone to bring back from shore and then forget to pay him. More than one man said Polanski was going to get what was coming to him someday, and hoped to be around to see it.

In Barranquilla we signed on a new engineers' mess man. We'd called there to load a few thousand bags of coffee, and an hour or so before we were due to sail, the engineers' mess man was rushed to a hospital with a kidney stone. The captain came back from the agent's with word that no replacement was available, and he had a beachcomber in tow.

I was having a word with the chief engineer by the gangway at the time, while watching my deck gang topping up number three derricks. The captain told the chief that the beachcomber claimed he'd sailed as mess man, and if the chief wanted to take him on, then to bring him along to the bridge to sign the articles.

The chief looked the beachcomber over. I didn't like the looks of him. He was rigged out in dirty whites, broken shoes, and grass hat, almost black from sunburn, and looked as though he hadn't shaved or eaten for a month.

"Any discharges?" the chief asked him.

"No papers, Chief," the beachcomber replied. He said he'd been mess man on a ship out of Liverpool, and had been given knockout drops and rolled in a *cantina*. When he came to in an alley, his ship had sailed, with his belongings and papers. He'd been bumming around the waterfront ever since, hoping to get another ship.

The chief, who ate in the salon with the captain, hadn't much choice but to swallow the yarn if his assistant engineers were to have a mess man for the remaining eight days or so of the voyage. The beachcomber gave his name as Evans, and spoke with a Welsh accent. The chief was Welsh, so that's probably why he took him on.

The assistant engineers learned at their next meal that the new mess man was a complete dud. He couldn't get an order right, or remember more than half an order at a time. When he made up the engineers' cabins during the forenoon, the bunks looked as though a gale-force wind had swept over them.

The juniors did little more than grumble, but Polanski flew into a rage at every meal. He'd make the mess man go back to the galley with each wrong order. Each day the man made up his bunk, Polanski would tell him to do it all over again, and if he had him below for five

208

minutes, he'd make him sorry he ever picked the *Orinoco* for a free ride to the States.

The mess man sometimes looked pretty grim, and seemed to be working up a slow burn. He had rigged himself out in khakis and cleaned himself up, so he looked better to me than at first. He was going bald in front, and with a black scrub mustache, he had a professional appearance about him. From his manner and speech, we figured he was someone who'd come down in the world. When asking the chief engineer for the job, he had spoken more like the average seafarer, to give the chief the right impression, of course. If anyone tried to get a line on him, he'd say it was none of his business what he'd been.

It wasn't until the night he hit the bottle that he let out anything about his past. He had come aboard broke, but one of the sailors sprang him to a fifth on the strength of his payoff at the end of the voyage. It looked as though Polanski was finally getting him down.

That liquor was local stuff—like firewater—and the new mess man was well away after a few snorters. He came staggering out of the glory hole into the crew mess room with a glass and the bottle, and banged them down on the nearest table.

"Come on, lads," he shouted. "Drink to a rising young surgeon."

A couple of the gang playing cards at another table laughed and said, "Hi, Sawbones!"

The mess man turned to them, swaying drunkenly. "That's what they called me—a rising young surgeon. Now what do you see? I'll tell you what you see—a flunky for that hounding swine of a first assistant. Damn his black sadistic soul!"

A wild look came into his face and suddenly he grabbed up the bottle and brought it smashing down on a sugar bowl as if it might have been Polanski's head, and then he fell across a chair.

The little Greek wiper helped me carry him back to the glory hole, while others cleaned up the liquor and broken glass. The mess man passed out, mumbling that a man who made life hell for others should himself be sent straight to hell.

The wiper said to me in his broken English, "I say same t'ing. He make life for me all time hell. Someday, he go too far, mebbe."

No one sprang the new man to another bottle after that. It was around the ship the next day that he was a doctor, and we started calling him "Doc," and "Sawbones." He didn't like it. He apologized for smashing the bottle in the mess room, and said it was only the liquor that had been talking. He said he'd sailed as a sickbay steward in a hospital ship, and it gave him big ideas when he'd had a drink or two.

One man who wouldn't let him forget he'd claimed to be a doctor was Polanski. The new mess man was improving at serving meals, giving Polanski less cause to fly into a fury, so the first assistant took to calling him "Doc" every time he spoke to him, and it seemed to have a maddening effect on the mess man.

We had clear summer weather all the way northbound until near Hatteras, and then we ran into dense fog about midnight. Toward seven-thirty the next morning, with ship fog whistles sounding from all directions, there was a terrific crash. I was sent flying across the fore well deck. A big Swedish freighter had stuck her nose into our starboard side. Her engines were going full astern when she hit; otherwise, she'd have sliced us in two. She backed away into the fog.

The chief mate yelled down from the bridge to the carpenter to take soundings, then ran down the ladder and aft along the boat deck to look at the damage. I made for the nearest ladder to the boat deck and followed him.

We could see there was no need to take soundings. Water was pouring into the engine room and the after hold. The Swede had cut into us by several feet. She had hit abreast the engine room bulkhead, gashing the hull from the upper deck right down below the waterline.

All hands were running up from below. The captain ordered the ship abandoned. The *Orinoco* was only a three-compartment ship, and with two of them filling, she wouldn't stay afloat long. The sea was smooth, and the Swede was stopped and blowing nearby; we knew we'd soon be picked up.

The first boat load, with the chief and second mates and the chief engineer, got off without any delay. The third mate, after having made a quick round of living quarters to make sure no one was being left behind, was checking the rest of us into number three lifeboat, which was alongside the engine-room skylight. All of a sudden we heard someone shouting for help. The voice was coming up through the skylight, wide open in that summer weather.

"It's my wiper," said Polanski, and he charged aft to the well-deck ladder and down to the alleyway leading to the engine-room door.

He was back almost within seconds. "He's trapped on the top grating. His leg's caught. He's over by the bulkhead. It would take a cutting torch to get him free."

There wasn't time for that. We could feel the ship settling by the stern and listing. Those of us not yet in the lifeboat looked at the captain. He was a gray-haired Norwegian of long experience, but had never been faced with anything like this before. The little Greek was now calling piteously to Polanski not to leave him. It was awful to hear him.

"I don't know what he was doing over by the bulkhead," said Polanski angrily. "I sent him up to call the watch just before we got hit."

"No chance of jacking him loose?" the captain asked.

"Not a hope of doing it in time. We'll just have to leave him."

"We could cut his leg off," said the captain.

That made me shudder, yet it was that, against leaving the little wiper to drown.

"Okay, if you want to let him bleed to death instead of drown," said Polanski callously.

One of the men not yet in the boat was Doc. He moved up to the captain, and said, "Sir, it's true I'm a doctor. I'll perform an amputation, if there's no alternative and there's time. How much would you say there is?"

The captain turned to him as to a godsend. "Anything from fifteen to thirty minutes. Maybe less."

"I'll need all the surgical supplies from the medicine chest. And a volunteer or two."

There were more volunteers than needed.

Polanski held back, said, "If you guys want to drown with that little runt, okay. He wouldn't have got trapped if he'd come straight up to call the watch. He was probably looking for a place to hide stuff from the customs. I'm sticking by the boat, ready to pull clear the minute the ship starts to go under."

He looked around for support. A few men murmured in agreement, but the rest of us ignored him. I ran along with the captain to his cabin for the medicine chest. Doc told the captain to give the wiper a shot of morphine. The second assistant engineer and the third mate started for the engine room.

"Get him calmed down," Doc said to them, "and just say we'll soon have him loose." He then headed for the galley.

By the time the captain and I reached the engine room, the wiper was pretty well calmed down. He was lying on the grating, moaning with pain. He was badly frightened, as who wouldn't be, with one leg fast and the sight of the water beneath him almost up to the middle grating?

While the captain was getting the morphine out, he told the little Greek that the mess man was a real doctor and was coming down to get his leg loose so it wouldn't hurt. The dynamos had stopped, but plenty of daylight was coming through the skylight, and the second assistant had grabbed up a flashlight from his cabin on the way down.

The little wiper told us in broken English that when going up to call the watch, he had stopped on the top grating to look at a motor which sounded as though it were having brush trouble. As he was bending over it, the Swede crashed in and he was knocked flat. His head hit hard against the grating bars. When he came to, he found his leg was caught.

We could see why. One of the bulkhead steel plates had curled in on the wiper's right shin, like the jaw of a trap. The buckled grating was a tangle of metal around it, forming the other jaw.

Doc came hurrying down with a cloth-wrapped bundle. He opened it beside the medicine chest, out of sight of the trapped man. It contained a galley knife and a meat saw.

Doc went to work fast. We still had our cumbersome life jackets on, but he threw his off. With the medicine-chest scissors, he cut the dungarees away from the wiper's leg and swabbed it with alcohol. There were few surgical supplies in that old freighter's medicine chest, barely enough for the emergency—tourniquet, forceps, procaine, sutures, dressings.

As Doc injected the procaine local anesthetic, he told the wiper it was more pain killer, and he wouldn't feel a thing when he began to work his leg loose. On Doc's instructions, I bathed the wiper's forehead with an alcohol-soaked wad, to keep his head down so that he couldn't see what Doc was doing.

Doc was as cool as though he were in an operating room ashore. I was far from being cool, feeling I should be bathing my forehead too. The sea was rushing in through that big hole nearby, and I tried to

212

stop looking at the rising water below. I kept glancing toward the few steps leading to the engine-room doorway and safety beyond, and I noticed the others doing it, too, making sure just where it was in case we had to make a sudden dash for it.

Doc did a swift job with knife and saw. The anesthetic was either weak or wearing off toward the end, and the little Greek began to scream. We had to hold him down. By the time Doc had finished, the wiper had passed out again.

He was lifted onto my back and I carried him all the way up to the boat, with Doc right behind me, keeping an eye on the bandaged stump.

Polanski had already ordered the boat lowered, and he was sitting by the tiller, ready to give the word to cast off.

"I wasn't going to wait much longer," he bawled.

We lowered the little wiper quickly but gently into the boat and soon were being pulled toward the sound of the Swede's siren. We had got away barely in time. We heard the racket through the fog as the *Orinoco* upended and sank.

The Swede began creeping through the fog, northbound for New York. Her bows had been stove in, but she was in no danger. She was a new motor ship with a well-stocked hospital, and Doc made full use of it looking after the wiper. He wanted him kept quiet—no visitors— but he did let those of us who had helped with the amputation drop in for a moment to say hello to the little Greek. He was taking the loss of half his leg in good spirit. He grinned up at me from the cot.

"Mebbe I be like old-time pirate wi' peg leg."

"No peg legs these days," I told him. "You'll get an artificial one and you'll like it better, because it won't grow corns."

He grinned at that. Then he looked over at Doc, who was preparing a dressing at a table. "I lucky Doc on ship. Cap'n he say Polanski tell him best t'ing do leave me go down wi' ship. Doc save me. I no forget."

Polanski didn't ask to look in on his little wiper, and when someone was praising Doc, he said, "Okay! So he saved the little runt's life. But doctors don't always save lives. Depends on the incentive."

I didn't see what was behind that remark until we docked in New York. The fog cleared during our first afternoon aboard the Swede, and the Coast Guard sent a seaplane out to fly the patient to a hospital in

Norfolk. The Coast Guard gave word to the press about the amputation, and as soon as we'd been cleared by the immigration inspectors in New York, some waterfront reporters and photographers came aboard. Our captain met them on deck with a group of us, including Doc and Polanski, and gave them the story. The photographers then called upon Doc to pose for pictures.

He didn't move. "I don't want any publicity," he said.

That was when Polanski got in what he was wanting to tell. "And now you might as well know why," he said. "His real name is Thorpe. He's wanted for murder in England."

I never before saw a bunch of men go so quiet and silent. We all stared at Polanski dumbly. He seemed to think it was because we didn't believe him.

"I read about him in a crime magazine," he said. "He murdered his wife and disappeared. When I heard he'd said he was a doctor, I remembered reading something like that and looked it up. He denied it to me. The magazine had his picture, taken before he grew that mustache. The magazine is offering a hundred dollars for information on him. I want all you guys to know I've got first claim on that hundred bucks."

Everybody looked at Doc now. There was little doubt how most of us felt. If Doc had made a dash for the gangway, I don't think a single one of us would have tried to stop him, but he probably knew he wouldn't have escaped for long.

"That man," he said to us in a tight voice, "would sell his soul for a hundred dollars—if he had one."

I don't know whether Polanski collected the hundred dollars or not, but I do know that he never sailed again. There were letters in the newspapers about him, some saying that he had acted like a law-abiding citizen, but ship crews showed how they felt about a man that had sold down the river a shipmate who had risked life and freedom to save another shipmate from death. The Line had to let him go, and he took a job in the machine shop of a Brooklyn shipyard.

Meanwhile, I'd shipped out under the American flag to get my time in for a license. The ship went around to the West Coast, but I corresponded with the third mate of the *Orinoco* who had helped me with my studies for a license; in fact, I might not have been a captain now if he hadn't encouraged me. While I was sailing out of the West Coast, he was on short trips to the West Indies from New York, and he kept me posted on New York waterfront news. It was he who wrote me that Doc had been hanged in England, an appeal for clemency having been denied. With his next letter he enclosed a clipping and told me to draw my own conclusions.

The clipping was from a New York daily, reporting that a man had been killed when he fell or jumped to the tracks into the path of an oncoming subway train. The man had been identified by a shipyard pass found in his pockets and was evidently on his way from work to his rented room. A woman said she had noticed the victim at the edge of the platform and leaning forward to see if a train were coming. She thought a little man stumbled against him. It might have been because—well, she couldn't be sure, for when all the excitement was over, she didn't see him again, but he walked as though he had an artificial leg.

A Very Cold Gimlet

by Frank Sisk

The phone was ringing as Osgood Chace approached the door of his hotel room. He got the key slantwise in the lock and dropped it, then recovered it. He finally got in, just as the ringing stopped. Closing the door behind him, he said aloud, "She'll try again, that's for sure."

He set his attaché case on a chair and his hat on the dresser, then shed his coat on the divan that was converted each night into a bed. Then he walked to a lowboy and took frowning note of the small assortment of bottles, an ice bucket, and a tray of clean glasses. He spoke aloud again, musingly. "Gin? Hmmm. Why not? But tonight with lime water. A very cold, very dry gimlet."

He uncovered the bucket. No ice. "I'll murder that maid," he said.

Osgood started toward the phone but it began to ring before he reached it. He knew who it would be. He had not noticed that about her at first, yet it was a trait that must have been there always. He had simply seen it as something else, girlish daring perhaps, or empathy. How else did two strangers strike up an acquaintance in a cocktail lounge unless they had something along those lines?

He addressed the phone's black maw. "Hello."

"Well, greetings to you too, Ozzie."

He wished she wouldn't call him that. "Janice?"

"Who else, honey?"

"I thought you were to attend a concert with your husband tonight."

"So did he. But you know how it is—I developed a splitting migraine."

"This may be one migraine too many, Janice. He's no fool. And I wish you wouldn't call me Ozzie. You know perfectly well what I prefer to be called."

"Okay, Buff. We'll play it your way. But I must see you tonight."

"I'm not too sure a meeting tonight would be in the best interests of either of us. Oh, and by the way, Janice, is your brother in town?"

"My brother?" A slight pause. "Ray?"

"Ray, yes. Have you got more than one brother?"

"Only one. Where did you think you saw him?"

"At a bus stop across the street from the hotel. Not more than twenty minutes ago."

"You're definitely mistaken, darling."

"Could be. A funny thing, though, I got the impression that this guy at the bus stop recognized me too. He seemed to turn his head away."

"That doesn't sound like Ray. And after all, Buff, you've met him only once."

"He'd shaved off that hussar's mustache of his."

She laughed. "That cinches it. Ray would rather part with his right arm than surrender a single whisker on his upper lip. Now let's get back to us for a moment. I have something important to tell you but I want to tell you in utmost privacy."

"Do you have a meeting place in mind?"

"A perfect place. And miles and miles away from here. Perfect!"

"Just how many miles, my love?"

"Say that again. The love part."

He said it again self-consciously. It was a word he had used with her quite naturally, if thoughtlessly, until a few days ago. He considered the word and its uses a bachelor's prerogative. It would come to his lips again some day with somebody else.

Janice was now employing the purr that was intended to give her voice a special intimacy. "I'll drive by and pick you up, lover, in twenty minutes."

"Okay." Smiling at his image in the dresser mirror, he shook his head resignedly. "But not at the hotel entrance. There's a shoe store halfway up the block, Deane's. I'll be there at five after eight, just twenty minutes from now."

He was there but she was ten minutes late. The interval gave him time to wonder at his foolishness in prolonging a relationship already dangerous to his career. He had not known how dangerous it was until the day before yesterday. Then he had discovered that Janice Sanford, the beautiful young blonde with whom he had recently worked out a most pleasurable arrangement, was the wife of M. P. Sanford, board

217

chairman of Carboy Dominion Incorporated.

Osgood Chace was temporarily working for Carboy Dominion. As an architectural engineer with a New York consulting firm, he had been assigned to Carboy six weeks earlier to make a preliminary study of the company's plans to build a new administration building. On his second night as a stranger in a strange city, he had picked up Janice in the hotel cocktail lounge. Or had she picked him up?

At the instant of contact, it seemed, each knew that chance was throwing them together for more than a single night. Hence, there was no effort to falsify basic facts about themselves. Chace knew from the beginning that Janice's last name was Sanford, and that she was married to a much older man who was very rich. But at the time, the name M. P. Sanford meant nothing to him; if he had ever heard that such a man was chairman of Carboy's board, he had forgotten it.

The affair marched well. Without concealment, it moved delightfully through the weeks from cocktail bar to restaurant to inn to motel and even to his own hotel room.

Chace was at that stage of bachelorhood when one lives to a large extent on whim continuously tempered by caution. In this case, however, he had been infected by Janice's delicious sense of the reckless. Flattery had dulled his instincts.

He should have recognized the trait of recklessness in her on that occasion three weeks ago, when he had accidentally met her in a New York hotel bar with her brother, Ray George. With that hussar's mustache and those wild blue eyes, Ray displayed the family characteristic as transparently as a glass of effervescent liquid.

The meeting, now recalled, was a strange one. Chace was in New York for the day to review a few radical construction ideas with his firm. He was to take a late-afternoon train from Grand Central. With fifteen minutes to kill before train time, he dashed into the hotel bar for a quickie and nearly collided with Janice and her fierce-looking brother coming through the entrance.

"What a surprise!" exclaimed Janice. "A small world."

Chace stared jealously at the tall man holding her elbow. "Small world indeed," he said.

There must have been the hint of accusation in his voice because Janice quickly said, "Oh, Ozzie, I want you to meet Ray George. My brother. Ray, this is Osgood Chace, the man I told you about."

Over a makeshift handshake Ray George said, "Hiya, Chace. Unexpected pleasure." He managed the impossible—to sneer behind his mustache. "I've heard a couple of things about you from Sis."

"Nothing derogatory, I hope," he said, more to Janice than to Ray.

But the brother answered, "All in the point of view, pal."

Disconcerted, Chace said directly to Janice, "I'm catching the four-sixteen. Like to join me?"

"Love to, but I can't. Family business. But I'll phone you when I get in tonight. Okay?"

"Fine."

She kept her word. That night, after eleven, she called to say goodnight and to explain that her brother, a compulsive gambler, was deeply in debt and that she had gone to New York that day to bail him out. "Otherwise," she added, "somebody might have killed him."

"Killed him?" Chace remembered how surprised he had been at her casualness. "Rather extreme measure, isn't it?"

"That's the kind of company he keeps," Janice told him.

He should have known then how unsafe it was to play around with somebody who possessed such a devil-may-care outlook. He knew now. But was it soon enough?

He was still balancing this question when a white convertible slid up to the curb. He got in. Janice gave his knee an affectionate pat as the car began to move.

Chace said, "Couldn't you have come in something else—the black sedan?"

"Still worried about Max?"

"Worried is hardly the word. I ought to have my head examined. Every time I think of that talk with Hanley the other day, I turn cold inside."

"You need a drink."

"I was just about to make one when you called. Yeah, I need a drink all right."

"Who's Hanley, honey?"

"The building coordinator at Big Daddy's plant."

"Oh, him."

"It's good he's a dumb slob or he might have put two and two together and come up with my finish."

"Tell me again what he said, Ozzie. Pardon me—Buff."

"He said that the hotel bartender told him that M. P.'s wife was playing right out in the open with one of the guests. And then he described the guest as the bartender had described him, and it was me to a T."

Janice laughed. "But you still didn't get it?"

"No, I didn't even know what the initials stood for. I asked Hanley who the devil was M. P., and he said M. P. Sanford, of course. But I still didn't make the connection. I thought of you as Janice, not Janice Sanford. Hanley even had to tell me—remind me rather—that M. P. Sanford was chairman of the board. That's how detached I was from reality. Once I caught on, though, I caught on good."

"And you've been running cold ever since."

"I'm only human, you know. I know what a man like M. P. Sanford could do to my career if the fancy moved him. He could cancel our consulting contract just like that." Chace snapped his fingers. "He could blame the cancellation on my moral turpitude or something. And that would finish me with my firm right on the spot. The boss is a real puritan. He wouldn't even give me a reference."

"I'd give you a reference, darling."

"The personnel managers might not be susceptible. Where are we going, Janice?"

"The place is about an hour's drive from here, in a grove of pines overlooking a lake. Cafe Tranquille. *Trés recherché*. And a superb cuisine."

Unsaid was the fact that Cafe Tranquille numbered among its regular clientele the M. P. Sanfords. Chace began to get the tip-off under the porte-cochere. The doorman, taking the car, was full of special deference. The girl at the cloakroom addressed Janice as Madame and flashed a speculative glance at Chace. The maitre d' inquired after the health of Monsieur Sanford, and the sommelier asked if he should chill a bottle of that champagne that had so appealed to Madame on the last occasion.

As soon as they were alone for a moment, Chace said, "We should have rented a window in Macy's."

"This is just as good," said Janice complacently. "Don't you like its charm, darling?"

"It's French enough for DeGaulle. But it's hardly a hideaway. Everybody in the place seems to know you and the old man."

"That's why I decided it was ideal for the purpose."

"What purpose?"

The discreet shadow of the sommelier again. Chace ordered a gimlet, and Janice, a champagne cocktail.

Chace asked again in a low voice, "What purpose?"

Janice took a cigarette from a beaded case. A waiter materialized with a lighter. "What purpose?" Chace asked for the third time.

Janice exhaled a gentle cloud of smoke and said, "Well, Ozzie, I may as well tell you the truth. Max has begun to suspect there is another man in my life."

Chace felt suddenly dehydrated.

"It was bound to happen sooner or later," she continued calmly. "As you have recently been observing, discretion is not my strong point."

Chace moistened dry lips. "Does he—Has he—"

"Has he done anything about it? Why, yes."

"Like what?"

"Well, he did the businesslike thing. He hired a private detective to follow me around."

"Oh, no!"

Janice laughed with genuine humor. "Oh, Ozzie. Don't take it so much to heart. You look like a frightened adolescent."

Chace strove for composure. "You don't understand the implication here, Janice. You don't see what's at stake."

"Oh, don't I now?" She smiled mysteriously. "I think I do. Your job is at stake for one thing."

"Exactly."

"And my life, my one and only life."

"Your life. Just what do you mean by that, Janice?"

"My life wouldn't be worth living if I let Max put together a case of infidelity. I'd end up with a besmirched reputation and not a sou of alimony. That's how a self-made man takes care of a self-made girl like me when his pride is injured." She gave him a gay wink. "When you grow older and richer, Ozzie, you'll be a bit like Max."

"Well, I'm not going to grow any richer as matters stand now. How long has this detective been on your trail?"

"For weeks."

"You mean ever since—"

"Ever since the night we first met in the hotel lounge."

The drinks arrived. Chace took a long swallow. The gimlet was very cold and quite dry enough. It fired a thought that seemed to start in his stomach and rise upward. "Let me get this straight," he said fearfully. "You mean that a private eye has been looking over our shoulders, at practically everything all these weeks?"

"Yes, honey chile."

"And you have been aware of it?"

"Again yes."

Chace finished the gimlet. "Then I am to assume that M. P. Sanford knows all about us."

"You assume right, Ozzie."

"He's got a report and—everything?"

"He received a full report yesterday. With pictures. All very vivid. Don't perspire, Ozzie. Order another drink, and stop trembling."

The waiter, not the sommelier, was approaching the table. Before he got within earshot Chace asked, "Did you also arrange for this detective to follow us out here?"

"The man was removed from my husband's payroll this morning. He had accomplished his task."

The waiter set a telephone on the table and stooped to make a connection with a jack on the floor. "A call for you, Madame," he said.

"I don't get it at all," said Chace.

With her hand still on the cradled phone she said, "All will be clear in a moment, Ozzie." She turned to the waiter. "We'll have another cocktail, please." And then she lifted the phone and said, "Janice here." Nothing more. She listened for a second and then hung up. Her eyes were dazzling.

Stunned at the quick change in her manner, Chace said, "What goes on here anyway?"

"Your worries are over, Ozzie."

"I bet."

"Really. You see I just learned, by prearranged code, that my husband was shot to death ten minutes ago in the men's lounge at Philharmonic Auditorium."

Chace heard himself say, "You must be kidding."

"I never kid in matters of life or death," said Janice. "That's why I provided us with such an ironclad alibi in advance."

"An alibi?" Chace was bemused.

"I thought we might need one," said Janice vivaciously. "After all, when the police begin nosing around and learn about that private detective's report, we will certainly be the most logical suspects. Don't you think so?"

"I do."

"But at the time Max was shot, here we were in the Cafe Tranquille, sixty-five miles from the scene of the crime, enjoying cocktails. Of course, there may be certain persistent investigators who may suspect that we hired a professional killer to do the job for us. But we know that's not true, don't we, Ozzie?"

"Do we?" he asked.

"Well, unless you say otherwise, I would never admit to such a conspiracy between us. It would be, as you say, indiscreet."

Chace's numb brain was beginning to think again. "But that call just now. It's little things like that which the cops get a hold of."

"Let them try. It was a call from a bookie giving me the results of the last race at Santa Anita. I bet five hundred on a loser, it seems. That can be checked."

"Who did the job, Janice?"

"Do you really want to know?"

"Your brother Ray, wasn't it?"

"I don't have a brother Ray," she said evenly.

"You know the man I mean. Ray George."

"I don't know anyone named Ray George."

"Well, whatever his name is," said Chace.

"Whatever his name is remains a secret." An icy note, that Chace had never heard before, crept into her voice. "It was to keep it a secret that we invented you."

"Just what do you mean invented?"

"Can't you guess even that much? We invented you solely for the sake of Max and his dumb detective. We gave them a sideshow that distracted them from the main event. And now I guess we've got to keep the show on the road a while longer for the benefit of the police."

A gimlet was set in front of him. He drank it in two gulps.

"Dry enough, darling?" Janice was asking, obviously for the sommelier's attention.

"And cold," he said dully.

Games for Adults

by John Lutz

It was seven P.M., and a fine, cool drizzle was settling outside the cozy Twelfth Avenue apartment building, when the Darsts' telephone rang. Bill Darst got up from where he'd been half-reclining on the sofa reading the paper and moved to answer the ring. His wife Della had been in the kitchenette preparing supper, and he beat her to the phone in the hall by three steps. A medium-size, pretty brunette, she smiled at her husband and stood gracefully with a serving fork in her hand, waiting to see if the call was for her.

Apparently it wasn't, but she stood listening anyway.

Bill watched her at a slightly sideways angle as he talked. "Oh, yes, sure I do. Yes," he said. ". . . Well, sort of short notice, but I'll see." He held the receiver away from his face and spoke to Della.

"Is supper so far along you can't hold it up? We have an invitation for this evening from the Tinkys."

"The what?"

"He's on the phone," Bill said impatiently. "Quick, yes or no." He smiled knowingly, aware that she hated to cook and seldom turned down an opportunity to escape the chore.

"Sure," she said, shrugging. "Why not?"

As Bill accepted the invitation and hung up, he watched her walk back into the kitchen, untying the apron strings from around her slender waist. They had been married only two years, and he still sometimes experienced that feeling of possessive wonderment at what he considered his incomprehensible and undeserving luck.

"They'll pick us up here in about twenty minutes," he called after Della. "Said the directions were too complicated to understand over the phone."

"Fine." Her voice came from the bedroom now, where she was

changing clothes.

Della appeared shortly, wearing the form-fitting but modest green dress that he liked on her. "Now, just where are we going?" she asked. "Who on earth are the Tinkys?"

Bill grinned at her. "Cal and Emma Tinky," he said. "Remember, we met them in that lounge on Fourteenth Street when we went there to escape the rain last week."

Recognition widened her eyes. "The toy manufacturer and his wife! I'd forgotten about them completely."

"Well, they didn't forget about us. Cal Tinky said something at the bar about inviting us for dinner and games some night, and I guess he meant it. I don't see any harm in us taking him up on a free meal."

"Games?" Della asked, raising an artistically penciled eyebrow.

"Tinky's the president and owner of Master Games, Incorporated," Bill reminded her, "and they're not toy manufacturers. They make games, mostly for adults. You know, three-dimensional checkers, word games, party games. They're the ones who make crossword roulette."

"We played that once," Della said, "at the Grahams'."

"Right," Bill said. "Anyway, the Tinkys live outside of town and Cal Tinky happened to be in this neighborhood, so he invited us out to his place."

"I hope his wife knows about it."

"He said she does." Bill picked up the paper again and began idly going over the football scores that he'd read before, but he didn't really concentrate on them. He thought back on the evening he and Della had met the Tinkys. Both couples had gone into the tiny lounge to escape the sudden deluge of rain, and they had naturally fallen into an easy conversation that had lasted as long as the rain, well over an hour. Cal Tinky was a large-boned, beefy man with a ruddy complexion and a wide, toothy smile. His wife, Emma, was a stout woman in her early forties. While friendly, she seemed to be rather withdrawn at times, the line of her mouth arcing downward beneath the suggestion of a fine moustache.

Only fifteen minutes had passed since the phone call when the doorbell rang and Bill went to answer it.

Cal Tinky stood in the hall, wearing a wide, amiable grin and a tweed sport coat and red tie that brought out the floridness of his complexion. "You folks ready? Emma's waiting down in the car."

"Sure," Bill said. "Come on in a minute and we can go."

"Evening, Mrs. Darst," Tinky said as he stepped inside.

Della said hello and they chatted while Bill went into the bedroom and put on a coat and tie. He could hear Della's laughter and Tinky's booming, enthusiastic voice as he stood before the mirror and ran a brush over his thick dark hair. He noted his regular-featured, commonplace appearance marred by a slightly large, slightly crooked nose and again counted his good fortune for having Della.

"We'll just take my car," Tinky said as Bill crossed the livingroom and got the coats from the hall closet. "You're apt to lose me in the fog, and it's not so far I can't drive you back later on."

"You don't have to go to all that trouble, Mr. Tinky," Della said, backing into the raincoat that Bill held for her.

"No trouble," Tinky said reassuringly. "And call me Cal—never did like that name Tinky."

Bill put on his topcoat and they left and took the elevator to the lobby, then crossed the street to where Emma Tinky was waiting in a rain-glistening gray sedan.

The ride to the Tinkys' home took almost an hour through the misting, foggy night. They wound for miles on a series of smooth blacktop roads surrounded by woods, listening to the steady, muffled rhythm of the sweeping wiper blades. Cal Tinky kept up an easy conversation of good-natured little stories as he drove, while Emma sat silently, gazing out the side window at the cold rain.

"I hope you won't go to too much trouble," Della said from the rear seat.

Bill watched Emma Tinky start from her silent thoughts, and smile. "Oh, no, I put a roast in the oven before we came into the city. It's cooking now."

The big car took another turn, this time onto a steep gravel road. Bill caught a glimpse through the trees of the distant city lights far below them. He hadn't realized they'd driven so far into the hills.

"I don't suppose you have much in the way of neighbors," he said, "living way up here."

"You're right there, Bill," Cal Tinky said. "Nearest is over two miles. Folks up here value their privacy. You know how it is when you work hard half your life and manage to become moderately wealthy—always somebody wanting to take it away from you. Up here we're not pestered by people like that."

By the looks of the Tinkys' home they were more than moderately wealthy. As the car turned into the long driveway bordered by woods, Bill gazed through the rain-streaked windshield at a huge house that seemed in the dark to be built something like a horizontal wheel. Its rounded brick walls curved away into the night in perfect symmetry on either side of the ornate lighted entrance. Off to the left of the car Bill saw a small beach house beside a swimming pool.

"Like it?" Cal Tinky asked. "I can tell you it cost more than a pretty penny, but we sure enjoy it, Emma and I."

"What I can see of it looks great," Bill said.

"You shouldn't brag," Emma said to her husband.

"Just giving them the facts," Tinky said heartily as he neared the house and a basement garage door opened automatically.

For just a moment the sound of the car's engine was loud and echoing in the spacious garage, then Cal Tinky turned the key and they sat in silence. Bill saw a small red foreign convertible parked near some stacks of large cartons.

"No fun sitting here," Cal Tinky said. "Let's go upstairs."

They got out of the car and the Tinkys led them up some stairs to a large utility room of some sort. After passing through that room they entered a large room containing some chairs, a sofa and a grand piano.

"Come on in here," Cal Tinky said, "into our recreation room."

Bill thought the recreation room was fantastic.

It was a spacious room, about thirty feet square, with a red and white checkerboard tiled floor and walls hung with large, decorative dominoes and ornate numerals. At strategic spots on the gleaming tile, four-foot-tall wood chessmen stood on some of the large red squares. Several tables were in the room, with various games spread out on them; chess, dominoes, and several complex games that were manufactured by Master Games, Incorporated. A smoldering fire glowed in the fireplace over which hung a huge dart board.

"Let's sit down," Cal Tinky invited. "Dinner'll be ready soon."

Bill removed his coat and crossed an area rug designed to resemble the six-dotted plane of a huge die. He sat down next to Cal Tinky on a sofa embroidered with tick-tack-toe symbols.

"Is there anything I can do to help?" Della asked Emma Tinky as the heavyset woman took her coat.

"No, no," Emma said, "you are a guest."

Bill watched Emma remove her own bulky coat and saw that she was wearing slacks and a black sweater covered with a heavy corduroy vest. There was something that suggested hidden physical power in her walk as she left the recreation room to hang up the coats and prepare dinner.

Della sat opposite Bill and Cal Tinky on a chair that matched the sofa. "Quite a decorating job."

Cal Tinky beamed. "Thanks. Designed most of it ourselves. After we eat we can make use of it."

"A house this big," Bill said, "do you have any servants?"

Cal Tinky stood and walked to an L-shaped bar in a corner. "No," he said, "we mostly take care of it all ourselves, fifteen rooms. Had servants, but they stole on us. Now we have someone come in from the city twice a week to clean. Course, most of the rooms we don't even use." He reached for a top-brand bottle of Scotch and held it up. "Good enough?"

Bill nodded.

"Make mine with water," Della said.

Cal Tinky mixed the drinks expertly. When he'd given the Darsts their glasses he settled down on the couch and took a long sip of his straight Scotch.

Emma Tinky came back into the room then, picked up the drink that her husband had left for her on the bar and sat in a chair near the sofa.

"You certainly must be fond of games," Bill said, looking around him again in something like awe at the recreation room.

Cal Tinky smiled. "Games are our life. Life is a game."

"I agree with that last part," Bill said, raising the excellent Scotch to his lips.

"There are winners and losers," Emma said, smiling at Della.

They sat for a moment in that awkwardness of silence that sometimes descends on people who don't really know one another. Bill heard a faint clicking that he'd noticed in the car earlier. He saw that Emma was holding in her left hand one of those twisted metal two-part puzzles that separate and lock together only a certain way. With surprisingly nimble fingers she was absently separating and rejoining the two pieces expertly.

228

"Winners and losers," Della said to fill the void. "I suppose that's true."

"The basis of life," Cal Tinky said. "Have you folks ever stopped to think that our whole lives are spent trying to figure out bigger and better ways to amuse ourselves, bigger and better challenges? From the time we are infants we want to play the 'grown-up' games."

Bill didn't say anything. It was something about which he had never thought much.

"And business!" Cal Tinky laughed his booming laugh. "Why, business is nothing but a game!"

Now Bill laughed. "You appear to be a winner at that game." He motioned with his hand to take in the surroundings.

Emma joined in the laughter. She had a high, piercing laugh, long and lilting with a touch of . . . Of what? "Yes," she said then in a suddenly solemn voice though a smile still played about her lips. "Material possessions are some of the prizes."

"Enough talk of games," Cal Tinky said. "I'm hungry."

Emma put the twisted pieces of shining metal into her vest pocket. "We can eat any time," she said, "unless you'd like another drink."

"No," Bill said, "not unless the food's so bad you don't want me to taste it."

Again came her high, lilting laugh, backgrounded by her husband's booming laughter.

At least she has a sense of humor, Bill thought, as they all rose and went into the large and well-furnished dining room.

The meal was simple but delicious; a well-done roast served with potatoes and carrots, a gelatin dessert with coffee, topped by an excellent brandy.

Throughout the meal they had kept up a running conversation, usually led by Cal Tinky, on the importance and celestial nature of games in general. Emma would join in now and then with a shrewd comment, a high and piercing laugh, and once, over the lime gelatin, Bill had seen her staring at Della with a strange intensity. Then she had looked away, spooning the quivering dessert into her mouth, and Bill heard again the soft, metallic, clicking sound.

After the brandy Cal Tinky suggested they go back into the recreation room for some drinks and relaxation. For a short time the Tinkys stayed in the dining room as Cal helped Emma put away some perishables, and Bill and Della were alone.

Della nudged Bill playfully in the ribs and moved close to him. "These people are weird," she whispered.

Bill grinned down at her. "Just a little eccentric, darling. Maybe we'd be, too, if we had their money."

"I hope we find out someday," Della said with a giggle. She quickly hushed as the Tinkys came into the room.

Cal Tinky was carrying a fresh bottle of Scotch. "The first order is more drinks," he proclaimed in his loud voice.

He mixed the drinks at the bar and served them, then he looked around at the many games and entertainment devices. "Anything for your amusement," he said with his wide grin.

Bill smiled and shrugged his shoulders. "You're the game expert, Cal."

Cal Tinky looked thoughtful and rubbed his square jaw.

"Make it something simple, if you will," Della said. "I don't feel very clever tonight."

"How about Bank Vault?" Cal asked. "It's a simple game, but it's fun for four people."

He walked to a shelf and took down the game. Bill and Della followed him to a round, shaggy rug, where he opened the box and spread out the game board. Emma spread four cushions for them to sit on.

When they were seated with fresh drinks, Cal Tinky proceeded to explain the rules.

It was an easy game to learn, uncomplicated, based like so many games on the advance of your marker according to the number you rolled on a pair of dice. The board was marked in a concentric series of squares, divided into boxes, some of which had lettering inside them: 'Advance six squares', 'Go back two', 'Return to home area'. Occasionally there were shortcuts marked on the board, where you had your choice of direction while advancing. Each player had a small wooden marker of a different color, and if the number he rolled happened to land his block on the same square as an opponent, the opponent had to return to the home area and start over. Whoever reached the bank vault first was the winner.

They rolled the dice to determine in what order they'd play, then settled down on the soft cushions to enjoy themselves.

Cal and Emma Tinky played seriously and with complete absorption. Cal would roll his number and move his red block solemnly while his eyes measured the distance his opponents were behind him. Emma would move her yellow block in short, firm steps, counting the number of squares as she moved it.

The game lasted through two drinks. Bill had rolled consecutive high numbers, and his green block was ahead until near the end of the game. Then he had landed on a 'Go back ten' square and Cal had overtaken him to win. Emma was second, only three squares ahead of Bill, and Della's blue block brought up the rear after an unfortunate 'Return to home area' roll.

"Say, I have another game similar to this only a little more interesting," Cal said, picking up the board. "Let's try it."

Bill reached to help him put the game away and found that his fingers missed the block he'd tried to pick up by half an inch. He decided to go easier on the Scotch.

Cal returned with the new game and spread it out on the soft rug to explain it to them. It was almost exactly like the first game. This time the board was laid out in a circle divided into compartments. The compartments were marked as rooms and the idea was to get back first to the room in which you started. This time the obstacles and detours were a little more numerous.

"Does your company manufacture this game?" Bill asked.

"Not yet," Cal Tinky said with his expansive grin, "but we're thinking about it. It's not the sort of game with mass appeal."

They rolled the dice in the same order. Bill rolled a twelve and moved well out ahead, but on his second roll he came up with a seven, landing him in the dining room where the lettered message instructed him to skip his next turn for a snack. Della moved out ahead of him then, landing in the den. Emma rolled a three, but landed in the utility room where she was instructed to advance ten squares. This brought her yellow block only two squares behind Della's and she emitted her high, strange laughter. Cal rolled snake eyes, allowing him a free roll, and he came up with a twelve. His red block landed on the den, and he placed it directly atop Della's blue block.

"Does that mean I go back to the entrance hall?" Della asked, smiling like a sport but feeling disappointed.

"In a manner of speaking," Cal Tinky said. He drew from beneath

231

his sport jacket a large revolver and shot Della.

The slam of the large-caliber bullet smashing into her chest sounded almost before the shot. Della flopped backward, still smiling, her legs still crossed. A soft sigh escaped her body and her eyes rolled back.

"*Della* . . ." Bill whispered her name once, staring at her, wanting to help her, knowing she was dead, finally and forever. A joke, a mistake, a horrible, unbelievable mistake! He turned toward the Tinkys. Cal Tinky was smiling. They were both smiling.

Words welled up in Bill's throat that would not escape—anger that paralyzed him. He stood unsteadily, the room whirling at first, and began to move toward Cal Tinky. The long revolver raised and the hammer clicked back into place. Bill stood trembling, grief-stricken, enraged and afraid. Cal Tinky held the revolver and the smile steady as the fear grew, cold and pulsating, deep in the pit of Bill's stomach. The floor seemed to tilt and Bill screamed, a hoarse, sobbing scream. He turned awkwardly and ran in panic from the room, from death.

He stumbled through the dining room, struggling to keep his balance. On the edge of his mind he was aware that Cal had put something in the drinks, something that had destroyed his perception, sapped his strength, and he tried to fight it off as he ran to a window. The window was small and high, and as he flung aside the curtains he saw that it was covered with a steel grill. With a moan, he ran awkwardly into the next room, to the next window. It, too, was barred. All the rooms that had windows were inescapable, and all the outside doors were locked. He ran, pounding against thick, barred windows that wouldn't break or open, flinging himself against doors that wouldn't give, until finally, exhausted and broken, he found himself in the kitchen and dragged his heaving body into a small alcove lined with shelves of canned goods, where he tried to hide, to think, to think . . .

In the recreation room, Cal Tinky looked at his wife over the game board. "I think he's had enough time," he said. "It never takes them more than a few minutes to run to cover."

Emma Tinky nodded and picked up the dice. With a quick, expert motion of her hand she rolled a nine.

Cal rolled a six. "Your shot," he said.

Emma rolled the dice again, a seven. She leaned over the board and, counting under her breath, moved her yellow block forward in short, tapping jerks.

"The kitchen," she said. "Damn! They never hide in the kitchen."

"No need to get upset," Cal Tinky said. "You'll probably get another roll."

Emma drew a long revolver exactly like her husband's from beneath her corduroy vest and stood. Stepping over Della, she walked from the recreation room toward the kitchen. Her husband picked up the game and followed, careful to hold the board absolutely level so that the dice and the colored blocks wouldn't be disturbed.

The sound of the shot that came from the kitchen a few minutes later wasn't very loud, like the hard slap of an open hand on a solid tabletop—but Emma Tinky's high, long laugh might have been heard throughout the house.

Farewell, My Brothers

by Theodore Mathieson

I've come a long, hard way to be where I stand now, in the bedroom of the man I've come to murder. I can hear him breathing irregularly in his sleep, sometimes gasping, as if he were having bad dreams, as well he should, for the burden he has on his conscience.

I can hear the clock on the night table, and I know why he set it for five-thirty, just as I know many other secret disciplines of his mind; as I know the trade he plies, the inexorable and victimizing nature of it, and how it has dehumanized him of all hope and love, even for himself. It is a kindness, really, which I do in coming to kill him now—as well as a release for me.

I move toward the bed, drawn by the profile of the man I hate. His white hair swirls up like a halo around his gaunt face. His great powers of will are dormant, banked like sleeping fires, as he struggles to catch his breath. He will not live long, I know (the doctor says he has emphysema), but I cannot wait another day, another hour, to be released from my bondage to him. For this man has dominated my life; he has kept me from marrying the woman I loved, forced me into a profession which, though I succeeded at it because I was young, intelligent, and adaptable, became in the course of years arduous and repugnant, so now I count the moments until I may be released from it—and only the death of my father will set me free.

I sit down on the bed and as I watch him gasp for breath, I think of my wasted years—forty of them; first, as policeman walking the beat on the San Francisco waterfront, later as detective sergeant in homicide.

You may remember I solved the famous Wentworth case (the first of many) in which the Texas oil man apparently hanged himself from the flagpole atop the Mark Hopkins Hotel, by shinnying up and fastening one end of his suspenders around the gold ball, and the other around his neck. I proved the pole hadn't been shinnied, and that the Texan had actually been throttled by his lawyer and his body juggled onto the pole from a helicopter in the middle of the night.

I met Dorrie at that time. She was Wentworth's niece, and as pretty a piece of luggage as you could imagine. For a while, it looked as if we were going to get married, too, in spite of the fact that my father was against it. Then I got involved in the Paxton murder (the chef of a famous downtown restaurant was found chopped up in the deep freeze) and when I turned around, Dorrie was gone. I always felt my father had paid her off or something, because I could never find any trace of her.

Other women came along afterward, but each time father would somehow get rid of them. I often wondered why I submitted to him—I, who was old enough to govern my own life, and doing a job in which I excelled in spite of my dislike for it; but my father was an unusual one, able to breed initiative, perseverance, and even ambition in a son whom he otherwise dominated completely. I didn't even remember my own mother.

I finally got my way, though, after about twenty-five years. I quit the force and formed my own agency at 101 Drumm Street. For a while, business was slack and I got a chance to start raising fuchsias on the side, which is a hobby I love, but with the close of World War II, there came a demand for my services at the foreign embassies, and I got busy again. A lot of secret agents, it seemed, were infiltrating into the United States, and killings among them almost rivaled the old gangland killings of the thirties!

After about fifteen years of private practice, I felt I was getting too old for my job. I was seventy, father was ninety-something, and I wanted to quit, but he wouldn't hear of it.

"If I can still do a day's work," he said, "why shouldn't you?"

So I, poor spiritless son, kept on, but not without an increasing ennui that sapped my physical vitality. Then came the day—two weeks ago—when I fell to the floor as I was potting a fuchsia.

I knew, then, that I could never take another case. I must stop. That was when I made up my mind to do what I am now doing—sitting at the side of my father's bed, and preparing to murder him.

Yet I want it clearly understood that it isn't for his money that I'm doing this. I could always get by somehow; but my office phone keeps ringing, and people keep asking for my help, which I can no longer give, because I know that if I take just one more case it will be the end of me. I'm worked out, burnt to a cinder of my former self, and yet my father has insisted that I take one more job, and then another—and another!

It is either he or I.

I reach out now and pick up a pillow. Father is gurgling and gasping, but it does not faze me, for I have seen death in a thousand forms . . . thanks to him.

Thanks to this *writer*, who for forty years has forced me, his creation, to try to rival the exploits of such investigators as Nero Wolfe and Hercule Poirot.

Farewell, my brothers!

Object All Sublime

by Helen Kasson

If the fellow at the filling station hadn't been such a talker, I would never have known Jessica was murdered.

Of course, there was the telephone call I made to Clarke's house at eleven the night she died, to tell them I had found Gambol over on Silver Spring. No one answered, so I kept the dog in my apartment until morning. Also, there was the feeling I had that one would have to try awfully hard to die accidentally in that garage; and, mostly, there was the fact that Jessica, of all the people I had ever known, seemed the least likely to commit suicide. But these facts, alone, did not add up to murder.

They didn't add up to murder in the Coroner's mind either. Jessica had no enemies. Outside of a faction in the Town Planning Board which wanted to put the park on the other side of the river, and the woman she'd beaten out for president of the Ladies League, she was pretty well liked.

The verdict was *accidental death*, but that was a euphemism, a misnomer, an evasion—just a convenient pair of words to blanket what had happened. Jeff had found her lying on the floor of the garage one morning when he went out to get his car, the garage door closed, the motor of her car still running. Yes, accidental death covered it neatly, and in the only way possible. Suicide was unbelievable.

Jessica had been buoyant, light-hearted, full of animal spirits, and she loved living. She had no financial worries, her health was excellent, she was busy from morning to night attending meetings—clubs, civic work—going to shows and lectures, and she had a pretty good husband, as husbands go. Maybe Jeff was a little set in his ways and a bit too concerned with pills and nostrums. He had been a bachelor for forty years until she caught him, but he was faithful and unobtrusive,

237

the perfect foil for Jessica.

During the first years of their marriage Jeff had tried to keep up with her, but after a while he just took to his easy chair after dinner, and let her bounce around from meeting to lecture to round table discussion, and finally home.

Jessica didn't like to go anywhere alone, however, so she was always after me. I'm a widow with no ties and, though I really didn't want to leave my own easy chair most of the time, she was so insistent, I would run out of excuses. Perhaps it was good for me; some evenings were pretty lonely, but I would have preferred a more leisurely companion, one who would dawdle over coffee, and who wasn't always driven by an irresistible compulsion to be somewhere else.

The minute Jessica got anywhere, she would start planning what to do next. There would be an art exhibit, or a concert, or a movie she just must make or, if she couldn't find any place she hadn't been, which was usually the case toward the end of the week, it would be a program on television which was "simply marvelous, my dear, we mustn't miss it. It's at six forty-five, a documentary on Zamboanga." Sometimes I thought the reason she kept moving so fast was that the moment she sat down she popped off. It was a vicious circle. She was so tired from chasing Culture, she had to keep on running to stay awake.

The "perfectly marvelous program" would usually turn out to be snatches from an old movie or else, due to technical difficulties, not Zamboanga but a couple of politicians talking about slum conditions in New York City, which is exactly one thousand miles from where we live. Still and all, I suppose being with Jessica was a cut above being alone.

Fleetingly, after she died, I wondered if perhaps she hadn't fallen asleep on the garage floor on her way out. Still, why then, was the door shut and the engine running?

Like many people in Milwaukee, the Clarkes had an automatic control on their garage door. The door began to raise when they pressed a button inside the car on the way up the drive (each car had one) and turned on a light in the garage ceiling when it reached the top. When the door closed, the light went out. When they came home at night, they'd leave the door raised so the light stayed on until they got inside the house through the back door and then press another button in the

238

kitchen to close it. When they went out, they reversed the process—opened the garage door with the kitchen button and closed it with the button in the car before they backed out the driveway.

It would have been possible for Jessica to close the garage door, after she got the car inside, by pressing the car button a second time. And if she wanted to kill herself, this is undoubtedly what she did. But if she pressed it inadvertently and the door closed behind her, why didn't she turn off the engine? Or why didn't she press the car button a third time to raise the door? Or why didn't she get out of the car and walk to the other side of the garage where there was still another button on the wall inside, put there for just such an emergency? There was even an extra light with a long pull-cord, in case the bulb motivated by the rising door burned out. The set-up was foolproof. There was absolutely no way of getting caught inside the garage, with or without the motor running.

Perhaps all this seems to go to prove that Jessica killed herself. But I know she didn't. I knew all along, even before I talked to Mike at the filling station. Jessica loved life and herself far too well to do away with that fulsome body before she had seen everything there was to see, and a bit more.

Jeff was her exact opposite. He was neat and quiet and pudgy and slow. He didn't have much *joie de vivre*. He was an estate lawyer, and he seemed to have taken on the characteristics of his old-lady clients. He liked to sit around in the evening with a book, a glass of fruit juice and his bottle of pills on a table beside him, and go to bed early. He did like good food, though. That's one way Jessica failed him.

I came home with her one day after a bridge game because she insisted. I'd much rather have gone to my apartment and taken off my girdle, but she won, as usual. It was around six when we got in. The bridge game hadn't lasted that long, but one of the downtown stores was having a sale which Jessica simply had to make. She bought a dress which, she decided on the way home, she didn't like. "I'll take it back tomorrow," she said, "after the Disabled Children's coffee and before the Humane Society lunch."

Jeff was sitting in a big chair with the evening paper. He looked tired. He greeted me, raised his cheek dutifully for Jessica's big kiss and then asked, "What's for dinner?"

"Oh, just left-overs," Jessica said.

239

"Left over from when? We didn't have any dinner last night."

"I'm not sure, darling. I'll have to look in the refrigerator."

"I've already looked," Jeff said irritably. "There's half a dish of cooked peas and a desiccated lamb bone somebody must have given you for Gambol. I know we haven't had roast lamb recently."

"Well then, that's dinner," Jessica said brightly. "Peas and lamb go well together."

"Do you mean to say," Jeff shouted, "that you brought Helen home for dinner with not a living thing in this house to eat?"

"There's always Gambol. Roasted, with an apple in her mouth."

"We haven't got an apple," Jeff yelled. "I just told you—"

"Never mind. Has she been walked lately?"

"No, she hasn't been walked. It's all I can do to drag myself around on this starvation diet. I'm no canary. I need food!"

"You need to relax too, darling. It's not good for you to get so excited. You just sit quietly and talk to Helen while I walk Gambol, and then I'll whip up some dinner for us all."

"Why don't you whip me up and feed me to that damned dog? She's all you think about."

"Because there are no apples," Jessica said blandly. "And no bread for stuffing."

"No bread?" Jeff was half out of his chair, but Jessica had left.

I sat down, as unobtrusively as possible. After a moment, Jeff said sheepishly, "I'm sorry I made such a scene. Jessica's a wonderful girl in many ways."

"I know," I said.

"And in many ways she is not," Jeff added, sheepish no longer. "Look at this house!"

I did. It was a shambles.

I'm quite neat myself. It almost amounts to a compulsion. But then, I live alone.

As if he had read my mind, Jeff said, "You'd never believe how I kept my apartment when I was a bachelor. A place for everything, everything in its place. It isn't so hard. There's no excuse for this!" He waved his hand in a futile, encompassing gesture.

"Jessica's very efficient," I said, "outside."

It was true. She kept everything in her head—figures, names, appointments, faces.

"She's efficient here too," he said, "if you mean by efficiency, saving work. About once a week she buys food, and we begin eating our way through to the last half dish of peas. Many a time I've had to have cheese for breakfast, or worse, sardines. I loathe fish. Then we starve or 'make do' as she calls it, for a couple of days, and finally she goes to the store again. But she won't go until everything is gone."

"Maybe she ought to have a big freezer. It's such a time saver."

"She has. It's the biggest I could buy. I looked in it tonight in the vain hope—" He broke off abruptly and asked, "Do you know what was in it?"

"No."

"Twelve boxes of frozen dog food. You can pretty well bet she sees to it that the dog eats."

"Nevertheless," I said pointedly, "you must be eating something. You're no wraith, and neither is she."

"You're right. I eat lunch, all I can hold, from soup to nuts. Sometimes three desserts. She must too, judging by her energy. She can put away plenty, if someone else fixes it. But this noon," he continued plaintively, "I didn't have time for lunch and I thought, inasmuch as we had pilaf last night (pilaf always means we're scraping the bottom of the barrel) she would go shopping today and we could begin to eat through again. Maybe a steak, or a couple of thick lamb chops."

His eyes looked wistful. He swallowed once, experimentally. I felt sorry for him. Jeff did love to eat.

There was a long silence.

"Helen," he said finally. I could tell he'd been wanting to say whatever it was he was going to say for quite a while. "You don't have any money lying around loose, do you, that you can readily spare?"

"No. I get an income from the business and that's it. That's what I live on. Why?"

"I'm on to a good thing, and I thought I might let you in on it."

Looking back, I can see that his voice wasn't as enthusiastic as it would have been if he were really on to a good thing, but I didn't notice it then. I said only, "I'm not much of a gambler, Jeff."

"Women shouldn't be. Neither should men."

Then I did fancy there was a certain ruefulness in his voice, but I didn't have time to find out why, because Jessica came back, carrying a big bag of groceries. "Don't worry, kiddies," she yelled. "I've got the makings here."

"Thank goodness," Jeff said. "I was beginning to live off my fat."

Jessica did whip up a pretty good dinner. The only trouble was, we didn't have time to digest it because, right before it was time for coffee, she had to rush off to a lecture and she took me along. I didn't want to go but, in the end, decided it took less energy than arguing.

It was a night about a month later that I found Gambol running loose. I tried to telephone the Clarkes but couldn't get an answer. The next morning Jessica was dead.

I called Jeff as soon as I heard about it.

"Merciful heavens!" I said. "What happened?"

"I don't know. I just don't know, Helen." He sounded dazed.

"But how—" I began, and then realizing that I'd only add to his misery by making him talk about it, I said, "Well, at least, I can keep Gambol for awhile."

"Gambol?" he asked. "What about Gambol?"

"I picked her up last night on Silver Spring. I tried to call to tell you, but you were out."

"No," he said, "I went to bed. I was in court all day and I was tired."

"I called around eleven."

"Oh?" There was a slight pause. Then, "Well, I didn't hear the phone. Maybe you dialed the wrong number."

"Maybe," I said, but I was sure I hadn't. I had dialed again, in fact, when I got no answer the first time.

"Why would she do such a thing?" he asked, with the same sort of aghast incredulity we all felt.

"I don't know. Maybe she didn't mean to."

"If she didn't, if the door closed due to some mechanical failure, there was still the button to open it from inside the garage. And the motor running . . ." His voice trailed off.

"Maybe the button didn't work."

"It did, though. The police tried it this morning."

"The police?"

I must have sounded shocked, because he said, "It was purely routine. They always investigate in—in these cases. She didn't turn on the other light either," he said after a moment. "She just—stayed there—in the dark with the engine running . . . waiting for the place to fill up with fumes.

"I should have stayed awake. I should have stayed up and waited for her . . ."

"Don't reproach yourself. You couldn't know—"

"Hold on," he interrupted. "There's someone at the door."

He came back to the telephone in a minute or two and said, "It was the insurance man."

"For the car?" It was a stupid question. Nothing had happened to the car.

"No, for Jessica. About her life insurance."

"But if it was suicide—"

"They won't honor it," he said dully. "But that doesn't matter. What matters is that Jessica—" He stopped, obviously in an effort to control his emotion.

"Don't talk any more," I said. "I'll be right over."

I spent most of the next few days with Jeff as many of Jessica's friends did. Jeff was pale and subdued but, all in all, held up well. On our insistence, he even managed to eat some of the food that people brought in, but you could tell his heart wasn't in it.

The inquest was held soon afterwards, and the verdict, accidental death, pronounced. Jeff went back to work, and things more or less returned to normal, except that I didn't have Jessica calling me every morning to try to get me to help her fill her day. I kept Gambol. Jeff had never been fond of her and she was company for me.

It wasn't until several weeks later that I stopped at my regular filling station for gas. Until then, I always seemed to run low when I was downtown or out in the country, so I would fill up there. At any rate, Mike, who had serviced my car when Jessica was in it, and Jessica's car when I was in hers, knew we had been friends. Naturally, he began to talk about her death.

He said, "I saw her that day, the day of the night she died. Him too. They came in for gas at different times. I never thought next time I'd see him, Mrs. Clarke would be dead."

"Nobody did. It was quite a shock. Dreadful for Mr. Clarke."

"It was the next day too," he said.

"What was the next day?"

"That I saw him again. He must have taken a pretty long drive."

"Why?" It was more or less of an automatic response on my part,

243

though I suppose my mind might have been beginning to percolate without my knowing it. Mike had to get his full quota of talking in before he'd creep around and do what he was supposed to do and, understanding that, I always tried to help him along to the end.

"Because, like I just told you, the morning of the night Mrs. C. died, Mr. C. was in here and got a complete fill. And then the next day he was back for more. So, I figure he must have taken quite a trip that day to use all that gas."

"Good thinking," I said absently, and then, all of a sudden, I heard Jeff saying, the morning after Jessica died, "I was in court all day." (Court is downtown, two blocks from Jeff's office.) I began thinking about that double garage and the two cars, and Gambol's running loose on Silver Spring at ten-thirty at night, and Jeff's not answering the telephone at eleven. He couldn't have been out looking for Gambol then, because he didn't seem to know she hadn't been there all night when I called the next morning. Of course, he was upset by then, because he had found Jessica's body . . . But still, if he hadn't left the house, as he claimed, why didn't he answer the telephone at eleven that night? And how did Gambol get out?

It took me a long time to figure it out. In fact, I had to come home and sit at my desk, and practically draw a diagram of all those buttons and light switches, and what worked what and what went out when, but when I had finished I had it clearly in mind—and I knew I was right.

Jessica had cooked dinner that night (a good one, Jeff said sadly the next day when we were all there paying our condolence calls) and then had left at seven for a meeting of the Zoning Committee. Right after, Jeff must have gone out to the garage, loosened the two light bulbs— the one that went on automatically when the door opened and the one manually operated by a cord—disconnected the button on the garage wall which opened or closed the garage door from inside, started the motor of his car, and then returned to the house and closed the garage door with the kitchen button. Gambol probably got out then. I didn't find her until ten-thirty, but Silver Spring is about a mile from Bayshore, where they live, and with all the stops and detours a dog makes, it could easily have taken her that long to get there.

Then Jeff must have just sat in the living room and waited for Jessica to come up the driveway in her car. She probably returned at ten-

244

thirty, or a little before, because when I called at eleven to tell him I had found Gambol, he wasn't there. At that time, he must have been back in the garage putting together everything he had taken apart earlier—and Jessica was already dead.

I figure that he let Jessica open the garage door from the driveway with the button inside her car, but the moment the car was inside, he pushed the kitchen button and closed the door behind it. So there she was, trapped in a garage which was already thick with carbon monoxide from the motor he had left running on his car. She was probably on her way over to shut it off when she was overcome. However, the chances are he waited a half hour or more, to give the running motor a chance to replace what little carbon monoxide had escaped in the moment the door was open. At any rate, when he was sure she was dead, or unconscious, he opened the door with the kitchen button (he had loosened all the bulbs so none of the neighbors would have noticed whether the door was open or shut) let the garage air out thoroughly, and then went into the garage.

The first thing he did, undoubtedly, was to switch off the motor of his car. Using a small flashlight, he reconnected the button inside the garage so that it would operate the door again, and shut the door with it so he could work inside in the dark without being seen. He tightened the light bulbs, and finally turned on the engine of Jessica's car. He could have been back in the house within ten minutes of the time he left—but it was during that ten minutes that I tried to call.

After I had figured it out, I sat for a long time, wondering. Why had he done it? Certainly not entirely because of Jessica's haphazard housekeeping. He had been happier as a bachelor, but that, alone, wasn't justification enough for murder.

Then I remembered about the good investment he had said he wanted to let me in on a month ago, and suddenly I knew what it was he wanted me to invest in. It was in his freedom—to keep him out of jail. He had probably been gambling with some of the old ladies' estate money and had lost it, and it was on the verge of being discovered. It was quite obvious.

I weighed the alternatives.

It wasn't pleasant to think of Jeff getting away with murder, but it wasn't pleasant, either, to think of his being electrocuted or put away for life. When you reach my age, men are at a premium. It seemed

245

sheer wastefulness to put a man out of circulation who, if concern with his health, pills and rest could do it, might live a good while longer. Besides, when I thought of all the nights Jeff must have gone to bed hungry . . .

I thought for a long time. Where did my duty lie? To justice? To law and order? Or to myself?

I still hadn't decided when, the next day, I took a complete dinner over to his house. The dinner was a gourmet's delight. A three-inch steak, verging on rare, sauce bearnaise, asparagus with hollandaise, watercress with Italian dressing and, for dessert, imported cheese, strawberry shortcake and Benedictine. He smacked his lips over every morsel.

As I watched him eat, it got more and more difficult to make a decision. It became almost impossible when, after he had run his tongue inside the cordial glass to savor the last drop, he said hesitantly . . . "Helen—"

"Yes?" I sensed what was coming.

"You're a wonderful person," he said, massaging his bloated stomach. "And you're neat, too. Living with you would be almost like—*almost* like being a bachelor."

This was praise indeed. I waited.

"Do you think," he continued softly, "after a suitable amount of time has elapsed, that you could—that you could possibly—"

I let the sentence hang. I was thinking—about my duty, and about Jeff, and about how long the evenings were when you were alone.

Then, in a flash, I had it. I could, in one action, solve both problems. I would take his punishment into my own hands, *and* I would have a companion.

"Yes, Jeff," I said sweetly. "On one condition," I finished.

"What's that, my dear?" He was looking at the empty plates, love in his eyes.

"That we live in my apartment," I said.

"Of course, angel. I know how you feel. Another woman's house."

"It isn't that. It's the garage. The one under my building has men on duty around the clock. I feel so safe," I paused for a long time, "when I come home alone at night."

"I see." His eyes flickered balefully. He knew his punishment had begun.

Galton and the Yelling Boys

by Hillary Waugh

"**H**uman nature," said Mike Galton, the captain of detectives, "is the key to man's universe. And," the old man went on, "if you want my opinion, a good, experienced cop knows more about human nature than a good, experienced psychiatrist."

Detective Bill Dennis, his young sidekick, said, "Oh, come on, Cap. That's stretching it a little."

They were having coffee with the desk sergeant and it was a mild May night with a full moon up. "I think he's right, Bill," the sergeant said.

"Given equal mentalities, of course," the old man cautioned. "But the reason I say that is because the opportunities are so great. We routinely encounter examples of human behavior the average man couldn't imagine, and psychiatrists have only read about."

The others couldn't gainsay that and were silent a moment, reflecting on personal experiences. Galton lighted his pipe and sat back enjoying the night. It had been a quiet one, with the citizens, for the most part, behaving themselves. There'd been a complaint of a fight over in the east end of town, but it was a husband and wife, and the appearance of a patrolman stopped it. There'd been a complaint south of City Park about a car full of boys helling it up, yelling and honking, but they were gone by the time the radio car went by. Even the missing child, reported by a frantic mother at six o'clock, had turned up fifteen minutes later. Violence had not gone abroad that night. The natives weren't restless and the police on duty could relax over their coffee, talk about non-cop things, and let the softness of the night steal through the open doors.

Then there was a screech of brakes, the slamming of a car door, and the clatter of racing feet on the outside steps. Galton sighed with regret, for the sounds told him peace was at an end even before the youth burst through the doorway and rushed up to the desk.

He was about nineteen, tall, with curly hair and good quality clothes. The clothes, however, were a mess, and so was his face. He was panting, and he looked in shock.

"Help me," he said, looking first at the detectives, then to the uniformed sergeant behind the big desk. "You gotta help me."

"That's what we're here for," the sergeant said easily. "What's the problem?"

"Three men!" the boy panted. "They kidnapped my girl."

"Whereabouts?"

"City Park. Hurry, hurry."

"We will," the sergeant said. "Relax, young fella. Calm down and tell us your name."

"But she's in trouble."

"And when we hear your story we'll know what to do about it. What's your name?"

The boy said impatiently, "Lawrence Wainwright."

"Where do you live?"

"Is that important? My girl—"

"You're wasting time, fella. What's your address?"

The boy told him, giving an address in one of the best sections of town.

"Now tell us what happened," the sergeant went on, writing in the blotter, keeping his manner calm.

"We were parked in the park, minding our own business, when all of a sudden three men appeared and dragged us out of the car. I tried to fight them, but they ganged up and knocked me out. And when I came to, they were gone and she was gone."

"When did this take place?"

"About twenty minutes ago. About quarter of eleven."

"What's the girl's name and address?"

"What does it matter?" the boy cried. "We've got to save her."

"We'll save her just as soon as we know she needs saving. What's her name and where does she live?"

"Her name is Helen MacKenzie and she lives over on Wells Street. Thirty-one Wells."

Galton moved behind the desk and thumbed through the phone

book as the sergeant recorded the information and asked where the youth had seen the girl last.

"In City Park. I told you."

"It's a big park, Mr. Wainwright. Just where in City Park?"

"Near the pond."

"That doesn't help much. It's a big pond."

"I've got my car outside. I'll show you."

Galton dialed a number and while he waited, said, "Did you know any of the men, Mr. Wainwright?"

"No. Of course not. Please, we're wasting time. Can't we go now?"

Galton said into the phone, "Mrs. MacKenzie? This is Captain Galton of the police department. I'm sorry to disturb you at this hour. Is your daughter Helen there, please?" He listened briefly, his face becoming still more sober. "What's the name of the boy she's out with?" he asked, and then, "Do you know where they went?" He listened for a bit and said, "When she comes in, would you have her call the police department? The moment she comes in. It doesn't matter what time." When he spoke again, it was to say, reassuringly, "No, she's not in trouble with the police, Mrs. MacKenzie. She hasn't done anything wrong. We just want to get in touch with her."

He put down the phone and said to Dennis and the sergeant, "It checks out and she's not home yet." To the boy, he said, "These men. What did they look like?"

"Two were dark and one was blond. They were my height but heavier."

"How old?"

"Maybe twenty."

"What were they wearing?"

"Sport clothes. Dark sport clothes. No jackets."

Galton's manner was brisk now. He took out a notebook. "Tell us exactly what happened."

The boy touched the blood on his cheek and absently wiped it on his shirt. "We were parked in the park doing a little—you know— smooching. All of a sudden I looked up and two men were staring at us through her window. Then, before I could do anything, they opened her door and at the same time the third man opened my door. He grabbed me and the others grabbed Helen. I fought with the one who grabbed me, but one of the others came and hit me and they both jumped on me and knocked me down and kicked me unconscious."

"What did Helen do? She scream?"

"No. I think they had a hand over her mouth. I heard her say, 'Stop it! Don't!' but that's all."

"You know if they had a car?"

"I think they did. I think they're the same men we saw when we went into the park."

The old man arched an eyebrow. "Tell us about that."

"Just when we were driving in, this cream-colored convertible went racing past us with three boys in it yelling and screaming. I think they were the same ones."

The desk sergeant said, "Say, that's the car we got a call on, Captain."

Galton turned. "When? What about?"

"We got a complaint." The sergeant looked back on the blotter. "Nine forty-two. Call from a Mrs. Stanley Turner on Westlake Avenue about a light-colored convertible with three boys in it driving around her neighborhood yelling and honking and raising hell. I sent Charlie car to respond, but they were gone."

Galton nodded. "Better alert all units." He said to the boy, "You didn't make the license plate, did you? Or notice what make of car?"

"No, sir. I just saw the three boys in it. Two dark and one blond."

Galton took a last swallow from his cup. "All right, we'll go out and take a look around. You feel up to it, son? Would you like some coffee?" he asked the boy solicitously.

"No, thanks. I'm all right."

"You'd better have a doctor look at your face."

"Later. Right now I want to find my girl."

Dennis finished his own coffee and tucked away his notebook. He and Galton led the way outside. A shiny new hardtop was against the curb with the lights on and the boy started toward it, but Galton stopped him. "We'll go in ours. It's got a radio."

They climbed into a black, unmarked cruiser, the detectives in front, the boy in back. They headed for the park, watching for convertibles. Dennis, driving, said, "What were you and the girl doing in the car?"

Wainwright hesitated and said, "A little necking."

"How were you making out with her?"

"Believe me, it's not what you think."

250

Galton said, "What was it?"

"We were kissing. That's all."

The detectives slid knowing looks at each other. Galton said, "You pick her up and take her out in the park and all you do is kiss?"

Wainwright swallowed. "No," he said. "We also talk. We sit and we talk and sometimes we kiss. When those men looked in the window, we were kissing."

"What kind of a girl is she?"

"A nice girl."

"What makes you so sure?"

"Well—what do you mean? I date her."

"What I mean is, she comes from another part of town. She comes from a different social station than you do. I'm not saying it's this way in your case, but usually when men date girls below their social class, it's for only one reason."

Wainwright said heatedly, "I'm not a snob. We happen to like each other. We've talked about marriage, if you really want to know. I mean, we aren't formally engaged and we haven't said anything to our folks, but we're serious."

Galton didn't push it. "Any chance she knew the boys? She call any of them by name?"

Wainwright said no, nor had her abductors used names. They hadn't said a word.

Dennis turned into the park and followed its winding roads. He looked at the moon and said, "If a bunch of boys want to raid neckers, Cap, this is the night to find them."

When they drove past the pond, Wainwright pointed to a stand of trees, black against the moonlit sky. "That's where we were," he said.

Dennis pulled off the road and crossed the fields some fifty yards to the trees. They got out and the detectives looked around by flashlight. Some grass had been flattened by wheels, but that was all.

Galton said, "You didn't see or hear anything before you saw them at the window? No car headlights? No motor?"

Wainwright shook his head. Dennis said, "They must have seen a girl in the car and doubled back with their lights off."

Galton agreed. He said, "In what direction did they drag her?"

Wainwright pointed toward black woods a hundred yards distant. "That way. At least, the last I saw."

"You see or hear a car any time after they slugged you?"

"No, sir."

Dennis said to the old man, "You think they might still be around?"

"It doesn't look like it. They probably took off after he did." Galton got back into the cruiser and picked up the microphone.

"Headquarters from Galton. The girl been heard from yet?"

The sergeant came on. "Negative."

"Anything on that convertible?"

"No, sir."

Galton depressed the mike button again and said, "Send all available units and all available men to City Park, the field opposite the pond. I want search parties prepared to go through the woods."

"Affirmative, Captain. All units. Calling all units—" in a monotone.

When Galton got out of the car, the youth said, "You think she's in the woods?"

Galton's tone was heavier, his voice distracted. "I don't know where she is, son, but you say that's where she was dragged, so that's the first place to look."

The two detectives and the boy reconnoitered the nearby areas while waiting and then, shortly after midnight, the squad cars began arriving and men poured out. By quarter past twelve, thirty policemen were on hand with flashlights and hand lamps, and the headlights of the cars gave a daylight look to the fields.

The men spread out and broke into the woods in a row, tramping through, throwing the beams of the lights in all the shadowy areas, calling the girl's name at intervals, looking for signs of her passing. The youth hunted with Galton and Dennis, but they made him stay in back of them lest his inexperienced bumbling destroy a clue.

They pushed through briars and bushes and trees for a long five minutes and then, from far on the left, there came a shout. Galton, Dennis and the boy started in that direction, following the others.

When they reached the spot, the other men were cluttered and mumbling, heads and shoulders bowed. The air was black and electric.

"You find her?" the old man said, pushing through.

"We found her."

They stepped aside so Galton, Dennis and the youth could see.

It was a sad and ugly sight. The young girl lay dead and cold under a tree. Her pants were down, her skirt was up and her blouse and bra

252

were off. Her once-pretty head was bloody and broken, and a red-stained rock, wrenched from the nearby earth, lay beside her.

The boy said, "No! Oh, God, no!" and turned away moaning. Dennis muttered a prayer under his breath, the captain shook his head and sighed.

"I was afraid of that," the old man muttered. "When she still wasn't home, I was afraid." He turned away and, with head down, started back. Dennis, the distraught youth and the searchers followed.

At the car they gathered around as Galton radioed in. The girl was dead, he reported heavily. The medical examiner was to be notified, the photo lab and the morgue. He got out of the car again, closed the door and leaned an elbow on the roof. He shook his head once, straightened a little and took a breath. "All right," he said wearily to the boy, "tell us what happened."

The boy said, "I did tell you."

The old mouth tightened and the tone grew firmer. "Tell it again, son. But this time tell it right."

The youth, glancing nervously at the large group of encircling men, said querulously, "What do you mean by right?"

"Tell it the way it really happened."

"I don't get you."

"You know, like this. You brought the girl into the park and a car with three yelling boys went by. You pulled off and parked under these trees. You took the girl down into the woods and started to pitch woo. Only she didn't want to go as far as you did and she tried to fight you off. But you were determined and you hit her with a rock to quiet her down, only, when it was all over, you found out you'd hit her too hard and she was dead. So you remembered the car full of boys and then you came in and told us the boys had kidnapped her." The old man turned his light on the youth's face. "That's pretty close to what happened, isn't it?"

The stunned boy blinked in the glare. "No," he whispered, his face white. "It's like I told you. They grabbed her. They hit me . . ." He looked around desperately, but all the faces were cold and disbelieving.

The old man shook his head impatiently. "Do you think you're the first person who's ever tried to sell the police a phony story? Do you think we con that easy? We get it all the time. All of us. I've heard so many phonies I could smell this one the moment you came in tonight. I hoped like hell you were telling the truth, but when she wasn't in by midnight, I was afraid you weren't."

The boy said heatedly, "You're crazy. I am telling the truth! I don't know what you've heard before, but this time you're wrong."

The old man snorted. "Are you kidding? All I have to do is look at her and look at you and I know the story's a lie. We all do."

"I defy you. What's not true about it? Show me what's not true!"

"The fact that you're alive and she's dead makes it not true."

He stopped and blinked in astonishment. "What's that got to do with it?"

Galton glanced helplessly at his grim-faced crew. "That's got everything to do with it," he explained to the boy. "Three guys, right? That's your story. There were three guys?"

"Yes."

"So what did they want? Did they want to kill people? Then why didn't they kill you both? That answer won't do. Did they just want to rape a girl? Then they'd mess you up to keep you from interfering. That's all right. But then they wouldn't kill the girl. They wouldn't do anything to her at all—outside of the rape, that is. She'd have gotten home alive."

"But she resisted! They hit her with the rock to subdue her!"

"Uh uh." Mike Galton shook his head. "One man, maybe. You, alone, might have to use a rock to have your way with her. But three men? What would they need a rock for? Two could hold her for the third so tight she couldn't move a muscle." The old man, studying the boy's face in the light, dropped the bitterness and said quietly, "Forget the fancy tales, son. That girl's body is going to be examined very, very carefully for physical evidence."

The boy's face crinkled suddenly and he started to sob.

Blind Date

by Charles Boeckman

She was in the trunk of my car and she was dead.

I stood on the lonely stretch of country road in the middle of the night with the rain drumming down on me and splashing around my feet, and I stared at the body. My flashlight was frozen in my hand. I forgot about being wet and cold.

A sheet of lightning split the heavy black sky with a clap of thunder that shook the earth. For a second the macabre scene was lighted by an eerie, blue-white flash. The perimeter of my vision registered a water-filled ditch beside the road, a rusty barbed wire fence and muddy field beyond.

But the center of my vision was focused on the dead woman in the trunk of my car. In the flash of lightning her chalk-white features and staring eyes were in bold relief. The image lingered, ghostlike, in the retina of my eyes for moments after the lightning passed, revealing to me more detail than was illuminated by the sickly, yellow glow of my flashlight with its out-dated batteries.

She was an attractive brunette in her early thirties. She was dressed in a suit of dark material and a light top coat that had fallen open. The cause of her death was apparent. There was a bullet hole in her forehead.

My numb mind struggled to sort facts out of the nightmare. She had undoubtedly ridden with me all the way from Kingsbury. I had not stopped once, even for gasoline, since I left there two hours ago. If highway construction had not forced me to take this detour where, in the darkness of the night, in a driving thunder storm, I'd hit a chuck-hole and blown a tire, she probably would have continued to be a passenger, unknown to me, for the remainder of my trip to New Orleans.

I realized I was standing in a frozen position like a statue, my left hand clutching the edge of the trunk lid.

My first reaction following the initial shock was one of instinctive self-preservation. I wanted to drag her out of there, change my tire, and put much distance between myself and this damned spot.

But logic warned me against acting so rashly. After all, she had not crawled into the trunk by herself. Someone had placed her there. This was a situation involving other people and matters I didn't know about. Running from this thing might have disastrous repercussions.

I bent closer, directing the feeble rays of my flashlight around the trunk's interior. The sickly glow touched briefly the spare tire, jack, and some odd rags stuffed in a corner, then returned to the dead woman. I noticed a dark stain on the trunk mat caused by blood from the back of her head.

I forced myself to study her features more closely. I had lived in Kingsbury for six months. It was long enough to have seen at least once every person in a town that size. But I was sure I had never laid eyes on this woman before I opened my trunk lid a few moments ago.

I noticed an object on the floor of the trunk near her feet. Her purse.

I reached for it. Then, temporarily, I closed the trunk lid and got back into the car out of the cold, driving rain. I started the engine and turned on the heater, one of the few things that operated properly on my old heap.

The warmth crept into my chilled body. I stopped shivering. I switched on the dome light, opened the woman's purse, and spread the contents out on the front seat, hoping to find some identification.

The first thing that caught my eye was a bundle of letters, about a half dozen altogether. They were held together by a rubber band.

I slipped the band off. They all were addressed to the same person, Cora Miller, 1216 Mayberry Drive, Encinal. That explained why I could not remember seeing her among the citizens of Kingsbury. Encinal was another town roughly the same size, about thirty miles from Kingsbury.

Then, as I was staring at the handwritten address, I became aware of a striking familiarity about the writing. Suddenly I felt the second shock of the evening. This was my handwriting!

Quickly, I opened one of the letters. My gaze raced down the page to the signature, "Frank." It was my first name. It was my signature.

Blood pounded at my temples. I started reading the letter. By the time I was halfway down the page I was shivering again, but this time not from being wet. This was a love letter of the highly personal, intimate type, the kind that would cause a judge to clear the courtroom before it was read aloud to the jury.

It was brief, but there was nothing vague about the message it contained. The writer, who had the same name and handwriting as myself, had committed himself on paper to being hopelessly in love with Cora Miller. References were made to clandestine meetings and to Cora's husband, Thurman Miller.

With unsteady fingers I flipped through the other envelopes. The postmarks covered the past two-month period and they had all been mailed from Kingsbury.

The most recent postmark was only two days ago. I removed the letter from that envelope. It was quite brief:

"My Dearest Cora,

I can hardly believe that in two days you will be mine completely. No more lies and slipping around for us. I'm winding up things here. Quit my job this morning. I'll pick you up at the corner of the bus station in Encinal at eight o'clock Friday night. I have made reservations for us in New Orleans.

Your lover, Frank"

I stared at the page, blinking slowly. The rain drummed steadily on the car top, splashed against the windshield, and leaked around the door. Thunder rumbled and lightning flashed. I had the eerie feeling of reality slipping from my grasp, of walking through a bad dream.

I *had* quit my job the morning the letter was written and mailed in Kingsbury. I *was* on my way to New Orleans where I had phoned ahead for reservations at a small hotel I knew.

But I had made reservations only for myself. I had not known I would be taking along a blind date—Cora Miller.

I pawed through the objects from her purse, lipstick, bobby pins, keys, face tissues, the usual female junk. Then I found her billfold. In it was close to a hundred dollars in cash. One of the compartments contained a driver's license and a number of credit cards all bearing the name, Mrs. Thurman Miller. Plastic sleeves on a spiral binder held an assortment of small photographs. There was a wallet-size snapshot of Cora Miller, and several of her with a beefy-faced man who I assumed was her husband, Thurman. Other snapshots were relatives or friends perhaps, but all adults. Apparently the Millers had no children.

I came to the final photo in the billfold. The face on it leaped up to my startled eyes. It was a snapshot of me. Written in a corner, in my handwriting, were the words, "I love you, Cora Darling, Frank."

The human mechanism can absorb so much emotional shock, after which it becomes numb and dazed. I had reached that point.

I sat half slumped against the wheel for several minutes. The heater fan whirred. Cold drops of moisture trickled down my neck. Finally I pulled myself together. I could not spend the rest of the night in this forsaken spot. The normal processes of survival demanded that I do something.

I stuffed the objects back into the purse, and placed it on the rear seat among my suitcases and clothes.

Then I switched on my flashlight, turned up my collar, and again sloshed out into the rain. I opened the trunk lid, hoping that some miracle would have caused Cora to dissolve. But she was still very much there. I swallowed a normal human aversion to dead people and pushed her out of the way of the spare tire. When I did that I noticed, for the first time, her green overnight bag wedged in a far corner of the trunk atop one of my suitcases.

I went about the wet, muddy business of jacking up the car and changing the tire.

Then I was behind the wheel again. I turned the car around. In a few minutes I reached a small town a few miles back on the main highway, which I had remembered.

I got a handful of change from an all-night service station. In a lighted street-corner phone booth I placed a call to the hotel in New Orleans. When the clerk answered I said, "This is Frank Judson. I want to check on a reservation I made."

"Yes, sir. Hold on just a minute, please."

He was back almost at once. "Yes, Mr. Judson. We received your phone call and later the telegram."

"Telegram?" I asked blankly.

"Yes, sir. The one asking us to change your reservation to a double because you'd have someone with you."

I stared at the water running in streams down the side of the phone booth. I suddenly found it difficult to breathe in the small enclosure.

"Did you wish to make any other changes, Mr. Judson?"

I wiped the back of my hand across my forehead where beads of perspiration were mingling with raindrops. "You might as well cancel the whole thing . . ."

I got back in the car. Cold perspiration was oozing out all over me. For a moment, reason gave way to wild fancy. I was a victim of amnesia. I'd had an affair with this woman. For some reason I had murdered her, and the shock of what I'd done had blanked out my memory.

Then I got a grip on myself. That was pure hogwash. I was turning into a hysterical fool. Somebody had murdered Cora all right, but it hadn't been me. An elaborate plan had been rigged to made it look as if I was eloping with Cora tonight, but had murdered her for some reason, perhaps because she was trying to back out at the last minute.

No doubt the police in New Orleans would be tipped off to check my car. If I hadn't accidentally had that blowout, I would have had no reason to look in the trunk before I reached New Orleans. They would have found Cora. I would have had some impossible explaining to do.

I mentally ran over the events of the past six months, trying to find a clue to this unpleasant mess.

I had driven into Kingsbury six months ago, broke and needing a job. I'd gone to work with the Kingsbury *Record*, a small daily newspaper.

The town and job had been pleasant, but, as usual, after six months I had the itchy feet to move on to greener pastures. I was twenty-six, no ties or responsibilities. I'd been out of the army four years now, and had spent that time seeing different parts of the country. There was still a lot I wanted to see before I settled down.

One thing had made leaving Kingsbury difficult—Emily Phillips. Every town had pretty girls. But only Kingsbury had Emily. I knew lately that she was falling pretty hard for me. What scared me was that I was starting to feel the same about her. I could hear wedding bells in the air. So I'd taken the only sensible course open to a guy with itchy feet. I'd quit my job and kissed Emily goodbye.

I hadn't known I'd be taking Cora Miller along as an uninvited

259

guest.

I could get rid of Cora easily enough. There were plenty of muddy ditches along the highway. And I could burn the letters and my snapshot that was in her billfold. But there were probably other letters and snapshots planted at her home. And how would I explain to the police the matter of the double reservation at the New Orleans hotel? And the blood stains in my car trunk?

It boiled down to this, that I had to find out what Cora was doing in the trunk of my car, and who had put her there. And the answer was somewhere back in Encinal or Kingsbury.

Two hours later I pulled into the city limits of the town I'd left earlier this evening, Kingsbury. By then it was almost midnight. Except for all-night service stations on the highway, the town had rolled up the sidewalks.

I drove to the home of Buddy Gardner, my best friend in Kingsbury. Buddy was a deputy in the sheriff's department. Like myself, he was an avid chess player. We'd spent many long hours drinking beer and waging battles over a chess board at Pop Lassiter's beer joint.

If anybody could give me information about Thurman and Cora Miller it would be Buddy.

He lived with his parents in a big, old ramshackle house on the edge of town. When I turned my mud-splattered heap into their yard, I saw a light on in Buddy's room. He was my age and a bachelor. I knew he had a habit of reading paperback novels most of the night.

There was a private entrance to his room. I knocked. His door opened and the light in the room silhouetted his heavy, six-foot frame and his bushy head. He was naturally surprised to see me. Only a few hours ago we'd bid one another a fond farewell over a last chess game and a few beers at Pop's.

"Frank! What the heck? Thought you were long gone."

Buddy talked in a slow drawl even when he was surprised.

"I was," I said. "I had to come back."

He pushed open the screen door. "Come on in here. You look soaked."

I stepped inside, dripping water on the linoleum. He had a typical bachelor room. Deer horns and other hunting trophies adorned the walls along with hunting rifles. A book shelf, extending all the way to the ceiling, was filled with paperback novels. On one cluttered table

260

was a portable TV set. A novel he had been reading was spread open on the rumpled bed. On the bedside table was a can of beer and his pipe.

"What happened?" he asked, peering at me curiously. "Have car trouble?"

"Something like that. I want you to help me with something, Buddy."

"Sure. How about a beer? Or maybe you'd better have a shot of bourbon. You look half drowned."

"The bourbon sounds fine," I nodded. My clothes felt clammy against my shivering body.

"You ought to get out of those wet clothes," he said, taking a bottle of whiskey out of a bureau drawer.

"Haven't got time. Thanks." I accepted the drink he handed me. I took it straight. I felt the warmth of the alcohol spreading into my bloodstream.

"Buddy," I said, "you've lived around these parts all your life. You ever hear of a guy named Thurman Miller?"

The bedsprings sighed as Buddy sat on the edge of the bed and picked up his can of beer. He was looking at me curiously. "Thurman Miller?" His brow wrinkled. "Do you mean the county auditor who lives in Encinal?"

"I guess I do. There wouldn't be two Thurman Millers in Encinal, would there?"

"Not that I know of." Then he chuckled. "I swear, Frank, if you ain't one for the books. This afternoon you and I were over at Pop's having a farewell beer together. Now here you are back at midnight, banging on my door, wanting to know about the county auditor in Encinal. What's up? You workin' on some kind of newspaper story?"

"Not exactly. Tell me about Thurman Miller."

Buddy shrugged. "What do you want to know? He's been county auditor over there a number of years. That's about all I know."

"Is he married?"

Buddy nodded. "Matter of fact, I think his wife's side of the family is from Kingsbury."

I took out one of Cora's wallet snapshots. "This Mr. and Mrs. Miller?"

Buddy studied the photo. "It looks like them," he said slowly, "though I wouldn't swear to it. I don't know them that well. The only times I see Thurman is when I run into him in the courthouse in Encinal when I'm over there."

"Do you think anybody in this town would know them?"

Buddy stared at me. "I swear you're acting mysterious. What's eating you anyway, Frank?"

"I'll tell you in a little while. The truth is, I'm in a kind of a jam. I thought maybe you could help me."

"Well, I'll sure try, Frank. I hope it ain't anything serious."

"It could be. Getting back to what I just asked you, do you think many people in Kingsbury know the Millers?"

Buddy massaged his jaw thoughtfully. "Oh, I guess quite a few people do. You know how folks in a small town are. And Mrs. Miller has relatives over here."

I swallowed the rest of the bourbon. I'd established who the Millers were, and that almost anyone in Kingsbury might know them.

But who, among my acquaintances, would be crooked enough or crazy enough to murder Cora Miller, and then try to make it look like I'd been having an affair with her over the past two months?

I paced around the room, trying to recall this afternoon in detail. If I could put my finger on the place where Cora's body was deposited in my car trunk I would be close to the truth.

I had packed my car late this afternoon. Cora had not been in the trunk of my car at that time because I had put a suitcase in it.

Then I'd driven to a service station to have the tank filled. But I had stood right beside the car. No one could have touched the trunk without my seeing them.

My next stop had been Pop Lassiter's, where I'd bid Buddy goodbye over our last beer together. Then I'd gotten in the car, and had driven steadily until I had the blowout.

The only time anyone could have tampered with my trunk was while I had my car parked back of Pop's place. That being the case, Pop Lassiter himself was the most logical suspect. He was a mean old devil, and an ex-con, and capable of anything. Furthermore, he knew all about my plans to quit and go to New Orleans.

"Buddy, will you come with me?" I asked. "You might say it's in the line of duty."

"Well, sure," he drawled. "I wish to heck you'd tell me why, though."

"Trust me," I said. It was a ticklish situation. Buddy was a good friend, and I knew I could trust him to help me. But he was also a deputy sheriff. If I told him about having Cora in the trunk of my car, he'd be forced to act in an official capacity. I couldn't afford to be arrested at this point.

Buddy pulled on a pair of cowboy boots and took a rain slicker out of the closet. We sloshed out to my car.

"Man, this heap of yours leaks," he muttered after he'd gotten in and felt rain splash down the back of his neck.

"I need a new top," I said, turning on the switch.

"That ain't all it needs," he said, looking around.

I drove down to Pop's beer joint.

"What the heck are you doing here?" Buddy wanted to know. "You know Pop closes at midnight. It's past that now."

"I want to talk to Pop," I explained.

The old sinner lived in a room behind the beer joint. I walked around to his door and banged on it. Buddy was right behind me.

The door opened. Pop stood there in his long underwear. He looked mad. "What in blazes you want? I don't sell no booze after closin' time."

He tried to slam the door, but I stuck my foot in it. "Since when did you get so legal?" I asked. I pushed it further open and walked in. "You used to bootleg the stuff, didn't you?"

Pop looked even madder at this invasion of his privacy. "What's buggin' you, Frank?"

Buddy came in after me. Pop's glare switched to him. "This some kind of raid? You got a warrant?"

Buddy laughed. "Pop, I don't know no more 'n you do. Frank said he had to see you and asked me to come along. I'm just here as an interested citizen."

"You didn't answer my question about bootlegging," I said.

Pop shrugged. "What if I did? That was back in Prohibition. Thirty years ago."

"You've done time since then," I reminded him. "Once for manslaughter, and once for peddling marijuana under the counter."

He looked mad enough to shoot me. "All right, you smart aleck young newspaper jerk. What business you got comin' around here insulting me in the middle of the night?"

"I got a reason." I shoved the snapshot under his nose. "You know this couple?"

Grumbling and swearing, he put on a pair of gold-rimmed glasses. He glared briefly at the photo, then shoved it away. "Course I do. That's the Millers from over at Encinal."

"How come you know them so well?"

"Hell, why shouldn't I? Cora Miller comes from this town. She's one of Ed Shelby's girls. I've known the Shelbys all my life."

I grabbed myself a fistful of his dirty underwear just under his breastbone and twisted it until his eyes bulged. "You knew I was going to New Orleans, didn't you?"

"Well, sure!" he yelled angrily. "That's all you been yappin' about the last two months every time you been in my place—about how fed up you are with this town, and how you're headin' for New Orleans. Good riddance, if you ask me."

I shoved him up against a wall and gave his underwear another yank until he was dancing on his toes. "Tell me what kind of a deal you're in to tie me up with Cora Miller?"

His gold-rimmed glasses were dangling from one ear. His adam's apple danced in his stringy throat. "Buddy!" he yelled in a high-pitched, frightened voice. "He's a-killin' me."

Buddy placed a huge paw on my arm. "Take it easy now, Frank," he drawled soothingly. "Don't you think you'd better tell me what's got you so upset?"

I released Pop. "You'll know all about it pretty soon," I said. "When I get this old coot to talk. You already heard him admit he knows the Millers, and he knew all about me fixin' to leave for New Orleans."

Buddy looked perplexed. "I can't help you if you won't tell me what's got you so steamed up. You want to prefer some kind of charges against Pop here?"

I looked at him in hopeless frustration. I'd come here, driven by desperation, with no clear plan in mind. I'd hoped that the surprise of seeing me back might shake Pop up and, when I confronted him, he might break down and admit he had a part in putting Cora in my car. I might have known that a guy like Pop, who'd lived on the fringe of the law all his life, wouldn't come unglued that easily. He hadn't even' looked surprised when I walked in.

Either he was putting up a good front, and with his criminal experience he'd be trained to do that, or I was totally wrong about his being involved.

We went back to my car. I drove out of town fast, headed toward Encinal. Again, I was motivated by fear and desperation, rather than any clear-cut plan. The only other person I could think of who might shed some light on this mess was Cora's husband, Thurman. If he proved to be a blind alley like Pop Lassiter, I was going to have to admit the whole thing to Buddy and let him arrest me, and hope the police would believe my side of the story—which was a pretty dim hope.

I thought about Cora getting stiff in the trunk of my car just a few feet behind us and I shivered.

Buddy could see he wasn't going to get any conversation out of me, so he patiently smoked his pipe and waited to see what I was going to do next.

When we arrived in Encinal, I drove around until I located Mayberry Drive. Then I found the address I'd seen on Cora's letters, 1216. It was a sprawling, ranch-style house worth at least thirty thousand dollars. That puzzled me. "A county auditor doesn't make much money, does he?"

"Not a heck of a lot, I don't think," Buddy said.

"Then how come Thurman Miller lives in a house like this?"

"He's well-fixed from some oil property his folks left him. That county auditor job is just local politics and prestige."

That explained Miller's obvious affluence.

"Come on," I muttered quietly.

We walked up to the house. I saw a light inside and I punched the doorbell. Thurman Miller opened the door. I recognized him from the picture in my wallet. He stared at me through the screen door. Then his face turned pale. He uttered a cry and ran out of the house. The next thing I knew we were rolling on the ground, and he had me by the throat. He was a big guy, and might have choked me to death if Buddy hadn't dragged him off me.

We got him inside, where he sank onto a couch and burst into sobs. I sat down too, shaken and weak-kneed from his unexpected, ferocious attack.

He raised his face from his hands and started cursing me. "What

265

have you done with Cora?" he cried.

"Do you know Frank, Mr. Miller?" Buddy asked curiously.

Miller glared at me with hate-filled eyes "I ought to. I've warned him to stay away from my wife. Tonight she eloped with him." He got up, walked heavily to a desk, took out a scrap of paper, and handed it to Buddy. "That's the farewell note she left me."

The nightmare had started all over again. I felt the hopeless, numb sensation creep through my body.

Buddy read the note, frowning. "Is this true, Frank? Did you take off with Mrs. Miller?"

"No," I said. But I said it without much conviction. I was ready to stop being sure of anything, including my own sanity. Those letters, the snapshot . . . now Thurman Miller recognizing me on sight. Did it mean my mind was playing tricks on me? Insanity takes many forms.

Was it possible that I had been running around with Cora Miller? Had I really murdered her in a fit of passion? Could a thing like that have been blanked from my memory by my sick, guilt-ridden mind?

My brain did feel feverish. My head throbbed. I pressed my fingers against my temples. For God's sake, what are the symptoms of madness? Is a mentally deranged person aware of his own illusions?

Dimly, I was aware of Thurman Miller demanding to know where his wife was. Buddy was staring at me intently, waiting for an answer.

What could I tell him? That I'd reached the point where I was no longer certain of reality?

"Buddy, come out here a minute," I said in a hollow voice. I felt wet and tired and scared. I dragged myself to my feet and started outside. Miller rose to go with us. "Make him stay here," I mumbled, stopping awkwardly.

Buddy shot a glance at Miller, who stared angrily at me, then shrugged and sank back down on the sofa.

I led Buddy out to the car. I gave him the keys. "Look in the trunk," I said. I sat in the car, listening to the rain drum on the roof. I stared straight ahead at nothing. I heard the trunk lid open. In a few moments it closed again. Buddy got in the car beside me. The springs creaked under his weight. His face mirrored the shock of what he'd just seen.

Slowly he let his breath out. "This is real bad, Frank," he said gravely. "Why didn't you tell me about it right away?"

"Because you would have been forced to arrest me, and I wanted to try and get at the truth first. I hoped I could get Pop to admit he had put her in the trunk of my car. When that didn't work, I came over here thinking Miller would be of some help to me." I made a useless gesture.

"But why Pop?"

"Because the only time her body could have been put in the trunk was while my car was parked behind Pop's beer joint earlier tonight, when you and I were having our farewell beer together."

"Are you telling me you didn't put her there?"

"Buddy, I had a blowout on my way to New Orleans. I got out to change the tire. When I opened the trunk I found Cora Miller's body. I swear that is the first time I ever saw her in my life." Then I admitted, "But I don't blame you if you don't believe me. I'm not sure I believe myself any more."

"What do you mean by that?"

I turned and dug Cora's billfold and the incriminating letters out from under my suitcase on the back seat. "Look at these."

He read them all carefully with the aid of a flashlight he'd brought along. Then he took the picture of me out of Cora's wallet and studied it.

"Buddy, I haven't been running around with Cora Miller. The only girl I've had anything to do with around here is Emily Phillips. I was sure those letters were forged, that the whole thing was an elaborate scheme to frame me for her murder. But when we knocked on Miller's door and he recognized me on sight—well, it's taken the wind out of my sails."

"He could have recognized you from a picture. Or somebody could have pointed you out to him on the street."

I looked at Buddy curiously. "You mean you think he's in on this scheme?"

"I don't think anything. I'm just saying that his recognizing you doesn't prove anything, one way or the other."

Suddenly, I felt better. I realized I must be emotionally drained, or I wouldn't be giving away to wild emotions like I had been for a few minutes.

Buddy had relit his pipe. He was puffing on it while he stared thoughtfully at my picture. "This is a close-up front view. You must have known when it was taken."

I shook my head. "I don't know how it was done. Nobody has taken a picture of me since I've been in Kingsbury. In fact, I don't remember having my picture taken since I was in the army."

"Hmm. This looks like a recent one, too." He puffed on his pipe and mumbled to himself, the way he did when he was analyzing a chess move. "Looks like it was taken indoors by available light." He bent closer, squinting his eyes. "Pretty grainy. Could be blown up from part of a negative."

He stared at it some more, turning it different ways under the flashlight, while puffing furiously on his pipe. Then he said, "Listen, I don't want to break the news to Miller about his wife like this. I'm going to tell him I'm taking you back to Kingsbury. I'll phone him from over there after the coroner has a look at her, and we have her some place decent like a funeral home."

He got out of the car. Then he thrust his head back in. "Frank, I have to tell you this. You're under arrest now, and anything you say can be held against you."

I nodded wearily. "Okay. I understand."

He went back into the house to talk to Thurman Miller. He was in there a few minutes, then came out and got behind the wheel of my car. He drove the car back to Kingsbury, which was fine with me. I was emotionally drained and physically exhausted.

When we reached Kingsbury, I expected Frank to take me straight to jail and phone the coroner from there. I was taken by complete surprise when he pulled up in back of Pop's beer joint instead.

"What's up?" I asked.

"Got a hunch. Come on."

For the second time that night, we banged on Pop's door. The old man jerked the door open. His disposition had not improved. "Now what?" he demanded.

This time he was dressed in shirt and trousers. "Going someplace, Pop?" Buddy asked.

"What makes you think that?" the old bar owner snapped.

Buddy shrugged. "Peculiar time of night for anybody to be dressed." Then he said, "Unlock your bar," his tone authoritative.

Pop stared at him as if he'd lost his mind. "At one o'clock in the morning?"

268

"Let's put it this way; it's an official request. But I can go wake up the J.P. and get a search warrant, if you want to put me to the trouble."

Swearing under his breath, Pop Lassiter got his keys, walked across the rain-drenched yard and opened his beer joint. He switched on the lights. It was still warm inside. Stale cigarette smoke lingered in the air from the night's business.

"Frank, sit over here at the bar," Buddy directed. He walked to a doorway leading to a room off the side of the bar. His voice came to me out of the dark room. "Glance this way. Can you see me?"

"No."

He emerged into the light. "That picture of you that you found in Cora's billfold—it was taken from this room."

I stared at him in amazement. "How did you figure that out?"

"The negative was blown up, and the background was cropped out, so your face and shoulders filled most of the print. But whoever did the enlargement left the rim of that clock, up there, on one corner of the print. I recognized it as the one on Pop's wall. All I had to do was figure what angle the picture was taken from in order to get your face in the foreground and that clock in the background and . . . well, I wound up in that room. A person could take your picture from in there and you'd never know it."

I felt myself growing excited. "Wouldn't I have seen the flash?"

"No flash was used. There's enough light here for fast film, and the right kind of processing. Isn't that right, Pop?" he asked, suddenly turning to the bar owner.

For the first time tonight the old man lost his composure. His face turned a dirty gray. "I—I don't know what you're talkin' about."

Buddy said, "Frank, earlier tonight you mentioned the things for which Pop has done time. Maybe you didn't know about this, but I did; he once served a stretch for forgery."

Old Lassiter groped at the bar with a trembling hand. He licked his lips. "Now wait a minute . . ."

"Forging those letters in Frank's handwriting was a snap for you, Pop," Buddy said. "So was putting Cora's body in his car tonight. You knew he and I would have one last chess game here before he left. We'd talked about it in here the night before." Buddy moved toward him. "Why did you murder Cora Miller, Pop?"

All the wind out of his sails now, Pop collapsed against the bar. He held out one trembling palm as if to ward off Buddy. "You ain't hookin' me on no murder rap!" he yelled in a quavering voice. "All right; I done the letters and the pictures. And I had a key made to fit the trunk of his car. That's all I had to do with it."

"If you didn't kill her and put her in the trunk, who did?"

The old man took out a handkerchief and shakily mopped his forehead. "Her husband—Thurman," he said hoarsely.

Surprise rooted me to the spot.

Buddy and I were staring at Pop. "It's the truth," he croaked. "He's got him some young blonde on the string. He wants to marry her. Cora won't give him a divorce. He come to me a couple of months ago, offerin' me money if I'd knock Cora off. I'm not going to get myself in that kind of big trouble. But I told him I could figure a way he could do it, and come clean himself. I knew about Frank here. He'd been comin' in my place shootin' off his mouth about gettin' fed up with the town an' wantin' to move on. I've seen 'em like him all my life. Drifters. Transients. I could see just as soon as he got a few bucks ahead he was going to scat out of town."

Pop Lassiter wiped his face with the handkerchief again. "Thurman paid me good money to set the thing up. I wrote those letters. He caught the mail before Cora got her hands on it. We waited until I heard you say you'd quit your job, and were leaving town tonight, Frank. Then I put in a call to Thurman. He shot Cora tonight, and brought her over here. He was parked back of my place in the dark, waiting for you to drive up and play that last chess game with Buddy. Then he put her in the trunk of your car, usin' that key I'd had made . . ."

Buddy took Pop down to the county jail, and phoned the coroner. Then, he drove over to Encinal to arrest Thurman Miller for the murder of his wife.

As for myself, I was chilled to the bone and close to nervous exhaustion. I drove back to the rooming house, woke my landlady, and got her to give me my old room. I took a hot bath, drank some more whiskey, fell into bed, and slept until about noon the next day.

When I woke, I phoned Buddy down at the sheriff's office. "Everything okay?"

"Fine," he boomed cheerfully. "Thurman gave us a complete state-

270

ment. You're clear, Frank. 'Course you'll have to testify at the trial."

"How about a chess game tonight?" I asked.

"Well, sure," he said, with a tone of pleased surprise. "You mean you're not takin' off for New Orleans now that this mess is cleared up?"

I didn't explain it to him then, but I wasn't taking off for anywhere. I had come to the conclusion that not only does a rolling stone gather no moss, it also does not gather friends. You have to stay in one place to do that.

I finished talking to Buddy. I had two more important calls to make. I had to phone my ex-boss at the newspaper to see if I could have my job back. And then I was going to phone Emily and see if I could have my best girl back.

The Blue Tambourine

by Donald Olson

In the shabbiest precinct of a city so long tainted by economic blight
that he is even denied the companionship of his own image in the
grime-crusted windows of its vacant buildings, Willie de Garde stoops
to snatch a starving cat from a dark doorway, pops it into the sack he
carries for this purpose, and then hurries on, for the night air is sharp,
winter close at hand. A cold fog shortens the streets and makes pretty
but useless golden roses of the street lights.

The young man cradles his furry prize tightly against his chest, as if
to revive it by contact with his own strong young heart, and his steps
quicken as he approaches an old brick building whose facade still bears
faint traces of a gaudy elegance. It is a theater called the Oriental Garden, the only theater in town which has made no concessions to the
changing habits of its patrons, and consequently has lost all but a special few. It has not modernized its marquee, nor improved its lighting,
nor installed retractable seats or refreshment stands, and it continues
to show movies consistently lacking in appeal to the general public.

The almost total darkness does not confuse Willie, who knows his
way around and can find his usual seat with no other guide than a few
spots of orange light where mandarin-colored bulbs glow eerily beneath
plaster bas-reliefs of Chinese maidens wearing kimonos that are now
chipped and paintless. Overhead, a similarly despoiled jet-black dragon
with only one red bulb of an eye holds in its teeth a huge black and
crimson Chinese lantern.

Those who still patronize the Oriental Garden seek something other
than entertainment: a place to sleep, a place to hide, a place to hope
for one of those exceedingly rare occasions when some black-sheep
cousin of Eros might lead to a nearby seat a figure whose needs, com-
municated by signals as universally understood by the initiated as the

272

Morse code is by the fraternity of wireless operators, might correspond to one's own.

Occasionally one might see, it's true, a white-skinned leg extended at a grotesque angle, and a spider-like hand creeping and crawling from ankle to thigh, but it is more often to the solitary passions that the Oriental Garden caters. It is a popular refuge, for instance, of lonely drunks who stumble into the orchestra to sleep off a binge after offering rumbling, gratuitous criticisms of whatever story is unfolding above them on the tarnished silver screen.

Like these others, Willie de Garde comes to the Oriental Garden for a purpose, and no sooner is he seated than his eyes peer through the gloom as anxiously as a seaman's through coastal fog until, perhaps from nearby, perhaps from the other side of the theater, he hears the jingle of the blue tambourine, a sound which violates the silence no more harshly than a discreet cough, and which is repeated at intervals until he has found his way to Mrs. Rainfyre's side.

Without the sound of the blue tambourine she might never be located, for she dresses always in black from head to foot, in garments as out of fashion as her face, a face rather like those that peer out of pre-Renaissance paintings, a Margaritone or a Cavallini, a somber, slant-eyed face as ravaged by time as the plaster faces of the Chinese maidens on the frieze above their heads.

"*Buona sera*, Poet," she greets him as he slips into the seat beside her. "What have you brought me?"

"A choice ingredient for your witch's brew. Another cat."

As usual, she ignores this little dig, just as she drops no hint of what she does with the creatures he brings to her. Nor does he ever ask. It's none of his business.

As he drags the unprotesting cat out of his sack, Mrs. Rainfyre settles her black umbrella against the farther seat and deftly plunges the animal deep into her own black leather shopping bag.

"Quick!" he whispers, for having fulfilled his part of the bargain he is eager for the customary payment; his eyes begin to water and his lips to burn as she rummages in yet another bag as if for some trifle requiring much fishing about to locate.

"*Ecce!*" she murmurs as a figure looms dimly beside them in the aisle, groping blindly along the dark, narrow row of empty seats.

"He can't see! Hurry."

"Ah, *pronto, pronto,*" she hisses, mimicking his urgency as her yellow fingers fasten upon the glimmering hypodermic, while the other hand grips his already bared arm pumping up the vein and finally puncturing it with a deft thrust of the needle.

As she puts away her instrument she engages in familiar small talk to which he scarcely listens. "How goes the poem? Soon finished?"

His body droops limply against the seat. "Soon . . ."

"Ah? But not *too* soon, one hopes."

He is so little aware of her now that he misses the faint note of alarm in her voice. "You have other—customers," he murmurs.

She strokes his thigh with an impersonal touch, cold and sexless. "You are my favorite, *care.*"

As soon as she departs, carrying her bags, her umbrella, and her blue tambourine, he too drifts out into a foggy drizzle in which the golden roses on their iron stems appear to expand and throb above him, and as he passes through squalid alleys, his mind in a state of swiftly laddering exaltation, a cascade of brilliant images floods his brain so that he fears it will explode before he reaches his own room and can transfer them onto paper. He moves very quickly now.

This creative mood is sustained for an unusually long period, and he is not aware of its passing until one garish dusk as he stands at the window of his room and watches the sun, like a mad arsonist lighting fires in the windows of buildings across the street, while the sky above this conflagration grows purple with news of an approaching storm.

Being above all else a poet, Willie de Garde seeks no logical explanation for the way in which Mrs. Rainfyre manages to be in the Oriental Garden whenever he has something—a cat, a puppy, a rat, a bird—to exchange for her ministrations; he is happy to grant to her occult powers of divination, in spite of having seen her on the street one day, all in black and carrying her usual luggage, stooping to crush a wad of bills into the grubby hand of a dwarf, who thereupon whispered something in her ear which sent her scurrying off in another direction. Apparently, Mrs. Rainfyre paid a whole brigade of street creatures to keep her informed of the desires and movements of her clientele.

When next he creeps into his seat at the Oriental Garden, Willie is shaking with something besides the craving of his burning nerves, for this time he harbors the secret of betrayal, the giddying knowledge that this will be the last time the odious harpy stabs him full of

274

dreams, for the poem is almost finished and he will spend a vagabond winter in the South. He speeds merrily toward the jingle of the blue tambourine.

"*Buona sera,* Poet."

Her perfume is as offensive and rank as the stench of brimstone in the halls of heaven. "Hurry!" he pleads. "I need it!"

She doesn't move. "Ah, Poet, we all have special needs tonight."

"Shoot me! Shoot me!"

"Slowly, Poet. Tonight you must pay for my merchandise."

He jabs at the bag in which she has deposited the gray squirrel he brought her. "I've paid, beldame!"

She jiggles a note of laughter out of the blue tambourine, "These pets you bring me—you think *they* pay for what you get?"

"Give it to me!"

"Will you pay?"

"I'll steal a lion from the zoo in broad daylight! But give—"

"Look. Empty." She opens the black bag and he plunges his hand deep inside, drawing it out damp and trembling.

"I must have it! Now!"

"So you will, *care,* so you will. We're going to leave this place together and go where you will be given what you crave—in return for a small service," she whispers.

They leave the theater and she leads him through a twist of streets and alleys to a tenement in an even more desolate part of town. In a filthy vestibule a dozen rusty mailboxes hang empty and unlabeled on the leprous wall. A bulb glimmers at the top of a long flight of steps.

A flight above this ill-fit landing they stop outside a door upon whose frosted pane has originally been painted in black letters the words:

RAINFYRE

PHOTOGRAPHER

However, the second word has been unskillfully scratched out and underneath has been inscribed the word, ESCHATOLOGIST. Mrs. Rainfyre pauses to let him read this before taking a key from her pocket and letting him in.

In a room as dismal as the Oriental Garden, a man sits quietly reading at a cluttered table. He looks as if he had been glued together out of miscellaneous pieces of chalk and string, for there is a curious incompatibility about his features; nothing seems to match. His glasses are so thick they give the illusion that his eyes are actually inside the lenses instead of behind them, rather like monstrous green buttons laminated in plastic spheres. The top of his head is covered by a cap made from a woman's silk stocking; the lobes of his ears sprout grizzled white whiskers. Willie scarcely notices any of this, so fascinated is he by the man's right arm, which ends in a flipper instead of a hand, an elongated tapering paddle of tissue and skin. The left hand is normal, although extraordinarily tiny and delicate, like a girl's.

"My husband," gravely announces Mrs. Rainfyre.

His voice is a passionate squeak. "Honored, dear boy. I know you well already, I feel." A nod toward his wife. "Forgive my not offering my hand, but, as you see . . ." and he deliberately waves the grotesque flipper in Willie's face, at the same time laughing with a sound like breaking glass. "A congenital inconvenience, most distressing at such a time."

"A crucial time," adds Mrs. Rainfyre darkly.

Willie feels faint. "I need—" he starts to say, and Mrs. Rainfyre, leaving her husband to help the youth to a chair, hurries into another room, returning with a hypodermic wrapped in gauze. She no longer has the blue tambourine. Willie tenses his arm, but she merely lays the instrument on the table.

"Yes," purrs Rainfyre. "You need your—medicine. Of course. The inconstant muse must be enticed, mustn't she? I can't tell you how thrilled Mrs. Rainfyre and I have been to have been permitted to play the role, so to speak, of patrons of the arts in the life of so gifted a young man."

In the silence following this remark there comes from behind an inner door the distinct sound of the blue tambourine. Rainfyre smiles at his wife. She consults a clock on the wall. "You had best tell him what you must, and quickly. It grows late."

Rainfyre gets up and circles the table, thumping its surface with that obscene flap of flesh, while with his good hand he removes his glasses and massages his eyes.

"Mrs. Rainfyre is right, Mr. de Garde, and though I deplore the necessity of offering so abbreviated an explanation of what we're going to do I have no wish to conceal from you the reason for which we require your services. At this very moment I am engaged in the most important experiment of my career, an experiment that will crown years of prodigious labor and research. Research, I might add, financed solely by the commercial enterprise of Mrs. Rainfyre, and the demand for that commodity which she has been abundantly able to supply."

Again, from behind the door, comes the jingle of the blue tambourine, and Rainfyre smiles and says, "Once we pass through that door there can be no turning back. I tell you now, young friend, you are here under no duress, nor will you be coerced into taking part in the experiment for which we require your assistance—provided you leave at once and never come near this place again. But hear me! Mrs. Rainfyre will make no further visits to a certain tawdry cinema where you have so liberally availed yourself of her services. You will never see Mrs. Rainfyre again. You must employ some new device to woo your muse, or find some other agency. Which will not be easy, for this service of Mrs. Rainfyre's is seldom extended on such generous terms. Am I not right?"

Willie's head droops forward onto his folded arms, his body racked by the savage pangs of his addiction. The poem . . . the poem . . . so near completion . . . if only . . . if only . . .

"Many poets have paid a higher price than you shall be made to pay," whispers Rainfyre, as if reading his mind. "You are the reincarnation of Poe. The shade of Baudelaire. The ghost of Verlaine. An artist to your soul. Your work is your life, as is mine. Upon fulfilling your part of this little business you will be given what you and your muse crave, and as a bonus—hear this—the very instrument of your pleasure in an exquisite velvet-lined case, and with a sufficient amount of that commodity of Mrs. Rainfyre's as will make you a king of dreams, and your muse a slave."

To Willie de Garde, writhing in misery, it sounds like the promise of heaven. He nods his agreement.

Rainfyre vanishes on his tiny feet into another room of the flat, and Willie raises his head and stares at the glittering receptacle of his anodyne, which Mrs. Rainfyre, sensing his intention, snatches quickly out of his reach. Then she removes a locket from inside the collar of her dress and hands it to him. Through the mist that stings his eyes he sees the picture of a young girl of not more than nine or ten, with luminous dark eyes and massive ringlets.

"Our daughter, Poet. She died less than a month after her father

277

took that picture. A drunken motorist ran her down in the street, crushed her little dancing legs. When they carried her to us in the house where we lived she was—"

"Still alive!" Rainfyre comes back into the room, wheeling before him on a squeaky-castored tripod a bulky crepe-covered object. "She lay for hours, broken, helpless, dying so very slowly. Near midnight she raised her little hand and weakly beckoned me. I looked into those eyes which had been rigid as stones with pain and saw such radiance she might have become an angel before death. Her eyes seemed to light the room, and she said in a strong, clear voice: 'Papa, papa, make them hurry. It's so pretty!' "

Behind his glasses Rainfyre's eyes expand like soap bubbles, seem sure to burst. "*It's so pretty!* Her precise words, Mr. de Garde. A moment later she was dead."

Raindrops tap against the black-curtained windows like the fingers of beggar children pleading to be let in. No one moves.

Rainfyre removes the shroud from the object and reveals an enormous camera of apparently antique vintage but fitted with innumerable shiny devices as terrifying as those that menace the waiting patient trapped in the dentist's chair.

Taking from his pocket three small pieces of stiff white paper, he lays them before the poet, who examines them gingerly, trembling. He sees nothing but over-exposed snapshots, dull on one side, glossy on the other, with vague bluish streaks on the glossy side.

"These, Mr. de Garde, are photographs of the last optical images in the brain of a dying guinea pig, one of the expendable creatures you so kindly procured for us. They're of no interest. I erred in the calculation of perceivable light ray intensity."

Again, behind the door, the jingle of the blue tambourine. There is a look of mild urgency in the smile that crosses Mrs. Rainfyre's face; her husband continues speaking, however, with no sign of haste.

"This, you observe, is a camera, with many sophisticated refinements. For several years I was a professional photographer. Now, as you may have read on the door, I am an eschatologist, an explorer of those ethereal regions my colleagues have heretofore ignored, although essentially it involves the same problems of timing and lighting. To oversimplify further, my boy, there is an instant between life and death when one is neither wholly out of this life nor entirely within the other. After the death of my beloved child, and with nothing but her deathbed cry to inspire me, I devoted myself to the exploration of that mystical borderland, and finally—yes, with this very camera!—devised a means of recording in black and white a picture of that afterworld whose radiant beauty illuminated my dying angel's face. With the brains of the animals you have procured for us I have mastered the enormous technical problems, and now—now, Mr. de Garde . . ."

Willie de Garde scarcely listens to this madness, so acutely painful are the symptoms of his body's deprivation. "Please! Give me . . . give me . . ."

"Yes, yes, soon, my boy. Very soon. Now come, observe."

Rainfyre takes the poet's arm and leads him to the door, pushes it quietly open. In the middle of a smaller room, a young girl sits on a straight-backed chair in a soft pool of light. She has long red hair and skin almost as white as the simple dress she wears. In her hands she holds the blue tambourine and she smiles with infinite sweetness as she gently taps it with her fingertips. She is totally blind, and sits stiffly, as if posed.

Though there was no perceptible sound as the door opened, she turns toward them. "Mr. Rainfyre?"

"Are you fatigued, child?"

"Oh, no. I've been listening to the rain and answering it with the blue tambourine. As long as I do that the rain won't turn to snow."

"Are you warm enough?"

"Yes."

"It won't be long," he promises. "We're nearly ready to take the picture."

Rainfyre motions Willie back into the other room and shuts the door behind them.

"You have glimpsed the rarest of treasures, Mr. de Garde—*total innocence*. A privilege, even for a poet. Our search for such perfect, pristine innocence makes a tale in itself, but we haven't time to entertain you with it now. Suffice to say it was most exhaustive and ended where it began—in this very building. She lives alone in a hole of a room on the floor above us, where she sits in the dark crocheting fancywork in exquisite designs, which she tries to sell by hawking them from door to door. If anyone deserves heaven, that child does."

The sight of the girl and the knowledge of what this madman plans to do with her momentarily distracts Willie from his own misery. He starts to protest, but Rainfyre hushes him with a threatening movement of the unformed hand.

"Don't distress yourself, my boy. The animals you brought to us died painlessly, and so will she." His magnified eyes roll upward in reluctant submissiveness to fate. "One would prefer to employ the brain of some hideous sinner, quite naturally. Alas, this is precluded by certain insurmountable technical problems. If you will pardon me for once again oversimplifying, and not to sound too flippant, one would need a most sophisticated flash device to take photographs of hell. So we had to skip that idea. And we needed, you must see, someone of unimpeachable purity in order to take pictures of heaven."

By now Mrs. Rainfyre is becoming quite agitated. She starts plucking at her husband's sleeve and casting urgent glances at the clock, but he goes on just as imperturbably. "Don't ask me to explain how the actual process works—a matter of electrical impulses flowing between the child's brain and the internal mechanism of this specially adapted camera. She thinks it's merely another picture. I've used her as a model for conventional photos on several occasions in order to dispel any qualms she might feel. She is patient and indefatigable. A saint. Her passing will be swift and humane, and at the last quick pulse of life the marvelously sensitive eye of this camera will register the visual image that flashes instantaneously across the optical nerves of her brain on the very threshold of the infinite."

Willie listens to all this with mounting nausea, while out of the corner of his eye he never loses sight of that fascinating steel instrument in Mrs. Rainfyre's hand. Loathing and revulsion serve only to quicken the burning appetite that has drawn him to this lunatic's room. He fights to keep alert.

"You are wondering precisely what you shall have to do?" says Rainfyre. "As you can see, I'm somewhat handicapped by this." He waves the flipper. "And I'm also afflicted with a coronary weakness that forbids undue exertion. Nor is my wife strong in anything but spirit. We must therefore rely on you, my young friend, to dispose of the—er—remains. You must carry the girl's body in a laundry bag down all these stairs to the alley. No one will see you, and once you've got to the river . . . You understand."

As he speaks, the photographer has been deftly, with his one good hand, rolling up Willie de Garde's sleeve, while Mrs. Rainfyre circles the table, the needle poised and ready.

"When you've completed your little errand you might wish to come back here and Mrs. Rainfyre will make you a lovely cup of tea. Yes. We might have a little celebration, just the three of us, and you could read us your poem. Wouldn't that be nice?"

Now he is opening the door into the inner room and Willie sees the girl in white playing happily with the blue tambourine, and then Rainfyre begins wheeling his terrible machine toward the door, pushing it along with the help of his tapering, fish-like flipper.

Willie's eyes are on the glittering shaft of the needle, but just as Mrs. Rainfyre extends it toward his naked arm he cries out and tears away from her grasp. Without realizing he is doing so, he snatches up the three photographs from the table as he lunges toward the door. Mrs. Rainfyre shrieks. An unlikely roar comes from the puny photographer.

Down, down, down the rickety steps he flies, crashing from wall to wall, bursting through the door and into the deserted street.

Breathless, he runs like a wild man through dark canyons of vacant buildings, big white crystals of snow settling upon his eyes and cheeks and lips like icy moths, and no matter how far and fast he runs he still hears in his head the mad jingling of the blue tambourine.

Near the end of the street a gust of wind tears the small white photographs out of his hand. He claws at the air to retrieve them, and thinks he has, but when he reaches the river and opens his fist he holds nothing but a handful of snowflakes.

Graveyard Shift

by William P. McGivern

The *Call-Bulletin*'s first deadline was at nine o'clock in the morning and by eight fifty-five everyone in the long brightly lighted city room was working under the insistent pressure of time.

Sam Terrell didn't look up from the typewriter when the phone rang; he finished the item for his column, then lifted the receiver.

The voice in his ear said, "I've got something for you."

"Who's this?"

"It doesn't matter, Sam. What matters is I got something for you on Caldwell, our lily-white reform candidate." The tipster's inflection was heavily ironic. Terrell's interest picked up; with elections two weeks off, anything on Caldwell had a priority value.

"I'm sorry, but this connection is bad," Terrell said. "Could I call you back?"

"I'm at a drugstore, so calling back wouldn't tell you much. Be content with the tip, Sam. Don't worry about me. Now: you know Eden Myles?"

Terrell did, slightly; she was a singer, the friend of a minor hoodlum named Frankie Chance.

"Well, she's been huddling with Richard Caldwell for the last month or so. Five or six times, all on the quiet. But somebody saw her easing into his hotel suite. You run this down and you got a story."

Terrell reached for his cigarettes. He was tall and nervous, and when he was working he usually looked angry. "Anybody else know about this?"

"Just you and me. Good luck, Sam."

"Wait a minute," Terrell said, but the phone was dead. He put the receiver down. Rich Caldwell and Eden Myles—an incongruous combination. Caldwell was the high-minded idealist, called to politics by duty and conscience. Eden Myles was a small-time tramp. Singer, hostess, model, all of it small time. Even Frankie Chance was small time.

"Ollie," Terrell said to the frail old man whose desk was beside his, "what do you think of Rich Caldwell? Someone was just trying to peddle a story on him."

"Caldwell's given up a highly profitable law practice to run for mayor of this benighted town," Ollie Wheeler said. "And he's got about as much political savvy as a sophisticated girl scout. Men like Ike Cellars, Mayor Ticknor—do you think they'll let this piece of cake fall into somebody else's fingers?"

"You're a cynic."

"You mean I've the capacity to see what's under my nose."

Terrell smiled, leaned back in his chair and lit a cigarette. Eden Myles and Rich Caldwell . . . The pressure had eased now that the first edition was in. Reporters and editors drifted down the long room toward the lavatory or water coolers. From his corner Terrell had a view of the rewrite section, the copy wheel, and managing editor Mike Karsh's huge, glass-walled office, which dominated both arms of the L-shaped city room. He had been a part of the city room's madness for eight years, and then Mike Karsh had called him in to tell him he would take over Kehoe's column when the old man retired to his farm to raise chickens. Karsh had been at his desk, beautifully groomed as always.

"It's a small piece of blank paper on page three," Karsh had said, glancing up at him with sudden intensity. "But multiply that space a half million times—our circulation as of this morning—and you've got a piece of paper big enough to sky-write on. I want you to do a good job. I think you will. You've learned this raunchy trade of ours pretty well."

"Most of it from you, Mike."

There had always been this strong bond between them.

Now Terrell glanced over his shoulder toward Karsh's glass-walled office and thought that he still felt a copy boy's hero worship for the man. He would have liked to get his opinion on the tip he had just received, but Karsh was in conference.

Terrell picked up his hat and coat, left word at the switchboard that he was going out, and cabbed across town to the Vanderbilt Hotel.

Caldwell's campaign headquarters were on the third floor, in an ornate ballroom. A dozen or so college girls sat at card tables distributing campaign leaflets, lapel buttons and automobile stickers to anyone who wanted them.

A blown-up photograph of Caldwell was at both ends of the room, smiling self-consciously down on his busy, cashmere-sweatered volunteer workers. He was a handsome man, forty-five or forty-seven, with even features, a good jaw, and mild, intelligent eyes. They should have tried for a better picture, Terrell thought—something more informal and engaging. But Caldwell's advisors were all dedicated amateurs. They scorned tricks. They were so sold on Caldwell that they didn't bother selling him to the people.

One of the girls came over to him with a button for his lapel, but Terrell told her no thanks. He gave her his name and asked for Caldwell.

"Mr. Caldwell's tied up in a meeting right now, but please don't go away. I know Mr. Sarnac will want to see you. He handles the press for us."

She hurried off, her pony-tail bobbing with excitement.

In a few seconds a small man wearing a gray sack suit and rimless glasses came through a door at the end of the room, and hurried toward Terrell. They introduced themselves, and Sarnac escorted Terrell to his office.

"What can I do for you, Mr. Terrell? Sit down, please." He indicated a straight-backed chair.

Terrell ignored the chair. "What I want," he said, "is to see Caldwell."

"Fine. Of course." That he was handling the press with care was evident in his manner. "I don't see why that can't be arranged. He's a busy man, but—"

"How do you fit into this setup?" Terrell asked abruptly.

Sarnac seemed somewhat flustered by the question. "Me? Why, I'm Mr. Caldwell's press secretary."

"Are you on a regular salary?"

"No, I'm on leave from Union College where I teach." Sarnac looked puzzled now. "But I thought you wanted to talk about Mr. Caldwell."

"Perhaps I was being irrelevant," Terrell said. There had been nothing accidental in his approach; he wanted Sarnac off balance. "Now, tell me about Eden Myles. I know she's been seeing Caldwell. But I'd

284

like the rest of the story."

Sarnac looked stricken. "I haven't the faintest notion where you came across such an absurd rumor, but I can assure you it's completely false."

Terrell nodded thoughtfully; then he said, "You told me I could get together with Caldwell."

Sarnac hesitated. "Yes." Again he hesitated. "Just a minute."

He left the office and it was a good five minutes before he returned. Caldwell followed in his wake. In addition to resembling the big campaign picture, Caldwell looked a bit like a bank teller or the high-minded agent in a life insurance advertisement.

Nervously, Sarnac introduced Terrell to Caldwell and then made himself scarce—quite obviously by prearrangement.

"Mr. Terrell," Caldwell said, "would you mind telling me where you heard this story? Sarnac just informed me about it and—"

"I would mind very much. However, since it's not true, what difference does it make?"

Caldwell was visibly disturbed; his face was white and there were tiny blisters of perspiration on his upper lip. "This is a very serious matter," he said. "Could I talk to you off the record?"

"No," Terrell said. "I'm not a bartender or a cab driver. I don't listen to gossip for the fun of it. I'm a reporter. What I hear I use. What you're saying is that you'll tell the truth, but only if I don't use it in my column. Isn't that your proposition?"

"I didn't mean it that way," Caldwell said. "You don't seem to want to discuss this. There's really nothing to be gained fighting about it."

"I'll tell you what." Terrell smiled slightly. "You convince me I'll get a better story by waiting a few days—then we ll stop fighting."

"Yes, I can do that," Caldwell said, something simple and honest and stubborn projecting from the man when he spoke. "I'll give you everything, all the details. Then you'll see that the important story is still in the making. Sit down, please." Caldwell cleared his throat and glanced at the door behind Terrell. Then he said, "Eden Myles called us six weeks ago. She had information concerning the incumbent administration, Mayor Ticknor and Ike Cellars. She wanted us to have it. Sarnac arranged a meeting between her and myself, in a suite at the Armbruster Hotel. Since then I have had five more conferences."

"Have you been meeting her alone?"

"Every time Eden Myles has talked to me there have been witnesses present—men and women of unimpeachable reputation. Also, every conversation between us has been recorded on tape."

"Does Eden want money for her information?"

"No. I gather it's revenge she's after. I understand that she's had a split with her steady friend, a man by the name of Frankie Chance. He works for Ike Cellars. Eden wants to pay them off."

"And what sort of information is she producing? Anything good?"

"Not at first. But recently she's been giving us more significant information. That Ike Cellars runs the rackets in town, that Ticknor has been re-elected for years by fraudulent registration in the river wards. That there's graft in high places."

Terrell got to his feet. "We've made a deal. If this girl comes up with evidence, I'll be surprised. But I'll be glad to use it. And here's a bit of free advice: Watch out for booby traps."

"We can manage, thanks."

Terrell hesitated at the door. He said bluntly to Caldwell, "What are you going to get out of all this?"

"I want to live in a clean city. To put it negatively, I don't want to live under an Ike Cellars-Mayor Shaw Ticknor axis, with the moral deterioration they've brought to our community. I don't want my children, and the children of others, to grow up sneering at conventional virtues and tolerating the fact that honesty and hard work mean nothing at all in the management of our public affairs."

"You won't start any arguments with those ideas," Terrell said. "I imagine you're all for displaying the flag on the Fourth of July and keeping marijuana out of the public schools."

Caldwell smiled. "Exactly."

The Gray Gates Development where Eden Myles lived was new and elegant and expensive. Terrell rapped on Eden Myles' door. It was opened by a blonde girl wearing brief white summer shorts and a man-styled yellow shirt. She smiled up at him.

"You want Eden, I imagine. My name is Connie Blacker. I just checked in last night." She was beautifully tanned, and her hair was bleached lightly from the sun.

"And when will Eden be back?" Terrell asked her.

"I don't know. She left while I was still in bed."

It was then that they heard the clatter of high heels in the outside hall. Connie said, "Here she is now."

Eden Myles stopped outside the apartment door, made her way slowly into the foyer, staring at Terrell.

"Hello, Eden," he said.

"What do you want, Sam?" She glanced at Connie, suspicion sharpening her eyes. "What's he snooping around here for?"

Connie said, "I was under the impression you were friends."

"Newspapermen are a notch below cops in my form book." She stood tall and angry, her flat model's figure framed effectively in the doorway. "Well, what do you want, Sam?"

"Why are you seeing Caldwell, Eden? That's what I stopped to check on."

Eden stared at him, and then she said, "Would you go now? I've got things to do."

Terrell shrugged. "Okay, Eden, if that's the way you want it." He studied her for a second or so, and then shook his head slowly. "I don't get it," he said. "You're a handsome woman, very elegant, very lovely. When Ike Cellars finds out that you've been indiscreet, you won't enjoy looking at yourself in mirrors anymore. Has that occurred to you?"

She looked suddenly weary and beaten; all of her careful grooming couldn't conceal the fear in her face. "I'm sorry," she said. "Can't we play the scene over with a little less volume?"

"Let's try," he said.

"I've been talking to Caldwell," Eden said. She sat down on a huge yellow ottoman and crossed her slender legs at the ankles. "I wanted to pay off Frankie Chance because he—well, there's no point going into that. It was a stupid thing to do—I know that. But after I got started it seemed the right thing to do. Caldwell's an honest man, and he's big and gentle and straight. I really fell for the guy. In a funny way, I respect him and I want him to respect me. I can't say I'm not afraid of what Ike Cellars will do. But I'm going ahead with it. He can't stop me, Sam."

"Tell me this, Eden," Terrell said, "do you have anything specific and serious to tag the opposition with? Gossip and guesses, you know, aren't going to hurt Cellars or Ticknor."

"I've got things that will hurt them."

"What?"

"It's for Caldwell. What he does with it is up to him."

Terrell was silent for a few seconds. Then he said, "Well, I wish you both luck. You deserve a medal, Eden. You may never get it, but you deserve it anyhow."

Terrell smiled at Connie, left and rode down to the lobby feeling depressed and irritable. The whole business stank. Dramatic revelations inspired first by vengeance, then a growing sense of duty and virtue. Eden's act was a scriptwriter's dream, preposterously pat.

But who was being cast as the fall guy?

Terrell cabbed back to the paper and ate lunch at his desk while he worked out the first draft of his next day's column. When he had it in shape he called Mike Karsh to get his reaction on the Caldwell story. Karsh didn't go for Eden Myles' tale of revenge and suddenly burgeoning conscience, but he did think that Terrell was onto something good.

That evening Terrell called Connie Blacker and tried futilely to get her to go out to dinner with him. He ended up grabbing something to eat at a diner and then headed for the *Call-Bulletin*.

At ten-thirty the newspaper's lobby was dark, and Terrell had to rap on the heavy plate glass doors to raise a watchman. This was the slow, graveyard stretch; the next edition, the Night Extra, wouldn't go in until one o'clock in the morning.

The skeleton crew was sitting at the long city desk with coffee before them and cigarettes burning away in ashtrays at their elbows. The big lights above the clock drew a circle of brightness around the men at the city desk and police speaker.

Bill Mooney, an old city hall reporter, was in charge of this shift. "Want some coffee, Sam?" he asked. "Prince here made it. It's what they hired him for, I guess."

Prince was a healthy looking young man with a degree in journalism from the University of Iowa. Mooney did not mind his youth, but he was in no hurry to forgive him for that degree in journalism. "I'll get you a cup, Mr. Terrell," Prince said.

"Never mind. I'll pass."

Ollie Wheeler, Terrell saw, was sitting just outside the cone of light that fell on the city desk. He wore an overcoat, and had his feet propped up on a wastebasket.

Mooney said to Prince, "Keep your eye on the radio for awhile and don't let anything slip by. Fires are indicated by the ringing of a bell and a strong smell of wood smoke. I'm going to the john."

Just as he disappeared into the shadows, the police speaker sounded. The announcer's flat voice directed the street sergeant from the Sixteenth District to an address on Manor Lane. A few seconds later he directed an ambulance to the same address.

Prince said, "It's rugged being treated like a stuttering cretin around here."

Terrell held up his hand. "Just a second."

Wheeler walked over to the city desk, a little frown on his lean old face. He bent forward to put his ear beside the police speaker. "Did he say two-twenty-four Manor Lane?"

"I believe so," said Terrell.

In the silence that followed, Prince said, "Mooney thinks it's indecent that I didn't start as a copy boy. He's got the idea that college . . ."

"For God's sake, keep quiet," Wheeler said. "They've sent an ambulance out to two-twenty-four Manor Lane. That's where Richard Caldwell lives."

"Go get Mooney," Terrell said to Prince. "Ollie, you better give the Sixteenth a ring and see if they can tell us anything yet." He picked up a telephone directory, then remembered that the house on Manor Lane belonged to one of Caldwell's friends who was now in Europe. Caldwell lived in the suburbs and used the town house when late speeches or meetings kept him in the city.

"Ollie, what's the name of Caldwell's friend—the one who owns the house on Manor Lane?"

"Just a second." Ollie waved for silence; he was connected with the Sixteenth. "Sarge, this is Ollie Wheeler at the *Call-Bulletin*. Say, what's happening? We just heard you sent an ambulance over to Rich Caldwell's house. Wait, hold on—just a hint, Sarge, for old time's sake. Sure, I'll hang on." He covered the phone with his hand and looked up at Terrell. "Scared little bastard. But it sounds big, Sam. What did you want? Oh yeah. Sims is the name of the guy who owns the house on Manor Lane. J. Bellamy Sims."

"That's it." Terrell flipped through the directory, found the number and dialed it quickly. A voice said cautiously, "Hello?"

"Who's this?" Terrell said. "I want to talk with Rich Caldwell."

"You can't—" There was silence on the line. Then: "Who is this?"

"This is Sam Terrell. *Call-Bulletin*. Where's Caldwell?"

"Look, I can't talk to you. You got to see the detectives."

"Wait!" Terrell yelled the word. "Is this a cop?"

"This is Paddy Coglan from the Sixteenth."

"Don't hang up! Don't. Are you all alone there? Just give me a lead, Paddy. What is it?"

"I was coming down the Lane when I saw a guy run out of Caldwell's front door." Coglan's voice was low and tense. "I chased him and lost him. So I came back to Caldwell's. The door was open, lights on in the front room. He's—" Coglan drew a sharp breath. "The Captain's here, Sam. Better get over." The connection was broken.

Terrell put the phone down and glanced at Ollie Wheeler who was still talking to the house sergeant at the Sixteenth. "Thanks, thanks a lot, Sarge," he said, getting to his feet. "Sure, sure. Thanks." He hung up and looked at Terrell. "Mooney had better call Karsh, and get some rewrite men and photographers on the way in. There's a dead girl over at Caldwell's. And Caldwell is dead drunk."

"Who's the girl? Eden Myles?"

"Head of the class, Sam. Eden Myles it is. Or was. Caldwell just strangled her."

Manor Lane was one of the select addresses in the city; the homes were small, old and expensive.

Terrell paid off his cab and walked over to a patrolman standing beside an ambulance. He recognized him and said, "Hello, Jimmy. They take her out yet?"

"Hi, Sam. No, not yet. Captain Stanko just got here. With one of your boys. The lab men are still working. It's brutal, I guess."

Terrell walked by a couple of squad cars and up the stone steps of Caldwell's home, nodded to the patrolman on duty and went inside. He turned from the foyer into the living room, where he saw shirt-sleeved lab technicians taking photographs and measurements.

The *Call-Bulletin*'s district reporter, a balding man named Nelson, was on the phone talking in a low urgent voice. Terrell nodded to him, then drifted into a quiet corner and lit a cigarette.

Eden Myles lay sprawled in the middle of the room, and Richard

290

Caldwell sat slumped in a deep chair with his head bent forward at an awkward angle; he was breathing noisily and raggedly, and every now and then an inarticulate little moan sounded deep in his throat. Captain Stanko, in command of the Sixteenth, was shaking his shoulder with a big red hand, and a police surgeon was peering into his eyes. The room was a shambles. Lab men moved around upended chairs with efficient speed. Terrell saw Paddy Coglan, the uniformed cop whom he had spoken to from the *Call-Bulletin*. Coglan was a small man, stockily built, with kinky gray hair and a round, red face. His eyes were switching around the room, as if seeking a place to rest.

"We can take her now," one of the lab men said to Captain Stanko, and Evans, the homicide detective, turned and looked thoughtfully at the body of the dead girl.

She hadn't died prettily, Terrell thought. The model, the singer, proud of her lean, elegant body and dramatic good looks—that was all over. She had fought hard; her dress was torn across the front revealing her starkly white shoulders. One of her slippers was off and a stocking had been pulled loose from its garter clip.

"Take her out," Captain Stanko said.

The *Call-Bulletin*'s reporter was winding up his story in a discreetly lowered voice. Terrell turned a bit to listen to Nelson. "Yes, that's all I've got," Nelson was saying. "What? Yes, Caldwell's got some scratches on his face. Look, I'll talk to Stanko when I can—yes, sure."

"Just a second," Terrell said. "What about the man who ran out of here? Did you give him that?"

Nelson looked at him blankly. "First I heard about it. What do you mean? A prowler?"

"Prowler?" It was Captain Stanko speaking. He turned toward them repeating the word in a cold, belligerent voice. He was a big man with a face like a block of dark wood, and his eyes were angry and suspicious as he stared from Nelson to Terrell. "Let me give you hot shots some advice. Don't start dreaming up angles. You'll get the story from my report."

Nelson put the phone he was holding back into its cradle. "I'm not inventing anything, Captain. I'm waiting for your report."

Stanko glanced at Terrell. "That suit you? Or do you want us to rush things up for your special benefit?"

The room had become very quiet.

"I'm not inventing things," Terrell said. "A man was seen running out of this house tonight. After the girl was heard screaming. That's part of the story, Captain."

Stanko studied him for a few seconds with no expression at all on his face. "Who saw him?"

"Your beat cop." Terrell glanced toward the patrolman. "Paddy, didn't you tell the captain what you told me on the phone?"

Coglan's face was brick red. "What do you mean, Sam?"

The silence in the room suddenly became oppressive and ominous; Terrell felt a little chill go through his body. Would they really try to get away with this? he wondered. Would they try anything so raw? "You know what I mean, Paddy," he said, watching the little man's shifting eyes. "You told me fifteen minutes ago that you saw a man run out of this house. You chased him and lost him. Are you changing your story now?"

Coglan's eyes slid past Terrell and focused on a spot just beside his shoulder. "I told you you'd better talk to the detectives. I remember telling you that, Sam. I was pretty jolted, finding her dead. Maybe you misunderstood me or got it mixed up."

"Sure, you got it mixed up," Stanko said, in a hard, derisive voice.

Terrell didn't take his eyes from Paddy Coglan's flushed and unhappy face. "Once more, Paddy; you didn't see a man run out of here?"

Stanko said, "He told you 'no' once."

Terrell hesitated, not sure of his next move. He knew Stanko by reputation, a cold, unemotional man with a blind and compulsive loyalty to the administration. What were his orders? To make certain that Caldwell was tagged with the girl's murder? To eliminate other suspects?

Terrell made up his mind. He said, "Captain, I'm using what Coglan told me. I don't know what he saw; but I know damn well what he *told* me he saw. And that's going into the paper."

"And your paper is heading for trouble," Stanko said. "Paddy's tried to set you straight. He may have been confused, or you may have misunderstood him."

"We'll print all of that, too," Terrell said, in a tone heavy with sarcasm. "He's been a cop for twenty years, but the sight of a body sends him into a state of incoherent shock. Readers will find that intriguing."

"Sam," Coglan said plaintively, "there's no reason—"

"Shut up!" Stanko yelled at him. "Print what you want, snoop. Now get out of here."

"We'll print all the versions," Terrell said. "Coglan's first account and Coglan's second account. Something for every edition. And when do we get the definitive official report? When the Mayor and Ike Cellars decide just how it should be shaded and tinted for public consumption?"

"Get out of here. Get out of here before I throw you out. You're a troublemaker, that's all. And, by God, I'd like to beat some manners and sense into you."

Terrell said, "I don't want trouble, Captain, I just want the truth. But those words mean the same thing tonight." He tossed him a salute, walked out of the room.

From Caldwell's house Terrell went looking for a telephone. He found an all-night drug store six blocks away, and called the paper. Wheeler was writing the first running story. Terrell gave him everything he had learned from Coglan and then headed for the Sixteenth.

There was an air of pressure and excitement in the old mid-town station house. This was where the preliminary hearing would be held; a magistrate was on his way to the Sixteenth now, and Caldwell had already been slated for murder and taken upstairs to the detective's bureau for additional questioning.

The atmosphere was carnival, Terrell realized, glancing around the smoky room. He wondered what poor, blindfolded justice would do, hampered slightly by a gun in her back.

Richard Caldwell was held for the Grand Jury without bail by a magistrate named Seaworth, who listened to Patrolman Coglan's testimony without taking his eyes from the prisoner's face.

The little patrolman, Coglan, stared at the floor as he gave his testimony. He told of hearing a scream and going directly into Caldwell's home. The front door was ajar and he found Caldwell in a dazed condition with the dead girl lying on the floor. He did not mention seeing anyone else in or near the house.

It went faster then. The police surgeon testified that Caldwell had been drinking. A lab technician gave the findings of his section.

293

Caldwell made no statement and his attorney waived cross-examination.

Magistrate Seaworth banged his gavel and gave his verdict.

And that was the end of act one, Terrell thought, as he watched Caldwell being led by the police toward the cell block. There was no expression on Caldwell's face; he stared straight ahead, his eyes were like those of a man on a rack.

Someone shouted, "Get out of my way!" in a high, raging voice and began to fight through the crowd toward Caldwell. Magistrate Seaworth banged his gavel as a man shoved forward and swung a looping blow at Caldwell's face. The blow landed, cutting Caldwell's lip and then a patrolman caught the man from behind and locked his arms to his sides.

Terrell recognized him as flashbulbs began exploding on all sides of the room. Frankie Chance. Eden Myles' friend.

Chance was tall and slim with wavy black hair and deep brown eyes that were soft as a child's. He was struggling like a maniac against the big cop who was holding him.

"You killed her!" he screamed. "Because she wouldn't let you touch her, because you're not even half a man! When they strap you in the chair. . . ."

"Take that man out of here!" Seaworth shouted. "This is a courtroom, not a—" He sputtered as he groped for words.

Terrell eased himself through the crowd and reached the public phone in the hallway. He called Wheeler and gave him a few paragraphs of atmosphere, including Frankie Chance's attack on Caldwell. When he finished, Wheeler said, "That's very juicy. Now here's a message for you. Karsh wants you to come in. There's been some confusion about that prowler Paddy Coglan did or did not see. The Superintendent called Karsh about it, and so did Stanko—they both said you'd gone off half-cocked. Also there've been certain implications that Coglan might have been loaded. Williams says he has a reputation as a rummy."

"So what happened?" Terrell said.

"Karsh killed the prowler angle just before we locked up," Wheeler said. "He wants to talk to you."

Terrell sighed and rubbed his forehead. "Well, there goes Caldwell's loophole," he said. "They've turned it into a noose." The disgust he felt was evident in his voice. "Tell Karsh I'm on my way," he said, and

294

dropped the phone back onto its hook.

Karsh sat down at his desk, twisted a cigarette into his holder, and then looked up at Terrell. "Well, it's a frame, eh?" he said. "Raw, clumsy and transparent. But effective. There's a lesson in that. If you want a man out of the way hit him with a meat cleaver, and go on about your business. Sit down, Sam."

"What do we do now?"

"We're going to save Richard Caldwell's neck. This is about the biggest story I've ever been near—and I want it. I want it all. Now let's go back a bit. Tell me just what Coglan told you, his first version, that is."

Terrell gave Karsh a detailed account of what he had heard and seen so far. And then he asked, "I may be out of line, but why in God's name didn't you use my story?"

"Because I don't want to waste ammunition on jerks like Coglan and Stanko. I want to know who paid the killer—and I want the killer. That's the big story, boy. It may turn this sovereign state upside down and shake a thousand grafters loose from their snug little perches—and among those thousands we may find Ike Cellars, and our beloved, corn-fed Mayor."

Terrell knew that Caldwell had a chance with the paper fighting for him. "We'll be on the side of the angels this time, Mike," he said.

"Don't kid yourself," Karsh said sharply. "I want the story for sensible, selfish reasons. I don't give a damn about public morality. As for you, your job is to find a killer. So get with it. But keep me posted, and take it nice and slow." He brushed Terrell's arm with the back of his hand. "I don't really care if they hang Caldwell, but I'd hate to lose you. Let's get to work."

Terrell went downstairs and found a cab to drive him out to Gray Gates. He hoped to talk to Connie before anyone else did.

When she answered her door he knew that she had heard the news; he could sense the fear in her voice.

"When did you get the news?" he said quietly.

"A friend of Eden's—" She moistened her lips. "A friend of Eden's called me."

"Were the police here?"

"Yes, a detective. He said he needed to know who should be notified. I gave him her mother's address. A reporter and a photographer were here a little later. They wanted snapshots of Eden, pictures of me, pictures of the apartment."

"That wasn't very pleasant, I guess."

"I couldn't think about anything but her." She began pacing restlessly, taking quick drags on the cigarette. "Eden knew so much, she worked so hard—and suddenly it's all over. Snuffed out. You know, she got me a job singing at the Mansions. I can't stand any room in the apartment. Everything is full of her things. Dresses, shoes—"

"Take it easy," Terrell said.

"I shouldn't be completely surprised that this has happened."

"No? Why not?"

"She was frightened by something." Connie sat down on the edge of the sofa. She wore pajamas and a blue robe, and looked very tired and very miserable. "I do know it was connected with a job she was doing. Tonight a man came here to talk to her. She was frightened. And she didn't want to go with him. But he insisted."

"Who was the man?"

"You're asking me to break the eleventh commandment," she said. "Keep thy mouth shut."

Terrell hesitated a second. "Take this on faith if you can," he said. "The man who killed Eden is walking free. An innocent man has been charged with—"

"You want the story, sure. That's your job. You'll get a raise and a pat on the back from your boss. Should I stick my neck out to make you look good?"

"Forget about me, for God's sake." Terrell sat down beside her and said, "An innocent man may die—that's why you've got to stick your neck out. Anyhow, you'll be protected. If you trust me, I'll see to it."

The phone began to ring and she started nervously and guiltily. She crossed the room quickly and raised the receiver to her lips.

Terrell lit a cigarette and watched her eyes; something changed in them as she stood listening. "Yes . . . yes," she said, and listened for a few more seconds. Then she said, "Yes, all right. I understand." She put the phone down slowly. Her face was very pale.

"Who was that?" Terrell said.

"A friend of mine."

Terrell took one of her hands. "Ice cold," he said. "What did he say? To shut up? To keep quiet?"

"Maybe," she said, pulling her hand free. "Why don't you go to the police yourself? They're paid to hunt killers. I'm paid to sing in a club."

"And I'll bet you're in for a raise pretty soon," Terrell said quietly.

She looked quickly at him, her expression guilty and defiant. "Don't bother needling me. I'm scared. Do you expect me to be ashamed of that?"

"I might feel the same if I were in your shoes," Terrell said. "I'm not sure. I wasn't needling you. I'm just a reporter at work. If you change your mind, you can always get me through the paper. Will you remember that?"

"It's no use," she said.

"Remember Caldwell then," he said, getting to his feet. "He's facing the loss of his career, reputation, his family, everything—even his life. And he's no more guilty than you are. Remember him while you're singing college songs to bald-headed drunks in Ike Cellars' joint."

"Why don't you leave me alone?" She was very nearly in tears.

Terrell sighed and picked up his hat. "You can reach me at the paper if you need me."

At nine-thirty in the morning, Terrell rapped on the door of an old-fashioned frame house in a poor and dreary section of the city.

The door was opened by a woman with graying hair and eyes that were large and anxious behind rimless glasses. "Yes?" she said, drying her hands on a pale blue apron. "Yes, what is it?"

"My name is Terrell, Mrs. Coglan, Sam Terrell. I'm a reporter with the *Call-Bulletin.*"

"You want to see my husband, I suppose, but he's not here. He's taken a trip."

"Yes, I know," Terrell said. "I stopped at his district first and Sergeant McManus told me Paddy had decided to use up some of his leave time."

"He wants to take what he's got coming before he retires," Mrs. Coglan said. "You know his pension's coming up in a few weeks."

"That's smart," Terrell said, smiling at her. "No point in giving the time back to the city."

"That's what I said to him."

"But you can help me out just as well as Paddy," Terrell said. "That's why I came by. We're doing a round-up of the Caldwell story in next Sunday's edition, and I want to use a piece on Paddy—a picture, a little biographical stuff, that sort of thing."

"I could find a picture of him."

Terrell took off his hat and followed her into the neat, plainly furnished living room that smelled faintly of floor polish.

"Just sit yourself down," she said. "And don't mind how things look. I haven't given the front rooms a lick yet."

"When did Paddy leave, by the way?" Terrell asked casually.

"Yesterday morning, around eight, I think it was. He'd been planning the trip for a long time. There was nothing sudden about it."

"Sure," Terrell said.

"Some people might think it funny him leaving just after testifying against Mr. Caldwell."

"He won't be needed until the Grand Jury hearing. No reason for him to give up his trip. Where did he go?"

"Well, he's visiting some relatives out in Indiana. Two of his sisters live there." Mrs. Coglan rubbed her hands briskly on her apron. "Well, I'll get you some pictures to look at."

"Is there any way I could get in touch with Paddy?" Terrell asked her. "That is, if I need to check an item or a date with him?"

"Well, he's driving," Mrs. Coglan said, looking at a spot on the wall. "He'll just meander along, taking his time. I don't see how you could, Mr. Terrell."

"It doesn't matter."

"I'll get the pictures now. You can take your pick."

When she went up the stairs Terrell stood and glanced around the room. His nerves assured him he was on the right track; his body was tight with tension. Paddy Coglan had been told to clear out. To stay away until after elections. His lie had destroyed Caldwell's only hope. And now he was gone safely away from Caldwell's lawyers or suspicious newspapermen.

The room told him nothing; it was tidy and unrevealing. He hardly knew what he was expecting—a letter or post card perhaps with a return address on it. He looked through the shelves beside the imitation fireplace, moving the dozen-odd books.

298

Terrell sat down as he heard Mrs. Coglan descending the stairs. "Well, here we are now," she said. She carried a bulky cardboard box which Terrell helped her place on the coffee table. "I've always kept everything," she said. "Newspaper clippings, transfer orders, letters from the pension officers. And here are the pictures. You should find something in that bunch."

"I'm sure I can." He sat on the sofa and began turning over snapshots of Paddy Coglan.

"He worked hard, if I do say so," Mrs. Coglan murmured, studying the photographs with a softened expression. "He'll take a drink. But as God is my judge, it was his only fault. He never, well—you know, had his hand out for favors, or anything like that. Just the drink."

"It's no crime to take a little nip now and then."

"I suppose not. But a man on a beat is different. Captain Stanko said—Oh, I shouldn't be bothering you with my chatter."

"Not at all. But could I use your phone? I have to check in to the desk."

"Just like a policeman," Mrs. Coglan said, shaking her head. "Always checking in. The phone is in the dining room."

Terrell followed her into the dining room and she turned on the overhead lights. The phone was on the sideboard.

Terrell dialed the Weather Bureau's information service, which gave a recorded weather report every fifteen seconds. He nodded and said, "Okay, okay, I'll check that, too."

Mrs. Coglan said, "I'll just be in the kitchen, if you want me," and left the room.

He smiled at her, and went on talking into the phone. When he heard her footsteps fade away, he turned quickly to a small table a few feet from the sideboard. There was a small stack of mail on a metal tray and with the receiver held between his jaw and shoulder, he went through it quickly. Finally, he came on it, an envelope postmarked the day before with the name "P. Coglan" written in the upper left-hand corner. The letter was addressed to Mrs. P. Coglan and the return address was the Riley Hotel, Beach City, New Jersey.

Terrell put the letters back on the tray, hung up the phone and strolled back into the living room. He made a selection of pictures, and was ready to leave when Mrs. Coglan came in to ask him if he would like a cup of coffee.

"Open up, Paddy," Terrell said, as he rapped on the hotel room door. "This is Sam Terrell. I want to talk to you."

The knob turned slowly, and the door swung back a few inches. Coglan stared up at him, his eyes shifting and his lips trying to work themselves into a smile. "Well, Sam boy," he said, laughing a bit. "You could knock me over with a feather. I needed a rest, and I ducked over here all by myself." He rubbed his mouth with the back of his hand. "That's all I wanted, some place where I could have a drink in private without scandalizing the neighbors." He smelled of whiskey, and he needed a shave.

"Can I come in?"

"Why sure, Sam."

Coglan moved away from the door and Terrell walked inside and took off his hat.

"You want a drink, Sam?"

"No, thanks."

Coglan smiled at Terrell. "Well, how come you're over this way?"

"You know why I'm here, Paddy. Me or somebody else—what difference does it make?"

"Yeah," Coglan said, in a gentle, whispering voice. "Yeah." He smiled again, blinking his eyes rapidly. "Somebody had to come, I guess."

"Because you lied, and an innocent man may die for it." Terrell sat down and took out his cigarettes. "You can't live with a thing like that. There's not enough booze in the world to give you a night's sleep."

"They had too much on me," Coglan said. "Too many times playing around with the booze instead of minding my work. And Stanko said he'd toss me out unless I lied. Unless I said I didn't see the man who ran out of Caldwell's. He said it was hush-hush business—that I'd understand later and that sort of thing. I didn't believe him. But I pretended I did. Even to myself." Coglan wet his lips and walked over to the bureau. "Sure you won't have a nip?"

"No thanks, Paddy. You go ahead."

"So I lied to you, to everybody, including the judge," Coglan said, measuring out his drink slowly and carefully. "I finish my twenty-five years in two months. Then my pension comes through. I want it, Sam, not for me, but for my wife. We never had kids, you know, but with the pension we could go out to California where her youngest sister is living. They've got a big family, lots of young ones. And that's what my wife's been thinking about all these years. You know how women are. It changes them not to have babies. It hurts them. And she wanted to be near those youngsters. So I was scared. Not of being slugged or shot. But of being out on my can, without a dime. Do you understand, Sam?"

"I think so," Terrell said.

"I was never a bad cop," Coglan said slowly. "I was just no good. There's a difference. You got to be lucky to prove you're any good. Did you ever think of that?"

"Sure," Terrell said. "But you're getting your chance. What happened the night Eden Myles was murdered?"

"I heard her scream," Coglan said in a weary, hopeless voice. "I had just turned the corner from Regent Square into Manor Lane. Well, I ran up to Caldwell's door and just then it was jerked open, and out came this big guy. I got a good look at him, Sam. He was surprised and he just stood there for a second. He was big, with thick black hair and a wide, tough face. A gorilla, Sam. Wearing a trenchcoat. No hat, so I could see a deep scar on his forehead. Then he pushed past me and ran across the street, angling toward those shadows from the wall around the church. You see how it was?"

"I see. So you lost him. Then you came back to Caldwell's?"

"That's right. The door was open. Caldwell was lying in a chair out cold, and she was dead on the floor. Her face was all swollen and blue. I called the district and Stanko answered the phone. He just told me to sit tight, and hung up." Coglan finished the drink and ran his tongue around his lips. "Then you called, and I gave you a line on what happened. When Stanko showed up he told me to forget all about the big man I saw running out of the house. So I lied. But sitting over here in this crummy joint I realized I couldn't stick it out."

Watching Coglan pour himself another drink, Terrell was touched by a deep, inarticulate pity.

"So what do I do?" Coglan said.

"You can give me the true story, and we'll run it," Terrell said. "That will take the heat off Caldwell, and put it where it belongs. But the cops who take orders from the Hall will boot you off the force as a liar and a drunk. And they'll hound you off any other job you try to get in the city. And they'll stop your pension."

Coglan stared at his empty glass. "You put it pretty hard, Sam."

"We're telling each other the truth, that's all." Terrell glanced at his watch. "Does anybody know you're here?"

"Just my wife. Stanko said get out of town for ten days and stay quiet."

"Okay, you just sit tight. I'll call you tonight—around eight-thirty. I'll tell you where to go then. Everything will be arranged for you. We'll put what you've told me on tape, and then let it fly." Terrell hesitated, looking down at Coglan. He said, "Have you got your gun?"

"Sure, I don't travel without it."

"Good." Terrell stood and walked to the door. "I'll call you at eight-thirty."

"Sure, Sam." Coglan smiled and put out his hand. "I'll be waiting. I've got nowhere to go . . ."

Terrell was back at the paper by five that afternoon, but Ollie told him Karsh was at the track. Finally, at seven, Terrell reached Karsh at home and told him about his visit with Coglan.

"Oh, brother," Karsh said softly. "Get over here fast, Sam. We've got our story now. Get moving . . ."

Karsh sat down in a leather chair before the fireplace. "Let's have it all in order," he said, glancing up at Terrell.

Terrell told him what he had learned from Paddy Coglan and when he finished Karsh looked at his watch. "Eight-fifteen," he said.

For a few seconds he was silent, frowning at the backs of his hands. Then he said, "Paddy Coglan is a ticking bomb, Sam. When he explodes the whole blazing city may go up in smoke. We'd better get him over here. Let's see, there's a train from Beach City around nine. Tell him to catch it. You can spend tonight getting his story and we'll cut loose tomorrow morning."

"How are you going to play it?"

"Straight, absolutely straight." Karsh stood and looked at his watch. "Get Coglan now. I'll fix us a couple of drinks."

The circuits to Beach City were loaded, the operator told Terrell, but she promised to call him back in a few minutes.

Karsh came back with two whiskies and soda and gave one to Terrell.

The phone began to ring.

"Get it," Karsh said.

The operator said, "I have your party now, just one moment." There was a click, and then a voice said, "The Riley Hotel, reservations."

"I'd like to talk to Patrick Coglan, please."

"Yes, sir." There was a silence, and then: "Who's calling, please?"

"Sam Terrell with the *Call-Bulletin*."

"Yes, just a moment."

Terrell heard a murmuring sound in the background, and then another voice came on the line. "Terrell? This is Tim Moran, Homicide. What did you want to see Coglan about?"

Terrell felt a chill go through him. "It's a personal matter, Tim. What's up?"

"Sorry to give it to you this way, but he shot himself about half an hour ago. Was he sick, or anything like that?"

Terrell covered the receiver and looked at Karsh. "Coglan's dead, suicide. I'd better get over there."

"See what they've got to say first."

Terrell uncovered the receiver and said, "I don't know if he was sick, Tom. Can you tell me what happened?"

"All right. He was found by a maid about eight o'clock. He shot himself with his own gun. In the left temple. The doc thinks he might have been dead a couple of hours though. Some shooting galleries across the street covered the shot."

"Did he leave any note?"

"We didn't find anything. What did you want him for, Sam? You were over this morning, I know."

"I was doing a piece on him," Terrell said. "Profile of an average cop, that sort of thing."

"Well, how did he seem when you talked to him? Depressed? Worried? Anything like that?"

"No, he seemed fine. Thanks, Tim." Terrell put the phone down slowly and looked at Karsh. "In the left temple, seven-thirty or earlier, no note. That's it, Mike."

"You should have got his story on paper. You should have taken a statement from him and had it witnessed and notarized." Karsh threw his cigarette into the fireplace, rose and began pacing the room. "Or you should have used a dictaphone."

"I'll remember next time."

The next morning at nine-thirty Terrell walked into the crowded lobby of the Clayton Hotel, which was an informal gathering place for Ike Cellars and his assistants.

Terrell didn't see Cellars in the lobby, but he noticed a number of his men standing around, portly, substantial types for the most part, studying racing forms, or chatting with one another in an atmosphere of money, cigar smoke and very special and formidable kind of privilege. Terrell went into the barber shop and settled himself in Nick Baron's chair. Nick was a voluble and intelligent little man, and one of Terrell's best sources. Every tip he heard went straight to Terrell's desk, installments against a debt he could never adequately repay. For Terrell had helped to save Nick's daughter when the child was dying of a rare blood disease; through his column he had alerted blood-donor services throughout the country, and enough of the girl's blood type was found to keep her alive for months. And during that time the disease responded to a new combination of antibiotics, and the girl's life was saved.

"How's it going, Mr. Terrell?" he said, putting a towel around his neck. "You look like you could use a facial, a little tone-up, eh?"

"No, I'm just a bit hung. How about using that vibrator on my throbbing skull."

Terrell had seen two of Cellars' men in the shop, but he knew the sound of the vibrator would cover his conversation with Nick. He and Nick had used this arrangement in the past. Nick switched on the vibrator and began massaging Terrell's forehead with his fingertips.

"I'm going to describe a man to you," Terrell said. "Tell me if he's been around."

"Sure, sure," Nick said, raising his voice slightly. "I bet him to win. Courage, that's what I got."

"He's big, black-haired, with a scarred forehead. Tough-looking gorilla. Have you seen him?"

"Well, I don't know."

Terrell saw the perspiration on Nick's upper lip and he realized that the little barber was frightened. "That's okay, forget I asked."

"No—he was in here two days ago with Ike. That's all I know. Want me to ask around?"

"Absolutely not. Forget it."

"Whatever you say."

Terrell glanced at his watch. "That's enough. I've got to be going."

He paid Nick, tipped him a quarter and slipped into his topcoat. He was turning toward the street entrance, when a man's voice said, "Sam boy, just a second."

He looked around and saw that one of Cellars' men, Big Manny Knowles, was smiling at him from the doorway that led to the lobby. Big Manny was a sheepish giant, with small, near-sighted eyes, and an expression that usually registered something just short of bewilderment. He strolled toward Terrell, and dropped a hand gently on his arm. "Ike wants to see you, Sam," he said. "Let's don't keep him waiting. You know how busy he is."

"I worry about it a lot," Terrell said. "All right, let's enter the presence."

Cellars was standing at the cigar stand, leafing through a magazine, a healthy looking man with a dark brown skin and hair as lustrous and beautiful as old silver. He wore a light gray flannel suit, a luxurious, well-cut garment, and a camel's hair coat with slash pockets and hand-stitched lapels. On either side of him were big, purposeful-looking men.

"Good to see you, boy," Cellars said smiling, putting out a wide, soft hand. "Here's what I wanted to see you about. We've got some really terrific pictures from the circus. You know, our big day with the kids. You know, eh, Sam?"

"Yes, I know," Terrell said. Each year Cellars sponsored a well-publicized outing for a group of the city's orphans. They were fed lavishly, entertained at the circus, and photographed extensively with Cellars, Mayor Ticknor, and other civic dignitaries.

"This year was the greatest," Cellars said, chuckling in a deep, confident voice. "Ben, let's have those pictures."

Ben Noble, his press agent, said, "Right off the griddle, Ike," and put a thick manila envelope into Cellars' outstretched hand. "Get a look, Sam." Cellars removed a dozen or so glossy prints. "How about that kid with the lion tamer?"

"It's great," Terrell said. "Moving."

"I'll have my girl send you the material you need," Cellars said.

Terrell smiled slightly. "I'll bet you've got enough material to fill my column for the next two weeks. Until after elections anyway."

"That's right," Cellars said, nodding slowly. "I hope you don't think

I'm being heavy, Sam. But fill your space with something sweet. You'll find that's a good tip."

"Maybe I should take a vacation for a couple of weeks," Terrell said. "Would that be a good idea?"

"Good's a funny word," Cellars said, watching him carefully. "I don't use good and bad. I use smart and dumb."

One of the big men beside him shifted restlessly. "I think he looks run-down, Ike. Maybe a vacation would be smart."

"Maybe," Cellars said.

"You two have a nice act," Terrell said. "Like an organ grinder and a monkey. Why don't you send him around the lobby with a cap and a tin cup, Ike?"

Cellars shoved the folder of pictures roughly into Terrell's stomach. "Don't be funny with me, snoop." The power of the man was suddenly naked in his face; Terrell could see the sadistic needs in his eyes, and in the turn of his cold, thick lips. "You take these pictures. And you look at them every day, and you remember what I been telling you."

Terrell's mouth was dry, and he knew that his forehead was damp with perspiration. But he let the pictures drop from his hands to the floor. "My space is booked for the next two weeks," he said. "I don't have a paragraph to spare."

Terrell stopped for coffee in a drugstore opposite the Clayton. He sat with the coffee until his fingers were steady, and then went out and hailed a cab. He had decided to see Sarnac; Caldwell and the reform ticket must have something damaging to use against Cellars. Otherwise Ike wouldn't have made such an obvious and stupid play.

The atmosphere of Rich Caldwell's campaign headquarters had changed drastically since his visit forty-eight hours ago. Then the mood had been one of missionary enthusiasm. Now the big room was almost empty, and the bunting and pictures seemed woefully incongruous against the dispirited silence.

A young girl escorted Terrell to Sarnac's office. Sarnac was pale and nervous.

"Please sit down," he said. "There's so much to be done, and at the same time there's nothing to do. Nothing, nothing—" He clenched his fists. "Nothing that will help. Nothing at all."

"What have you been doing?"

Sarnac removed his glasses and pressed the tips of his fingers against his closed eyes. "We've hired a firm of private detectives. They're checking everything—Eden Myles' background and that patrolman—what's his name—Coglan, who shot himself. They're going over all the testimony for loopholes. The National Committee has offered us a blank check—they believe in Mr. Caldwell. Money, TV time, their best writers, best investigators, anything they've got."

"Well, to be as cynical as hell, he's their baby. They can't dump him. That would hurt the ticket from one end of the country to the other. Have you talked to Caldwell today?"

"Yes, early this morning. He still has no idea what happened. He believes he was struck down from behind. The police obviously don't agree."

"They've got their story all wrapped up," Terrell said. "Paddy Coglan is dead, but his evidence at the preliminary hearing is a matter of record and admissible in court. Caldwell doesn't have a prayer as things stand. As a loyal friend, all you can do is tidy up his affairs and comfort his widow."

"Does his helplessness give you any satisfaction?" Sarnac was angered and disturbed by Terrell's tone. "Are you pleased that the life of an innocent man is in jeopardy?"

"I want to make a deal with you," Terrell said. "But you've got nothing to bargain with. I want that understood. It will save hedging and double-talk. I think Caldwell was framed. I'm not going to tell you why I think so. But I'm going to try to prove it. I want what you've got on Ike Cellars. On the present administration, up to and including Mayor Ticknor."

"Now just a minute, please." Sarnac looked confused and excited. "I can't agree to those terms. I can't give you information without knowing what to expect in return. You've got to consider my position."

"That doesn't interest me at all. I want what you've got on Ike Cellars. I want the information that he's afraid of. I'm offering one thing in exchange for it—a chance to keep Caldwell out of the electric chair."

"You think Caldwell was framed?" Sarnac said. His hands were shaking. "Is that a guess, Terrell?"

"I know he was framed," Terrell said quietly. "Understand? I *know* it. He could have hurt someone important so he was stopped dead in his tracks. Stepped on. Smashed. Now are you going to tell me who he

307

was about to hurt? And how? Frankly, I don't see what you've got to lose. We're after the same thing for different reasons. I want the story, you want Caldwell cleared. Why shouldn't we work together?"

"I don't know," he said. "All right, all right." His voice rose sharply; Terrell had stood and turned to the door. "Sit down. But for the love of God and truth don't deceive us, Terrell. Don't offer us hope if none exists."

"I'm offering you a chance, which depends on what you tell me. So let's get with it."

"If Caldwell had been elected, Ike Cellars and Mayor Ticknor would have gone to jail for life. Along with dozens of smaller thieves in the administration." Sarnac's voice strengthened as he went on. "That's what they feared. That's why they've committed murder to keep him from office."

"That's a good, husky charge," Terrell said. "Now for details. How were you going to do this?"

"I'll make it as clear as I can. First, let me tell you that our Municipal Parking Authority is one of the neatest civic swindles you'll ever come across. And the public's indifference to it has cost the community—the public itself—millions of dollars."

"Okay, I'm shocked. How does it work? And how do you tie Cellars and Ticknor to it?"

"I'll try to explain." Sarnac stood and came around his desk, frowning thoughtfully.

"The Parking Authority was established by City Council at the request of Mayor Ticknor," Sarnac said, in a careful, precise voice. He paused, as if giving Terrell time to take notes, and then continued, "This was about four years ago, shortly after the present administration had been returned to office. Mayor Ticknor was supported by dozens of experts in traffic management and city planning. Their arguments were clear and logical. More cars are being licensed each month. Parking space is contracting steadily. Traffic problems can only worsen unless drastic and imaginative steps are taken. And so the Authority was created, with broad powers to pass laws, condemn property, build traffic arterials, and so forth. On paper all these proposals look fine."

"But they weren't put into effect."

"That's putting it too simply. Let me give you an example from our files. Three years and six months ago it was announced that a parking

308

drome would be built at Ninth and Morrison. This was just one unit in the overall plant, of course. But we'll take Ninth and Morrison to simplify things. That's a slum neighborhood, fairly close to the center-city shopping and business districts. A logical place to provide parking space, close to the main north-south boulevards, and well integrated into the master circulation system. The architects approved the site, and got to work on plans. The Authority stepped in to confiscate the land. Next the buildings were torn down, the ground cleared away, and it appeared that a certain amount of traffic relief was on the way."

Sarnac paused and sighed. "Well, that's step one. As you know, there is no parking drome at Ninth and Morrison. Here's what happened. The architects submitted a new recommendation. Ninth and Morrison wasn't the best spot after all. Twelfth and Fitzgibbons was much more logical, it seemed. This didn't dismay the Authority. Not a bit. They okayed the new recommendations, and scrapped the plans for Ninth and Morrison. They sold the land at cost—apparently losing nothing on the deal."

"But where's the swindle?" Terrell asked him.

"First, they write off the legal expenses of acquiring title to the land. And secondly, they write off the costs of clearing the ground, wrecking the buildings and so forth. These costs are absorbed in their operating expenses. Thus the land becomes a magnificent bargain. You see, there's a vast difference between land with homes and shops on it, and land that is physically and legally clear of all encumbrances. A private firm might spend years, for instance, merely trying to acquire title to the land—but the Authority can set a price and take possession."

"And Ike Cellars snapped up these bits of property?" Terrell said.

"Cellars, Ticknor and others, all operating under various disguises. They've gobbled up acre after acre of our most important center-city property—using the Authority as their price-fixer and enforcer. And here's another angle. The firms that did ninety-eight percent of this work were Acme Construction and Bell Wreckers—firms that no one knew anything about four years ago. They've blossomed overnight into two of the biggest outfits in the state—solely on contracts they've received from the Parking Authority. The legitimate, or should I say established, companies have never had a chance on Authority jobs."

"Why didn't they gripe?"

"They have, but it's done them no good at all. Dan Bridewell, for

309

instance, has fought them on every contract. He's been in business here forty-five years, but he's never gotten a dime's worth of work from the Authority."

"Can you prove all this?"

"If Caldwell is elected, yes. Our auditors could make out a criminal case in twenty-four hours. And that's why Caldwell was stopped."

"We're back where we started," Terrell said wearily. "In the area of rumor, gossip, what-have-you."

"Every word I've told you is true," Sarnac said.

"But you can't prove it—not in time," Terrell said. "Look: who owns those companies you mentioned? Acme Construction and Bell Wreckers?"

"Again, we don't know. But we'd know the day after Caldwell took over the Mayor's office."

"Okay, okay," Terrell said. "Where did you get this story? Eden Myles?"

"No. A clerk in the Property Tax Office came to us with the lead."

"Did you get anything significant from Eden Myles?"

Sarnac shook his head. "No, just a few rather small odds and ends."

"That's the most interesting thing you've told me."

"I don't understand," Sarnac said.

Terrell got to his feet. "Well, it doesn't matter." It had occurred to him that Eden Myles had probably been framed, too; she hadn't been killed for informing, she had been killed to incriminate Caldwell. It was a chilling and terrible thought.

"What can we do?" Sarnac said, in a desperate rising voice.

"If I find out, I'll let you know," Terrell said. "That's a promise."

After leaving Sarnac, Terrell phoned Gray Gates and asked for Connie Blacker, but learned that she had left Eden Myles' apartment the day before. She had given the Beverly Hotel as a forwarding address, but the desk clerk there told him she wasn't in.

"Do you know when she'll be back?"

"Is this by any chance—" The clerk's small laugh telegraphed the joke. "Is this by any chance *Mr.* Chance?"

"Yes, that's right," Terrell said. "Why? Is there a message?"

"She'll be in around two o'clock, Mr. Chance. She's at the city morgue now, I believe—she asked me for directions, you see."

"Thanks very much."

Terrell took a cab to the morgue. He glanced into the general offices, which were separated from the waiting rooms by a high, wooden counter. Clerks were busy at typewriters and filing cabinets. One of them was talking to Connie Blacker, pointing to a line on the blank she was studying. She was nodding her blonde head slowly. The clerk seemed eager to help, and it was obvious why, Terrell thought. She wore a simple black suit and a short tweed coat, but with her figure and legs she might as well have been wearing a bikini.

Terrell wondered if Frankie Chance had moved into her life. It figured; his girl was downstairs with the iceboxes and running water and he would need a replacement. Connie might just fit. She was young, lovely and manageable. Everything required for the job, including a strong stomach. He sighed, wondering why in hell he felt so bitter about it.

She would be busy for awhile, he knew, completing the arrangements to send Eden's body home. He drifted down the wide corridor. As he turned back toward the general offices he ran into a cleaning woman he had known when the morgue had been his beat, a big and cheerful colored woman who had worked in the morgue for the past thirty years. He was pleased to see Martha. They talked for a few minutes and then she said, "You coming back to work here, Mr. Terrell?"

"No, Martha. I'm waiting to talk to a person who's signing the forms on Eden Myles."

"Wasn't that a shame? That poor thing, so pretty and all. What do you suppose is the matter with that Mr. Caldwell? You think he went crazy or something?"

"I don't know, Martha."

"But why did he have to do it? She's so pretty. And expecting a little baby. That made it worse, if you ask me."

Terrell's expression didn't change. He lit a cigarette, and said, "It's a damn shame. But how did you know she was pregnant? That's supposed to be a secret."

"Oh, oh." Martha put a hand over her mouth. "I've done it again, Mr. Terrell."

"It's nothing serious."

"I heard one of the doctors talking the night she was brought in. I didn't know it was to be kept quiet. You don't say I told you, will

311

you?"

"Of course not, Martha."

Terrell walked back down the corridor, covering ground with long strides. In the Coroner's reception room, Terrell told the secretary he wanted to see Dr. Graham, who was the city's chief coroner. She smiled mechanically at him, spoke into an intercom telephone, and then nodded at the door behind her. "Go right in, Mr. Terrell."

Dr. Graham, a tall man with a long, thin nose, came around his desk and extended a big, but seemingly boneless hand. "We don't see you around much these days, Sam," he said. "Too busy being an important columnist, eh?"

Terrell smiled. "It's a nuisance keeping the space filled every day. It's like an extra mouth to feed."

"What can we do for you?"

"I'd like to look at the report on Eden Myles."

"That's all been in the papers, Sam."

"I know, but I'm running down an angle. I'd like to see the report."

"I read the autopsy report to the press," Dr. Graham said, rather irritably. "You think I've left out something?"

"You left out the fact that she was pregnant," Terrell said. "I'm wondering if you left out anything else."

Dr. Graham fumbled through his pockets and finally brought out cigarettes. His face had become white. "What kind of a bluff do you think you're running?"

"Now, now," Terrell said patiently. "I know she was pregnant, Doctor. I want to know how far gone she was. I want to see the report."

"No, that's impossible. We don't pass out autopsy reports anymore. It involves too much clerical help."

Terrell swore in disgust. Then he said, "I'm going over to the Hall and get a court order to pry that autopsy out of you. And I'll bring back a photographer with me. And the character on our front page with the rosy, embarrassed look won't be me, Doc."

Dr. Graham sighed heavily and sat down behind his desk. "I don't want trouble. I don't want to be in the middle. As God is my judge I've done nothing wrong. The girl's condition had no bearing on her health or Caldwell's guilt."

"She was pregnant then. How many months?"

Dr. Graham sighed again. "Almost three months."

312

"Why didn't you give it to the papers?"

"Captain Stanko said—" Dr. Graham took a handkerchief from his pocket and wiped the damp hollows under his eyes. "Well, he said there was no point in blackening the girl's name."

"The old softie," Terrell said. "This girl has been travelling with hoodlums since she was about twelve, but Stanko doesn't want her reputation besmirched. Come on, Doc, try again."

"The case is open and shut," Dr. Graham said in a hurried, pleading voice. "The girl's a martyr now. Sweet kid, innocent victim, that sort of thing. Why not leave it that way? Why worry about messy details? Caldwell killed her—that's what counts."

"Well, maybe Stanko's got a point," Terrell said. "Don't worry about me broadcasting any family secrets."

"We'll just forget it then?" Dr. Graham said, smiling nervously.

"Sure. Why bother the public with details. So long and thanks, Doc."

In the tiled lobby Terrell looked into the reception room and saw that Connie Blacker was collecting her gloves and purse from the counter, smiling a thank-you at the clerk. He didn't know how to use the information about Eden Myles; he couldn't fit it into the rest of his theory.

Connie pulled open the glass door of the reception room and Terrell walked toward her. "Hello there. All through in there?"

"Yes, I'm through."

"Can I buy you some lunch?"

"No, I have a date."

"With Frankie Chance at two o'clock. But couldn't you be a little late? I'd like to talk to you."

"I'm sorry. I don't have time."

She started past him but he caught her arm.

"Let me go!" Her eyes were mutinous and angry. "Do you want me to start screaming?"

"I want you to start talking," he said. "Who was the man who came to Eden's apartment the night she was murdered? What job did he want her to do? Why was she afraid?"

"Let me go. I don't know anything."

"You're lying, Connie. You can save the life of an innocent man. You can put Eden's murderer in the death house where he belongs. But if you keep quiet nothing will happen."

"Nothing will happen to me," she said tensely.

"And how about Eden?" Terrell's voice sharpened with anger. "You've signed the forms and off she goes by fast freight. Is that the end of it? Have you gone downstairs to look at her? She's lying like a piece of frozen meat with a name tag tied to her ankle. Like something in a butcher shop. Only they kill animals a bit more humanely."

"Stop it, stop it." She turned away, tears starting in her eyes.

Terrell released her arm. "Okay, I'll stop." In his heart he couldn't blame her; why should she risk her life to help him. "I'll drop you at your hotel."

At his desk Terrell typed out an item for his column. He described Eden Myles' killer, the big man with the thick, black hair and scarred forehead, and suggested that the police were looking for him in connection with the Caldwell case. For several minutes he sat frowning and staring at what he had written. This was risky business. Karsh wasn't in or he would have asked his advice. As it was, this had to be his baby. He called a copy boy and gave him the item as an insert for his column; it would be squeezed in in time for the next edition, the two star, and be on the streets around four o'clock. And after that there would be an eruption in the Hall.

Karsh was waiting at Terrell's desk the next morning, looking fresh and handsome in a Chesterfield overcoat with a white silk muffler knotted about his throat. "Why didn't you tell me you were going to toss a grenade?" he asked Terrell. "I might have put my fingers in my ears."

"You heard repercussions?"

"Yes, Jack Duggan, our distinguished superintendent of cops, called me about it. I told him you'd talk to him this morning. Now listen to me." He glanced about the busy room, then looked back at Terrell. "Play it safe. You know about that gorilla who was seen leaving Caldwell's. You're the only one who does. If that gets around you'll become a lousy insurance risk." He patted Terrell's shoulder, in a clumsy and awkward gesture. "You're the staff for my declining years. Remember that, and don't be a damn fool."

"Sure, don't worry." Terrell was touched by Karsh's concern. Without his customary cynicism, Karsh seemed defenseless and vulnerable.

314

He likes me, Terrell thought, and that embarrassed him.

"Don't let them trick you into popping off what you know," Karsh said. "Tell 'em you printed some talk, without checking it."

Jack Duggan was seated at his desk, a large, solidly built man with bold, direct eyes. He wore a uniform with golden epaulettes.

"Sit down, Sam," he said. "This item of yours—" He fingered a clipping on his desk. "It's a strange business. You describe a man in detail, and say we're looking for him in connection with the Caldwell case. Did you make that up? Or what?"

"I gather then the item isn't accurate," Terrell said.

"We aren't looking for anybody," Duggan said. "Let's don't be cute with each other. The Mayor raised hell with this. I know you're a good newspaperman. You don't print gossip or guesses. So it figures that someone gave you the item—someone you trusted. We want to know who it was."

"You and the Mayor, that is."

"That's it. Don't bother reading anything into his interest. He's within his rights. Your item indicates we don't have a complete case against Caldwell. Or that there might be something unexplained and mysterious about it. Neither conclusion is justifiable. The person who peddled this story to you is—a vicious, deliberate troublemaker. And we want to know who it was."

"The tip came in anonymously."

"I wouldn't advise you to stick to that," Duggan said. "This time we aren't interested in anything cute or cryptic. We want the truth."

"So do I," Terrell said. "Supposing we trade."

"What do you mean by that?"

Terrell hesitated, frowning slightly. Duggan was personally honest, Terrell was sure. But Terrell also knew that Duggan was a victim of something that might be called moral inertia; he was honest to a point and beyond that he was neutral.

"I'm waiting," Duggan said. "Who gave you the story?"

Before Terrell could answer, the door opened and Mayor Shaw Ticknor sauntered into the room. Ticknor was grinning widely and scratching the inside of his leg. The grin disappeared when he saw Terrell, but he continued to scratch his leg. "Well, you're the culprit I've been looking for. I hope for your sake you don't mind the taste of

315

crow. Jack, did you put our position to Sam?"

"We were just discussing it," Duggan said.

"There's nothing to discuss," Ticknor said easily. "Not a damn thing." He strolled across the room toward Terrell, smiling again, a tall angular man with shaggy, iron gray hair and big features that looked as if they had been hacked roughly from coarse red rock. The voters seemed to be amused by his calculated oafishness, for they had returned him to office four times running. But he was a man who loved dirty stories, all-night poker games and sadistic practical jokes. He was also a thief on a large scale, and the ruthless enemy of anyone who stood in his path.

"Now let's get squared away," Ticknor said, still smiling at Terrell. "I guess Duggan's made our point by now—long-winded as he is. Somebody peddled you a bum story. The least you can do is print a retraction. Just a line or two. And then tell me where you got the story from."

"That's all, eh?"

"I hope you're not being sarcastic," Ticknor said, and he wasn't smiling any more. "I've been mayor of this city for twelve years, Sam, and I'm not letting you throw mud at my work and my reputation. There's nothing wrong here—but you're trying to stir up dirt. Well, you'll find that doesn't pay off here. Not in my city."

Terrell glanced at his watch. "That all you have to say?"

"Now listen to me," Ticknor said slowly, holding onto his temper. "I want to know where you got that phony story about a man with a scarred forehead. I'm going to get it, Sam. Or you'll wish you'd never crossed me."

"I'm double parked," Terrell said casually, "so you'll have to excuse me. I don't want to get in real trouble." He glanced for a second at Duggan, who was staring at the backs of his hands, an expression of shame and anger on his face. Then he walked to the door.

When Terrell returned to the paper it was almost ten o'clock; the second edition was nearing its deadline and tension was building through the long room. Everyone was conscious of the big clock above the city desk. Karsh waved to him from his office, and Terrell crossed the floor and joined him in that soundproofed command post.

"Don't tell me," Karsh said. "His Honor just hung up." He shook his head. "Corn-fed ass."

"They're worried sick," Terrell said. "Even Duggan. I've never seen them this way before, Mike."

"More bad news is on the way." There was a gleam of devil's humor in Karsh's eyes. "Paddy Coglan's wife came in a while ago. She's waiting upstairs to tell you her story. It's a beaut, a fat, cream-fed beaut. Come on."

Mrs. Coglan was waiting for them in an empty office on the ninth floor. She stood awkwardly when they entered and began plucking at the skirt of her rusty black dress. Terrell could see that she had been weeping.

Karsh said, "Please sit down, Mrs. Coglan, and tell Sam what you've just been telling me."

"They asked me to come in yesterday, to the Hall," Mrs. Coglan said. "And they hemmed and hawed, but finally they came out with it. I could have the pension if I said that Paddy was of unsound mind for the past while. They said it would make the difference. Taking his own life might disqualify him, they said. But if it could be proven he had been upset, crazy so to speak, for some little time, then they thought it would be all right."

"She told them she'd think it over," Karsh said.

"Why do they want to say the poor man was insane? Isn't it enough he's dead?" She clenched her work-worn hands and her lips began to tremble. "Why must they ruin his name? Make him a figure of ridicule?"

"Your husband saw something the night Eden Myles was murdered," Terrell said. "Or someone. That version may be brought forward yet. But it can be discounted if you testify he had been acting oddly. Lunatics aren't very good witnesses."

"How long did they give you?" Karsh asked her.

"Until tomorrow morning."

"If you don't hear from me before then, stall them," Karsh said. "You can be down with the flu, if necessary. We're working on a story that yours is part of. Terrell is putting it together. We won't cut loose until we get everything. Okay?"

She said yes and smiled uncertainly.

Terrell took her to the door. "Paddy would like what you're doing," he said.

"Yes, he was a good man, a good man. Thank you, Mr. Terrell."

Terrell spent the rest of the morning studying clippings on the Municipal Parking Authority. It was a tedious business. He even read the Act itself, straining his eyes over the small print.

Finally he collected the pages of notes he had made, and went upstairs to the financial section, which was one of the long arms of the city room, between Karsh's office and the Sunday departments. The financial editor, Bill Moss, was speaking on the phone, but he smiled and waved Terrell to the chair beside his desk.

Moss wound up his call in a hurry, hung up and smiled at Terrell. "Want a tip on the market? Buy low, sell high." Moss was a handsome man with graying hair and dark, alert eyes. "What can I do for you, Sam?"

"I'll remember that—buy low, sell high. Bill, our Municipal Parking Authority has begun to fascinate me. Mind if I ask you a few questions?"

"Go right ahead."

"Well, I've just read through the Act. Isn't it a pretty loose setup?"

"I would say so, yes. That isn't too unusual, though."

Terrell smiled faintly. "Here's another point I'm curious about. Most of the Parking Authority contracts went to two firms—Acme Construction and Bell Wreckers. I'd like some dope on those outfits—everything you can turn up."

Moss made a note of the firm names, and said, "I'll put somebody on it. I assume you're in a hurry?"

"Sorry, but I am. I'll have lunch and drop back. Okay?"

"I'll try to have the information for you then."

At two o'clock Terrell was back at Bill Moss' desk.

"Here's your information," Moss said, tapping a neat stack of folders with his pencil. "I can probably give you a synopsis faster than you can dig it out for yourself. To start with, and I imagine this is one thing you wanted to know, both companies are legitimate. But there is something queer about them. For one thing, I'm not satisfied by their statements of ownership. I'll explain that in a minute. And secondly, they've been too lucky. Starting from scratch, they've mushroomed into huge organizations, with all of their work coming from the Authority."

318

"How about their ownership? You said something was odd there."

"Well, they list four or five men as owners. I know a couple of them, and well—" Moss shrugged lightly. "These men, in my opinion, don't have the brains and backing to have pulled these companies into shape."

"They're figureheads, you'd say."

"That would be my guess."

"How do I find the real owners then?"

"That's a tough one. The arrangements may be verbal and you can't very well examine or analyse a verbal contract."

"Well, thanks a lot."

Moss nodded. "Let me know what else you find out. I'm always interested in larceny."

"Me, too," Terrell said. "Particularly grand larceny."

At his own desk, Terrell sat for awhile smoking and mulling over what he had learned from Moss. Finally, he picked up his phone and dialed the downtown office of Dan Bridewell's firm. One of the state's largest contractors, old man Bridewell had started as a bricklayer and worked his way to the presidency of the company. He had come a long way, but he had fought for every foot of it.

"Yes? Who's this?" It was Bridewell's voice, high, sharp and irritable. "Terrell? With the paper?"

"That's right, Mr. Bridewell. Sam Terrell. I'm doing a piece on the Parking Authority, and I've come across a point or two I'd like to check with you."

"I'll save you some time, Terrell. The Parking Authority won't give me a contract—they prefer dealing with fly-by-nights. I use the wrong kind of bath soap, or I don't vote right. I've said all this a dozen times, and it's all on the record."

"I want to ask you about Bell Wreckers and Acme Construction—the firms who do the Authority jobs. Do you know the men who own these companies?"

"You'd better go down to the Hall and ask that question, son. They must know. But they never told me. I've got work to do now. Goodbye." The receiver clicked in Terrell's ear.

Terrell smiled and put his phone back in place. For another fifteen minutes he sat at his desk, staring out at the activity and tension that radiated from the city desk and copy wheel. There was only one way to

319

get the information he wanted; he had to make a deal. He picked up the phone and called Superintendent Duggan's office. He mentioned a trade to Duggan and arranged to meet him in five minutes at the north annex to the Hall.

The Superintendent was waiting when Terrell arrived, his face ruddy but rather anxious under the gold-embossed peak of his cap. They fell into step and walked toward Seventeenth Street, moving at a leisurely pace through the crowded mall.

"Do we trade even?" Terrell said. "I help you, you help me?"

"Let's try it."

Terrell put a cigarette in his mouth, hesitating; Karsh's words had come back to him: *"You know about that gorilla . . . if that gets around you'll become a lousy insurance risk."* Could he trust Duggan? That was the gamble. He said, "I talked to Paddy Coglan over in Beach City."

Duggan stared at him. "The day he shot himself?"

"That's right. He described the man he saw running out of Caldwell's house. That's the description I used in my column. The man I described was in town huddling with Ike Cellars a few days before he murdered Eden Myles."

They walked along in silence.

"You happen to know," Terrell said, "who owns Bell Wreckers and Acme Construction?"

"That should be on record some place."

"The owners of the records are dummies," Terrell said. "I want to know who they're fronting for."

"I can put some pressure on," Duggan said. "I'll get the information."

"I need it by tonight. Can I call you at home?"

"That soon, eh? Well, I'll do my best. Around eight?"

"Eight o'clock it is. So long now."

Terrell watched Duggan as he shouldered his way through the hurrying crowds, a big military figure, a picture of power and precision. And what was he thinking? Terrell wondered. How to weasel out of this challenge? Whether to take his information to Ticknor and Cellars, and close his eyes to what would happen?

Terrell was wryly amused at his academic attitude—because there was nothing academic about his position. If Duggan let him down, he

320

wouldn't have a prayer.

At eight sharp Terrell dialed Duggan's home. Duggan answered. "Who's this?"

"Terrell. Well?"

"I've got what you wanted," Duggan said. "And I've got a load of trouble for myself. I picked up two of those dummy owners, and put them through the wringer. Ticknor heard about it and blew his stack. When the Council meets tomorrow I'll be suspended. A nice pay-off, isn't it?"

"Well, you're a cop, not an ostrich," Terrell said. "Incidentally, who owns those companies?"

"It jolted me. I've been on the inside for years and I wouldn't have guessed it. Ike Cellars is a half-owner and that figures. But the other half-owner is old Dan Bridewell. Can you figure that?"

"Are you sure? Dead sure?"

"Christ, give me credit for being able to handle a routine investigation," Duggan said wearily.

"Sorry. For what it's worth, you've got friends in our shop. You may look pretty good in our story."

"Thirty-five years in the business and our Huckleberry Capone of a mayor can break me for doing ten minutes of honest work. It's nice, isn't it?"

"Very. But don't quit. Make them fire you."

"I've already done that."

Terrell hung up and began to dress. Bridewell—that was a sleeper. The posturing puritan, the do-gooder, the angry denouncer of mobs and grafters—in thick with Ike Cellars!

As he was about to leave, the phone rang, and he scooped it up irritably and said, "Hello? Terrell."

"You told me to remember the name," she said.

He recognized Connie Blacker's voice. "I'm glad you did. What can I do for you?"

"I want to see you. I've . . . well, changed my mind."

"Where are you?"

"I'm at the club, The Mansions. Could you come over and have a drink with me?"

She didn't sound right, he thought. Scared maybe. Or worried.

"How about nine or nine-thirty?" he asked.

"That's perfect. It's between my numbers. Please don't let me down."

Terrell looked at the phone and raised an eyebrow. She sounded very odd indeed. "Don't worry," he said. "I'll be there."

Terrell drove to The Mansions, Ike Cellars' big and brilliant night-club in center-city. The headwaiter, Miguel, greeted him cordially and sent a message back to Connie Blacker with a busboy.

The busboy returned and told him Miss Blacker was waiting in her dressing room. Terrell nodded a so-long to Miguel and crossed the floor to the corridor that led to the entertainers' quarters. She was waiting for him at the door of her room.

"I'm glad you could make it," she said.

"You sounded pretty urgent."

"Come in, please. It's cluttered, but there's a spare chair and an extra ashtray."

"Men have lived and died with a lot less," Terrell said. She was nervous as hell about something, he realized. Shaking in her boots. "How's your job coming along?"

"Pretty well. I'm about one notch above a cigarette girl. I do a chorus with the band in the closing number—and I have a little stooge routine with the MC." She smiled rather quickly. "Please sit down."

"You'll get along," he said. "Places like this always need icing." She wore a ribbon in her short, yellow hair, and her skin was like a young girl's, flawless and clean without make-up. Her costume gave her figure an assist it didn't really need. But Terrell had an illogical feeling that she didn't belong in Ike Cellars' elaborately camouflaged clip joint. She was decorative certainly, but she was more than that. She belonged in a home that smelled of clean babies and a pot roast for Sunday dinner, with maybe a log fire and martinis thrown in. But he could be wrong.

"Why did you want to see me?"

She glanced at the door. "If I told you something you could use— what would I get out of it?"

"The usual tawdry things," he said wearily. "Peace of mind, self-respect, an easy conscience. It's a good trade."

She sat down slowly, watching him now. "Nothing else?"

322

"You mean something clean and idealistic—like cash?"

She crossed her legs and moved her foot about in a quick circle. "That's it," she said. She glanced toward the door again, and Terrell saw her hands were gripping the edges of the chair.

"I think we might make a deal," he said. "But I'll need an idea of what you've got."

She leaned toward him suddenly. "Get out of here," she said, in a breathless, desperate voice. "Get out fast."

Terrell stood quickly, but the door was already opening and he realized that he was too late. Frankie Chance came into the room, his deceptively gentle brown eyes alight with anger and excitement. Behind him was one of Ike Cellars' bodyguards, a tall, wide man named Briggs.

"I told you not to bother her," Frankie said.

"She wasn't complaining," Terrell said.

Frankie glanced at her. "Soft-hearted, doesn't want to finger you, that's all. But I know the story. You had a few drinks, Sam, and you began to get ideas."

"This is pretty stupid—even for you," Terrell said.

"Two things Ike won't stand for are drunks and guys who molest his girls."

Briggs put a huge hand on Terrell's arm. "We'll just escort you to your car."

"Thanks for nothing," Terrell said. He tried to pull his arm free but Briggs' hand was as firm as a concrete cast. He looked at Connie then, but she turned away from him. "Nice going," he said.

Briggs led him through the doorway, and glanced at Frankie Chance. "Back way?"

"Sure," Frankie said, taking Terrell's free arm. "It doesn't look good dragging drunks across the dance floor."

They took Terrell through the kitchen and out to the parking lot in the rear which was used for overflow business. Now it was empty and quite dark. An attendant came out of the shadows and flipped his cigarette aside. He seemed to know what was expected of him.

Briggs pushed Terrell against a brick wall, and the attendant and Chance held his arms.

"Sam, you've been a nuisance," Frankie said.

Briggs opened a flask then and splashed whiskey over Terrell's face

323

and shirt front. "Shame to waste it," he muttered. Then he hit Terrell in the stomach with his free hand, bringing the punch up with a kind of lazy power. Frankie and the attendant tightened their grips as Terrell pitched forward, gagging against the pain spreading from his loins to his throat. Briggs hit him a dozen times, methodically and thoughtfully, and then paused and took a pull at the flask he held in his left hand.

"Take him home," Frankie said to the attendant. "We don't want him cluttering up the alley."

Terrell lay on the sofa in his apartment, breathing with infinite care against a frightening pain that moved up and down his body with the rise and fall of his chest.

He wasn't aware of dozing off, but suddenly a chill went through him and he sat up shaking his head and staring about the dimly-lit room. The illuminated hands of his wrist watch stood at two-thirty. He had been asleep an hour or more. What had wakened him?

Then it came again, a soft tap on the door. Terrell got stiffly to his feet, pressing one hand against the pain in his side. He crossed the room, and stood beside the door with his back to the wall. "Who's that?" he said.

"It's me—Connie."

Terrell put the burglar chain on, and opened the door a few inches. She was alone, looking young and pale and frightened.

"What do you want?"

"I was worried. Can't I come in for just a minute, please? I want to explain."

"I'll bet your story's cute," Terrell said. But he was interested. He unhooked the burglar chain. "Come on in." When she slipped past him he closed the door and bolted it and then limped back to the sofa.

"You're hurt," she said. She came up behind him and touched his arm. "Can I get you anything?"

"You've helped enough. Any more help from you and I'll need a complete set of new parts."

"I'm terribly sorry. They made me call you. You—you'd better sit down. You look sick."

"Stop fussing," he said foolishly.

"Well, you stop acting like an idiot." She turned him toward the

324

sofa. He tried to pull away from her but the strength was flowing out of him in giddy waves. "Cut it out," he said. He was on his back then and she was adjusting a pillow under his head.

"They made me do it," she said. "Can't you believe that?"

"Sure, that's how concentration camps got built. People were made to do it."

"They said they just wanted to talk to you. Frankie said you wouldn't see him. So he told me to call you and arrange a date. I—I shouldn't have done it. I wouldn't have if I'd known they were going to hurt you. Would you like some coffee?"

"I don't need anything. All right, coffee then." He knew she wouldn't be able to find things, so he decided to get up and help. But instead he went to sleep. He didn't wake until she shook his shoulders gently and said, "Here's your coffee, Sam."

He had been asleep half an hour, and the rest had revived him considerably. The apartment smelled pleasantly of coffee and cigarette smoke, and Connie was sitting in a chair beside the sofa.

"Do you feel any better?" she asked him.

"I'm all right, I guess." He sipped the coffee and looked around for a cigarette.

"Here," she said.

He took one, accepted a light from hers, and nodded his thanks.

"You should go to bed," she said. "I've put out your pajamas and turned back the covers."

"That's fine."

Terrell stood and limped into his bedroom, aware of her following close behind him. He slipped out of his suitcoat and let it drop to the floor, but the shirt was another matter; he could barely raise his hands to his collar.

Without a word, she stepped forward, and facing him, she took off his tie and unbuttoned his shirt. Her nearness felt good; it was warm and soothing. She said something in a little whisper when she saw the bruises along his ribs. Her lips began to tremble. "They might have killed you," she said.

"A small price for a good story," he said. "That was our class motto. Martyrs in the cause of fearless reporting. A fine, clean way to go, don't you think?"

"Lie down and stop it. Should I call a doctor or something?"

"No, I don't think so. Nothing's broken. It will wear away in a day or so."

"Why are you putting yourself on a spot? Isn't there someone who could help you?"

"Sure," he said, "you for one. But you said no."

"It wouldn't do any good. You can't change things."

"Maybe, maybe not. But I can change into my pajamas, if you'll excuse me."

"Yes, certainly."

Terrell got under the covers a few minutes later and let his body sink into the soft warmth of the bed. A knock sounded gently on the door, and he said, "Come in."

She had her coat over her arm. "I'm going now," she said. "Anything else I could get for you?"

"I don't think so."

She came to the side of the bed and looked down at him with a grave little frown. "I made fresh coffee. All you have to do is turn up the burner when you want it."

"Okay, thanks." They looked at each other for a few seconds in silence. She was very pale and her short yellow hair shadowed her face.

"I'd better go."

"So long, Connie. And thanks again."

But she stood watching him and made no move to leave. Finally she sat on the edge of the bed and looked down at the tips of her brown pumps. "I'm running out of small talk," she said. "I thought—don't you want me to stay?"

"Just like that?" he said.

"Sure—just like that." She spoke almost flippantly, but a tide of color was moving up in her pale cheeks.

She started to rise but he caught her arm. "Why do you want to stay? A tender breast for the wounded warrior? Something like that?"

"I don't know. I didn't figure it out." She looked at him and the light from the bedlamp glinted on the tears in her eyes. "You made me feel cheap and useless, that's all. I wanted to do something for you, something I could do—" She shook her head quickly. "It doesn't make sense. I'm sorry."

"It was a very decent impulse." He was oddly touched and grateful, and that made him feel awkward. "Would you like a cigarette? Some-

326

thing to drink?"

She shook her head again. "No, I've got to go."

Terrell took one of her hands. He didn't want to hurt her any more than he had already, but he couldn't find the words to express his feelings. "Couldn't we forget the bitterness?" he said.

"Can you do that?"

He touched her cheek and then the smoothness of her throat. When she turned and smiled uncertainly at him, Terrell felt very lucky and just a bit humble. "We'll try," he said . . .

The ringing phone woke him much later. He got up on his elbow and switched on the bedside lamp. The room was dark but lines of soft, gray dawn framed the drawn blinds. He lifted the phone and the operator said, "Mr. Terrell?"

"That's right."

"One moment. Beach City is calling."

Terrell swung his legs over the side of the bed and lit a cigarette. Then he looked over his shoulder and saw that she was watching him with a sleepy little smile. "Sorry," he said.

"And I was having such an elegant dream."

"Close your eyes and pick up where you left off. It's still early."

She snuggled into the pillow, her face small and pale in the frame of her tousled bonde hair.

The receiver clicked in Terrell's ear, and a voice he knew said, "Sam? Sam Terrell? This is Tim Moran, Beach City homicide. Sorry about the time."

"Never mind. What's up?"

"That little cop who shot himself over here, you remember? Coglan? Well, I don't think he did. I don't want to say more now, but if you come over here I'll give you the story."

"There's no traffic. I can make it in two hours."

"Fine. I called you because I just got a brush-off from your police department. They want that suicide tag to stick."

"Who'd you talk to?"

"A cop named Stanko."

"That figures. I'll see you in two hours, Tim. And thanks."

Terrell put the receiver down and said, "I've got to shave and get rolling. You try to sleep."

"You must go?"

"Yes, it's important."

She sat up smiling and pressed her cheek against his arm. "I wanted to help you," she said. "And it was the other way around."

"It was much more than that," he said. "I'll tell you about it when I get back. In loving detail."

"Sam . . ."

"Yes?"

"I want to help you. I want to tell you what happened that night at Eden's."

He was silent a moment, watching her. Then he said, "Does anybody know you came here last night?"

"I don't think so. Why?"

"Listen to me: if I let you help, will you promise me not to stick your nose out of this apartment? And to keep that door locked until I get back? And promise not to let anyone in, up to and including the Angel Gabriel?"

"Yes, I promise." She was smiling. He cared about her, and that made what had already happened much more important. "Ike Cellars came to the apartment that night. He wanted Eden to do a job for him."

"And that job was?"

"To help frame Mr. Caldwell."

"Are you sure of this?"

"I was in the bedroom. I heard it."

It was nine o'clock when Terrell pulled into the parking area reserved for police and press at the Beach City courthouse. He had already relayed Connie's story to Karsh, and the presses were ready to run. He needed Tim Moran's story, but he had everything else; the why and how of the frame around Caldwell, the Parking Authority mess, everything. And it was Connie's eye-witness account that tied it all together.

Terrell went up to Moran's office on the second floor. Moran was in his shirtsleeves, his tie loose, his collar open, and he looked gray with exhaustion. But his eyes were narrow and sharp with a hunter's excitement.

"Well, you made pretty good time," he said. "Sit down, Sam. I'll tell you what I've got. Then I think you can tell me something. Is that fair enough?"

"Sure," Terrell said.

Moran picked up a glossy print from his desk and handed it to Terrell. "There's the mug who shot Paddy Coglan. Know him?"

Terrell studied the dark face, the low, scarred forehead, the bold, angry eyes. He shook his head slowly. "I don't know him. Where did you get the picture?"

"You know something about him though, Sam. I saw your expression."

"This could be the guy Coglan saw leaving Caldwell's." At Moran's puzzled frown he said, "I'll sketch it in for you, don't worry. But tell me the rest of your story. Where did you get this picture?"

"It's a weird thing, Sam. As odd as I ever ran into in this business. We wrote Coglan off as suicide, you know. Well, two days after his death I got a call here in my office. It was from a guy who'd been registered at the hotel at the same time as Coglan. He was on the same floor, just a room away, and he heard the shot. He looked out into the corridor and saw a man closing Coglan's door. He saw only the man's back. But he was able to describe his overcoat, the color of his hair and general build."

"Why did he wait two days to speak up?"

"He was plain scared. But his conscience obviously bothered him a bit. I took the description to the hotel, and talked to the bell-hops, elevator men and desk clerks. They'd seen this man, all right. He'd been in the lobby in the afternoon and right after suppertime. And an elevator operator remembered taking him to the floor above Coglan's. Then I played a long hunch. You know there are quite a few sidewalk photographers working this area, so I rounded them up and looked at the shots they'd taken the day that Paddy Coglan was shot. That's how we got this picture. The photographer remembered the guy. He thought the big boy looked like a fighter or a wrestler, someone who might be flattered by a picture of himself. But it didn't go. Our guy stopped and glared at the photographer and then walked off fast." Moran grinned without humor. "I like to think of what that did to his nerves. Anyway, we sent the print to Washington, and they traced it. He's Nicholas Rammersky, Alias Nick Rammer, age forty-two, with two convictions and a record of minor stuff stretching back twenty years.

He's a paid killer. And I want to know who paid him to kill Paddy Coglan."

"I said I'd fill you in," Terrell said. "I had everything but Rammersky's name when I came over. It goes this way . . ."

Twenty minutes later Moran came to the door with Terrell. He said, "Rammersky will burn for the murder of the girl or the cop. Either way, I'm not particular. He can't hide after your story breaks. And neither can those other crums in your backyard . . ."

Terrell drove back through heavy traffic and reached the city shortly after two-thirty. He parked in front of his apartment, and checked the time as he went up the stairs. They would need a couple of hours to get the story organized. By working fast they could make the three-star final at four-thirty. The editions establishing Caldwell's innocence would hit the city like sledge hammers.

Terrell unlocked the door and said, "Hey!"

There was no answer, no stir of life in the apartment. He stood with his hat in his hand, feeling the grin stiffen on his lips. For several seconds he waited, and then he closed the door and walked slowly through the little apartment. Empty. The blinds were still drawn, and the bed was unmade. There was the light fragrance of her perfume in the air. But that was all.

He lit a cigarette and looked around the living room, a frown touching his face. She didn't have any reason to risk her neck, he thought. Why shouldn't she clear out? But he was surprised, Terrell realized sadly. He would have bet anything that she'd stick.

It was then, as he was putting his cigarette out, that he saw the note on the telephone table. He picked it up, feeling the leaden disappointment moving in him. It was written in pencil, in a neat and careful hand: "Maybe I picked sides in too much of a hurry. I'm trying to be sensible now. Forgive me for backing out. Give me that much of a break."

Terrell stared around the room, shaking his head like a weary fighter. Without her testimony much of his story fell apart. The Rammersky part was intact, but that only proved that Coglan was murdered; it wouldn't help Caldwell. Not in time.

He sat down and called the paper, but Karsh wasn't in. His secretary told him he was at the game. The Game. Terrell had forgotten;

Dartmouth was playing and Karsh was there with a party of friends. It irritated Terrell; a game, any game, seemed silly and insignificant while Caldwell was in jail, and the truth couldn't be told . . .

Terrell stood and looked around, frowning again; something was wrong. The unmade bed—that was wrong. She wouldn't leave without tidying up. Terrell looked at the note he had dropped on the coffee table. That was genuine. His heart was beating faster. He was suddenly hoping that she *had* walked out on him. That she had left of her own free will.

He sat down and dialed her hotel. When the clerk answered Terrell said, "Is Connie Blacker there?"

"She's checked out sir."

"When was this?"

"Let me see—that was around ten this morning."

"Did she leave a forwarding address?"

"Just a second—no, I'm afraid not."

"Was she alone?"

"Sir, I can't tie up this phone indefinitely. I—"

"Was she alone?" Terrell repeated sharply.

"No, sir—there were friends with her. Two gentlemen."

"Was Frankie Chance there?"

"There's a call waiting, sir. If you could stop by—"

Terrell put the phone down and picked up his hat. He went downstairs to get a cab.

At the hotel, the desk clerk described the men who had been with Connie: one was large, with dark skin and hair and the other was sharply dressed, with light hair and thin features. The big man sounded like Briggs, Cellars' bodyguard.

Terrell went outside and stopped on the busy sidewalk, wondering what to do next. He was caught between two fears, the first that she had walked out on him, and the second that she had been picked up by Ike Cellars' hoodlums. The first fear was selfish, but the other thing was a matter for the police or FBI—but he had no proof beside his illogical conviction that she wouldn't have run out on him.

Terrell went back to his apartment and called Karsh, but the maid told him everyone was still at the football game. Karsh's son was in with a group of friends, she said, and everybody was coming back after the game for a buffet dinner and some drinks.

Terrell paced up and down the apartment, smoking one cigarette after the other. Finally, he turned decisively and scooped up the telephone. Superintendent Duggan wasn't in his office, his secretary said; he could be reached at home if it were important. Terrell broke the connection and dialed Duggan's home number.

Duggan's wife answered, and said just a minute, she'd tell Jack, and then Duggan was on the phone, speaking in a soft, worried voice. "Sam, it's been a wild day. I guess you've heard all about it."

"I haven't heard anything. I've been working. I want to report the kidnapping of a girl named Connie Blacker who worked for Ike Cellars."

Duggan paused, and Terrell heard his heavy breathing. "Why come to me?" he said at last. "It's a Federal charge."

"Aren't you interested? Did Ike Cellars dampen your flaming official zeal?"

"Who the hell do you think you're talking to?" Duggan said, in an angry, rising voice. "I've been kicked around all day, and I'm sick of it. The Council didn't suspend me—but only by three votes. Ticknor told me off like I was a rookie cop he'd caught drunk on a beat. I'm not taking any more of it—from you or anybody else."

"You're going to take a lot more," Terrell said. "Ticknor can scare up three more votes, don't worry. And after that you're through—another ex-cop whining that he got squeezed out by political pressure. But if you find that girl you've got a chance."

Duggan said, "What do you mean? What's she got to do with me?"

Terrell was aware of the quickened interest in his voice; then suddenly he realized that he'd been beaten on this story from the start: Paddy Coglan, Connie—someone was always ahead of him.

"I don't understand," Duggan said. "What did you say her name was?"

"I forget," Terrell said. "Smith or something like that."

"Why the cute stuff? I asked you a question. What's the girl's name? What's she got on Ticknor and Cellars?"

"Nothing at all," Terrell said. "I was dreaming."

"You sound wide awake to me."

"It's a trick I learned in college. Take it easy." Terrell put the phone down on Duggan's protesting voice, and picked up his hat and coat. Duggan wouldn't help. No one would help. She was trouble, and the

332

smart boys would want no part of her. A pillow over her face, the pressure of a finger on her throat—that was the best thing all around. So the smart boys would figure it. But there was still a chance, Terrell knew. He had enough to print now. Enough to blow a loud whistle on Cellars.

When Terrell reached Karsh's apartment it was late in the afternoon, and the early winter darkness had dropped over the city. The crowd was back from the game and a party was underway.

"Where's Mr. Karsh?" Terrell asked the maid.

"He's talking on the long distance in his bedroom, Mr. Terrell. Can I bring you a drink or something to eat?"

"No, thanks. I'll forage."

Karsh's son and a half dozen of what obviously were his friends had grouped themselves about the massive record player, the young men in dark flannels and white buck shoes, the girls smooth and sweet in tweeds and cashmeres.

At the opposite end of the room Karsh's mistress and an assortment of friends and sycophants were standing in front of the well-stocked bar. To each his own, Terrell thought, as he went over to get a drink. But he felt sorry for Karsh, who seemed to make sense only at work. There he operated with brilliant precision, keeping every department of the paper under meticulous supervision. But the rest of his life was chaos. His marriage had ended in divorce several years ago and he had been bled white by his wife's lawyers. He had never been close to his children—a son and daughter—and saw very little of them now; the girl had married and moved to the west coast, and the son was a smooth and expensive youngster who dropped in at the office occasionally to discuss his financial needs.

Terrell's thoughts turned from Karsh to Connie. It was now after six: Connie had been gone since ten that morning. Eight full hours. Anything could have happened to her in that time—anything might have been done to her.

The bedroom door opened and Karsh walked out. He was fairly drunk, Terrell guessed.

He wore a superbly cut gray flannel suit with a Dartmouth pennant in the lapel, and was groomed to glossy perfection. "Let's have a drink, for God's sake," he said.

333

Terrell crossed the silent room and took Karsh's arm. "Mike," he said, "listen to me. Will you please?"

"Sam, old boy, glad to see you. Did you meet my son? He's ashamed of me, but he's a good kid in spite of that—or because of it, I should say."

"Mike, listen," Terrell said. "The girl is gone. The witness. Cellars has her."

But Karsh was lost to him. "Old college songs, Sam, that's the spirit of the evening. There's one from the ole U. of Peiping—" He laughed as an ad-lib struck him. "The University of Peiping Tom, actually."

Karsh's son joined them and said easily, "Dad, we've got to peel off. I didn't get a chance to tell you during the game, but we're driving up to Skyport tonight." Young Karsh was tall, dark and his manners were impeccably casual.

"That's all right," Karsh said. He smiled and patted the boy's shoulder. "Sorry you have to be on your way. I missed a briefing, I guess. I thought this was to be a real holiday. Well, have a nightcap anyway. And a bite of something to eat. Make your friends live it up a bit."

When Karsh turned back to Terrell his manner had changed; the boozy good fellowship was gone, and his eyes were empty and cold. "I go on kidding myself," he said. "Thinking there's something besides work. But there's nothing." He shook his head quickly. "The girl is gone, eh? When did this happen?"

"Around ten this morning."

"How important is she to your story?"

"She's it. But I can start without her."

"Are you sure Cellars picked her up? She worked for him, you said. Maybe she's still working for him."

"No, she's on the level. I know, Mike."

"It's a question of how far we can trust her. She may have walked out on you—keep that in mind. Scribbled a note and walked out. There's no proof that Cellars grabbed her. Is there, Sam?"

Terrell hesitated, frowning faintly at Karsh. "How did you know she left a note?" he said.

"Clairvoyance, pure and simple. They all leave notes. Now look. Wait for me in my bedroom while I make another call. I'll put the call through out here and say good-bye to the boy. Then we'll go to work. Could you get everything together in two or three hours? For the

334

Night Extra?"

"I'm ready now," Terrell said.

"Good." Karsh winked at him and walked briskly to a telephone on a table beside the record player.

The room was noisy with talk and music. When the connection was made and Karsh was speaking, Terrell turned and walked into Karsh's bedroom. He closed the door behind him and leaned against it, hearing the hard, laboring stroke of his heart. The music from the living room poured around him, but he was aware only of the reactions of his body; the beat of his heart, the tight, cold feeling in his stomach, and then something in his mouth that was like an essence of fear and betrayal and death.

The extension telephone was on a table beside Karsh's long, wide bed—just a foot or so from Terrell's hand. He looked down at the smooth, black receiver, and a little shudder went through him.

But Terrell's hand moved slowly, almost of its own volition, raising the receiver to his ear. He heard music first, a noisy background sound from the record player, and then he heard Karsh's voice, sharp and hard over the music, and insistent to the point of desperation.

"—it can't be covered up, Ike I'm telling you, it's impossible. Be reasonable, man."

The music beat strongly in Terrell's ear, a pulsing rhythm that matched the quick beat of his heart. And then he heard Ike Cellars' voice, bigger than Karsh's, thick with convulsive anger.

"Don't tell me anything, understand! You keep it out of your paper."

"But Terrell's got everything."

"You keep it from being printed then. That's your job. Don't worry about anything else."

"Just a minute—hold on a second." Karsh's cry was desperate and futile; the connection was already broken.

Terrell heard Karsh's ragged breathing for an instant before he put the receiver quietly back into its cradle. He stood perfectly still, rubbing his hands on the sides of his trousers.

When he heard the knob turn, he put a cigarette quickly between his lips and raised his hands to cup the flame of his lighter. The door swung open and Karsh walked into the room, his manner brisk and business-like. "I'm squared away now," he said. "Tell me what you've got, Sam."

Terrell couldn't make himself turn and face Karsh. He stood in profile to him, almost physically sick with a blend of shame and anger and pity.

"Well?" Karsh said. His tone was puzzled. "I asked you a question, Sam. What've we got? Provable stuff we can back up with witnesses and written evidence?"

Terrell turned at last and stared at Karsh. The silence stretched out until Karsh made a worried little gesture with his hand, and said, "What's the matter, Sam? I'm just asking you what we can use."

"Why not ask Ike Cellars?" Terrell said, softly. "From the weather to classified ads—he's the boy to ask. Isn't that right, Mike?" His voice rose suddenly in anger. "Well? Isn't that right?"

"What the hell are you talking about?" Karsh's puzzled smile was a good effort, but his face had turned clammy and white.

Terrell said bitterly, "Don't lie and squirm. Spare me that. You knew the girl wrote a note. How? How did you know that?"

"I told you—"

Terrell pointed to the extension telephone. Karsh's voice trembled and then he wet his lips and stared at Terrell in silence.

"I heard you talking to Cellars," Terrell said.

"Listen to me—you've got to understand."

"Understand what? That you're working for him? I know that now."

Karsh took a step toward him and raised his hands in a clumsy and incongruous gesture of supplication. "Sam, I was trying to save you— you've got to believe me. From the moment you talked to Coglan and got his story about the prowler—from then on you were slated for the morgue."

"I brought you the whole story," Terrell said. "You could have smashed them to bits with it. But you killed it. We'd wait until we had it all, you said, the drama and the color, the whole thing in one piece, like a beautiful symphony." Terrell's voice became savage and ugly. "But you were lying. I had the guts of the story the first night, but you threw it out. Threw away Caldwell's only chance. Then I traced down Paddy Coglan, and got the truth from him, a scared, drunken little cop hiding in a cheap flea trap in Beach City. But he was dead before his testimony could do any good. Then Mrs. Coglan came in with her story, and you buried that too. More lies. Wait till we have it all, the drunks singing Faust, the symphony of news." Terrell pounded a fist into his palm.

"I fell for it like any prize fool. But I was too close to you, Mike. I believed in you. You taught me this business. For a dozen years you were my model—I even tried to dress like you when I was a copy boy."

"Sam, listen for God's sake."

"Then the girl talked," Terrell said bitterly. "And we had them cold. But you squealed to Cellars again, and now she's gone. Where?" Terrell caught him by the lapels of his expensive suit and shook him with all of his strength. "Where is she? What have they done with her?"

"I don't know—I don't know."

Terrell let him go and Karsh turned away and sat down slowly and wearily on the side of the bed. His face had gone slack, and he was breathing with a definite physical effort, like a man in pain. "I needed money, I always needed money." The travesty of a smile twisted his lips. "The pleas of the absconding bank teller, the defense of a kid who snatches a purse. You'd think I could come up with something more original." He sighed and a little shudder went through his body. "Gambling, alimony, that little fop of mine outside—they suck money out of me every minute of the day and night. Cellars offered to chip in a few years back. At first it was simple. Kill a divorce story, ease up on some characters in trouble with the tax people—favors I could do with a pencil or a telephone call. But I got in too deep. I couldn't pay him back." Karsh looked up at Terrell, his eyes pleading for understanding. "Then the Caldwell story broke. You stumbled on the truth, and Cellars expected me to keep it out of the paper. If it was just my job at stake I might have told him to go to hell. I don't know. But it was your life, Sam. Cellars wanted to kill you. I convinced him it would be smarter to kill the story. So we played you for a fool. Everything you dug up went back to Cellars—and nothing went into the paper. But you're alive, remember that, *I saved your life*. Maybe you don't believe me." Karsh tried to smile, but his face was a mask of despair.

"Where's the girl now?" Terrell said.

"I don't know. I swear it." Karsh got slowly to his feet and moistened his dry lips. "Is she important to you?"

"What difference does that make? She's important to herself. She's a hundred pound girl who got in trouble with hoodlums because she was willing to tell the truth."

"She won't be hurt, Sam. She'll be all right."

"Is Paddy Coglan all right? Do you want the girl's death on your conscience too? Where is she?"

"I don't know, I don't know."

Terrell turned to the door.

"Wait, Sam, wait. Please."

Terrell looked back and saw the tears trembling in Karsh's eyes. But nothing could touch him any more. He walked out and slammed the door on Karsh's entreating voice.

Terrell stopped at a bar near Karsh's place, and drank two double whiskies, but the liquor failed to dissolve the sickening coldness in his stomach.

The story would break, of course. Nothing could stop it now. When Rammersky was picked up for Coglan's murder, he would talk—he wouldn't go to the chair and leave Cellars in the clear. And when Cellars fell he would drag old man Bridewell and Mayor Ticknor with him.

Terrell didn't need a newspaper to print his story. He could give it to Sarnac, and the national committee of Caldwell's party would splash it across the country.

But would that help Connie? No. He needed something that would stampede Cellars tonight; that would be sure to take his mind off everything but survival.

"Another one?" the bartender asked him.

"Yes, thanks." An idea had occurred to Terrell. There was something cruel and destructive in it that appealed to his need for reprisal. He walked to the phone booth at the end of the room and looked up the number of the Weston Hotel, where Frankie Chance had an apartment.

The hotel operator connected him with Frankie's room and after a few rings Frankie Chance said, "Hello?"

"Frankie? This is Sam Terrell. I'd like to see you for a few minutes. Can I come over?"

"You feeling unhappy about the beating you took the other night?"

"Live and learn," Terrell said. He began to smile, but his eyes were cold and hard. "This is another matter. I want to tell you who killed your girl. I'll be over in five minutes."

"You dirty, filthy scum, I'll—"

338

Terrell laughed shortly and dropped the receiver onto the hook.

At the Weston Hotel, he walked through the crowded lobby, took the elevator to Frankie Chance's floor. He went along a clean, warm corridor to the apartment and rapped lightly with the back of his knuckles. Frankie pulled the door open and said, "Come in, snoop. I prayed you'd come. I swear to God, I prayed." His hand was in the pocket of a gaudy dressing robe and Terrell knew he was holding a gun.

"There's no point in being mad, Frankie," he said. "I'm not here to needle you. I'm here to do you a favor."

Chance closed the door and took the gun from his pocket. "Don't stall," he said. "What are you trying to tell me, Sam?"

Terrell sat on the arm of a chair, smiling faintly. "I could do this leisurely, but I never got my kicks pulling wings off flies. Your girl was murdered on orders from Ike Cellars. A thug named Nick Rammersky did the job. That's it, Frankie. The guy you work for, the big boy who tosses you your bones—he had Eden killed."

"Shut up!" Frankie said softly. "You already said too much."

"Ask yourself one question, Frankie. Would I come here without proof?"

Chance stared at him for seconds, digesting this, and then he sat down slowly on the edge of the bed. "Proof—what kind of proof you got?"

"It's an interesting and devious story," Terrell said casually. "Eden Myles was peddling a few innocuous facts to Richard Caldwell. You follow me? Or do words like 'innocuous' tax you, Frankie?"

"You keep talking, or I'm going to beat it out of you," Frankie said.

"She was peddling them on orders. You were probably in on it that far, Frankie. And Eden thought it was as simple as that, too—get Caldwell's ear, give him a few bum tips. Wheels within wheels, a bit of standard political flimflam. But she didn't see the end of the script," Terrell said, watching Frankie's hot dark eyes. "Ike planned to have her killed in Caldwell's home—and frame Caldwell for her murder. Cellars had no animus against your girl, Frankie, but she could have been troublesome later. So that's the story. Rammersky came in the back door and knocked Caldwell out. Then he strangled Eden and left."

339

"You mentioned proof." His voice trembled. "Where is it?"

"First, Rammersky was seen bolting away from Caldwell's by a little cop named Paddy Coglan. Secondly, Connie Blacker heard Cellars explaining the phony deal to Eden. You know Connie, Frankie. You know she's straight."

"She's a square, an oddball," Frankie said, but a tide of angry color was moving up in his smooth brown cheeks. "What'd she tell you?"

"She was at Eden's apartment the night Eden was killed. Staying there as Eden's guest. Cellars arrived about ten-thirty, and told Eden she had to put on an act at Caldwell's that night. Get him drinking, and then start screaming and pretend that she'd been attacked and so forth. And as an added precaution, Cellars went on, one of his men would come in the back way and knock Caldwell unconscious, make it look as if he and Eden had struggled around a bit till he fell and hit his head. Cellars' man would disappear—leaving Eden alone to face the aroused neighbors and eventually the police. Eden would testify that Caldwell had become abusive, and had attacked her. This, Cellars assured her, was all she had to do or say. Connie heard this conversation, and talked to your girl when she came into the bedroom to change. Eden was frightened. She thought the whole deal was raw. She didn't know just how raw it was going to be."

"They didn't have to kill her," Frankie said. Tears were starting in his eyes. "She never hurt anybody. She was kind to everybody. We were together for five years and she never looked at another guy. We were going to buy a six-flat over in Eastport next year. Live in one flat, and live off the rent from the others. It was what she wanted. Something solid."

"Did you know she was pregnant?" Terrell asked quietly.

Frankie began to pound the foot of the bed with the flat of his hand, gently at first, but the blows fell harder and harder. "She wanted it. I didn't. I was scared. For her."

"What were your plans for the kid?" Contempt put an edge to Terrell's voice. "A job running numbers, or maybe selling programs and peanuts in a burlesque joint? Then take him back to Sicily to show the old folks how well you'd done in free, democratic America. Were those your dreams, you bastard?"

Frankie seemed hopelessly confused; he opened and closed his mouth but he couldn't manage anything but incoherent grunts.

340

"Beautiful dreams," Terrell said. "Then Cellars put his foot down, and there's nothing left but a grease mark on the floor."

"I got to ask some questions around," Frankie said, forming the words slowly and laboriously. "I'll find out the truth."

He dropped his robe on the floor and took down a raglan topcoat from the dressing room alcove. "Nobody ever talked to me the way you did," he said. "So I'll see you again, don't worry." He transferred the gun to the pocket of his topcoat.

"Wait a minute," Terrell said wearily. "Don't be a sucker, Frankie. You start after Cellars or Rammersky and you'll get your head blown off."

"Sure," Frankie said. "They're tough guys."

"I've been steaming you up for personal reasons."

Frankie turned and looked at him then. "What kind of personal reasons?"

"Cellars picked up Connie Blacker. She came to my apartment last night and that's where he found her this morning. I wanted him to start worrying so hard about his own skin that he'd forget her. I thought you were the boy to worry him."

"You're brainy. Using me to save her hide."

"It's no good, Frankie."

"Why not? I'll worry him plenty. And if I get my head blown off, what difference does it make? You'll have your girl. I'm a nothing to you. A bastard, wasn't it? The kind of slug who'd raise a kid to run numbers or work in a burlesque joint." Frankie was smiling but he sounded very much like a child trying not to weep. "Wasn't that you talking a few seconds ago?"

"I shouldn't have," Terrell said.

"You don't know me. You don't know Eden. But we're tramps to you. Isn't that right?"

"For Christ's sake, stop being so emotional."

"I think I'm going to die tonight." Frankie shrugged lightly. "That's why I'm talking like an oddball. It's important. You think she was a tramp, eh?"

"I think she loved you," Terrell said. "She wanted to have your baby. She was no tramp."

Frankie nodded slowly. "That's a logical way to look at it. It's funny that what you thought of her should matter to me. But you may be the

341

last guy I'll ever talk to about her. So it makes a difference."

"You're selling yourself a deal," Terrell said. "You'll die all right. You'll be hit by a truck wandering around talking nonsense."

"No, it won't be that way," Frankie said. His hand turned the knob slowly and the door opened an inch or so. "You bought yourself an address," he said. "Bancroft's Nursing Home, on Madden Boulevard near the city line."

"What's that?"

"It's where Ike sent the little blonde," Frankie said. "You should know how close you came to not getting it. So long now." He opened the door and slipped quickly into the corridor.

Terrell listened to his heels clicking sharply toward the elevators, and then he picked up the phone.

He got the police board, but it took him almost five minutes to get through to Duggan. Finally Duggan's voice cracked in his ear. "Yes? Who is this?"

"Sam Terrell. Listen, I've got an address I want you to take down."

"Sam, you must live under a rock. Don't you know the whole goddamn city is upside down? We picked up a hoodlum named Rammersky who tells us he strangled Eden Myles. Caldwell's clear."

"The Bancroft Nursing Home," Terrell said, raising his voice over Duggan's. "There's a girl being held there. Connie Blacker."

"Wait a minute," Duggan said. "We already got that tip. The Bancroft Nursing Home. Hang on."

"What are you talking about?" Terrell yelled, but Duggan was off the line.

He returned a full minute later, and said, "I just checked with Radio. A couple of cars are on their way to pick her up."

"Where did you get the tip?"

"Mike Karsh called about ten minutes ago. Told us the girl was being held against her will, that she was an important witness against Ike Cellars."

"When will you know if she's all right?"

"When the cars report to Radio. Sam, I'm busy as hell."

"I'll call you back," Terrell said, and put the phone slowly back in place. He sat on the bed and lit a cigarette. Mike Karsh . . . He shook his head, completely bewildered.

Five minutes passed. He called Duggan again, and was another couple of minutes getting through to him. Then he said, "Have you got the girl?" His voice was high, and he could feel the uneven lurch of his heart.

"Yes. They've taken her over to St. Anne de Beaupre's and made three arrests at the Bancroft Home. It's a phony joint."

Terrell's hand tightened on the phone. "What's the matter with her?"

"Christ, I don't know," Duggan said impatiently. "She's in bad shape. That's all they told me."

Terrell said to the nurse in the accident ward at St. Anne de Beaupre's hospital, "Connie Blacker. How is she?"

"Admitted," the nurse said. She looked up at him and smiled quickly. "Hello, Sam. You're a stranger. She's under oxygen, I think. She was having some kind of respiratory trouble. What's the matter? You look pretty rocky yourself."

"Nothing," Terrell said. "Where is she?"

"Just down the hall. In Emergency."

"Thanks," Terrell said, and turned into the wide white corridor. He knew his way around every hospital in the city; he had sipped coffee in this one, and kidded with the nurses while waiting for an accident victim to die.

Now it was all different. A tall, balding doctor came out of the emergency ward, and Terrell caught his arm. "The girl they just brought in," he said. "How is she?"

"Not too good. You're a friend of hers?"

"That's right, I'm a friend."

The doctor removed his glasses and polished them on his clean white smock. "She was injected with considerably too much morphine," he said. "That was sometime this morning, I gather. Then she spent the day in a tank—the treatment for violents, you know. Wet sheets from head to foot. She's completely disoriented now. Out of sheer fright, I'd say. And the morphine has affected her respiratory center."

"Will she be all right?"

"I don't know. I'd say yes, with some qualifications. We're giving her oxygen, and an antidote for the morphine. She's had the raw material for a lifetime of nightmares packed into a very short period of time— that will give her trouble. She'll need help."

"Yes, sure," Terrell said. "When can I see her?"

"Not for a couple of hours anyway. You can leave a message if you like."

"Thanks, I'll give a phone number to the desk."

As Terrell entered the reception room the door opposite him opened and a *Call-Bulletin* photographer named Ricky Carboni came in with his bulky camera.

"Sam boy," he said, "how goes it?" Ricky was an old-timer, a big, balding man with dark eyes and a warm smile. "Where's the girl?"

"You mean Connie Blacker?"

"Yeah, how is she? Ready to be immortalized?"

"She's in no shape for pictures, Ricky. Not for a couple of hours."

"Karsh said to get a picture—regardless or irregardless."

"Karsh? What the hell is going on, Ricky?"

"Don't ask me. Karsh just tore the Night Extra into tiny scraps. Everything's out except the want ads. And the whole damn daytime staff is back putting a new edition together. I thought you were working when I saw you. Well, I'm going to find the poker game. Take it easy."

"Sure," Terrell said.

He went outside and a patrolman said, "We're riding in, Sam. Need a lift?"

"Thanks, I'm going back to the shop." He was in no hurry to see Karsh. But he had to see him. One more time . . .

The lights were on in the city room, and the atmosphere was one of hectic tension. Normally the Night Extra was put to bed by a staff of three. But now everyone was in; Williams handling the city desk, Tuckerman hunched massively beside the police speaker, and all of the top writers and reporters from the daytime shifts.

Karsh stood directly behind Williams, one foot propped up on a chair, talking urgently and imperatively to Ollie Wheeler.

Terrell dropped his coat over a chair and walked toward Karsh and Wheeler.

Karsh turned, a quick, easy smile lighting his face. "You're just in time, Sam. I want you on the main story—every detail in chronological order. Don't waste time on the Parking Authority—just mention it as if the readers knew all. They will when they read Ollie's piece. He's doing a special story."

344

"I'll get started, Mike," Ollie said.

"Yes, get with it." Karsh was still looking at Terrell, but his manner was business-like and impersonal. "Bridewell issued a statement half an hour ago—owned up to all his crimes, including not curbing his dog several years back. The mayor can't last much longer than it takes city council to get in session. They're licked, Sam."

"And I'm supposed to write the big, hot story," Terrell said. He lit a cigarette and flipped the match aside. "The works, eh? All stops out?"

"Certainly."

"And how do I handle you?" Terrell asked him coldly. "How do we tint and shade the image of Mike Karsh? Are you portrayed with an arm around Ike Cellars' shoulder, and a hand reaching for the public trough?"

Karsh winced slightly. "No metaphors, please. Never oversell a good story. Play my part for what it's worth. No cover-ups—but don't get off on a tangent. Caldwell was framed. Here's how and why. Bang that home."

Tuckerman looked up then and covered his phone with a huge hand. "Mike," he said. There was an unmistakable significance in his tone and as Karsh turned to him, a silence settled around the immediate area of the city desk.

"What's up?"

"Ike Cellars," Tuckerman said. "For you."

Karsh smiled complacently, and began to screw a cigarette into his holder. He glanced at the clock above him, and said, "I expected to hear from him before this." He touched Terrell's arm. "Now look: you get on an extension and take down our talk. This may be good." He waved to the switchboard operator sitting behind the police speaker. "Nell, put Tuckerman's call through to me here and hook in one of these front desks. All right, Sam. Ready?"

Terrell said, "Yes, let it fly." He sat down and put on earphones.

Karsh picked up a phone and leaned against the city desk. "What's up, Ike?" he said. His voice was almost respectful, but an ironical smile twisted his lips. He winked down at Terrell, and he seemed completely strong and confident. "Something wrong?"

"I hope you're not being cute." Terrell heard the suppressed anger in Cellars' voice. "Photographers from your paper are hanging around my house. They say you sent 'em."

"That's right," Karsh said. "You're going to look nice on page one."

"I pay you to keep me out of the paper. You cross me, and you're through."

"What do you want me to keep out? That you paid a killer to strangle Eden Myles? That you framed Richard Caldwell to keep the city in your own pocket?"

Cellars said softly, "I'll settle with you, don't worry."

Karsh began to laugh. "You're heading for the front page of our next edition. Murderer, perjurer, pickpocket, pimp—have I forgotten anything?"

"Just your good sense, Mike." And Cellars broke the connection.

"Okay, okay, let's get going," Karsh said, putting the phone down and slapping his hands.

Terrell worked slowly at first, getting his lead down right. He had clips on Eden Myles and Cellars and Caldwell sent up from the morgue, and a bit later called the detective division in the Hall for background on Rammersky's arrest, and a direct quote from his confession. A detective he knew well filled him in and said, "A big night, eh, Sam? We got another dead one, you know. Frankie Chance."

Terrell took the cigarette from his mouth. "What happened?" An illogical sadness welled in him.

"It happened out near Cellars' home," the detective said. "One of Ike's bodyguards got him. There's more to it, but I can't give it to you now. Maybe in a half-hour or so."

"Sure," Terrell said. He told Karsh about Frankie Chance, but Karsh said, "Never mind him. We'll run something about it on page six. Don't clutter up your pieces with the bit players."

"Okay. Here's the lead then."

Karsh scanned it quickly, a little grin on his lips. "This is okay. Fine."

Terrell went on working, and Karsh took the pages as they came from the typewriter and handed them on to Williams, who proofed them and funnelled them to the copy wheel.

The minutes ticked away.

Terrell finished his last paragraph and took the paper from his machine. "This does it," he said. A copy boy took the page up to the desk where Williams was standing waiting for it. Terrell looked around for Karsh but didn't see him. He went up to the city desk.

Tuckerman said, "A call came in for you from St. Anne's. A doctor there says to tell you that you can come and see the girl. She's asked for you." Tuckerman grinned amiably. "Connie Blacker, a long-legged blonde. A real dish. You're lucky."

"Yeah, sure," Terrell said. He was staring about the crowded, noisy room. "Where's Karsh?"

Tuckerman twisted his big body around in his chair. There was a small frown on his long, placid face. "He wouldn't go out," he said. "Not alone. Not tonight."

A copy boy said tentatively, "I saw Mr. Karsh at the elevators a few minutes ago."

"Was he dressed for the street?" Tuckerman asked.

"Yes, he had his coat and hat. I met him when I was coming up with coffee."

Tuckerman swore softly. "He's crazy." He was reaching for the phone when it began to ring. He picked it up, listened for a few seconds, and then let out his breath slowly. "Sure, Mike." Tuckerman turned and handed the phone to Terrell. "Karsh. For you."

Terrell took the receiver and said, "Where the devil are you?"

"Just across the street. Lindy's. That all-night dope den that sells us our coffee and reefers. It's the first time I've been in here. God! A foul smell of—"

"Mike, call a cab and go home," Terrell said. "Or come back here and we'll have a few drinks." Terrell glanced around the desk. "Everybody's in the mood."

"It sounds fine," Karsh said. "But not tonight, Sam. I've got a date."

"Where? With who?"

"I don't know. It's a face behind a windshield. That's all I saw. I'll know more about him later."

"You damn fool," Terrell said. He covered the receiver and spoke quickly and softly to Tuckerman. "Karsh is in Lindy's. Get a squad over there. I'll try to keep him on the line." Tuckerman grabbed a phone and Williams stood and stared at the clock above his head. They were still four minutes from deadline.

"Mike?" Terrell said. "You still there?"

"Sure."

"Don't go outside. Sit in that booth. You hear?"

"Sure, you're yelling like a fishwife," Karsh said. "But you listen to me. Remember what I taught you about the newspaper business, will

347

you?" Karsh's voice trembled slightly, and then he recovered himself and said quickly, "Will you do that? Remember what I taught you on the job? And forget everything else? Everything I did?"

"Of course, Mike. Of course. But sit still. We're coming—" Terrell stared at the phone in his hand. The connection was broken.

"A squad is on the way," Tuckerman said.

"Sam, come here!" Ollie Wheeler called. He was at the big, floor-to-ceiling window staring down at the street. Terrell went to Wheeler's side, jarred by the urgency in his voice. Tuckerman and Williams came up behind him.

The street below them was dark except for a patch of light that fell on the shining pavement from the all-night restaurant.

Terrell saw Karsh standing in that square of brilliance, his figure square and blocky, his face shadowed by the brim of his homburg.

A car swung into the street a half block away and came toward Karsh with its lights turned off; it rolled silently through the darkness, angling toward him. The car picked up speed suddenly and shot past Karsh. When it was gone, swaying on its springs at the next intersection, Karsh lay in the gutter, looking small and unreal.

For an instant Terrell didn't realize what had happened; he thought Karsh had thrown himself out of the car's path. It wasn't until he saw the fragments of glass gleaming on the sidewalk that he knew Karsh was dead; the bullet that killed him had also smashed the window in the restaurant.

Terrell turned and sat down wearily at a desk. Karsh didn't have to . . . This was the thought running through his mind. Except to prove—to prove what? That he was Mike Karsh. That he could make the gesture. The Night Extra was a writ of habeas corpus for Caldwell, an epitaph for Mike Karsh.

Ollie Wheeler said, "I'd like to get drunk tonight. Anyone interested?"

"Sure," Williams muttered. "Why not?"

The tears stung Terrell's eyes. Later he would go out to the hospital to see Connie and that would be all right. But now he hurt all over.

Above him the illuminated second hand made its last circuit before deadline and the loud, warning bell rang shrilly. Everyone looked up at the clock. The forms were locked up, the presses were ready to start rolling. The Night Extra was just about in.